A BREACH
IN THE
WATERSHED

A BREACH
IN THE
WATERSHED

DOUGLAS NILES

ACE BOOKS, NEW YORK

This book is an Ace original edition,
and has never been previously published.

A BREACH IN THE WATERSHED

An Ace Book / published by arrangement with
the author

PRINTING HISTORY
Ace edition / August 1995

ISBN: 0-441-00208-0

ACE®
Ace Books are published by The Berkley Publishing Group,
200 Madison Avenue, New York, NY 10016.
ACE and the "A" design are trademarks
belonging to Charter Communications, Inc.

PRINTED IN THE UNITED STATES OF AMERICA

10 9 8 7 6 5 4 3 2 1

For Fred Baxter,

and watersheds from
the Crazies to Durango

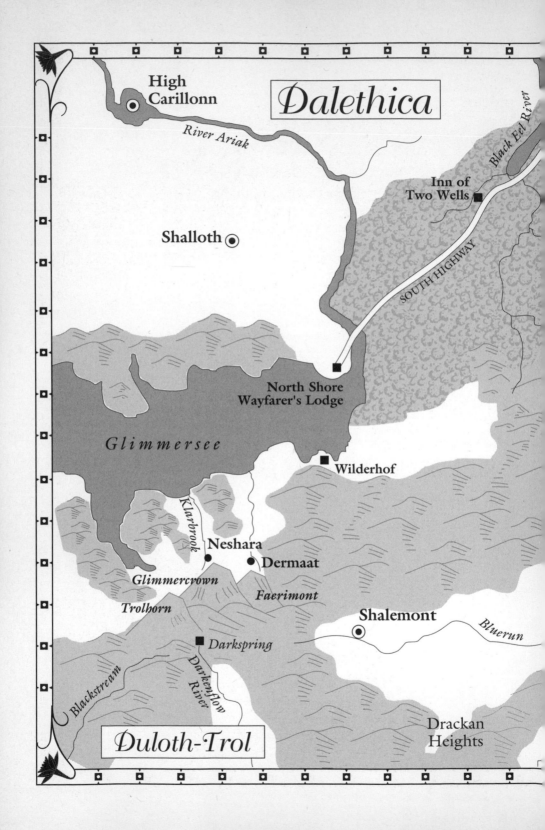

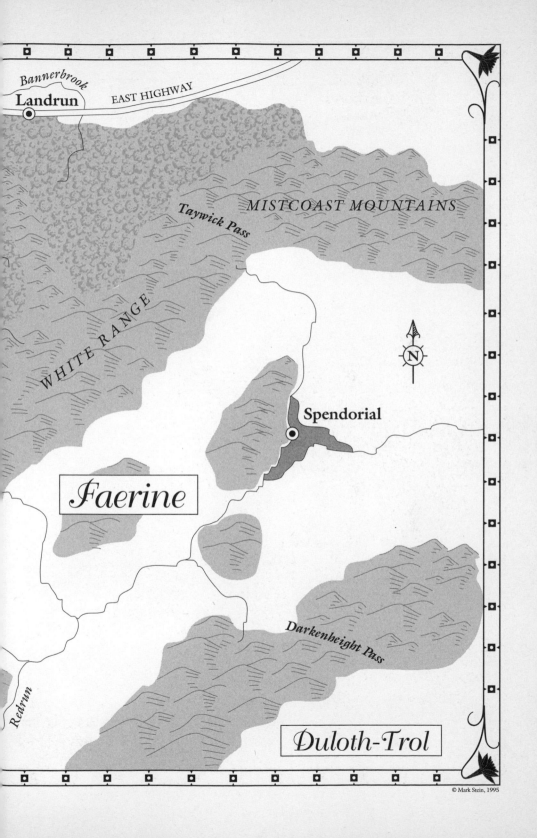

© Mark Stein, 1995

A BREACH IN THE WATERSHED

PROLOGUE

When destiny takes a mortal by the soul, life swerves
onto a substantially unalterable course. In its fashion,
such a fate imprisons one more securely than the
deepest dungeon.
—Songs of Aurianth

Old Pheathersqyll was the great constant of my early life. I must have been a great trial for him—from my first steps as a rambunctious girl racing at high speed, wide-eyed with wonder, through the Academy of the Sun's sanctified halls. Many are the times Pheathersqyll found me in discussion with the Knifemaster or the Lord Pilferer, practicing techniques with little application to temple life.

High Acrobat Theapos was my favorite instructor. Teaching me the tumbles and leaps of his art, Theapos drilled me until I could climb a wall of almost seamless brick, or land, unhurt, following a high fall. Pheathers pretended dismay, but I know now that he tacitly sanctioned these activities, understanding them to be an important part of my preparation.

More difficult for my beloved mentor were the later years, as I chafed against the restrictions of the Academy order. Why did I have to be different from the other girls—to bury myself in the studies of a hundred disciplines? "The prophecy," Pheathersqyll would mumble mysteriously. "You are the girl born under Three Stars Rising."

Often I begged him to tell me more, but—prior to my twelfth birthday, at least—the old sage would simply harrumph in dismissive refusal and change the subject. His favorite diversion was study of the Three Mighty Gods; Pheathers always reminded me that nowhere else in Dalethica were Aurianth and Dassadec acknowledged as powers equal to Baracan, God of Man. He told me I was lucky to be raised in such an enlightened environment—and sternly bade me cease complaining.

In the remote and pastoral gardens surrounding the Academy of the Sun, I came to know a life unfettered by prejudice or doubt. The Sun Lord, King of Myntar Kosh, was our liege, and he was curious about the workings of all the gods. Indeed, I remember his visits, always in the height of the summer festivals, when he would ride out from Myntercairn with his entourage of ladies and lords. Though to Baracan went the most elaborate—and ponderous—ceremony, the Sun Lord always requested a grand dance in the name of Aurianth. I think he would have dispensed with the ceremonies and extended the dancing, but for the disapproval of ambassadors from the eastern realms.

I, too, found the God of Man uninspiring. I was expected to master the *Scroll of Baracan*—which I did—but I much preferred the more lyrical verse in the *Songs of Aurianth*. My lessons concerning the Mistress of Magic were relentlessly fascinating. Often they caused my imagination to spark, and I would sing, dance, or whistle, making music in tribute to that gentle goddess.

I learned about Dassadec, too—though these studies were more apt to cause me nightmares than to inspire song. Still, when I objected, Pheathers quickly pointed out that all the rest of humankind had forgotten about the Sleepstealer centuries ago. Dassadec had not been a threat for a thousand years, and so to people he seemed like an impossibly ancient thing, with no bearing on real life. Even as a young girl, I learned differently.

And despite my petty rebellions, some internal compulsion insured that, in every one of my pursuits, I excelled. Nor do I wish to claim that these disciplines were odious or frightening. More often than nightmares, my sleep was visited by dreams. Usually they included a lanky, shyly smiling man, with wavy brown hair and a curious glint in his ice-blue eyes. I did not know this man, but he had been my nocturnal visitor since the days of my first conscious memories.

Though I now understand the reasons for the mystery, many years would pass for that growing girl before she was to learn the truth. And even now, in the twilight of my days, how much of this tale can I as a mere mortal truly claim to comprehend? However wise a person becomes, that person remains a lone individual, with but a single point of view; and any tale must inevitably be altered by the shifting of the teller.

Of course, the three gods had some history in common, and my lessons began there, with the tales of the creation and betrayal. Many of these made up my early studies, and include stories that have stayed with me through the sum of my years. My favorite has always been the foundation legend:

When time began, oceans roiled across the world. Lands rose from the torrent only to vanish beneath surging tempest. Life struggled to survive on the edge of chaos. Slowly, chaos prevailed.

The gods, finding more pleasure in the destruction of each other's works than in the accomplishments of their own, fought ceaseless and brutal wars. Each of the multitude of deities aligned under one of the Three Mighty Gods; and each of these factions was sustained by one of the waters of the world.

These are the precious liquids of the primordial seas: crystalline Water—pure and clean, the key to all life, everywhere; Aura, rainbow brilliant, surging with the raw power of magic; and Darkblood, the flowing effluence of evil, violence, and decay.

The waters burst forth at the beginning as they will flow together at the end, fuming in chaos as terrible as the Immortal War itself. Maelstroms swirled across entire oceans, and no rock could long survive above the waves.

Until, finally, the gods created the Watershed and brought order to the oceans and the world. They made land firm, raising huge mountains to channel the storms into their proper places. The three waters flowed apart, and so could bring no harm to the Watershed. Instead, each shaped the surrounding land into its own image, creating the Three Realms: Dalethica, Faerine, and Duloth-Trol.

As their task was done, the gods made a pact: they would leave this place to mortals, and journey to a far, ethereal home. This they did—all save Dassadec, the Sleepstealer, who treacherously remained behind. His act is known as the Great Betrayal—but here I venture into a different tale, a story for another occasion.

Still, I cannot recite the old refrains without a thought of Pheathersqyll. There is a wistful peace and serenity to my memories of those days, all those years. It was a time when I knew everything about much, but nothing at all about the thing that really mattered.

From: *Recollections*, by Lady Raine of the Three Waters

ONE

Clouds of Steam or Darkblood

For so long as the Watershed stands intact, the
Sleepstealer can touch the mortals of the world only
through their dreams, or—rarely and at some risk—by
the agency of his Lord Minions.
—TOME OF VILE COMPULSIONS

— 1 —

"It's a great day to be outside, isn't it, Uncle Rudy?"

The lanky young man lowered the axe to the ground beside his chopping block and wiped the film of sweat from his brow. "Certainly is—especially if you're a prattling little girl with nothing better to do than pester your elders!"

"Rudy!" Anjell's mouth opened indignantly, then clamped tightly shut as she realized he was teasing her. "I'm not pestering," she claimed. "I came here to give you a message—but now I'm not certain I'll do it."

Twin braids whirling, Anjell tossed her head. Her nose, up-turned by nature, now pointed straight toward the sky. "After all, I don't know why a Prince of Galtigor should have any interest in a mere woodcutter. . . ."

"I'm an *Iceman*—" Rudy began his irritated retort before realizing that his brother's daughter had achieved exactly the result she sought.

With a sigh, he looked at the mound of stumps behind him and acknowledged that, today at least, he was a woodcutter. "What's this about a prince?"

"I thought I was pestering you," the girl said coyly. "I'd better go. . . . "

"Anjell Appenfell! I've a good mind to take you off to the Wilderhof—and leave you there!" Rudy declared in exasperation.

"You don't scare me! Besides, I'd just find my way back to Neshara. It would be kind of an adventure."

"When Umma threatened me with the Wilderhof, she used to get some obedience!" Rudy grumbled.

"Silly. Nobody's afraid of it anymore."

"All right," groaned the young man. "I give up! But can you tell me—when's the prince coming? Is it to make a climb?"

"That's my news!" Anjell continued, satisfied to get a small rise out of him. "A Prince of Galtigor is coming—and yes, he wants to climb a mountain."

"Did Beryv send you to tell me? What did he say?" Rudy could scarcely contain his excitement. His older brother—Anjell's father—would naturally handle the arrangements with the nobleman. It was Rudy's devout hope that Beryv would invite him along to help work the ascent.

"Of course." Anjell looked at him with the condescension only a ten-year-old girl could muster. She added, almost as an afterthought: "Papa said you'd have to get all the wood done in the next week. After that, he's going to need you for a few days. 'Course, he didn't say what for."

With that announcement, she was gone, skipping down the lane toward the central road of Neshara, where she could no doubt boast to her friends about the family's imminent, illustrious guest. Rudy watched her go, a warm glow of excitement rising in him. He knew why he'd be busy next week—Beryv would ask him to climb the mountain!

Mindful of his woodcutting tasks, Rudy allowed his eyes to drift across the ornate chalets of Neshara, past the sparkling ribbon of the

Klarbrook to the irregular, steeply rising slopes of the mountains beyond. Even the lesser heights loomed lofty and remote; crags of rock and snow crowded shoulder to shoulder, and impassive granite faces turned not toward Neshara or the other towns of Halverica, but upward to witness the trio of great summits known, collectively, as the Crown of the World.

Faerimont to the left and Trolhorn to the right. Tendrils of white cloud trailed like horsetails from each peak, so impossibly high. Each of them dwarfed all the other mountains of Halverica—yet they looked like mere foothills beside the Glimmercrown, the hulking dome of ice-covered rock that loomed even higher than its two mighty neighbors.

Though the base of the massif lay ten miles from Neshara, so lofty were the trio of summits that they seemed to lean over Rudy's head. Halverica was a land defined and shaped by mountains, yet nowhere else in all the free cantons—or in all the Watershed—did three such peaks exist. And, in the case of Faerimont and Trolhorn, not just passively observed, but climbed! True, only the most skilled Icemen—and their wealthiest clients—ever ventured onto those precipitous slopes. Rudy felt certain, beyond any shred of doubt, that the Lord of Galtigor was such a client. He already knew that his brother Beryv was the most skilled climber in Neshara and that the Icemen of Neshara were the best in all Halverica; he needed no further information to make his deduction. The upcoming ascent would be made on the Crown of the World.

And now it seemed that he would be invited along! Drawing a deep breath, aware of energy tingling throughout his body, Rudy lifted a stump to the block and split the weathered pine with one smashing blow. In moments he reduced one half, then the other, to eight hearth-sized logs.

Mechanically Rudy reached for the next stump of wood and then the next. Lost in his labor, he split log after log while time whirled as fast as his axe.

When Anjell came racing up the lane some hours later, the pile of split wood stood higher than Rudy's head; the mountain of stumps had dwindled to a few gnarled specimens. The girl swerved, shrieking, behind Rudy, who watched in amusement as several younger boys charged into view, and then halted abruptly at the sight of Rudy. He noticed they were all soaking wet.

"You should be more careful when you cross the stream!" Anjell taunted, secure behind the lanky barrier of her uncle.

"We'll get you, Anjell Appenfell!" one boy, a husky eight-year-old, shouted.

"It's not *my* fault you can't stay on the top side of a log!"

Recognizing a lost cause, the boys wandered off in search of mischief. A picture of innocence, Anjell batted her eyes at Rudy. "That old log bridge over the Klarbrook is getting rotten," she explained. "It wobbles a little bit."

"If you work at it hard enough with a pry-bar," Rudy responded, chuckling at her protestations. "Maybe it won't have to be me—maybe the boys'll cart you off to the Wilderhof!"

"Hah! As if they could catch me." Anjell squinted up at Rudy, as if insuring that he was joking with her. "Besides, I told you—the Wilderhof doesn't scare anybody anymore. Those are just old legends and fairy tales about monsters. The Wilderhof is just a bunch of mountains on the other side of Dermaat. That's in Dalethica, and even I know that all the magic stays in Faerine."

"You know a lot more than that," Rudy acknowledged, still laughing.

"Do you think the Lord of Galtigor will be coming with a princess? Or maybe actors and musicians?" Anjell asked, abruptly changing tack. "Or perhaps even a twissel from Faerine?"

"A twissel?" Rudy scoffed. "There hasn't been a twissel, or any other Faerine, come over the Watershed in my lifetime—I don't know why one would show up now."

"To make music!" Anjell insisted. "Everyone knows that Faerines have wonderful songs!"

"Though why they should share them with humans is beyond me. No, I think if you want to hear a twissel sing you'll have to go to Faerine. Your chances of seeing one here are about the same as meeting Aurianth, Mistress of Magic herself!"

"Well, if the prince won't bring a Faerine, what about a minstrel or some actors? *Human* ones. Do you think he might bring some of *them* along?"

"You can't take an entourage up the Faerimont. It's my guess he'll come with a few servants, a squire perhaps—but it won't be a big party."

"Why does he come all the way to Halverica to climb a mountain?"

Rudy chuckled. "They don't have mountains—at least, not like the Crown of the World—in Galtigor, that's why."

Anjell looked at him as if uncertain that he was telling the truth. "Well, what *do* they have, then?" she asked suspiciously.

Rudy shrugged. "Trees, I guess. At least, I've heard that their king built highways through huge forests. They're supposed to be the widest roads in Dalethica. And armies and knights—Galtigor's men are always busy fighting a war someplace. The River Ariak flows past the border of Galtigor after it leaves the Glimmersee. Maybe we'll go there sometime and see," he added with a wink.

"I don't *want* to see a place with no mountains," Anjell replied firmly.

"No . . ." Rudy looked up at the peaks, feeling the excitement tingle along his spine. He tried without success to picture life in a place that was flat.

"No," he repeated. "Neither would I."

— 2 —

Nicodareus hated the cold. He loathed these icebound heights, despised the ceaseless winds roaring through passes, scouring even the loftiest peaks. Involuntarily he shivered, a wrenching convulsion that rippled through his black, scale-covered body. Digging the talons on his feet into the hard rock of the trail, he snarled in rage until the trembling passed.

Folding his leathery wings across the ridged hump of his backbone, the Lord Minion tried to insulate his skin from the force of the gusts. Fanged jaws clamped in determination, he faced ever upward, the twin horns on his forehead jutting, goatlike, toward the lofty ridge as he maintained his steady ascent.

He remained alert for Guardians—the Power of Three empowered him to cross the Watershed, but it would have no effect on the stony beasts who patrolled the high divides. One or two Guardians he could kill; if he encountered more than two, he would have to outdistance them. It was galling to have to face such a threat—one of the few foes he couldn't easily master. Nicodareus knew that he would have to be vigilant; at least he, who was called the Eye of Dassadec, would have no difficulty remaining alert.

Finally he reached the crest, the knifelike ridge of stone that divides waters and worlds. As a Lord Minion, Nicodareus would never know fatigue, yet he paused here to reflect on the drastic differences of the worlds before and behind—and to muster the spiritual strength to leave his native realm behind. The Power of Three would sustain for a time after he crossed the divide, but travel beyond the realm of Darkblood was inevitably draining and debilitating.

To the rear sprawled Duloth-Trol, realm of Dassadec the Sleepstealer. Glowering tarclouds billowed over the land, forming black, ominous mountains in the sky. Lightning crackled beneath the thunderbanks, and Nicodareus well knew the force of pounding hail and blistering whirlwind that scoured the land in the smoky mists. He could see the Blackstream below, an inky line that etched like acid ever deeper into the bedrock of Duloth-Trol.

Before him now, in stark contrast, sprawled the vast, well-watered realms of Dalethica. Humans in countless thousands dwelled there, Nicodareus knew, laboring in the pathetic belief that they were safe from the reach of Dassadec the Sleepstealer. Perhaps for a time they had been. But now, thanks in part to this mission of Nicodareus, that was about to change.

From the ridge, the Eye of Dassadec let his Sight probe the world before him. To the east stood the heights of Faerine, where the presence of the accursed Aura screened the land from the Lord Minion's view. Ahead, however, he could see every detail of Dalethica, including the insides of human houses, scores, even hundreds, of miles away. Yet these puny mortals held no interest for Nicodareus. They were featureless beings, identical in most places except for an occasional flicker of defining essence—what the mortals might, arrogantly, describe as the "soul."

The Lord of Duloth-Trol allowed his gaze to shift toward the tallest mountain in all the Watershed. The Glimmercrown, they called it. The summit, the only place in the world where the three Watersheds met, was too high for Nicodareus to reach—even a Lord Minion would be defeated by that extreme cold.

But that did not mean it was unattainable. He studied the crystalline frost at its peak with keen interest. Growling subconsciously, he looked across the nearer slopes, relieved to see no sign of the Guardians.

Fields of white snow draped the foreslope of the ridge, plunging away across rocky slide zones into green valleys. Through those lowlands flowed sparkling streams, dammed where the ridges of the mountains curved inward, forcing the rivers into long, serpentine lakes. Such an extent of water always unsettled Nicodareus, and he was relieved that his route to the meeting would not take him near any of the larger tarns.

Wings spread behind him, the Eye of Dassadec hurled himself from the ridge, plunging past cliffs draped with snow and ice, gliding heavily downward toward the lower regions. He aimed for a meadow in a thickly forested vale, and dropped catlike onto his hands and feet as he came to rest, allowing the darkness of the forest floor to cloak him. Though Duloth-Trol was a treeless realm, it remained constantly screened by dark, heavy clouds—so much so that the Lord Minion found the sunlit skies of Dalethica most irritating.

He padded soundlessly through the forest. Around him sprawled a region of thick pine woods, broken by bleak gorges and shadowy caves. Full darkness descended as he jogged up a winding trail toward a rock-bound summit. This was the appointed place of the meeting, and as the Lord Minion stepped onto the crest he knew immediately that the human had arrived before him. A scent—sweat, perhaps, or even rank fear—permeated the air. The Eye of Dassadec stared into the shadows, and quickly made out the shape of a man standing beside a proud, tethered war horse.

"You are here at the appointed hour," Nicodareus observed. "You are wise."

His voice rumbled deeply, like the creaking of heavy stone hinges that had long been unturned. Though he spoke softly, the words carried clearly to the human's ears.

"I made my vow to my—to *our*—master," the man replied simply. He wore a travel-stained cloak and muddy boots; an air of confidence swirled about him as if he were a master of men who, nevertheless, understood that he was now in the presence of a higher power. Yet it did not escape the minion's notice that this human had dared to remind him that they both served one who stood even greater.

"Dassadec gave to me a dream; in that dream I knew that I was to come here on the night of the next new moon." The human gestured toward the clear night sky, where a dazzling array of stars, untroubled by competing moonlight, began to sparkle into view. "Was there doubt but that I would obey?"

The man was tall, his narrow face tapering into a pointed beard. The chiseled features, Nicodareus suspected, would appear handsome to a human female. Now the fellow looked up questioningly, as if surprised that his loyalty might have been suspect.

"There is always doubt where humans are concerned," the Lord Minion noted. "Nevertheless, you are doubly fortunate. Your arrival here at the appointed time pleases me; and, know this, *human*: when the Sleepstealer sends a dream, the one who slumbers does not always awaken."

For the first time, a glimmer of fear flicked across the man's features. Still, he stepped toward Nicodareus. The Lord Minion thought privately that his master had chosen well—the fellow was not lacking in courage.

"I understand the price of my devotion. I intend to give my lord no cause for displeasure."

Nicodareus, standing half again as tall as the human, curled his beastlike face into a sneer as the fellow came closer. Most mortals would have recoiled from that look, but this warrior simply placed his hands on his hips and waited, expectantly.

"You display wisdom. Yet there is another thing you should know: though we owe fealty to Dassadec, *I* am your master. When we must meet, it is *I* who will find you. The Power of Three gives me the means to come here now; it shall do so again, two more times. And know that, if you fail, your punishment shall be delivered by me."

"As you wish, my lord," the fellow said. He nodded his head and then, as if reconsidering, dropped to a knee.

"Very well." Nicodareus was pleased. "You may rise."

"The dream showed an image . . . did you bring me something?" the man asked audaciously.

Scowling, Nicodareus pulled the long, leather-wrapped package from his back, wordlessly extending it to the man. The mortal reached out and took the object reverently, kneeling again to lay it gently on the ground.

Carefully he peeled back the layers of oiled skin, finally revealing an object so black that it seemed lost among the shadows of the night.

"A Sword of Darkblood," Nicodareus said softly. "You will use it to gain that which Dassadec commands."

"Indeed," said the man, barely breathing. He reached out and took the weapon by its leather-wrapped hilt, raising it from the ground and holding it before him. An expression of wonder grew upon his face.

The blade itself was a complete, perfect black, absorbing every speck of light that touched it. As slender as a blade of the strongest steel, it moved through the air with keen, supple power. Slowly the man reached out a hand, as if to touch the inky perfection of the blade itself.

"No—not yet!" commanded the Lord Minion, his voice cracking like thunder. "Even the slightest contact could prove fatal—it would certainly weaken you to the point of uselessness. The grip is guarded by the cured skin of a terrion; touch only the hilt, and wield the blade only against those you wish to slay."

"Aye, lordship," said the man slowly, and there was real reverence in his voice.

"Now I will make you proof against that poison—if you have the courage. I offer you a test you must choose of your own will. Success will offer you gifts of Darkblood. But know this, human—failure will cost you your life."

"I accept!" the man declared.

Nicodareus nodded, again pleased. Extending one brawny forepaw, the Lord Minion turned the palm upward. He touched the black, gnarled forefinger of his other hand to that palm, gently tracing the curving talon of his nail in an X across the surface.

He froze for a moment, and then plunged that claw through the black skin. A single drop of oily black liquid spurted from the wound, pooling on the minion's skin even as the wound seamlessly vanished.

"Kneel."

The human obeyed immediately.

Extending his huge hand, cupping the precious droplet, Nicodareus lowered his fingers, tracing the talons along the underside of the man's chin. The fellow stared unblinkingly upward, eyes wide. Yet he did not tremble.

"Open your mouth."

When the man obeyed, the Lord Minion wiped the drop of blackness across his lips. Then he stepped back, crossing his arms and watching for a reaction.

The human's head rocked backward, his mouth working in reflexive, soundless gagging. Flipping from his knees onto his back, the man shuddered and kicked spasmodically. The lanky body thrashed on the ground for a long time, and—though they twisted with unspeakable agony—the man's lips never made a sound.

When the tremors ceased, the human lay limp but breathing. His chest rose and fell with trembling speed, more like a panting dog than a man. Yet Nicodareus knew that he would survive.

Indeed, within a few minutes the man sat up. When he climbed to his feet, his legs were strong, his breathing regular.

"What—what did you do to me?" he asked.

"The Darkblood of a Lord Minion protects you against every form of poison. Too, it will shield you against the powers of that which Dassadec commands you seek."

"That blood should have killed me."

"It usually kills a mortal," Nicodareus said casually. "It would seem that the Sleepstealer has chosen well. There is another thing you should know—because you drank of my blood and lived, you shall never know thirst. Nor can you drink water or anything bearing water as its root—such liquid would cause you . . . extreme difficulties."

The final piece of knowledge Nicodareus kept to himself. There would be a time, later, when he could tell the human of the additional condition: now that the man had tasted the blood of a Lord Minion, he must take an additional drop before a full year passed, and every additional year thereafter—or his painful, inevitable death would commence.

"You know your mission?" the Lord Minion asked.

"Indeed—and with this blade and your protection, my success is a certainty. I am to meet the Icemen in a week, and we will begin the climb immediately. Yet why am I to make this ascent? What is the purpose of this ice?"

"For now, it is enough that you get it—you do not need to know the reasons, nor should you ask again. Just know that the Ice of Three Waters is the rarest of elements, a substance that combines Aura, Darkblood, and Water in a single compound."

"It is enough to have your command," the man declared, bowing humbly. "I shall not rest until the ice is mine."

"Excellent." Nicodareus was impressed with this human. The scheme of Dassadec, he realized, had strong potential for success.

"Another thing," the Lord Minion noted, indicating with a hooked claw the black-bladed sword. "This weapon is blessed with the power of Darkflight. Use it with care—it is a power usually bestowed only upon Lord Minions. Point the blade at a place you can see—a place within a hundred paces of your current location—and pronounce my name, *Nicodareus*, loudly and firmly. The weapon will grant you the power of instantaneous flight, carrying you precisely to the place you indicate."

An expression of awe crossed the man's face as he studied the ink-black, shimering blade. Slowly, reverently, he tucked it back into the scabbard.

"I am unworthy of this terrible gift. Why do you give it to me?"

"It will aid you in making the climb—during the upper reaches, when you will be on your own. Without the power, it is unlikely you could reach the top."

"I will use it wisely," the human pledged. He paused, awkwardly. "I've made my camp below. Would you . . . care to share the comfort of my fire?" The question, sensed the minion, was asked with a notable absence of sincerity. No matter; the Eye of Dassadec had better things to do than waste precious hours in contact with a mortal, however capable he might seem.

"I need no rest; I start back to Duloth-Trol immediately."

The human nodded with a palpable sigh of relief.

Nicodareus turned to the edge of the knoll, spreading his wings in preparation for a dive into the night. Though to the human, utter darkness yawned beyond, the minion clearly saw the course of his gliding flight. Abruptly he paused and turned back to the man. The fellow caressed the hilt of the sword reverently, but looked up as he sensed the minion's continuing presence.

"About the Icemen," Nicodareus said. "You will need them to make the climb. But before you descend, make certain that there are no survivors."

"Aye, my lord," pledged the man, his response but a distant whisper to the great, bat-winged form that had already vanished into the night.

TWO

An Iceman of Halverica

A rope must be discarded at the first sign of fraying or
wear; remember that, by breeding false confidence, a
weak rope is more dangerous than no rope at all.
—CREED OF THE CLIMBER BY DUNKAR KALLAND

— 1 —

Rudy slapped the red paint across the gate outside the Appenfell chalet,
admiring the sleek crimson sheen even as he hurried to get the job
done. Anjell, bored, sat under a nearby tree and watched.

"How about getting me a cup of water?" the uncle asked his niece.

"I will—for a copper," she said.

"I'll get my own water, at those prices!" he snapped, stopping to
wipe his brow.

"Oh, I'll get it," Anjell grumbled, climbing to her feet. "You've
got red paint all over your forehead," she said, giggling as she headed
for the pump.

Several alphunds barked and howled down the street, the sound
originating where the bridge over the Klarbrook welcomed visitors to
Neshara. Though a track extended to the north from the other end of
the village, that route led only to a wilderness of towering mountains—
and to the impassable barrier of the Watershed, beyond.

Chickens squawked, and then came the unmistakable sound of hoofbeats pummeling the dirty ruts of the road.

"That's *him*! That's the Prince of Galtigor!" cried the girl, turning and running down the lane.

Rudy, conscious of the dignity expected of him now that he was twenty and one, sauntered in his niece's wake. Nevertheless, he wiped his hands and face on a corner of his shirt, heart pounding in anticipation He, too, was certain that the rider was the Lord of Galtigor. And he would be coming to the Appenfell house!

The horseman swept into sight, cantering easily up the town's main street. People emerged from the houses and shops to watch—children with expressions of shock and awe, elders inscrutable, showing only cool interest. Yet even those outwardly calm demeanors masked a good measure of curiosity and wonder.

The charger, a black, powerfully built stallion, slowed to a trot and snorted disdainfully as if to assert that it would have much preferred to gallop. Muscles rippled under the big horse's satiny coat, bespeaking an easy power that, to Rudy, made every other steed seem a worm-infested nag.

But the stallion was no less than a fitting mount for the rider. The Lord of Galtigor sat high in the saddle, casting his head this way and that—always seeming to look over the heads of the Halvericans now lining the sides of the narrow street. His hair and beard were black, well-combed, and gleaming with oil. He looked as though he had just come from a visit to his barber instead of completing a long ride over a rough, steeply climbing track.

A woolen cloak of black and red flowed from the horseman's shoulders. Heavy leather boots protected his feet; black, supple gauntlets did the same for his hands. The leather-wrapped hilt of a sword jutted from a bejeweled scabbard at his belt. That gem-encrusted sheath was the man's only sign of nobility or wealth; while his garments and accoutrements were well-made, none of the rest bore any obvious symbol of status or power. Still, Rudy felt certain beyond doubt that this was the Lord of Galtigor, of whom his brother had spoken.

The horse halted with an angry snort as the man pulled back on the reins and spoke to plump Hermann Kruk, who stood outside his breadshop.

"You there—baker. Where can I find the house of Appenfell?" The rider's tones were clipped, typical of the flatlander accent that Rudy had heard only a few times in his life.

Nervously, Hermann wiped his hands on a floured apron, then palmed his hand over his heart in a silent prayer to Baracan. It had been a long time since anyone on a horse had come to the village.

"Here!" cried Anjell, before the flustered Hermann could answer. "We live up this lane!" she added with a wave.

The horseman's eyes turned to the girl as he nudged the horse into a walk. Rudy felt an irrational fear; worried that his niece would be trampled beneath the great hooves, he stepped forward protectively.

"I am Rudgar Appenfell. I will lead you to my brother's house."

The lord nodded. Rudy was about to explain that he and his brothers lived with their mother—since his father's death on the mountain, ten years earlier, Beryv had been the family patriarch. Yet something in the rider's bearing convinced him that any such conversation would be viewed as trivial prattling, so he held his tongue.

"What an extent of flower gardens," remarked the lord, as Rudy led him up the lane. "Yet the steepness of your country must limit your pasturelands. Could not something more practical be grown in these plots?"

"We Halvericans have a tradition with flowers—and we don't lack for food," the young man replied, a little defensively.

"That's what comes from living on the border of Faerine. Flowers—and songs, too, no doubt."

No one in the village could make any kind of music worth listening to, but Rudy didn't feel compelled to admit that. "The Watershed stands at its highest between Halverica and Faerine—we don't mix with the folk of magic. I should think that Galtigor would have more relations with Faerines than we do—isn't there a pass through the Watershed on the border of your realm?"

"Taywick Pass—bah! You can't cross there—the Faerines have it enchanted with all kinds of protections. Any man who tries will either stumble back down again a few weeks later, or wander around until he starves. But tell me—how can men have a tradition based on flowers?"

"The First Hero of Halverica is Dunkar Kalland," Rudy explained. "He came down from the mountains—some say the Glimmercrown itself—and united the ten cantons. Everywhere he spoke, blossoms rose from the fields—a different variety in each of the cantons. It's Kalland who gave us the freedom that's lasted until today; and we remember him with our gardens."

"Freedom?" The lord looked skeptical. "I should think you'd want to have a king. Who speaks for your people to masters of other realms? How do you handle matters of war and peace?"

Rudy shrugged, reflecting privately that—without a king to stir up trouble—peace was the comfortable norm.

Shortly they reached the sprawling Appenfell chalet, one of the largest houses in Neshara. Surrounded by drackanblooms, tulips, and columbine, the building's ornately carved shutters, eaves, and doors gleamed in the daylight. The structure nestled into the sloping ground, and from its wide porches and balconies one could overlook all the town and see the rising heights of the mountains beyond.

"I'll see to your horse," Rudy offered, indicating the small shed that would serve as a stable.

"Cyric will allow no one but myself to handle him," the lord replied, dismounting with the smooth ease of a natural horseman. "Tell your brother that Prince Garamis of Galtigor has arrived."

Surprised, Rudy nodded and went to the house. Anjell had already carried the news, so he encountered Beryv on the side porch as the senior Iceman came looking for his client.

Beryv Appenfell was only average in height—several inches shorter than his youngest brother—but he outweighed Rudy by a stone or two, carrying the greatest mass of his body in his broad shoulders and strapping arms. A craggy chin and sharp nose gave his face a look like one of the mountain faces on which he came most truly alive. Now Beryv's black eyes flashed with irritation.

"Why aren't you tendin' the lord's horse?" he demanded. "D'ye want to make him think he's come to some manners-forsaken backwater?"

Swiftly Rudy explained, though Beryv seemed only slightly mollified. "Wait here," commanded the elder Appenfell as he started toward the small stable.

Coyle and Donnial came out of the house, and Rudy waited with his two other brothers while Beryv went to meet Garamis.

"He called himself a prince?" Coyle, who was only five years older than Rudy, asked in wonder.

"He's one of the three royal sons of Galtigor," Donniall noted smugly. Obviously, Beryv kept him better informed than his younger brothers. "First in line for the throne, from what I hear. He's got his own army—they all wear black mantles over their armor—and they've done most of the fighting with Carillonn in recent times. It's said that Garamis has won every battle he's ever fought."

"They must've had some real campaigns," Rudy added. "I heard that war between Carillonn and Galtigor has been going on for fifty years."

"There hasn't *been* a real battle in ten centuries—not since the Nameless One was stopped at the shores of the Glimmersee," Donniall said. "Still," he allowed, "some of these fights along the River Ariak have been pretty savage—hundreds killed, and Galtigor usually victorious. And it seems that Garamis is their big war leader."

"He didn't bring servants, escorts?" Coyle asked Rudy.

"He was alone—probably traveled plenty fast, too. I don't know how anyone else could have kept up with that horse!"

"So—are you ready to put on your climbin' boots?" Donniall inquired playfully, clapping Rudy on the back. "This'll be the first of the big ones for all four Appenfell brothers."

The note of pride in his brother's voice touched Rudy, warming him with determination. "It *is* one of the Crowns?" he asked. "Faerimont?"

"None other," Donniall replied, his eyes unconsciously swinging to the great massif rising into the southern sky, with only Glimmercrown standing higher.

"It's the first time in ten years there's been a client wanting to go there," Coyle noted, then coughed awkwardly. The climb of a decade earlier was a thing not often mentioned in the Appenfell home. "Let's hope this is the start of good times again."

"As long as Galtigor and Carillonn stand at the brink of war, I don't think we'll see climbin' as it used to be." Donniall shook his head. "Since these flatlanders have each other to worry about, they're not going to look for the challenge of the high mountains."

"How about this prince—Garamis?" Rudy wondered. "If he's a son of the king and such a great war leader, you'd think he'd be on the battlefield."

Donniall chuckled, grimly amused. "From what I hear, he usually is. Those Black Mantles have a reputation for butchery that's carried as far as the Glimmersee. I'm glad he's here as a client, and not an enemy."

"Lucky we are to live in the free cantons, I say," Coyle observed, to a chorus of assenting voices.

Their conversation halted as Dara, Beryv's wife, swept up to the door and summoned them inside for dinner. Rudy quickly went to his room, changing out of his paint-stained tunic into his only pair of trousers and a cotton shirt that had been patched in many places. Still, the clothes were clean and comfortable, and that was the best he could do. Soft moccasins completing his outfit, he hastened to the huge dining room, where Beryv and their guest had already taken seats.

"Ah, the fellow who guided me through the maze of your city streets," Garamis acknowledged, smiling thinly as Rudy and his other brothers sat at the table.

"It was my privilege—and honor," the young Iceman replied, not certain if the lord was mocking or not.

"Not the last guiding you'll be doing for me—I presume you are the fifth member of our party?"

"Rudy will be making his first climb on the Crown," Beryv interjected.

"Splendid!" The lord turned toward the warm loaves of bread that Dara had placed on the table. Scooping a large dollop of butter onto his plate, he tore half a loaf away before passing the basket to Beryv. As he chewed, the Prince of Galtigor remarked about his enthusiasm for the upcoming adventure.

"Greetings, my lady," Garamis said abruptly, and Rudy turned to see his mother enter on Dara's arm. Umma Appenfell gingerly took a chair at the far end of the table. She did not speak to the men, and as she flashed Rudy a wan smile he was surprised at how old she looked. In the decade since her husband had perished on the high face of Faerimont, the woman seemed to have aged with unnatural haste.

Rudy quietly ate a slice of bread, surprised at the lord's garrulousness, when he had seemed so taciturn, even forbidding, on horseback and in the stable. In a way it was a relief, but he couldn't get out of his mind the picture of Garamis as an aloof and condescending nobleman.

". . . now that peace is near at hand," the lord was explaining, as Rudy blinked, returning to the present. Anjell stood beside him, nudging him as she offered a plate of steaming potatoes.

"Here—take some while you can!" she whispered, with a meaningful look at Garamis. Rudy suppressed a smile, noting that the lord's plate was piled high with pink, freshly roasted ham. Dara, supervising Coyle and Donniall's younger wives, saw that all the food was placed on the table. Only when each of the men had been served a warm bottle of beer did the women sit.

"The war might be ending? Oh, that's splendid news!" For the first time, Rudy's mother spoke. "It seems so strange, in a way. Do you know that it's been going on since before I was born?"

"I shouldn't think the affairs of Galtigor and Carillonn would be of great interest here in remote Halverica," the lord remarked.

"Oh, but this war has carried a cost for us as well as you," Beryv noted. "In my grandparents' time the River Ariak was a great throughroute of trade. The North Shore Wayfarer's Lodge was a small citystate in its own right, offering a gateway to the rest of the world. Since your war has made the river impassable, we have become an isolated land, surrounded by the Watershed to the south and our battling neighbors to the north."

"Did it really last for fifty years?" asked Anjell boldly.

Garamis nodded. "Still lasts, actually—I only said that there was a *chance* of a settlement."

"What kind of chance?" pressed the girl.

"There is a noblewoman of Carillonn, Bristyn Duftrall—Duchess of Shalloth. Her father's realm is a small place, but well-defended, near the border of Carillonn and Galtigor. She is reputed to be a woman of fabulous beauty, though I have not seen her myself—yet," the lord explained. His eyes flashed as he spoke; Rudy sensed that he had devoted a lot of thought to this duchess. "She has agreed to lead a diplomatic mission to Galtigor."

"And that's enough to make peace? Why did it take fifty years?" demanded Anjell.

"It's not enough." Garamis smiled, and with the pointed beard and neatly trimmed mustache Rudy thought that he resembled a fox. "But this princess shall wed one of the sons of Galtigor—and in that bond will we find the path to a lasting accommodation.

"But enough of these matters—it is precisely to escape such political conundrums that I have sought the pristine escape of the mountains." His smile deepened, the foxlike resemblance becoming more pronounced. "You should know that the reputation of Neshara's Icemen has extended even to distant Galtigor and beyond."

Beryv waved his hand modestly, though a flush of pleasure crept across his clean-shaven cheeks. "Baracan has favored us. We are fortunate enough to stand at the foot of the greatest mountain in the Watershed—it is to this geographical good fortune and the favor of the God of Man that we owe our proficiency."

"Be that as it may, when I reached the North Shore Wayfarer's Lodge, I already knew that my destination was your village. And when I asked, there, about the greatest Iceman in Halverica, I was told to contact Beryv Appenfell of Neshara."

"Your message from the lodge was most welcome," Beryv said. "I am sure that your confidence in my brothers and myself will not prove misplaced. Indeed, I began the preparations for the climb as soon as I heard from you. We can leave as soon as you wish."

"Tomorrow morning, then."

Rudy felt a tingle of excitement, and looking across the table, he saw that Coyle, too, was grinning like an eager bridegroom. Only then did he notice that Beryv did not share his instant enthusiasm.

"I would suggest that you spend a time—at least a few days— here in Neshara. You will find the transition to the extreme heights of the mountain much easier if you accustom yourself to the town first. After all, we are a great deal higher than the Glimmersee here—and the Glimmersee is very much higher than Galtigor."

"The altitude will cause me no difficulty," declared the lord, with a self-assurance that forbade any dissent. "And there are matters in Galtigor—matters relating to war and peace—which allow me no un-due delay. I am needed there constantly, as my brother Takian has been away from home for several years—a circumstance that has placed the burden of the campaigning upon myself. So let us begin with the sunrise."

Beryv hesitated, but finally nodded. "Very well."

Rudy, remembering Donniall's remark on the porch, blurted a question. "Don't you have *two* brothers?"

Garamis' face darkened and for a moment the Iceman wondered if he'd said something terrible. Then the lord blinked, his expression becoming impassive again. "Yes, I have two brothers—Takian and Boric. Matters of governance, however, are left to Takian and myself."

The prince offered no more information on this topic, instead turning to Beryv. "How long will it take to make the climb?"

"I expect five days, though we'll take food and provisions for seven. It will take us a full day to reach the foot of the peak, then another to reach a secure ledge about halfway up. It is the only place to camp on the whole north face, so from there we will commence the final assault on the summit. This will be the most dangerous part of the climb."

"This route, I understand, follows a ravine between the summits of Faerimont and Glimmercrown?"

"Aye—your information is good, my lord. We will reach the ridge that connects the two peaks, and from there it is a relatively easy ascent to the summit."

"And you will place the ropes for the climb up the ravine?"

"Surely. I myself shall make that portion of the ascent, so that you will have well-anchored lines to follow for the entire route."

"Am I correct—you are the only man alive who has made this climb?" inquired the lord.

"Yes." Beryv's face was blank, but there was a hesitancy in his voice. "My father made it before me—but the last time he tried, it cost him his life."

"I am certain that Baracan will smile upon us—and our expedition will meet with great good fortune," declared Garamis, with an expansive gesture. "To the adventure—and the accomplishment!" He flourished his bottle, though Rudy noticed with surprise that he hadn't drunk any of his beer. "And to the five us, standing on top of the world!"

"A good toast," agreed Beryv, taking a long swig from his own bottle. "Though there will only be four of us at the summit."

Rudy's heart sank even as Beryv turned his face toward his youngest brother. "You will remain at our halfway camp, below the Twin Steps, where you can follow the course of the climb. If anything should go wrong, you will be our eyes and our voice."

"But—!" The objection died on Rudy's lips; even if the look in Beryv's eyes hadn't quelled his argument, he knew his stubborn brother well enough to realize that there would be no changing his mind.

"Finally, my lord," continued Beryv, already dismissing Rudy from his mind. "There's the matter of the Palefee—"

"I understand about that," replied Garamis. "I shall pay you forty sovereigns for your services. I have the gold with me, and you will receive it before the expedition departs."

"The Palefee is different from the guide fee—and it is not a thing that you must pay us now. I devoutly hope it will *never* be paid," Beryv explained with a grim expression. "The Palefee is incurred only in the event of a fatal accident. The reasons behind it are thus: tomorrow we begin a dangerous climb. I want it well understood—should an Iceman perish in your service, his family will receive a Palefee sufficient to address any future question of debt."

Garamis blinked in surprise, as if he hadn't considered the possibility of real bodily harm. "So I will swear—a hundred gems of indigo—or their equivalent—as compensation to the family of any man who dies."

"I'll take your sigil on this writ," continued Beryv, as if he had not heard the lord. The Iceman pulled a sheet of filmy skin from within his tunic, extending it toward Garamis. "Anjell—fetch my quill and inkwell."

The lord of Galtigor signed and put his seal to the compact, his face blank of expression.

"Now," Beyrv noted, pushing himself back from the table with an expression of deep satisfaction. "I would suggest that we get to bed. Tomorrow we depart with the dawn."

— 2 —

Moonlight filtered through icy walls, casting the snowbound cavern in a bluish, twilit glow. A naked figure, hulking, blunt of skull, its flinty skin rippling like a soft layer of stone, stooped through the entrance and came to a squatting position in the center of the cave. Similar figures emerged from alcoves of the icy shelter, gathering in a circle about the newly arrived scout.

That one raised his broad-snouted face, staring with stark blue eyes—orbs like pure turquoise in a wall of granite—at the greatest of the apelike shapes.

They come.

No words were spoken, but all present understood the report of the Guardian.

They will turn away from the Crown—as they always have before. The leader's reply, similarly soundless, carried clearly to the gathered council.

These . . . are different. There is a thing that speaks of danger in their presence—something as grim as Darkblood, as terrible as the Lord Minion. I feel the menace all the way from the summit itself. The Ice of Three Waters might be endangered.

The hunched figures shuffled awkwardly, awaiting their leader's response. That fellow stroked a stony finger across the rough, knobby bumps covering his chin.

They may come tomorrow, the scout indicated, scowling for emphasis.

With a sigh, the chieftain sagged, slumping his massive, white-frosted shoulders. Yet his reply was phrased in an undertone of grim determination.

I do not believe they will challenge us, when none has done so for a thousand years. Yet we are the High Guardians—if they come, we shall have to stop them.

— 3 —

The full moon had already vanished behind the ridge when Rudy awakened. Knowing that his fur-lined bedroll offered him the only chance for warmth on the whole majestic mountainside, he could not force himself to lie still and wait for dawn. Though the camp lay in shadow, the nearby mountainside and all Halverica below was revealed clearly in stark moonglow.

Perhaps it was the memory of the stag that had disturbed his sleep. He had seen the magnificent animal yesterday morning, when he had been the first to rise in their base camp. The great deer had stood still in the dawnlight, a broad rack of antlers spreading like branches from its head. For a brief moment Rudy had felt the touch of those dark eyes, and the feeling left a magical glow that had lasted throughout the previous day.

Remembering that emotion, he rose, quickly throwing a fur parka over his tunic and leggings. After thrusting his feet into ice-crusted boots, he left the lofty camp and worked his way carefully along the adjacent ledge.

The camp nestled in a niche between Faerimont and Glimmer-crown, a narrow shelter where humans had never been meant to venture. Yet last night, halfway up the mountain, the five climbers had slept here, restoring energy for the even more audacious ascent planned to begin with the coming dawn. They had left Neshara two days earlier, spending the previous night at the foot of the mountain itself. The sky remained clear, the temperature no colder than one had to expect at this altitude.

This was probably the highest patch of nonvertical ground in all

Dalethica, Rudy decided. A narrow crack descended at this point from the ridge between the two peaks, with each summit looming more than a mile overhead. The chimneylike crack, at its base, provided a shelter no more than eighteen feet deep, less than half that in width. At least it had served to block the stiff afternoon and evening breezes that otherwise would have burned their skin and sapped their strength.

Now, in the predawn hours, the wind had died away to a tickling breeze. Despite the chill, Rudy was warm and comfortable as he walked along the narrow ledge. He retraced the end of their previous day's route, looking down the steep shoulder that had carried the party to this height. The mountainous ridge was very high, but not so steep that the climbers had needed to rope together for protection.

Rudy's heart pounded with excitement, amplified by the beauty of the scene before him. Far away the Glimmersee, the vast lake that formed the central valley and major highway network of Halverica, sparkled in the moonlight. Wide, forested valleys led upward from the lakeshore, linking the towns of ferrymen and fishers with the highland villages of Icemen and herders.

Above, still limned in the bright moonlight, soared the Glimmer-crown, highest summit in all the Watershed. Flanked by the lesser height of Faerimont, that lofty pinnacle formed a snow-swept dagger of chiseled gray stone. A series of steplike ledges dropped away from the summit; each shelf was separated above and below by ice-draped walls of sheer rock. Beyond the great summit, the forbidding north face of the third lofty peak, Trolhorn, was just barely visible as it curved down to form the opposite shoulder of the Crown.

A quick glance back at the camp showed that Rudy's three brothers still slept. Perhaps their experience enabled them to relax while he, on his first major ascent, was forced to pace anxiously away from the tight confines of the camp. Or perhaps the others, with the climb before them, simply knew that they needed the sleep. With his own day to be spent waiting here in the camp, Rudy would have little to do but rest.

A vague restlessness urged the young Iceman to walk a little distance. At least then he wouldn't run the risk of trampling one of his older brothers—or, even worse, Lord Garamis. Despite his friendliness at the dinner table, the Prince of Galtigor had demonstrated several times during the previous two days that he possessed a fiery temper. Once, when a buckle had frozen shut, the lord had been so angry that he almost drew his sword to strike the offending clasp. Now, the mere prospect of arousing that temper drove Rudy along the narrow ledge leading outward from their niche.

The ledge was wide and relatively level as it curved outward along the broad, mountainous shoulder. After a few dozen paces Rudy reached a portion of the mountainside where the moon was visible in all of its fullness. He stood above the sweeping cliff, drawing deep, satisfied breaths and overlooking all Halverica.

A shape moved along the mountainside, instantly drawing Rudy's attention. Something bounded from one rock to another with feline grace, and a feeling of awe came over the Iceman. A snow lion! None of his brothers, so far as he knew, had ever seen one of the rare and beautiful creatures. Rudy's father had described a lone encounter in his childhood, which had taken on an almost mystical quality in the young man's mind. Now he himself beheld the creature!

The snow lion was the epitome of feline grace and power. The animal's broad paws, insulated by tufts of fur, rested easily on the rocky slope. Its wide, wedge-shaped head swiveled toward the young Iceman, and for a moment it held Rudy's eyes—much like the stag had done on the previous morn.

Again the snow lion leaped, extending its long, supple body as it crossed a yawning gulf, coming to rest on a narrow ledge. The broad face turned toward Rudy, as if sensing the Iceman's presence. Then the creature sat, leisurely licking its paws and running them across tufted, upturned ears. Scarcely daring to breathe, the man watched raptly, knowing he might never again have a chance like this.

A sound pulled his attention back to the shadowy niche. Something stirred in the camp, and Rudy saw a man starting along the ledge. He felt a sense of disquiet as the shadowed figure stepped into the moonlight and he recognized Lord Garamis. Taking a quick glance along the mountainside, the Iceman saw that the snow lion had already disappeared.

The Prince's black hair shone like oiled silk in the crystalline light, and his teeth flashed in a smile as he approached.

"I see I'm not the only one too tense to sleep," Garamis murmured. These were the first words he had directed specifically to Rudy since the expedition had begun, and the younger man found his tongue utterly paralyzed when it came to responding.

"Oh, yes," Garamis continued, as if he hadn't expected a reply. "The prospect of this climb excites me—and frightens me, perhaps more than I'd care to admit to your brothers."

"Me, too," Rudy agreed.

"It's a shame that Beryv won't allow you to join our approach to the summit," the prince observed quietly. "I should think that, once you've come this far, it would be only natural to join in the final ascent."

Though these echoed Rudy's own feelings, voiced to Beryv the previous night as forcefully as he'd dared, he now felt strangely compelled to come to his brother's defense.

"It's usual—for an inexperienced Iceman to only make a portion of the climb on his first attempt. Later, I'll have a chance to get to the top."

"Yes . . . I'm sure you will."

Rudy shivered, uncomfortable suddenly. The young noble stepped past him, stalking to the lip of the trail, staring from the edge of the precipice with a nonchalance that astounded Rudy. The lowland lord was nothing if not courageous, the Iceman admitted to himself.

"It seems as though you can see all Dalethica from here," noted Garamis. The long black hair puffed back from his face, driven by a suddenly increasing breeze. "Is that your village down there?" He gestured to a tiny collection of cottages and farms visible in the moonlight that washed the valley. A few windows glowed, where farmers had begun their early milking.

"No—that's Dermaat," Rudy explained. "Neshara is over the ridge to the west, the one that we crossed yesterday. You can't see it from here."

"And to the right—a wilderness, it would seem."

"That's the Wilderhof, to the east of Dermaat," Rudy confirmed. "It's a trackless place—so rough that not even the woodcutters live there." Rudy laughed softly, remembering his conversation with Anjell.

"We used to claim it was haunted, use it as a threat for unruly children. That doesn't work anymore."

"There's water—streams—all over. You can see it shine in the moonlight," Garamis declared, gesturing to all the broad sweep of Halverica.

Rudy gestured to the stream below that sparkled in the moonlight "There's a creek like this in every valley flowing down from the mountain—all coming from springs in the sides of Glimmercrown. Everybody says it's the purest water in all Dalethica."

Garamis didn't really seem to be listening, but now that he had found his voice, Rudy was not about to relinquish it. "Neshara is actually at the foot of the Glimmercrown. This valley here, that goes past Dermaat and down to the Glimmersee, ends at the ridge between Glimmercrown and Faerimont, above us."

"No one's ever climbed to the top of Glimmercrown, have they?" the lord inquired.

"No!" Rudy replied, shocked. "That's sacred ground—the only place in the world where the three Watersheds come together! The summit is protected by curses and Guardians. To climb there would be certain death!"

"Indeed," murmured the lord. "Thus we turn our energies to Faerimont—though in fact the Glimmercrown doesn't seem like a much more difficult climb. After all, both peaks are connected by the ridge above us."

"It's not the difficulty of the climb," Rudy explained. "It's just—well, it's *always* been sacred. No one even thinks of going there."

"Naturally." Garamis turned back to Rudy, his mouth twisted by a private smile. "You know, I could order your brother to bring you on the climb today."

Rudy shook his head helplessly. "The chief Iceman is the authority on all decisions, once the climb has commenced," he said—though Beryv himself had made this point to Garamis on several occasions. "I'll have to live with his decision."

"Yes . . . well, it does seem unfortunate. I'm sure the experience will be unique—and moving," the lord remarked.

Rudy, feeling vaguely disloyal even discussing this subject, gave

Garamis no further chance for conversation. Seeing signs of movement in the camp, the young Iceman started back on the ledge. Silently the Lord of Galtigor came along behind.

Beryv Appenfell saw his youngest brother approaching and nodded gruffly as he climbed out of his bedroll. "Daylight's less than an hour. We'll want to be started by then, so see that the lines are coiled," he ordered.

The elder Iceman hawked and spat, then turned to pulling on his frost-caked boots and gloves. Rudy, picking up the lines that would belay the lead climber—today that would be Beryv—began to carefully arrange the supple ropes into coils, shaking out every trace of a snarl or knot.

Garamis stepped past the young Iceman to confront the expedition's leader. "I think the young man should accompany us today," he said firmly.

Beryv blinked stoically. "We been over that already."

Pacing a step or two in the narrow niche, the nobleman shrugged his shoulders where they were chafed by the scabbard of his sword. Rudy, as he had many times since the climb began, wondered why Garamis had decided to carry his weapon. The sword—at least the hilt, which was all he had seen—was wrapped in leather, free of adornment. The jeweled scabbard he had left below, keeping the blade wrapped in soft leather. Except when he lay down to sleep, the prince constantly wore it in the sheath strapped to his back.

"From here on it's straight up—all the way to the saddle between Faerimont and Glimmercrown. He's not ready for a climb like that— not that it's any concern of yours. *I'll* tell him when he can go."

Listening as he worked, Rudy's heart sank—though he could have predicted his brother's response with complete accuracy. Still, briefly, he had allowed himself to hope. Rudy looked back at the camp, hoping that the lord would have the decency to drop the argument.

For a moment Lord Garamis met the flashing eyes of Beryv Appenfel, but finally the flatlander looked away. "Very well," he declared, his tone even. "I defer to your expertise."

Sunrise painted the snow-swept peaks in subtle shades of rose and lavender. Stars vanished into pale light as dawn framed the mountains and teased with the suggestion of distance so great that even the far horizon seemed near. Gradually, the cobbled surfaces of the surrounding peaks appeared, revealed in the clarity of the air like remote witnesses gathered to observe an example of human audacity.

Sharing the tension preceding the climb, the Icemen and the Lord of Galtigor ate their cold breakfast in silence—a silence that Rudy was in no mood to dispel. Even Coyle supressed his characteristic joking. Rudy's three brothers were obviously strained and uneasy, and for a moment he thought of suggesting that they delay the ascent. They wouldn't, he knew, and he also understood that his asking would only lower their estimation of him. Pulling his cloak tight against the growing wind, Rudy bit his lip and remained silent.

Only Garamis seemed ready: the young lord's eyes flashed as he looked upward, baring his teeth in a sharp grin.

"All my life I've dreamed of this summit," he declared. "It brings a sense of awe, now, to think that I'm finally about to stand upon the crest."

"A place few men can claim to have been," agreed Beryv.

"Only one place higher in all the Watershed," Garamis muttered, his gaze shifting slightly until it came to rest on brilliant Glimmercrown.

As ropes and lock rings were attached to each man's belt, Beryv pulled his youngest brother to the side.

"Hold the low belay until Coyle reaches that ledge, there—about a hundred feet up. Then we'll be on our own. Be careful down here, Rudy."

"*You* be careful," Rudy retorted, feeling a stab of irrational fear. He could see that his brother was gravely worried. Though he felt that he should try to ease Beryv's fears, his own apprehensions choked his throat and tied a knot in his tongue.

"Save some of the sausage," the senior Iceman said, forcing a smile. "We'll be back afore sunset."

Beryv Appenfell secured a rope to his waist and turned toward the cliff wall at the rear of their camp. Stepping with one foot onto a rock, he reached upward to wedge his right hand into a crack. His other foot caught the lip of a tiny outcrop, and then the fingertips of his left hand grasped a tiny knob over his head.

Carefully, in a series of smooth, short moves, the Iceman began to climb. He never reached with more than one limb at a time, yet neither did he ever cease moving. In meticulous, careful fashion, Beryv slowly inched his way up the wall.

The veteran Iceman trailed the rope as he selected a series of hand- and footholds in the broken face of the cliff. After thirty feet he stopped and drove a piton into a crack, through which he ran a metal ring and then passed the rope. Then he continued inching his way upward.

After Beryv had anchored the second piton, Donniall began to follow. His job was to belay any fall of Beryv's, as well as to assist the man who would climb behind. Donniall, steady hands on the rope, watched his brother proceed on the long ascent to the first of the Twin Steps. Those two ledges were the only resting places on the long, sheer face of the mountain—until the climbers reached the saddle of the connecting ridge, thousands of feet overhead.

After Donniall started upward, Prince Garamis clipped the rope to his belt. Rudy noticed, with a jolt of surprise, that the nobleman still wore his leather-hilted sword. Though it was strapped to his back, out of the way of hands or feet, it still seemed like a needless encumbrance on a dangerous ascent.

Soon Coyle departed, while Beryv already negotiated heights hundreds of feet above. Alone in the windswept niche, Rudy heard a grim warning in the gusts—but it was an alarm that could only increase his unease, not provide information on any threat. He kept the rope tightly around his waist, paying out the line as Coyle ascended along the route Beryv had established. Finally, when all the climbers had begun the higher stages of the ascent, all Rudy could do was wait.

By moving back to the mountainous shoulder flanking the camp, Rudy found that he could keep the party of climbers in sight. Soon Beryv reached the lower of the Twin Steps, the first place he could sit and rest on the long cliff. Anchoring a secure rope for the other climbers, Beryv paused for only a few minutes before starting the next phase of the ascent. He reached the second Step—a similar ledge, though narrower than the lower slab—after another hour's meticulous climbing. There he barely paused, perhaps because the ridge line was only a few hundred feet farther.

Four hours after beginning the climb, Beryv reached the saddle between the two summits. Quickly, following the ropes left by the lead climber, Garamis and the two other Appenfell brothers joined him. The ridge line snaking to the Faerimont soared upward from the gap, but that route, Rudy knew, lay beyond his view.

The young Iceman started to scramble down from his rocky perch, when a flash of movement overhead caught his eye. He saw a tiny figure, with a black object in its hand. For a moment he was puzzled, and then he gasped as a stab of fear pierced his bowels.

Lord Garamis had drawn his sword!

But where were the Icemen? Rudy could see only that lone figure, carrying the weapon as if he expected to use it. Resolutely, Garamis started along the ridge—and only then did Rudy realize the full import of the nobleman's presence.

Garamis did not disappear from sight because he had not started along the ridge to Faerimont. Instead, he stalked boldly along the crest leading to the main summit of the Glimmercrown! But how could he proceed—that ridge was too steep for an unskilled climber!

"No!"

The word reached Rudy's ears across a gulf of mountainous space, yet still he recognized his brother's voice. Beryv came into sight then, approaching Garamis from behind.

The nobleman turned and raised the black blade.

"Beryv—look out!" cried Rudy, though the climber must plainly see the danger before him. Still Beryv advanced, arms raised, apparently pleading with Garamis to turn from his sacrilegious course.

The black blade fell once, chopping into Beryv Appenfell's shoulder, and the Iceman vanished from view. Whether he lay on the rocks of the ridge top or had plummeted down the other side of the incline, Rudy could not see.

Garamis turned back toward the main summit, and now Rudy saw Donniall and Coyle scrambling in pursuit. They were armed only with the hammers and picks that were their climbing tools, and the nobleman easily held them at bay with his long, shadowy blade. The two Halvericans quickly went down, leaving Garamis alone on the crest.

Rudy saw the prince gesture upward with that horrible sword—but then Garamis disappeared! Stunned, the Iceman saw the treacherous nobleman appear farther up the steeply climbing ridge. Again the prince pointed, and once more he blinked out of sight, only to reappear still farther up the slope. Rudy feared he was losing his mind—and still Garamis continued to point the weapon and flash instantaneously upward.

Fear, disbelief, and fury wrestled within Rudy's heart and mind. Every instinct urged him toward the rock wall, but he knew that he lacked the skill to match his brothers' climb—and with all the Icemen so far above, there was none to offer him a rope or belay.

Then another sight sent a shiver of terror through him. Several large, pale figures came into view, moving along the icewall below the ridge. Larger than Garamis or the Icemen, the newcomers moved with nimble ease across the treacherous terrain. Their tan-white color, he discerned, was the shade of the jagged, rocky surface that covered their otherwise naked bodies.

It was only another moment before he realized that these climbers intended to stop Lord Garamis from reaching the summit of Glimmercrown. Others, he saw, moved onto the ridge crest and started downward, cutting off the nobleman's retreat—or perhaps advancing on any of the Appenfell brothers who might still be alive, hidden from Rudy's view.

Who were these strange people—or were they people at all? The mystery was added to the myriad other questions swirling through Rudy's brain. He remembered tales of Guardians, charged with protecting the sanctity of the Watershed—could he be seeing them now? Even as he wondered, he saw Garamis raise that awful blade, striking twice—and sending two of the hulking creatures tumbling away. The route to the summit was clear.

Lord Garamis disappeared behind a swooping cornice, an overhanging shelf of snow that swept outward from the ridge. Because of the curling edge to the cornice, Rudy knew that the drift was snow that had been blown upward from the far side of the mountain, in the high valley of Faerine. Now it hung like a precarious shelf over the valley of Dalethica.

A sharp, urgent growl carried to his ear, and Rudy turned in shock to see that the snow lion had returned. The animal's broad paws, claws retracted, pounded smoothly across the rough, snow-covered rocks. It bounded toward Rudy, then spun and pounced away. After several leaps it turned and looked back, with an expression that struck the Iceman as strangely beseeching.

A *crack*! resounded through the air, returning in a few seconds as an echo from the surrounding peaks. Looking upward again, Rudy saw the cornice of snow break free from the ridge. A huge slab of icy crystal plunged downward, tearing away rock and snow as it fell.

Garamis stood at the rim of the slide, and Rudy saw him scrambling to retain his balance. In another moment the cloud of snow exploded outward, sweeping more and more of the mountainside into its furious cascade. The ridge, the peaks overhead, all vanished in the growing chaos—chaos that Rudy now realized was plummeting straight toward *him*.

The young Iceman looked around desperately for some kind of shelter. The camp was doomed, he knew—the funnel of the two shoulders would carry the brunt of the slide straight into the niche. On the ledge the snow lion pounced away, turning back to look at Rudy after each leap. Outward, the cliff grew steeper and steeper.

Any choice in the matter suddenly vanished as a heavy slab of ice smashed into his head. He felt himself toppling backward, plunging away from the mountain and, for a brief moment, mingling in free fall with the careening force of the avalanche.

The first impact was a jarring smash against his shoulder, the next, a blunt crash into his back. The pain grew duller with each blow, until he was wrapped only in a cocoon of whiteness, pressure, and cold.

At last, all he knew was the cold, and then even that slipped away.

THREE
Wardens of the Watershed

During the chaos of Godswar, before the raising of the
Watershed, much immortal blood spilled across the
land and mingled with the sea. Thus did Darkblood
and Aura come to the world.
—SONGS OF AURIANTH
VOL. II, GODSTOME

— 1 —

Slowly the naked, rock-limbed figures made their way down the sheer
face of the Glimmercrown. They climbed with neither rope nor hammer, instead relying on long limbs and powerful, dextrous fingers and
toes to grip the slick surfaces of rock and ice. No spider ever clung to
a wall more certainly than did the High Guardians as they descended
from the mighty peak that was their home.

Even the gray, slate-scaled chieftain, who had reigned for more
years than the typical human could count, moved with grace and ease.
On the shallower slope at the base of the cliff, he dropped onto the
snowfield and ambled easily over the wet, slushy surface. He approached a group of his scouts, who stood around a body packed in
heavy, wet snow.

None of the Guardians save the chieftain carried anything; that
illustrious leader wore a series of pouches suspended from a rope belt
around his waist.

The killer chopped free a block of ice, reported one of the scouts. *He bore it away with him, leaping down the ridge faster than our eyes could follow.*

The chieftain turned to regard his stony fellows with pale blue, milky eyes. *How many of my children were slain by the blacktooth?* The speechless question reached each of the assembled warriors.

One, a hulking figure nearly eight feet tall, bowed his head before replying in the same fashion. *The human killed six of us. His weapon bore powerful medicine, and all of our protections were void. With it, he danced like the wind, passing us by and reaching the top. He has the power of Darkblood within him.*

Or at least, in the black claw that he bore in his hand, amended another. *It was that talon that did all of the killing.*

Perhaps that weapon was the portent of the Lord Minion we felt; it has been long since any of the Sleepstealer's spawn challenged us.

You may be right or wrong; it matters not, anymore.

We pursued with all haste, another Guardian reported. *But the dark one fled too fast—and always that talon struck out, when one of us drew too close. The other humans had left him ropes, and with these he could descend faster than we could follow.*

The leader turned his broad face skyward, and as his ice-blue eyes scanned the slope of the mighty peak, they filled with tears. His once-proud form slumped, the broad shoulders curving down as if they bore a great load—a weight too heavy to be carried by any one individual.

The failure is ours, Great One. Again the huge scout spoke, lowering his own head abjectly. *Allow us the penance of our lives—when we have given up our breath, then may the honor of the Guardians be restored.*

With a sigh, the chieftain shook his craggy head, his mane of layered shale swinging with regal grace. *This is not a matter of honor. It is true that the sacred ice has been taken by a mortal, and that is a matter of concern to all the Watershed. But more deaths among us—and we are already too few—will do nothing to assuage the harm.*

Groaning, the huge scout collapsed onto the snow. The others sat motionless, staring bleakly downward, their best hope of absolution taken from them.

What of this one? inquired the leader, gesturing toward the body in the snow. *It has not perished yet?*

It is near death, with many broken bones.

This one is innocent, the leader proclaimed. He bent down, allowing his long fingers to trail across ice-crusted jowls, to lift a floppy, snow-filled ear. *This one should not die.*

Reverently the other Guardians tucked their heads, while their chieftain squatted beside the motionless form. Reaching into one of his pouches, he withdrew a handful of snow—snow that sparkled when the sun touched it, reflecting the brilliant colors of the rainbow. The High Guardian dusted the creature's head with this glittering snow, and with his fingers he spread a trace of the frozen Aura across the wide black nostrils. *Now rise, Snow Lion, and return to your life.*

The others leaned forward, touching the shaggy coat of the great animal. They felt breath return to those powerful lungs, heard a huffing snort as air was expelled from the black nostrils.

With a startled growl, the snow lion sprang to his feet. His dark eyes swung warily from one Guardian to the next, but the animal sensed that these were not enemies. Still, hackles rose on his shoulders as, stiff-legged, he slowly backed way.

The Guardians made no attempt to restrain him. Instead, they watched him sympathetically. Their voiceless words could not reach him, but their blue eyes silently urged him to go, to turn and run back to a life on the mountain.

With a nervous growl, the animal retreated until he was well out of reach of these mysterious beings. Then he turned and leaped away, racing across the wet snow, broad paws easily bearing his weight without sinking through the soft crust.

But the snow lion did not race upward, back to his mountain home. Instead he loped along the slope, traversing the wide snowfield where the avalanche had spilled its fury. The Guardians understood what he did, and they respected his courage and loyalty—even as they knew he was doomed to fail.

— 2 —

Nicodareus looked for the other Lord Minions as he entered Dassadec's cavernous throne room. All around, spuming falls of Darkblood, a score in number, poured from niches high in the black walls. Shadows shrouded the wide gallery, a mile or more long, where the hosts of the Sleepstealer's lesser warriors could gather in uncounted thousands. Once, fourteen centuries earlier, hundreds of thousands of those minions had gathered here. Nicodareus still recalled the great ceremony that had sent the massive legion of minions off to war.

That war had lasted for four hundred years; when it was over, nine out of ten of those minions had perished. Even now, after a full millennium of rebuilding, the numbers of minions were only approaching their earlier maximum. Though the beasts of Darkblood did not die—other than from violent cause—neither could they be quickly and readily created.

The great plaza of Agath-Trol was broken only by the dark oval of the Bloodpool, where black liquid bubbled and seethed with barely contained power. Beyond the plaza, the floor sloped upward into a wide flight of stairs and a platform that was itself as large as any mortal palace. The vast surface was adorned only by three towering thrones, each mounted on a spire of black stone, while overhead a jagged ceiling was lost in shadow. Two more pillars, cracked and splintered, stood beside the three and showed clearly the effects of violence done a thousand years before.

A throne for each of his Lord Minions, Dassadec had declared, and raised the stone pillars from rock and Darkblood. Once they had been five, but Balzaracc and Karthakan had been slain by Guardians during the Four Century War; now there were only the three of them left.

The Sleepstealer himself required no support—indeed, no physical framework could hope to contain his mighty presence. Still, from this chamber Dassadec followed the progress of his minions, and from here he worked the schemes that brought him, each day, closer to his single goal.

The surrounding fortress, called Agath-Trol, was a mountain rising from the heart of Dassadec's wasteland. Not quite so high as the Glimmercrown, the massif nevertheless covered a huge area, and much of its interior had been excavated to form huge chambers and myriad passageways. At its heart was this massive throne room.

Nicodareus skirted the circular, bubbling pool—as big as a small lake—that seethed and percolated in the center of the great chamber. Darkblood erupted in geysers, then swirled into riotous whirlpools as it plunged back to the depths. Great flights of stairs led to the lake's surface from each of the four directions. Grimly the Lord Minion reflected on the singular direction of those steps—many had descended, but few, if any, had climbed back up.

As he approached the vast dais, Nicodareus sent his Sight before him and saw that the two other thrones were already occupied. To the right the massive, serpentine bulk of Reaper overflowed his wide bench. Known as the Talon of Dassadec, Reaper was an aloof and regal wyrm, all curved claw, scaly skin, leather wing, and wickedly knowing smile. Now Reaper nodded his massive head, as if sensing the presence of the Eye in the air before him.

Still stalking imperiously, Nicodareus moved his Sight to the throne at the left, where Phalthak hissed and slithered. The Fang of Dassadec possessed none of the imposing presence of Reaper; nor did he exude the bestial pride of Nicodareus. As if sensing his own grotesqueness, Phalthak now bobbed uncomfortably, his myriad heads darting this way and that as he perceived his cohort approaching.

The Fang's apelike body sprawled awkwardly across the throne. His tail was bare of fur, like a rat's, and it thrashed through the air in obvious agitation while his huge hands pawed himself roughly between his legs. Each of his necks was a sinuous snake. More than a dozen of them writhed and lashed, emerging from a single moist aperture between the ape-body's shoulders. The snake-mouths were studded with tiny fangs, each of which bore a different type of venom.

By the time Nicodareus completed his remote inspection, he had reached the foot of the broad stairway. Flapping his wings—more for show than for lift—he rapidly ascended the steps, crossed the dais to the center pillar, and stalked up the stairway that spiraled around the pedestal of his own throne. At the top he paused to nod once to Reaper, again to Phalthak, before he took a seat in the gleaming black chair.

For a long time they waited. The Eye and the Talon rested patiently, immobile yet alert, while the Fang of Dassadec continued to seethe and twist in his chair.

Their master's arrival was nothing seen, or sensed with any other overt evidence—it was more like the subtle gathering of cloud that precedes a violent storm. Dassadec's presence seeped through the air, insinuating into the Lord Minions' awareness with awe-inspiring might.

Each lord climbed down from his throne to sprawl in obeisance, and the will of their master wrapped them in an embrace of pleasure . . . and anticipation.

Greetings, my lords. I have summoned you for a momentous beginning. The voice of Dassadec reached into the minds of his Lord Minions, touching each.

"Master—you have but to command," they replied in unison.

The Four Century War ended one thousand years ago. That struggle has been all but forgotten by humans—certainly none of them know how close we came to ultimate victory. Know this, my Lord Minions: only two factors stopped our complete triumph. The stubborn resistance of Halverica, and the untimely intervention of Faerine.

Nicodareus shuddered. When he remembered the deaths of Balzaracc and Karthakan, he knew that the Guardians, too, had been terrible foes of the Sleepstealer. But the Lord Minion remained silent, attending as Dassadec continued the message for his lords.

Reaper . . . my bold son, my Talon . . . you are to fly to the west. There you will rally the hosts of my minions to the banner of the Sleepstealer, assembling a mighty host along the Dry Basin. When you have mustered an army, you will await my further command.

"As you wish, Master." The wyrm's voice was a ground-shaking rumble, yet it was quickly swallowed in the vast chamber.

And you, Phalthak . . . you are my Vile One. For you, it is to the border of Faerine, to the slopes below the Darkenheight. There you will watch and wait—and when I give my command, you shall kill.

A dozen snake-heads bobbed, tongues flickering forth in ready acknowledgment of the Sleepstealer's command.

And you, my Eye—my most perceptive lord . . . The soundless voice of Dassadec turned toward Nicodareus, penetrating every pore, thrumming in his torso like a steady drumbeat of power. *You have made good use of your journey—the first of the Power of Three.*

"Yes, Great Lord. I preserve the powers of the second and third journeys until you make known your purposes and command me to go."

You shall not wait long—very soon it will be time to begin.

"You have only to wish, my master, and I obey."

But now—before you again cross the Watershed—you must go to the Spring of Darkblood. My laborers have toiled there for five decades—now it is time the task was done.

Nicodareus' body grew taut. His ember-eyes flared at the thought of the power so imminent. He had inspected the canals of Darkblood himself, but had not suspected the moment of release to be so near. Now he found it difficult to contain his excitement.

"The breach will be made immediately!" promised the Lord Minion.

Splendid. A thousand years ago it was one human realm—Halverica—standing between myself and ultimate triumph. The . . . diversion of Darkblood shall insure that, this time, it will not happen again.

Nicodareus stood at full attention. He himself had barely survived that great campaign, ten centuries past, and now he suppressed a memory, picturing the hateful Guardians who had come so close to killing him. Darkblood pulsed through his veins, in full fever with the knowledge that he would soon have the chance to avenge that disaster.

The Stormfleet awaits your departure. Do not give me cause for regret. Now, go!

— 3 —

The outside of Dassadec's palace rose as a great darkstone mountain, jutting from the wasted plain of Duloth-Trol. Massive turrets of rock surmounted jagged shoulders on the lower flanks, but the ultimate central pillar rose as a slick-sided tower of obsidian. A great flock of terrions wheeled through a circle, patiently soaring over the fortress, spiraling and diving among the ships of the Stormfleet.

The flagship of that mighty armada was the *Dreadcloud*—the great, black vessel currently moored to the high tower of Agath-Trol. A huge expanse of the mountain/fortress lay beneath the *Dreadcloud*'s shadow, while the lesser shades of Dondercraft scudded back and forth, downwind of the mighty battlecloud.

A cloaked brutox threw the line free as Nicodareus stepped to the top of the tower. One of the terrions squawked, its cry a harsh arrow piercing the air, and the Lord Minion recognized Slasher. He felt an emotion as close to affection as any he would ever know.

"Fly well, my terrion," Nicodareus murmured. "This is another voyage I must make alone."

The *Dreadcloud* surged overhead, and as the Lord Minion waited, a whirling cyclone descended from the lower hull of the dark, seething cloud. Twisting down, the black funnel swooped over the Eye of Dassadec.

Nicodareus felt the tug of the whirlwind and allowed it to raise him from the tower. Within moments he came to rest on the low deck within the massive cloudship. He stepped carefully to a ladder, quickly adjusting to the spongy nature of the surface beneath his feet.

"Welcome aboard, Lord Minion," said a helmeted brutox, offering a hand—which Nicodareus ignored—at the top of the ladder. "Would you care to watch the flight from the bridge?" The brut's lower jaw sagged, revealing a pair of long, yellow tusks; sparks trickled from its talons, leaving the stench of ozone acrid in the air.

"I'll go to the forebattery," Nicodareus declared. "Tell the captain to meet me there."

On his rare flights in the *Dreadcloud*, the Lord Minion had discovered this platform, and preferred its vantage to any other. Thrusting outward from the bow, the forebattery was a circular surface of black cloud. Six columns of smoky vapor, arranged hexagonally around the deck, loomed and seethed upward, turning inward on themselves in a constant, angry flow. These columns, Nicodareus knew, could each spit a powerful bolt of lighting from the underside of the battery, striking a target anywhere on the ground.

Now he made his way to the battery, through long, lightless tunnels walled with seething black smoke. He met several stalkers, who raced about bearing messages or busy upon other errands, but the reptilian humanoids quickly ducked from the Lord Minion's path. Soon Nicodareus reached the more open passages near the bow.

When he emerged at the prow of the massive sky vessel, the wind whipped his cloak and wings back from his broad shoulders. The kroaks who manned the forward battery bowed humbly at the Lord Minion's arrival, but Nicodareus ignored them to stride directly to the forward edge of the massive, solid cloud. The smaller Dondercraft were already under way, bucking and pitching through the storm-spattered sky as they took up their escorting positions to port and starboard. The *Dreadcloud* would lead the way, as was the mighty ship's due.

Far below, sprawled the wasteland of Duloth-Trol. Occasional chasms, many belching clouds of sulphurous gas, yawned in the broken ground. Black lines of glistening Darkblood trickled across the steaming plains, forming the "rivers" of the Sleepstealer's realm. Toxic to any creature of Dalethica or Faerine, the vile liquid was the nectar of sustenance to the minions, even the Lord Minions, of Dassadec.

The prow of the *Dreadcloud* rose and fell as the mighty craft plowed into the wind, and Nicodareus lost himself in the sheer majesty and power of the flying ship. The wind roared around him, and a higher layer of overcast prevented the irritating presence of the sun from becoming too intense.

Shortly he sensed a presence beside him and looked down to see a broad-shouldered brutox clad in shining black plate armor. The creature raised its hand in a brusque salute, sparks cascading from its claws, describing a glowing arc in the air.

"Ah, Captain Direfang . . . you found me."

"We are honored to have such an eminent passenger, my lord," declared the brutox. "I trust that you are making yourself at home?"

"Naturally. It seems we're making good time—is that the Tarlake I see already?"

"Indeed, lord. The sturmvaults are fuming at maximum capacity—

we'll have enough momentum to carry you almost to the Watershed."

"Would that you could carry me over that vexing barrier," Nicodareus muttered, half to himself. At the captain's worried look he chuckled. "I jest. If you can bring me to the slope below Glimmercrown, I should be quite content."

"Aye, my lord—it is as you wish."

The sun rose and fell twice as Nicodareus stood like a figurehead on the *Dreadcloud,* watching the realm of Duloth-Trol flow beneath. For the Eye, light or dark conditions mattered little; his Sight could at all times examine the lands below, and those hundreds of miles away. Lava rivers flared against the black ground. Huge flats of tar bubbled and steamed, vaporizing Darkblood into the air. The land rose steadily toward the great ranges of the Watershed. By the second day the distant ridge of mountains had come into view even for the mundane eye, their peaks smeared with the black frost of Darkblood. Gradually the summits took form and detail as, true to the brutox captain's word, the massive cloud surged across the foothills, plowing up the valley of the Darkenflow River. Soaring mountains now rose to either side, but the floating ship easily negotiated the narrowing channel, until it reached a terminus at the base of a towering massif of stone. The face of the mountain was scarred by many surfaces of black ice.

"Behold the Glimmercrown," offered the captain. "And you see the Darkspring below. That is where you wish to descend?"

"Indeed."

Nicodareus looked back, absorbing the familiar vista of Darkblood's realm. How much of the world would look like that, he wondered, before the Sleepstealer was through? Neither Dassadec, nor his Lord Minions, would be satisfied with less than the entire Watershed.

— 4 —

Once again the Lord Minion rode the whirlwind. This time the howling spiral carried him slowly to the ground, where Nicodareus came to rest beside a huge quarry. Hundreds of kroaks excavated and hauled stone under the watchful eyes of many brutox overseers. Two brutox flanked the wide, dark mouth of a mine shaft extending straight into the mountain, its course boring directly under the summit of Glimmercrown. The guards snapped to attention as Nicodareus approached.

The Lord Minion observed a stack of bodies—kroaks—piled to the side of the tunnel mouth. He counted at least a dozen individuals, and noted a pile of assorted arms, legs, and other body parts. He indicated the gory mounds as he reached the guards.

"Another Deep Guardian attack?" he inquired.

"Yes, Lord Minion," sparked the brutox. "A large one—near the terminus of the shaft. They grow increasingly agitated by our progress. I am happy to report that this individual has been slain."

"And it killed only kroaks, eh?" Nicodareus chuckled, watching the brutox guard squirm under his fire-red gaze.

"Indeed, my lord. Only kroaks."

"Good." Nicodareus marched past the guards to enter the tunnel and stalk along the channel of dark stone. Inspecting the smooth walls and floor, the precisely arched ceiling, his mouth curled into a wicked smile. The minions had indeed performed their work splendidly.

The Lord Minion walked many miles from the entrance at the Darkspring. He was impressed by the careful excavation, the diligent use of stone pillars to shore the ceiling—all the sturdy features that marked the long, precise tunnel. The shaft had been started four dozen years ago, and had cost numerous kroak and brutox lives during its long period of construction—but once Nicodareus completed his immediate task, that tedious labor would be behind them.

Beside the smooth walkway, thick, sludgelike liquid flowed in a deep channel. The Darkblood bubbled like syrup, seething and foaming along the slightly descending trough, as if it sensed the nearness of its release.

For simplicity's sake, Nicodareus shifted his outer form and traveled in the guise of a kroak, round-shouldered and strapped with muscle. The mouth of the craven beast gaped slightly open, revealing short, blunt, canine teeth, while his slightly bowlegged lower limbs clumped him steadily forward. The characteristic knob on his forehead formed the prominent bone of the thick-skulled humanoid.

Often he met parties of real kroaks, marching to or from the head of the tunnel. At these times Nicodareus lowered his face so that the minions could not see his eyes—for, if they noticed the fiery gleam there, they would know that the one of the Lord Minions of Dassadec walked among them, and the kroaks' fear would only complicate Nicodareus' task. Also, word of his approach would reach the worksite— and when the Eye of Dassadec inspected a labor crew, he wanted his arrival to come as a surprise.

For hours, Nicodareus walked in solitary silence, yet never did the disguise of his stooped, ignoble form waver. He passed great reservoirs of Darkblood, and here he saw kroaks standing beside sluice gates and capstans. The beasts paid him little notice—he was just another slavish laborer, trudging toward the terminus of the long shaft.

Crossing a network of stone bridges, the Eye of Dassadec knew that he neared the end of his march. Now the sounds of chisels and hammers came to him, and he saw the sparking illumination that could only mean the presence of at least one brutox.

In a few minutes Nicodareus approached a team of kroaks, led— as he had known they would be—by a swaggering, hulking brutox. Though the craven laborers had not suspected his true nature, Nicodareus knew that their overseer would not be so deceived. At the same time, it now suited his purposes to show himself.

The kroaks chopped at a wall of black rock, wielding hammers, picks, and shovels with the stolid, uncomplaining patience of their kind. The brutox, fully a foot taller than its human-sized drudges, leaned against a pillar of rock and watched. The tusks jutting from the brut's wide jaws were yellowed with age, but its talon-studded hands swiped quickly at any kroak foolish enough to slow the pace of its work. Sparks dripped from those claws as the brutox idly traced them across the surface of the Darkblood.

Nicodareus changed shape as he reached the workers, his size increasing smoothly, shoulders straightening and limbs extending. The leathery wings sprouted from his shoulders, while the clublike feet of the kroak-body expanded to form his great paws.

As he had known they would, the kroaks trembled and gawked as Nicodareus approached. Even the mighty brutox bowed deeply, gazing upward at its approaching master with eyes that could not conceal the brut's abiding fear. Two other brutox held back, lurking in the shadows and letting their fellow speak to the powerful visitor.

"Greetings, O Mighty One," gurgled the brutox, rising to stand at a semblance of attention. "It is always a great pleasure to behold a Lord Minion of Dassadec," he added, lying smoothly.

"Of course," murmured the winged creature, his bestial face curling into a sneer. "How fares the excavation?"

"We grow near to the waters of Dalethica," the brutox replied, nodding with enthusiasm. "No more than a hundred paces of rock remain before us. A week—two at the most—and the canal will be completed."

Nicodareus was known for good reason as the Eye of Dassadec. Now he turned those penetrating organs onto the rock wall at the end of the tunnel. His vision pierced the slick, dark surface, passing through a few spans of stone until he recognized a subterranean spring of pure, transparent water. The Eye of Dassadec could see that the spring was considerably closer than the hundred paces estimated by the work captain.

"Redouble your efforts," Nicodareus commanded. "I want your crew to make contact as soon as possible."

"Of course," agreed the brutox, offended by the implication that his kroaks weren't working at their utmost pace—yet intelligent enough to conceal these feelings from the powerful Lord Minion who commanded him.

"Work, you slugs!" bellowed the tusked overseer. Sparks showered and snapped from his claws, emphasizing the commands, and the kroaks bent to their task with redoubled effort.

Grimly contented, Nicodareus moved back along the black tunnel, away from the laborers. He inspected a complicated series of sluice gates and valves. Made from dark iron, the heavy barriers restrained the reservoirs of Darkblood from the end of the tunnel, though as soon as the gate opened, the thick liquid would surge all the way to the terminus. Now, where it met the metal barrier, Darkblood seethed and bubbled angrily, though the iron resisted the liquid's corrosive effects.

The Eye of Dassadec grew impatient. Only a few feet of rock remained, and though the kroaks made a great clamor of tools and curses, the work progressed too slowly for the Lord Minion's increasing agitation. Already a sheen of pure water glistened on the rock wall, as pressure in the spring beyond the mountains sought release. Nevertheless, the chisels and hammers would require days of continuing labor before they would excavate a passage large enough for the canal.

Nicodareus reached forth a huge, taloned hand, cupping a pool of Darkblood and pouring the liquid over his skin. He repeated the process until the glistening stuff coated his entire body. Next he seized the lever of the first sluice gate. Behind that barrier the great reservoir of putrescent, seething liquid pressed, urgently seeking release. With a wrenching twist, Nicodareus pulled open the iron palisade.

Darkblood immediately surged through the channel, frothing along the chute that led downward toward the workers. All the weight of liquid in the miles-long trough pushed forward, into a growing, ink-black cascade.

Even over the din of their labors the kroaks and brutox felt the disturbance. Gaping blankly, the former turned from the wall to stare incomprehendingly at the approaching wall of Darkblood. The brutox, conversely, sensed the nearness of disaster. Sparking in agitation, the three overseers tried to press through the ranks of workers, seeking an escape that did not exist.

The oily flow of Darkblood swept workers, tools, and loose rock into its cascade, roaring toward the wet wall at the end of the tunnel. Already, crystalline water from the spring beyond trickled into tiny streams, pooling on the floor.

When the stuff of darkness met the pure water from beyond the mountains, a rumbling explosion convulsed through the long tunnel. The force of the blast tore kroak and brutox into pieces too small to distinguish. Pressure erupted before and behind, twisting the bedrock of the mountains, cracking shelves of stone that had lain intact for thousands of years.

Most important to Nicodareus, the eruption blasted the rock barrier out of the way, allowing the Darkblood to continue its downward flowage—though none of the ignoble laborers remained alive to witness the successful conclusion of their half-century-long task.

The Eye of Dassadec, however, stood and gloated in the full force of the blast. His skin slick with Darkblood, Nicodareus remained immune to the physical hurts of rock, pressure, and blast. When the chaos of the explosion had settled, he made his way slowly through the smoldering wreckage. The Lord Minion stepped across the hissing confluence of liquids, to where the water—now polluted with Darkblood—bubbled outward toward the release of a mountain spring.

Abruptly the bedrock shifted beneath the Lord Minion's feet. Nicodareus pitched to the side, scrambling to retain his balance as the passageway trembled. Rocks splintered free from the ceiling, tumbling to the floor, while dust and steam clouded the air, obscuring even the Eye of Dassadec's vision.

The earthquake rumbled through the mountains, heaving with a force that rocked even the mightiest peaks. For a dark, terrifying moment Nicodareus wondered if a million tons of rock were about to smash downward, crushing him in place now, when he stood so close to victory.

But soon the temblor faded, and the ceiling of the passageway—coupled with the protection of the minion's Darkblood-slick skin—shielded Nicodareus from serious harm. Stepping over the mingled carnage of brutox and kroak, the Lord Minion reached a bubbling pool, where the liquids of two springs mingled. Water and Darkblood formed a spiraling pattern, flowing away in a steady, powerful stream.

The Watershed was breached, Nicodareus observed with fierce exultation. For the first time since the gods carved the mountainous barriers into the bedrock of the world, Darkblood flowed beyond the boundaries of Duloth-Trol! It did not matter that the breach was, for the time being, a slow trickle. Spilling into Dalethica, the Darkblood would join the confluence of water flowing into the mountain stream, and then merge into the lake and river beyond.

Nicodareus tried to use his Sight to examine the slopes of the Glimmercrown, far overhead, to be certain that the human prince had done his work. Unfortunately, the convulsions had caused a great amount of Aura to slide across the divide; as always, the water of magic—snow, in this case—blocked even the potent vision of the Eye of Dassadec.

As the rubble and chaos settled, more minions marched into the tunnel, drawn by the Lord Minion's unspoken summons. A reptilian stalker led the way, followed by dozens of kroaks.

Nicodareus met the slitted eyes of the stalker with his own fire-red gaze. "Lead these kroaks into the valley beyond. You will have to remain near the breach, for that will be your only source of pure Dark-blood. Yet venture as far into Dalethica as you can. Learn if there were any survivors of the climb on the Glimmercrown; if so, kill them."

The stalker nodded, its snake-head bobbing up and down on a long, flexible neck. Under the force of its master's gaze, the creature shifted its shape, until soon it resembled a long-limbed human. Hissing eagerly, the minion started through the breach in the watershed. Dozens of growling, snapping kroaks followed along behind.

— 5 —

During my earliest lessons about the gods, I learned that Aurianth, not Baracan, was the source of all prophecy. Though Pheathersqyll had still not shared the details of his auguries regarding my own life, I knew that these prognostications had guided, even dictated, my entire existence thus far. Since so much of my fate was controlled by these mysterious words, I turned to the Mistress of Magic as the great cornerstone of my faith.

If not for the dreams, during those years my faith probably would have flagged. I was frustrated when Pheathersqyll turned my questions aside—little did I want to hear those words "wait" and "patience."

My escape came with each night, when that tall, brown-haired man would visit my slumber. He was young, his smile pleasant but very shy. I felt as though I began to know him then—even to love him a little bit, though of course I knew nothing about love. Yet he gave me the strength and the faith to wait, when waiting was the most difficult thing in all the Watershed.

Finally, in my twelfth year, Pheathersqyll told me of the prophecy he had divined at the time of my birth—the dictates that had initiated my course of study:

Find the girl of Three Stars Rising.
Daughter of the goddess, sister of man;
Mother of years, and child of time.
She must learn well, and completely;
For her strength shall bear the fate of ages,
*   and man.*

At the time he shared this verse with me, Pheathersqyll admitted it was but the first of three parts. The second part, he said, I must wait for more years to learn; and the third part would come from he knew not where. Naturally, the verse did not tell me nearly as much as I wanted to know; indeed, to my mind it told me nothing at all.

"How will I know when I can learn the rest of the prophecy?" I challenged Pheathers.

He gave me, again, that supercilious smile. "Patience, girl. You will wait, and you will grow, and Aurianth will know when you are ready."

Yet that very night I failed to dream. In my remaining years at the Academy of the Sun, the nocturnal visage of that brown-haired man never visited me again.

From: *Recollections,* by Lady Raine of the Three Waters

FOUR

Mourning Gardens

When water mingles with a great concentration of
Aura or Darkblood, chaos results. Our two ranks were
created to protect against this destruction of order . . .
High Guardians, to watch the peaks and ridges atop
the world; and Deep Guardians, as sentries warding the
Watershed's foundation and roots.
—CODEX OF THE GUARDIANS
VOL. I, GODSTOME

— 1 —

Something jarred Rudy's face, striking a hard blow—an assault that he
somehow didn't feel through his skin, but sensed as a dull pressure
against his head. He tried to blink, but his eyes refused to respond.
He heard nothing, saw only darkness.

Very gradually that inky shadow lightened to a dim gray haze. A
tingling sensation of pain worked through his limbs, irritating his skin
as if a thousand hot pins pricked at him. Yet as memory returned, that
pain became a source of disbelieving wonder—could it be that he was
still *alive*?

The young Iceman offered a small prayer of thanks—and hope—
to Baracan. Straining, he tried to raise an arm, to kick with his legs,
but still he couldn't move. He struggled to clench his hands into fists,
realized that they were already tightly balled, and attempted instead to
extend his fingers.

Amazingly, one of them moved—not much, but enough to convince him that returning consciousness brought him back to the body that he knew. The tingling burn intensified, cramps seizing his muscles as vitality spread. He tried to open his mouth, but firm pressure against his cheeks and jaw prevented any movement beyond the wiggling of his tongue.

Then, abruptly, brilliant light shot through the grayness of his vision. Involuntarily, he squeezed his eyelids shut, which only partially dimmed the brightness. A sense of warmth spread across his brow, as if someone had pressed a warm cloth onto his face.

At the same time, his nostrils picked up an odor of hot, unfamiliar breath. Again that warm presence swept across his face, wiping more of the snow away. He saw a great, shaggy form silhouetted against an impossibly bright sky. A big paw, surprisingly gentle, cuffed him across the face, and finally Rudy recognized his benefactor.

The snow lion! Rudy choked, spitting frosty pieces of snow away from his lips. His face came free as a huge tongue, sandpaper-rough, wiped the icy crystals away.

Sputtering, Rudy opened his eyes again, squinting against the brightness of the sky. He felt velvet paws scraping across his shoulders and chest as the animal clawed away great chunks of packed snow, pawing at the icy cocoon with fanatic intensity. Dazed, the Iceman contented himself with deep breaths of air, letting his eyes adjust to the brightness of the world.

Far above loomed the Glimmercrown, with the neighboring peak of Faerimont soaring to almost equal altitude. He realized—with a shock strong enough to penetrate his numbness—that the avalanche had carried him all the way to the foot of the immense mountain.

He had plunged nearly two vertical miles, and yet he was still alive. *That* fact seemed too unreal for him to grasp; instead he focused on the struggle to escape his ice-bound cocoon. The snow lion dug valiantly and soon Rudy's arms and shoulders came free. The weight of snow encasing his legs had set like icy mortar, and briefly the young Iceman feared that he had regained consciousness only to realize the nature of his fatal trap.

For a moment he wondered something else—why did this creature, so wild, so shy and solitary, make an extraordinary effort on a human's behalf? Lowering his broad snout into the channel scraped by his paws, the snow lion gnawed at an outcrop of ice. With a loud *snap!* a chunk bigger than Rudy's head broke free. Prying with his hands, the man pulled enough snow out of the way to squirm free of the frigid trap. He was thankful that he'd laced his boots so tightly; otherwise they would certainly have been left buried in the tightly compressed snow.

The snow lion stood over him, almost protectively, as the young Iceman crawled out. Rudy still wondered why the animal had saved him. Only when he had rolled free of the ice-encrusted depression and scrambled to his feet did other, darker thoughts begin. Were Beryv, Coyle, and Donnial alive? His emotions flamed into rage as he remembered the brutal treachery of Prince Garamis. Through growing despair he faced the truth: his brothers must certainly be dead. Like his father, they had perished on the high faces of the Crown of the World.

But *why?* The Prince of Galtigor had caused the disaster—that much was obvious. But for what reason had he turned toward the Glimmercrown, instead of Faerimont? As to the strange creatures who had defended the peak, Rudy had an idea. He had heard legends about the High Guardians, protectors of the peaks and ridges of the Watershed who emerged from cracks and crevices in the rock to fight for their mountain. Still the central question remained: why did Garamis turn toward the sacred peak and trigger their assault?

The snow lion prodded Rudy with a massive paw, a rumbling purr gurgling in the deep, broad chest. The big animal rubbed a shoulder against the man hard enough to knock him off balance.

"Easy, big fellow." Rudy scratched the snow lion behind his drooping ears and the purrs increased to ecstatic growls. "I guess you saved my life—I wish you could tell me why."

The animal dropped to the ground and rolled onto his back, allowing Rudy to kneel and scratch his tender belly through the coat of long, silky hair. At the same time, Rudy continued to wrestle with a multitude of questions. His thoughts raced from one puzzle to another, buzzing around like fat flies in his head, making him desperate for answers—just to relieve his agitation.

Indeed, his muscles thrummed with growing energy, building on a vague sense of urgency. The snow sparkled like none he had ever seen—an illusionary effect, he believed, brought on by his miraculous rescue. Probably he had never appreciated the beauty of sunlit snow before. Now the frozen crystals gleamed and glittered like a field of diamonds, their countless tiny facets reflecting all the colors of the rainbow.

The Iceman no longer felt any pain in his limbs; he looked at his hands and arms curiously, aware that he should be suffering some evidence of frostbite, or damage from the plunge. Yet he couldn't find even a scratch or a scrape, much less any sign of a significant wound.

An unusual tear in his fur jacket caught his attention—a tiny cut had been made, directly over his heart. The hairs turned inward, as if the coat had been punctured with great force. Pulling the outer covering aside, he was frightened to find his shirt stained with blood; checking quickly, he saw a hole in that garment to match the outer puncture. When he lifted his shirt, he saw that his chest, too, was bloody.

Where the puncture would have entered his skin he found the strangest thing of all—a tiny patch of ice, frozen hard, nestled in a small groove in his skin. There was no wound, nor did he feel any pain when he probed the area. The ice was cold to the touch of his finger, yet it didn't chill the skin of his breast, nor did it seem to melt from his body heat.

Rudy tore off his jacket to look at it more closely, and only then did he notice the second hole—in the *back*, where the fur had been pushed outward. Wonderingly, he reached a hand behind himself, stretching until he felt a similar tiny patch of ice below his shoulder, indicating—what?

That not only had he tumbled down the sheer mountain and been trapped, unconscious, under the snow—he had been *stabbed*, actually run through with a blade!

But who could have done that? Garamis? Certainly the prince must be dead—it didn't seem possible that any man could survive the attack of so many fierce Guardians. Too, if the prince had survived, he must be up near the top of the mountain. It was barely possible that the man could descend from the mountain's summit to its foot in a single day, but he would not get down until after dark. Rudy could see that there was still a lot of daylight left.

"What *happened* to me?" He asked the question of the snow lion or himself; neither could provide an answer. The animal huffed in sympathy, pricking up his long ears.

Nearby, Rudy recognized the lake at the head of Dermaat Valley. He saw the spring at the base of the mountain. Like all of Glimmer-crown's fountains, the Dermaat spring was fabled for its pure water—yet now Rudy could see that its outflow was dark and murky. Of course there was a logical explanation: the landslide must have dumped a good deal of mud into the spring, and it would take some time to flush clean. Still, the ugly liquid gave an even more sinister cast to his apprehensive mood.

What about the others? He thought about his brothers, knowing the truth, yet still finding it impossible to believe they were dead. Certainly they would come tromping down from the peak, raucous with the laughter of a climb well-made, thirsty for beer and ready to boast all night in the Black Bull Tavern. But when he looked upward, he saw only the sheer side of the greatest mountain in the Watershed. There was no sign of any living man. His brothers would never make another climb; he would never hear that laughter, or listen to the boasts or share the beer. A picture of the big Appenfell chalet, horrifyingly, devastatingly empty, filled his mind and, with an anguished sob, he collapsed.

Gradually, the grief gave way to a vast emptiness, a numb sense of disbelief that insulated him against ultimate despair. The sun had fallen behind the western ridge, and late afternoon shadows stretched across the valley floor. A sliver of evening's waning moon would soon follow the sun past that horizon; most of the day was gone. Rudy knew he'd have to start on the trail to Neshara, getting back to the village as quickly as possible, bearing the bleak news of the disaster. He dreaded the grief he would bring to his brothers' wives and children. Yet at the same time he felt a growing sense of animation—a need to be on his way. The snow lion padded in a circle around him, pouncing and whoofing as if it shared Rudy's desire for movement.

Only then did he wonder at the rapid departure of the day. The slide had occurred no later than late morning. Had he lain entombed by snow for the better part of a day? Obviously, he had—yet how was it that he was still alive?

Avalanches were a common threat in Halverica, and Rudy had gone out many times with his brothers and a team of stalwart alphunds to seek unfortunate mountaineers caught in these treacherous cascades of ice and snow. Always, time was of the essence, for even if the victim had managed to create an airspace under the snow, death by freezing was certain within a few hours. And if the poor fellow was packed into heavy, wet snow, with no air, suffocation would end his life in a much shorter time.

Yet Rudy, unconscious, with no air pocket, had somehow survived for eight or ten hours. Survived a great deal more, he reminded himself, touching again the snowy poultices in his chest and back. The icy slivers had not changed in shape or size since he'd first noticed them.

Before starting for home, he once again examined the mountain overhead for any signs of life. His heart quickened as he saw a long, slender line—a rope!—dangling from a lower ridge. Plunging through the deep snow, heart pounding, he made his way to where the rope terminated. Could some of the climbers, perhaps Beryv, have made it down from the summit?

His high hopes were dashed as he saw a single set of footprints leading away from the line. The edges of the prints had melted and refrozen numerous times; Rudy estimated they had been made at least a week earlier. Obviously, the rope had been left by a previous climber. He thought it strange that they hadn't noticed the line on their way up, but Rudy knew he was not mistaken in his belief that these footprints had been here for at least seven or eight days, quite possibly even longer.

Shaking his head in wonder, he trudged through the wet, heavy snow until he had passed into the shelter of the forest. The snow lion, no longer agitated, paced along beside him. Rudy found a south-facing clearing where the ground had been exposed by snowmelt, and he wondered if he should build a fire and rest before beginning the long hike to Neshara.

Yet he felt no fatigue, nor any sense of hunger. His clothes were soaked through to his skin, but even in the growing shadows he felt not the slightest chill. If his endurance held, he could reach the village by dawn. The moon, which had been full just last night, would provide him with plenty of light for the walk.

At that memory, a violent trembling took hold of Rudy, shaking him to his core. The tremor was produced by his profound desire to cast away an impossible piece of knowledge. Yet he could not. Inevitably, his eyes rose to the sky, toward the stark crescent he'd seen near the mountain ridge.

The tiny sliver of moon caught his eye as it touched the horizon. A day or two past new, the crescent slowly slipped below that lofty ridge line.

Rudy stared upward, gaping in shock at the luminous curve. Vividly he remembered the moon on the previous night, the full circle cresting upward from the east at sunset. Yet now it would set on the very tail of the sun!

With growing shock, he understood the import—though he had difficulty in accepting what he now knew: it was not "yesterday" when he had camped on the shoulder of Glimmercrown; not "this morning" that the climb had begun. The moon had cycled far since then.

The day when he had been swept into the avalanche, Rudy understood, must have been at least two weeks before.

— 2 —

Darkness slowed Rudy's progress down the mountainside trail, but he had no desire to stop and wait for dawn. He wanted neither rest nor the warmth of a fire—instead, he plodded tirelessly toward Neshara as if there he would find the answers to all his questions. He found himself whistling a little tune—which surprised him, for he had never before made any kind of music. The light melody was strangely soothing.

Thick pines of the highland forests surrounded him, and though the trail was lost in shadow, somehow Rudy's feet never tripped over any unseen obstacle. Instead, they carried him with a kind of detachment, as if they were vehicles charged with safely transporting the rest of his body.

The snow lion padded silently before him, unerringly selecting the proper fork at each of the branches in the trail. A short bit of climbing carried Rudy over the intervening ridge, and by midnight he was started on the long, downhill pathway that would lead him to Neshara.

Yet still he walked like an automaton, his mind wrestling with a multitude of inexplicable occurrences—the figures on the peak, his amazing survival, his rescue by the great mountain creature. And, finally, the long time he had lain under the snow—that fact, undeniably proven by the moon, was the final, most baffling mystery.

Perhaps he'd only imagined it all, and had in fact gone mad. What other explanation could there be? A part of him even longed for insanity, wished for this dark fantasy to vanish when he returned home and saw the familiar faces of his brothers. But even that dark hope was futile—whatever the explanation for his survival, Rudy knew in his heart that he was in full possession of his faculties. Perhaps, he noted wryly, that was the first sign of madness.

Also left unanswered was the question of why Lord Garamis had started for the higher peak, after he had been clearly warned of the dangers. Rudy remembered the nobleman's sword, inexplicably carried up the lofty peak. Now he knew—the Lord of Galtigor was no more than an assassin, and had borne the weapon so that he could complete his murderous task!

But *why?*

His mind drifted to the memory of the rope, dangling from the side of the mountain. He had discounted it as irrelevant, since the tracks below the line had been more than a week old. Now he realized they had probably been made shortly after the avalanche.

Garamis. Desperately Rudy wished that one of his brothers had lived to place that rope, had survived the avalanche and that awful sword . . . but he knew beyond any doubt that the man who escaped had been the Lord of Galtigor. Remembering the way the prince had moved with that black sword—a hundred paces in an eyeblink!—the Iceman knew that the Guardians would not have been able to catch him.

The waters of the Klarbrook babbled and splashed beside the trail as Rudy drew near to Neshara. He remembered countless outings along this stream—fishing with Coyle, or hunting with Donniall. Beryv, who had been like a father to Rudy for the last ten years, had often accompanied him on long walks beside the chuckling rapids, claiming that an Iceman couldn't really think clearly unless he got away from his home, his woman, and all the trappings of village life. Beryv claimed that only in the deep forest, or on the shoulder of a mighty peak—places where he could hear the music of the mountain streams—did a man truly come alive. Rudy had listened, rapt, knowing that, like his brothers, his own destiny lay in the high places.

Dawn blossomed into full daylight before Rudy heard the cowbells of Neshara. He looked around, realizing with a start that the snow lion had disappeared. Why had it come this far, he wondered, only to vanish? Immediately he missed the big feline, feeling at the same time a powerful, if irrational, sense of guilt, knowing he had never adequately expressed his gratitude to the animal that had saved his life. He could only add one more unanswered question to his list.

Shortly the streamside trail brought him to the first cottages of the village. Each neat wooden house was surrounded by lush gardens, with windowboxes bearing more blooms and clean-swept walkways inviting passersby to brightly painted front doors.

Such gardens were a constant feature of Halverica—every little town taking great pride in the extent and variety of its blossoms. Now they mocked Rudy with their cheery colors, and as he turned up the lane toward Beryv's house he tried, unsuccessfully, to prepare himself for the sight of his own family's home.

Reaching the end of the lane, he saw the chalet standing in stark contrast to the rest of the village, surrounded not by blossoms, but by gardens of green stems and barren stalks. In the traditional mourning ritual of Halverica, the widows had stripped every flower from the yard, rendering it into a bleak and lifeless mirror of the tragedy that had struck the family within.

They'll see me—and they'll wonder why their husbands—their fa-

ther—had to die. They'll wish I was Beryv, or Coyle, or Donniall.

At a small sound he turned to see Anjell staring up at him, her eyes wide and wondering. One of her blond pigtails had come unraveled, and the lacy embroidery that trimmed her dress was stained with dirt.

"Hello, Anjell," Rudy said to his niece. "Does your mother know you've been playing in the mud?"

Solemnly the girl nodded her head. The young man squirmed under her scrutiny, at last turning to approach the door of the house. Looking behind, he saw that Anjell stared after him, though the normally boisterous girl showed none of her usual inclinations to leap into his arms, or to inquire about the contents of his rucksack.

"How . . . is your mother?" he asked quietly.

"My daddy died," she said finally. "Up on the mountain."

"I know." For the first time since emerging from the snow, Rudy felt a powerful urge to cry. He tightened his jaw, resisting the impulse. "I'm sorry."

"How come you didn't die?" Anjell asked innocently. "Mama said you were dead too. Are you?"

"No." Rudy could not help smiling, though tears clouded his eyes. "I don't know why I didn't, but here I am—still alive."

"I'm glad," she said, still solemn.

He knelt down, holding his arms out to embrace the girl as she fell into his arms. He groaned his grief into her shoulder, feeling her tiny arms clasping his neck. Anjell sobbed, her sorrow giving him the strength to hold back his tears.

"Come in the house now?" she asked, and dumbly he nodded, allowing her to take his hand and lead him to the door. Vaguely he was aware that other villagers had come up the lane behind him, staring in wonder—as if he were a ghost returned from the dead. In a sense, perhaps more than he fully understood, he was.

The door opened before he reached it and he saw Dara, Beryv's widow, standing ashen-faced, one hand held to her mouth. Mutely the woman palmed her heart, mouthing a prayer to Baracan.

"Look, Mama!" Anjell cried. "Uncle Rudy's back! Does this mean Daddy's coming home too?"

Dara, a tall woman with arms and hands strong from a lifetime of work, stared into Rudy's eyes and read the tale. "No, sweet one—I'm afraid it doesn't. But how did . . . what happened?"

The young Iceman shook his head. "I—I still don't understand."

He saw Payli, Coyle's young bride, and again the grief tugged at him. The women escorted him toward the family hall, as neighbors—apparently reassured as to his mortality—filtered through the door and gathered around. The Appenfells had been a large, prosperous family, and the deaths of the brothers had touched nearly everyone in Neshara, one way or another. Now the community gathered to celebrate the return of one from the dead—and to hear the tale of the doomed expedition.

Surrounded again by friends and family, Rudy nevertheless felt a strange sense of distance—as if he remained alone, trapped in the snow on the mountainside. The warm house, the hopeful faces, all seemed vaguely alien to him.

"What—what day is it?" he asked, looking into Dara's face as if he hoped to find the answers to all his questions there. "How long have I been gone?"

"It's Loamday now," she replied, her brow creasing as she calculated. "Three Cairndays past, now, is when the Lord of Galtigor came to town—and you left on the Godsday morn. You've been gone sixteen days."

Anjell appeared through the press of family and neighbors—somehow she had carried a pitcher of milk and a plate of cheese and cakes. "Here," she whispered. "These were for dinner—but I think you need something to eat before they make you talk all day."

"Thanks," Rudy replied, deeply touched by her concern. For a moment he couldn't see, as tears blurred his eyes and his throat grew tight with grief.

A wrinkled face leaned forward from the crowd of neighbors, and Rudy blinked away his tears and recognized Old Karlsted—a veteran Iceman who had been a comrade of Rudy's own father. Now Karlsted scowled as he spoke.

"The mountain has never given up her dead . . . until now. How did she come to do so, lad?" The old Iceman's watery blue eyes fixed upon Rudy with penetrating force.

"Don't ask him to explain," Jonn, a neighbor and friend of Rudy's, interjected. "Accept that it's a miracle—as much a miracle as Dunkar Kalland coming down from the mountain to unite the ten cantons!"

No one spoke for a moment. Rudy felt a powerful sense of awe and unworthiness—in his own mind there was no comparison between himself and Halverica's greatest hero.

"Aye, all right," Karlsted said quietly. He studied Rudy, and the younger man wondered what depths of memory and understanding were masked by the faded blue of the old man's eyes. "But tell us what you know, lad."

Slowly, haltingly, Rudy told them everything he remembered—Garamis' treachery, the prince's magical ascent of the Crown, the avalanche, and the young Iceman's inexplicable rescue by the snow lion on the previous day. Not a sound broke the concentration of his listeners, save for an occasional gasp of surprise, or murmurs of shock or dismay.

"I'm on my way to Dermaat tomorrow—I'll look into it over there, see if they've heard anything," pronounced a deep voice. Rudy recognized Roggett Becken, a veteran Iceman who was also the best carpenter in Neshara. "They've called me over to help repair some damage from the earthquake last fortnight—but I'll see if they know anything about this avalanche, as well."

Rudy believed the search for an explanation was fruitless, but his neighbor's courageous gesture heartened him. More than a dozen men, including Jonn, were quick to offer their aid.

"Did Garamis return through the village?" Rudy asked.

"His horse disappeared nearly two weeks ago, but we never saw him," Dara said, shaking her head. "At the time we thought it the act of a thief."

"It was," Rudy declared grimly. "D'you remember the compact—the Palefee?"

"Yes—the parchment is still in Beryv's study—" Dara's voice

caught, and Umma gave her a strong hug.

"It's a miracle you're here—Baracan himself must have watched over you," Payli declared, her eyes reddened by the tears shed when she'd heard the tale of her husband's demise.

Rudy looked at her, recognizing the God of Man's name but feeling terribly confused. The faces around him blurred, whirling through a circle until they blended into one vaguely concerned expression. For the first time since his awakening, his throat was parched with thirst.

Then the whirling faces dissolved into Dara's wide-set eyes. She reached forward and cradled him against her breast as everything around Rudy slowly faded into black.

— 3 —

Would *he* be there? All other questions paled to insignificance as Prince Garamis of Galtigor galloped toward the great city of Landrun, home to his father's palace. Two more times Nicodareus would come to Dalethica, the Lord Minion had promised—but would it be so soon? Nothing else mattered but this one crucial question: would Nicodareus be in Landrun?

Garamis couldn't know the answer, but he felt a desperate, consuming *need* for the Lord Minion—for his praise, his attention. This thought occupied all of his attention as he spurred Cyric into a racing canter along the road.

Secure in Garamis' saddlebag, and every bit as large as it had been when he had chiseled it out of the frozen crust atop the Glimmercrown, rode the object of the nobleman's quest—the Ice of Three Waters, which he had first beheld in the dream of the Sleepstealer.

Vividly Garamis recalled his struggle on the ridge of Glimmercrown. The act of slaying was not new to the prince—indeed, he had killed on many battlefields, fought dozens of skirmishes against the encroaching farmers of Carillonn, but never had the lethal work been as *personal* as this. Yet beneath the strike of the black blade Beryv Appenfell had given up his life as easily as any farm-raised bumpkin fighting to protect his home.

Then the power of Darkflight contained in his mighty sword had carried Garamis up the slope, blinking instantaneously past the Guardians who tried to block his path. The distance to the summit was great, but the magical power of the blade had carried him to the top in a dozen abrupt leaps. After chiseling free the block, the prince had blinked downward again with the sword, until he reached the high ridge line where Beryv had died. Since the range of his dramatic teleportation was too limited to carry him all the way to the bottom, the prince had been forced to rely on his hands and feet, on his skill and courage—not to mention the ropes left by the Appenfell brothers—to get down.

Indeed, the hardest part of the whole business had been that terrifying descent. That experience blended into a collage of horrible images—huge, sweeping faces of rock plunging below; his life suspended by a thin rope, attached to some impossibly frail spike driven into a crack of the mountain wall. The climb down had tested every reserve of the prince's courage—and in the end that courage had been the master of the task.

Carrying the heavy block in his rucksack, he'd easily taken Cyric from the Appenfell stable. Though he would have killed anyone who discovered him, his passage through Neshara had been discreet and free of incident. Then, onto the road, riding the fleetest horse in all Galtigor!

But when he reached Landrun, would Nicodareus be there, to hear the tale, to offer even the faintest word of praise . . . or, perhaps—and this deeper hope only came to Garamis in moments of giddy delight—joy of joys, another taste of that pure, inky blood?

Earlier on this day he had taken the ferry across the River Ariak, then passed the border watchpost into Galtigor. He rode hard along the South Highway, knowing that he was no more than six days' fast ride from the city. By noon he reached a small clearing, distinctively marked by several tall stones. Here he reined in, allowing Cyric to breathe as his own dark eyes searched the perimeter of the field.

Several armed men came into view, emerging from the trees and leading their war horses toward the prince. They wore the black capes and red shoulderboards that signaled all the many companies of Garamis' personal troops, the Black Mantles. In addition, the metal breast-plates and red helmet-plumes marked the elite status of these troops—they were the Redsteel Guards.

Garamis recognized Wilfriz in the lead, and in a few moments the captain of the prince's personal warriors had approached his liege. Wilfriz bowed deeply.

"Greetings, my prince." The captain of the Redsteel Guards wore a full red beard, and hair of similar copper sheen flowed from beneath his helmet. Now he removed that metal cap and ran a hand across his scalp, squinting curiously up at his leader.

"I knew you would be here," Garamis replied—a statement that passed for praise, since he had ordered nothing less of his men. He noticed traces of rusty red on the captain's belt, and saw that several of the other guardsmen wore fresh scalps around their neck. "You found some action on the way, I see. More of the pests of Carillonn?"

"Aye, lord. A sort of 'welcome home' gift for Your Highness. A group of 'em tried to settle a strip of land east of the Ariak."

"None are left, I can assume?" Garamis probed.

"Not anymore. Some of the women were pretty, so they lived for a few days," Wilfriz said with a grin.

"You do good work in my absence." The prince was pleased, but not surprised. All the companies who wore the Black Mantle were primed, ready for important fights—but the Redsteel Guards were the most savage, most capable men under his command. He admired their blatant audacity, their cruel sense of triumph.

"There is bad news, as well," the captain added, as Garamis dismounted and stretched his legs. When the prince replied only with a raised eyebrow, Wilfriz continued. "Your brother has returned home. He arrived barely a week after you departed."

Garamis stiffened. "Takian." He spoke the name coldly, showing no emotion, though suspicion, envy, and rage stormed within him. "My father welcomed him warmly?"

"Aye, lord. Of course, the young prince asked after you. He was told the same thing as everyone else—that you had gone hunting. The deception has worked well in the city and the palace."

"Of course. Only now the truth can be told. When we reach

Landrun, I shall display the Ice of Three Waters as proof that we are on a great course of destiny." He thought of the other sign of his destiny—the Sword of Darkblood. That potent weapon, the prince had decided, he would keep a secret for the time being, most especially the power of Darkflight.

For five days the prince and the forty riders of his Redsteel Guard paraded through the towns and past the inns that lined the King's Highway. The citizens of each town turned out dutifully to applaud the royal heir, but Garamis led the procession at a full canter through all but the largest of these communities. His eagerness to reach Landrun compelled the company to depart with each dawn and ride for an hour or two into the night.

Finally they crossed the broad Black Eel on the ferry, and rode the last miles toward the city. The prince raised his head, let the wind blow his black hair into a trailing plume, and spurred Cyric to a gallop. Abruptly the close-pressing forest ended, still some miles from Landrun's walls, and the thundering column of horsemen raced between fields of grain. Scythe-wielding harvesters paused to stare, openmouthed, at the royal procession.

The prince relished the familiar views of home. The great Black Eel River bustling with barges, ferries, and fishercraft swept through its low valley. Before them the walls of the city—heavy wooden palisades layered over dirt and rocks—rose from the flat pastureland. The palace itself surmounted a low, rocky knob overlooking the city's waterfront, with one grand tower rising as the highest point in Landrun and for a hundred miles in any direction. Soon the gates creaked open, and trumpets blared a welcome as the prince and his escort thundered onto the long, wide avenue extending toward the city center.

Landrun, capital of Galtigor, sprawled along both banks of the meandering Black Eel. Buildings of wood crowded shoulder to shoulder against a few stone edifices—mostly temples, though a mint and several armories also stood lordly guard over the less permanent structures. Even the palace of the king was a lodge of great wooden beams.

Garamis led his column through the streets at a fast trot, toward the slopes and summit of the rocky knoll. Soon the riders swept around the last curve on the twisting, precipitous road.

Regally astride his charger, looking neither to the left nor right, the black-haired prince led his company through the towering gates of the palace. These portals formed the only gap in a wooden palisade some thirty feet high; now they swung open at his approach. Garamis and his escort had no sooner filed into the courtyard than the gates shut with a boom that shuddered through the ground.

The prince dropped from his saddle with casual ease, noting with disgust that the sound of cheering dropped abruptly as he disappeared from sight. A palace hostler rushed forward to take the reins of his horse. Garamis recognized Dalik, one of the few stablemen Cyric would allow to handle him.

"Leave that for me!" the prince barked as the man reached for the saddlebag. Though the weight bore him down, Garamis would accept no assistance as he slung the bulky satchel over his shoulder and made his way into the palace proper.

"Hi, Garam! Are you back?" A round-shouldered young man came bouncing from the wide entry hall, his guileless face split by a grin of sheer delight.

"Hello, Boric." Garamis was pleased to see his youngest brother. "Yes, I am."

"I'm *real* glad!" Boric fell into step beside Garamis, his rolling gait a humorous contrast to the older's prince's smooth, confident step. Boric's eyes, huge and round—as they had been since the birth that had squeezed his skull and permanently dulled his mind—stared at every sight in the courtyard, seeing the marching guards, the hurrying courtiers, as if they were wonders beheld for the first time. "It's been so *boring* since you went away. Except Takian came home! That's great, don'tcha think?"

"Yes." Garamis kept his tone neutral.

"Are you going to take me to the war now?" asked Boric, suddenly excited.

"Soon—soon I will," the elder prince replied, restless.

"You always say that!"

"I mean it. Now tell me—did Takian say anything to you about where he went—what he was doing?"

"Oh Garam—he went *everywhere*! He was gone so long! I almost didn't know him when he came back—but I did."

Boric saw one of the royal hounds and went off to play while Garamis walked quickly past the guards at the palace doors. Takian's mysterious travels were much on his mind—for three years his middle brother had been gone, and those had been good years for Garamis. Yet now, if he was back, the elder prince vowed to remain alert for treachery.

Garamis, still carrying the weighty satchel, continued down the wide, smooth-paneled hall of the entryway, into the huge, vaulted great-room. A throne of wood, ornately carved with images of horses and weaponry, stood vacant at the far end of the room, and a hooded figure stood beside that seat. The man now advanced to meet the prince.

"Greetings, your lordship. A thousand welcomes on your return." The man's voice emerged from the deep cowl of colorful silk. His robed form bowed forward, offering respect but not obeisance to the proud prince.

"Thank you, Terral. Is my father in presence?"

"Indeed, my lord. He awaits you in the private audience room. And may I be allowed to congratulate you on your success."

Nodding in acknowledgment, the prince didn't bother to wonder how Terral knew that his task had been successful. Terral had ways of learning many things, most of which proved useful to Garamis; the advisor's small liberties must be indulged.

Garamis moved resolutely toward a door in the wall behind the throne. The barrier swung open as he approached—though no attendant was in sight, the prince knew that his father's bodyguards could see the entire throne room from concealed slits in the wall. These loyal men-at-arms controlled the door, which had no visible latch.

Garamis stepped through the doorway, made his way down a short hall, and continued through another door that opened silently as he approached.

An old man rose to his feet from a well-cushioned chair, tottering on frail legs toward the prince. Garamis dropped to his knee as the king pressed his hand against his son's brow.

"There will be rejoicing and feasting on the occasion of your return. It has been too long since the three royal sons of Galtigor were in presence together," King Larriac said, his voice tight with emotion. "Did you not hear the joy in your subjects' throats?"

"Aye, Father—though the joy seemed to vanish quickly, once I was out of view," the prince replied wryly. He stood quickly, swinging the heavy satchel off his shoulders. His eyes swept the small room, probing the shadows of several darkened alcoves.

"Greetings, Garamis."

"Hello, Takian." Stiffening, Garamis tried unsuccessfully to smile.

The younger prince stepped forward, the lamplight reflecting from his golden hair. As always, Garamis resented his brother's smooth self-confidence, the easy smile that he suspected concealed a wealth of envious schemes and treacherous designs. After all, if Garamis had been the second in line for the throne, *he* would certainly have worked to change the circumstance of birth.

"How fared your hunt?" asked Takian, without an obvious trace of guile.

The older prince drew in a full breath; now he could smile. "It was an unqualified success," he declared. "I'll let you admire my trophy."

Garamis hoisted the heavy saddlebag onto a wooden table and pulled the leather back to reveal an irregularly shaped block of ice. Tendrils of steam drifted upward as the surface was exposed to the air.

The two princes and the king stood mute as they examined the steaming chunk of frost. Indistinguishable from normal ice—except, perhaps, that even in the warm room it showed not the slightest sign of meltage—the block of unnatural ice held them spellbound.

"What kind of a hunt was this?" Takian asked, breaking the long silence.

"A quest—commanded by the gods themselves," declared Garamis.

"What do you call it?" Takian asked.

"This is the Ice of Three Waters, formed at the peak of the Glimmercrown—the only place in the world where all the Watersheds meet."

"You *climbed* that summit?" The younger prince shook his head in amazement. "But . . . *why?* The gods, you said—why would Baracan send you on such a mission?"

Garamis' smile grew broad at his brother's mistaken assumption. "It has a use—an important purpose that, for now, must remain secret." *Even from myself*, he added silently.

"It—it doesn't melt," the king observed, reaching forward a finger.

"Don't touch it!" Garamis snapped. "It causes a burn on the skin, quite painful. But you're right—for three weeks it has been exactly the size it was when I cut it free of the mountaintop.

"But enough," he broke off, turning to Takian. "Tell me about your own travels. Did you go the breadth of Dalethica? Up to the Watershed?"

"I saw a hundred different lands, Garamis! Homes and realms across Dalethica! So many people that you'd never believe it! Spice lords of Zanthilat—the Sun Lord's palace at Myntercairn. I sailed on a Corsari ship around the shore of the Circled Sea! And then I ended up—stayed for the last year, in fact—in Carillonn."

"Did you spy on the knights?" Garamis inquired sarcastically. "Perhaps bring back some information about their army's weaknesses?"

"Better than that!" Takian replied with apparent sincerity, taking no note of his brother's tone. "I have met the Duchess of Shalloth herself—and given my word that she shall have safe passage on her mission to Landrun."

"This mission was arranged a year ago. You seek to steal a chance to woo the duchess early?" demanded the elder son. "Do you fear my luck if she meets us both fairly?"

"Perhaps," Takian acknowledged with a sly grin. "Or perhaps I realize that you're the firstborn prince. I need any kind of advantage I can get."

"Advantage is better helped by battles won than by pleasant promises," Garamis replied tartly. "And among all the duchies of Carillonn,

Shalloth has been our most stalwart foe."

"That's because we keep taking more of their land," Takian observed.

The older prince laughed, his voice a sharp crack. "Those knights of Shalloth have made a worthy test, it must be noted—they've helped my Redsteel Guards keep ready for a *real* war!"

"But why?" Takian objected. "The Bordermen hold Falteran at bay—we have nothing to fear from the east. To the north, Andaran is suing for peace—and Carillonn now sees the wisdom of that course as well. What need do we have of claiming another miserable steading, or tiny crossroads? The wars are won!"

"Until the war is *over* we need to hold their backs to the wall!" declared Garamis. He cast another look at the Ice of Three Waters, and then looked despairingly around the room. His brother infuriated him; his father was an annoying nonentity. Why did they have to bother him thus?

Only in the depths of his heart did he recognize the true nature of his distress—the fact that Nicodareus, Eye of Dassadec and Garamis' one true master, was not here to welcome, to praise, to reward him.

FIVE

A Stalker at the Gate

To flee a battle that offers no hope of victory is neither
a failure of courage nor of skill; instead, to sacrifice
blood and treasure to a lost cause is a failure of
rationality and leadership.
—Scroll of Baracan
Vol. III, Godstome

— 1 —

Dara's face . . . a mist of pale light . . . the unfamiliar curtains of a bedroom . . . His mother's stoic presence, gray and silent and sad . . . The
snow lion, lifting his head toward the clear, twilit sky . . . These images
rose and fell in Rudy's consciousness, and they gave him hope. At times
he saw them against a background of swelling music—music unlike
any he had heard before. The melody was pleasant, soothing, healing.

But at other times the music disappeared and the pictures in his
mind became dark, frightening. . . . He saw the black sword of Garamis, suspended above his neck, and he knew that the merest touch of
that midnight blade would kill. His visions were haunted by mysterious, bestial creatures. The monsters snarled and snapped in pursuit of
him, and when he eluded them they killed his family. Helpless, he
watched his brothers reborn in his dreams, only to perish once more—
this time beneath the claws and talons of unspeakably vile beasts.

Once he saw the face of Old Karlsted, peering forward and squinting in concentration. Dara stood beside him, and they pointed to Rudy's chest. Only later did he understand that this was real, not part of his feverish imaginings.

The first time he truly awakened it was mid-morning, an unknown number of days after his return home. Anjell sat beside him, and when he opened his eyes and said her name, she raced from the bedroom to return in a few moments with her mother.

"How are you feeling?" Dara asked, sitting down and touching a hand to his forehead.

"All . . . all right, I guess." Rudy was surprised to realize that in fact he felt quite robust. "I guess I was kind of out for a while, there."

"We were terribly frightened," his sister-in-law said seriously. "For a time we almost lost hope. . . . "

"How long was I sick?"

"You've been in that bed four days. D'you want something to eat?"

Rudy shook his head. "I'd rather know what *happened* to me! How could I walk all the way home from the mountain, and then collapse in the family hall?"

"Did you . . . ?" Dara was hesitant. "Did you look at your chest, after you came out of the snow?"

Immediately Rudy remembered the tiny groove in his skin, packed with ice that had not melted. Silently he nodded, pulling aside the sheet to see if the wound had changed. Seeing that the silver of sparkling snow remained, he reached around to his back. When he probed his skin, he felt nothing. Sensing his unspoken question, Dara leaned over him.

"There's nothing there."

"When I woke up in the snowfield, there was a piece of ice there, just like on my chest."

"There's not even a scar, now," she declared. "Of course, I don't know when it might have disappeared. We noticed the other mark the day after you got sick, when we changed your bedding. But why doesn't it melt? Can that be what made you sick?"

"I don't think so—if anything, it was the melting of the one in my back that made me *well* again."

Old Karlsted pushed the bedroom door open and hobbled to the bedside in time to hear Rudy's guess. Dara shook her head, but the neighbor put his hand on the widow's shoulder. "The lad might have something, there," he pointed out. "Tell me, son—was there anything strange about that avalanche? Anything you didn't tell us that night?"

Rudy shook his head. "Not that I remember."

"The snow—where did it come from?" Karlted pressed.

"The mountainside, of course. It started with a cornice at the very top of the ridge—I saw it break off."

"The ridge between Faerimont and Glimmercrown?"

"Aye."

"You know that Faerine lies on the far side of that ridge, don't you?" Karlsted asked.

"Yes, of course . . . but what does that have to do with—?"

"Aura. The snow that encased you was not frozen water, but frozen Aura—the essence of Faerine's magic."

"But the Watershed—that should prevent the Aura from escaping, shouldn't it?" Despite his doubts, Rudy felt a growing certainty that Karlsted was right.

"Aura can't *fall*, not as rain or snow, on our side of the divide," the old man argued. "But who's to say that snow on the ground can't be blown by the wind—at least enough to make a cornice off of the high ridge!"

"Well, all I know is—it's *still* a miracle you're here," Dara said. She glared at Karlsted, who chuckled at her concern. "The lad needs rest—let's leave him be for a bit. You sleep as long as you want," she told Rudy. "Just let us know when you want something to eat."

"I will—and thanks, Dara."

For several hours Rudy tried to rest, but found that his energy increased rapidly. He forced himself to stay in bed, fearing a relapse, but at heart he knew that his malady had passed.

Anjell came to bring him tea, cheese, and cakes, and after he ate he did fall asleep briefly. He awoke to find her staring solemnly at the bed, as if she had tried to wake him up by mere force of her will. He smiled wryly at the thought; obviously, she had succeeded.

"Is it time for lunch already?" he asked, realizing that the sun spilled into the west-facing window.

"Oh, that's past," she said. "I brought you some bread, but you were sleeping so well that I took it back to the kitchen. Do you want it now?"

" 'Sleeping well'?" he quoted with a chuckle. "Do I sometimes sleep *un*well?"

"Oh yes—mostly always," the girl replied, unaware of his intended humor. "You thrash about like you're fighting something, or groan like you're afraid."

Rudy flushed. "I'm *not* afraid," he snapped, immediately regretting his tone when he saw the hurt on Anjell's face.

"Well, I'm only saying what it *looks* like," she replied, pointedly turning toward the window.

"Do you think I could have that bread now?" he asked, much more gently.

In a few moments she returned, and sat watching him while he hungrily munched several rich, grainy slices. She offered him two apples and he ate them both, surprised to find that he was still hungry.

"When are you going to get up, Uncle Rudy?" she asked.

"Now!" he declared, flinging back the covers and swinging his legs toward the floor.

"Marvelous!" she cried, clapping her hands.

"How are you feeling, lad?" At the new voice, Rudy looked up to see Roggett. The big Iceman filled the door of the room, ducking under the lintel as he entered. "I got out of Dermaat after half a day— joined the other fellows up on the mountainside." One look at Roggett's face told Rudy that the searchers had found no sign of any other survivors.

"We saw the chute of the slide, all right," the big Iceman said with a nod. "It's a miracle you weren't killed! And you're right about that rope—it looks like that flatlander made it down. But there's no sign of him, now—and from what I remember of his horse, there's no one in Halverica likely to catch him."

"What else did you see?" Rudy wasn't surprised by the news, but it brought back his sense of despair, which Anjell, for a brief time, had almost dispelled. Even as he asked the question, his misery began to develop a focus, building gradually from the banked coals of his anger into an all-consuming rage. An image of Garamis' face rose up before him, and the prince's eyes seemed to be chips of black ice, as cold as the soul of the Sleepstealer. Only vaguely did he realize that Roggett was talking, answering Rudy's question.

"Nothing much. That slide that brought you down must have had a *huge* amount of snow. There's still a big snowfield there, where the rest of the slope has already been cleaned by the spring melt."

"That's strange," Rudy commented. The head of the valley was exposed to the south and west, and the hillside received a lot of sunlight. It should have been among the first of the winter snowfields to disappear.

"Jonn and Pater went back down to Dermaat to see if anyone there had heard anything more, but they didn't get back by last night. Probably wenching it up in Dermaat House, if I know them. I wasn't about to wait another day for 'em, so they'll just have to meet us here."

"That reminds me!" Anjell said. "There was a man here looking for you," she told Rudy. "Mama said you were sleeping—he wanted to talk to you bad, but she sent him away."

"A 'man'? Who was he?" Rudy asked. Neshara was a tiny village, and strangers were rare. "How did he know my name?"

Anjell shrugged, rolling her eyes.

"Lord Garamis—or his agent?" he wondered aloud, with a renewed flash of hatred.

"It wasn't Garamis—he wouldn't dare show his face around here," Anjell declared. "And he wasn't dressed like any lordly agent *I* ever saw."

Rudy reflected that Anjell had probably never seen a lord's agent; still, he respected her judgment enough not to challenge her. "What *did* he wear?"

"Mostly black, though his cloak and boots were all gunked up with mud and stuff. He spoke with a funny voice."

"What do you mean, 'funny'?"

"Well, he was sort of a hisser; kind of like his esses were extra long. 'Is thissss the housssse of Appenfell?' " she parroted.

Roggett narrowed his eyes. "Where did this stranger come from?" he inquired.

Again Anjell rolled her eyes; the capacity of adults to ask stupid questions apparently never failed to amaze her. "He was here this morning," she said. "So he must have been staying at the Black Bull."

Rudy knew the Bull well; as the only inn in town it seemed a logical choice. But Roggett's next words disputed the guess.

"We stopped for a drink there, when we first got back to town— well, you know, it's the first place you come to off the mountain, if you take the long way around," he added sheepishly. "Barton was there himself, remarked how business has been so slow. If he had a guest, he would have told us."

"Could the stranger have come from Dermaat?" Rudy wondered.

"He would have to have left in the middle of the night—I *told* you, he was here right after breakfast this morning!" Anjell retorted.

Rudy knew that she hadn't actually mentioned the time, but being well acquainted with his niece's ways, he was sensible enough not to debate the issue. "Well, he'll come back if he really wants to see me."

"Know what?" Anjell inquired coyly.

Rudy raised his eyebrows queryingly.

"I hope he *doesn't* come back!" Anjell declared, forcefully enough to dispel her uncle's lighthearted manner.

"Why?"

"There was something, well . . . *spooky* about him. I wouldn't mind if he left Neshara today and never looked back! His eyes—they stared right at me, but it wasn't like he was looking at a *person*! I felt like a mouse being hunted by a snake. I even started to get dizzy, till I quick looked away."

The news sent an odd sense of disquiet through Rudy, and he was strangely reluctant to see Roggett and Anjell depart. He wanted to get up, to move around. Grateful that his strength had returned, he rose and walked to the window.

From here, he looked across the flower garden that swept around the back of the house, and he saw Anjell run down the walk and out the gate. She scampered up the cobbled street, calling gaily to several of her friends.

Suddenly weary, the young Iceman collapsed into the rocking chair, pushing back and forth in agitation. His body was healed, but he recognized that the malady still gnawed at his spirit.

His whole life, it seemed, had, in a disastrous few moments on the mountainside, been reduced to a maze of unanswered questions. And now this mysterious stranger, asking in sibilant tones to see him. For the first time, Rudy considered that information in light of his recent experiences.

He came to the inescapable conclusion that the visitor presented a threat. The fellow would return, Rudy believed, and when he did, it seemed unlikely that he would come for a pleasant social visit. *Why* anyone should harm him became just another unanswered question to add to those of the last few weeks—yet he couldn't shake off the feeling that a very sinister reason lay behind the stranger's request.

Fear stabbed through him as he thought of this villainous presence questioning Anjell. The girl would defend her uncle ferociously, he knew—but that determination only served to increase her danger.

He went to the chest that held his belongings, lifting the lid and quickly finding a heavy, long-handled hunting knife. The hilt seemed awkward and unbalanced in his hand, but Rudy nevertheless felt better as he took the weapon and crossed back to the rocking chair.

Again he thought of Garamis. The man was no doubt safely back in the lowlands by now—probably secure in the knowledge that he had left no witnesses to his brutal crime. A grim resolve settled into Rudy's soul: the Prince of Galtigor *would* pay for his brutality. The knife in his hand lent weight to the thought, and he considered the prospect of driving it into the nobleman's bejeweled breast. Could he do it?

Night settled across the garden, but the Iceman felt none of the weariness that had been his constant companion. Now his senses were keen and alert, and he knew that he could maintain his watch throughout the hours of darkness without succumbing to sleep.

When he pictured Garamis or remembered the prince's murderous acts, his pulse pounded and his hands curled of their own accord into fists. Restless, he forced himself to remain still and watchful; all the while his determination to do *something* increased tenfold.

The sun set, but he lit no candle, for in the full darkness of the room he could plainly observe the gate, and the garden. He heard sounds of dinner in the main wing of the house, and knew that his own food, brought by Dara or Anjell, would be arriving shortly. He leaned toward the window, trying to stare through the shadows of the darkened village.

His first warning was a vague sense of disturbance, like one shadow moving in an unnatural pattern among its fellows. He stared, muscles taut, clutching the heavy knife in his hands. There! He saw it again—a fluid form, darting from one tree to the next, advancing like a floating blanket down the lane. Across from the Appenfell house it paused, blending into the darkness below the wide-spread pine standing sentinel on the lane.

Staring at that dark figure, Rudy shuddered with the distinct impression that it glared back at him. He crept back from the window, crouching low, with only his head above the sill, straining to penetrate the darkness.

Again he saw movement, as the shadowy form glided across the street, resolving itself into an apparently human body swathed in a dark cloak. This was the visitor Anjell had described—the Hisser, he thought.

The figure hopped over the gate with smooth grace. If it was indeed a man, the fellow possessed a degree of acrobatic skill that Rudy had never before observed. In another moment he lost sight of the form as it came up to the wall of the house.

For long seconds the Iceman remained still, straining to hear, or to see. The only sound to reach his ears was a kind of sniffing, and he was reminded of a hound seeking the trail of some elusive quarry. With a chill, he heard the sound approach the window.

The door of the room burst open and Rudy spun on his heel, raising the knife in an instinctive attempt to parry attack. His heel caught on the rug and he twisted, cursing, to the floor.

"Why are you sitting there in the dark?" demanded Anjell, holding up a candle as she advanced with a steaming tray. "And get back in bed!"

"I—I'm feeling better," Rudy stammered, slipping the knife under the bed as he clumsily got to his feet. Stepping to the window, he quickly slammed the shutters. His night vision destroyed by the light from the candle, he saw nothing except blackness outside.

"Well, at least you can eat something," Anjell clucked. She reached down and pulled the knife from beneath the bed. "And what in the Watershed are you doing with *this*?"

"Never mind!" Rudy snapped, more harshly than he intended. He snatched the knife from her hand and set in on the chest beside the bed. "Um, thanks for supper," he added, chagrined. "You should leave now."

"Well! You won't have to tell me twice!" huffed Anjell, turning and marching from the room.

The aroma of onion soup and steamed trout drew Rudy's attention to the tray she had brought. Despite his apprehensions, he greedily gulped down the food, keeping a wary eye on the shutters. Once, he thought he heard a snuffling sound again, but when he crept to the window and listened carefully the sound had disappeared.

When he finished eating he doused the candle, and sat in the dark clutching the knife. He tried to imagine that he was ready for any attack, but he couldn't fool even himself on that point. If someone— or some *thing*—came in the window for him, he realized that he'd be lucky not to stab himself. At the same time, he felt a buzzing, nervous tension that compelled some kind of action.

The nameless sense of terror grew with each passing minute. Rudy knew beyond any doubt that the thing lurking outside was not only an enemy but a potent force of evil. He didn't question the deduction; after his recent experiences, he found it easy to reach conclusions without any rational basis for doing so.

Yet, even so, there *was* a real foundation for his fear: the sounds he had heard at the window had not come from the mouth of man or woman. There had been a sense of *hunger* in those noises, and Rudy knew that he was the object of that craving.

Only then did he realize the potential threat to others: by staying here, in the Appenfell house, he put all the surviving members of his family at risk. If they were attacked, they would fight bravely—and all might perish horribly. He would have to leave—he could not be responsible for bringing further tragedy down on the heads of his loved ones. The thought of Anjell in the clutches of some despicable beast chilled the blood in his veins, and once more brought him to his feet.

Where could he go? If he stayed anywhere in Neshara, he exposed the whole town to this nameless menace. Wherever he went in Halverica, he might well draw the inhuman pursuer after him. Baracan only knew what kind of threat this would pose to his innocent countrymen!

Where *could* he go? He cast about the room, as if the walls or ceiling might offer him a suggestion. His thoughts returned to the Prince of Galtigor, and the cold fire of vengeance flared upward again. If he could find Garamis, face him—and kill him!

Abruptly he remembered the parchment signed by Garamis, pledging the Palefee—Dara had said that it was on the desk in Beryv's study. In that instant he had the answer to his question. He felt strong and fit, well able to stand up to the rigors of a long journey. And with that compact, he had proof that the ruling house of Galtigor owed his family a considerable sum of money. He would find Garamis, claim the Palefee—and then he would kill him!

The hallway outside his room was quiet. Leaving his door ajar, he slipped down to the study and found the scrolled parchment on Beryv's desk. Treading quietly he returned to his room, certain that he hadn't been observed.

Going to the chest in the corner, he found the sheath for the heavy knife, and he fixed the weapon to his belt. Next he removed the flint box and a coil of supple rope, dropping the former into his pouch and wrapping the latter about his waist. Knowing he'd be sleeping on the ground, he stuffed a thin bedroll—his plush, fur-lined sleeping bag had been buried in the avalanche—into a worn haversack, slinging the pack easily from one shoulder. In the bottom of the chest he found a short-handled ice axe, and this he stuck through the wide leather strap of his belt.

An old waterskin lay beside the axe. Rudy picked it up and inflated it by blowing air through the nozzle. Satisfied that the skin had no leaks, he slung it over his shoulder.

Last he took up a tiny coin purse. Loosening the drawstring and looking inside, he saw an array of copper and silver disks. Below those were several octagonal gold sovereigns. The coins, whose total value amounted to very little, represented all of his life's savings. They would have to do.

Dropping the precious sack into his belt pouch, he went to the window and quietly pushed open the shutters. He stared into the night for several minutes, satisfied at last that the stranger did not lurk nearby. With a last look at the door to the room, Rudy remembered Anjell's kindness and knew with a stab of pain that he'd miss her, very much.

Then he lifted himself over the sill, dropped to the ground, and started into the darkness beyond.

— 2 —

Rudy crouched beside the house, straining to hear any unnatural sound. The noises of village life had faded with the close of day, Halvericans being a people active mostly between sunrise and sunset. Raucous laughter from across the stream marked the Black Bull Tavern; there were always exceptions, Rudy reminded himself.

Except for the boisterous sounds of the drinkers, the village apparently slumbered. If the watcher at the window was still hiding in the garden, he was capable of absolute silence. Yet when Rudy remembered the palpable sense of menace he had felt before, he knew that— for now, at least—the intruder was gone.

Quickly he darted down the walkway, leaping the garden gate so as not to use the noisy latch. On the street he darted from the shadows of one tree to another, following the back lanes all the way to the end of town.

Only then did he consider a pertinent question: how did one get to Galtigor? With chagrin, he realized that he wasn't at all sure of the answer. Despair threatened, and he fought the sense that his mission was doomed even before it began.

Don't be a fool! he told himself. *To start, I just need to reach the lowlands. When I get to the Glimmersee, I can ask someone for directions.*

Of course. All travel into and out of Halverica passed around the edge of the great lake, through the crossroads of the North Shore Wayfarer's Lodge. He would go to that great, legendary inn, and find out what to do from there. The solution seemed easy and natural, and once more he relaxed.

Nothing stirred in the street behind him. Crossing the wooden bridge before the Black Bull, he stopped at the stream to fill his waterskin. He kept to the shadows as he passed the tavern and moved onto the forest road. Tall pines loomed overhead, shrouding the ground in layers of darkness.

After tripping over ruts and roots, he was forced to walk slowly in order to avoid a painful fall. He had the tinderbox, but he didn't dare light a torch—its flame would broadcast his presence to every curious interloper within a dozen miles.

Soon he reached the fork in the road. The most direct route to the Glimmersee, he knew, was straight ahead. That path followed the Klarbrook valley, down through the midvale villages of Auric, Daylo, and Timberheight, until it plunged the last few miles into the great valley of the Glimmersee. That huge, cold lake was the great waterway of Halverica, into which all the highland streams poured, and out of which the great River Ariak commenced its majestic course toward the lowlands.

Yet the right fork, lesser used than the valley trail, offered a possibility as well. That road climbed steeply to the forested crest of the nearby ridge called the Dermaathof. From there it descended into the next valley and the village of Dermaat. In that valley began a road that paralleled the Klarbrook route, descending to the shore of the Glimmersee.

Since it seemed logical that anyone seeking to follow him would continue down the Klarbrook Creek road, Rudy immediately turned toward the Dermaathof, feeling that the long climb would be more than worth his increased security.

The trees thinned somewhat on the slopes of the rock-bound ridge, allowing more starlight to penetrate to the road. Rudy picked up his pace, often looking back into the shapeless darkness below. His imagination conjured many threats, and—propelled by these lurid fantasies—he reached the high crest of the ridge shortly after midnight.

Here he paused to breathe in the night air, to stare at the wonders of the mountains that rose all around. A few twinkling lights in the valley signaled the location of Neshara. The trail curved around a shoulder of the ridge, masking Dermaat, so he could see no sign of his destination. Breathing hard, Rudy acknowledged that the exertion felt good; at the same time, he recognized that he was tired.

The voice of reason suggested that he get some rest before the night was over. He was not familiar with the road before him, and even in the starlight, irregularities underfoot were hard to detect. Leaving the road, he poked his way between several trees until he found a small bower where the forest floor was thickly lined with fallen pine needles.

Gratefully he spread his bedroll on the ground, using a cushion of moss to serve as a pillow. Removing his pouch and the rope, he laid the knife within easy reach of his right hand. He wondered briefly about the possibility of a pursuer, but quickly convinced himself that he would be safe. Within moments he fell asleep.

— 3 —

Rudy awakened suddenly, to the sound of stealthy movement in the forest. The sky glowed a pale blue to the east, though starlit darkness still yawned overhead. What had he heard?

There! A twig snapped, very close to where he lay. Slowly, Rudy's hand groped for his sheath. He drew the blade, cursing silently as it clinked against a nearby rock. The woods remained utterly still, but, straining to hear, he detected sounds of low, measured breathing.

Drawing up his legs, Rudy wriggled out of the bedroll and curled into a squat. The cold steel of the knife blade gleamed, shiny even in the dim twilight. He listened, trying to gauge what he heard, to discern from which direction the threat came.

A dry branch snapped under his foot and he grimaced, certain that he had betrayed his position. Then it came; the crackling of branches as something pushed them out of the way, the scuffling of feet on the rocky ground as whatever it was headed straight toward Rudy's bower.

Fear compelled him to move. He dove forward, stabbing with the knife, then grunting as the blade bit solidly into the trunk of a tree. Desperately he tried to pull the weapon free, but his hand slipped off the hilt and he tumbled backward, gouging his back on a sharp branch.

"Imagine! What a person has to do to find a person around here!" snapped Anjell, peevishly stepping into the bower.

Rudy looked up, gaping in shock, still not quite certain that he wasn't about to be torn into small pieces. He looked beyond Anjell, but nothing moved in the darkness.

"How . . . wha—what are *you* doing here?" he finally managed to blurt.

"I thought you'd be hungry," she said, offering him half a loaf of bread. "It was a whole loaf," she admitted, "but I got hungry too."

Rudy wanted to laugh, but the seriousness of the situation stifled the impulse. "When did you notice that I'd gone? And how did you *find* me here?" he demanded.

"Well, I wanted to tell you about that," Anjell explained. "About how we saw you were gone, I mean. You see, that stranger—the hissy fellow—came back looking for you. He was, well, even *spookier* than before. He talked to Dara at the door. At first she argued, but then she got all quiet and said she'd go get you. There was something strange about the way she said it—like he was *making* her do it or something, even though she didn't know it. I remembered the way he made me dizzy when I looked at his face; it made me afraid for Dara— and you. So I went to warn you, but you weren't in your room."

Rudy nodded. "And what about the stranger?"

"Well, I came back and told everyone, and—guess what? He was already gone! He must have heard Dara talking to the rest of us, and he took off. Though not before he trampled through the garden to look in your window."

A chill of apphrension passed through Rudy's gut. He had been right to leave, he saw—but he hadn't reckoned on the complication of Anjell! "How did you find me?" he asked again.

She shrugged. "You snore. I knew there weren't any bears up here, so that growling in the woods had to be you! Oh, and I just guessed you'd come by the Dermaat Road—anyone who was following you would probably go straight on down to the Glimmersee."

Rudy's cleverness sounded considerably less brilliant when he realized that Anjell had followed the same reasoning. Still, he *was* hungry.

"Thanks for the bread," he acknowledged, tearing off a crusty piece and chewing.

"Where are we going?" Anjell asked, in wide-eyed innocence that Rudy sensed was a sham.

"*You're* going back home," he said. "As soon as it's light, I'm taking you back to the village."

"That's not fair!" she complained, but he held up his hand to halt her protests.

"There's no debate. The most dangerous place you could be right now is with me. I'm not going to let you take that chance."

Though Anjell sulked, argued, and pouted in rapid sequence, her uncle remained firm. When dawnlight had swept across the full dome of the sky, Rudy rose and led her back to the road. They were about to start back toward Neshara, when movement in the valley below caught Rudy's eyes. A familiar, dark-cloaked figure crossed the bridge before the Black Bull and started into the forest. Again the Iceman was struck by the fluid grace of the creature—and the growing conviction that it wasn't human.

"That's *him*!" whispered Anjell, though Rudy had immediately sensed that fact. "That's the Hisser—the one who was looking for you!"

"*Ssst!*" Rudy hissed for silence, clapping a hand on his niece's arm.

Other figures moved in the shadows of the wood. Hulking forms, larger than the Hisser, cloaked in furs, hoods, and boots, emerged from the trees only to vanish from view as the road twisted into the steep-sided valley below. The newcomers fell in behind the stealthy Hisser, lackeys apparently, who had waited in the woods while their leader investigated in the town.

"Was he alone, yesterday?" Rudy asked.

Anjell shrugged. "He's not alone anymore. Those guys looked *big*!"

Rudy was forced to agree. "Big, and dangerous." Immediately he realized the folly of returning Anjell to Neshara—they stood an excellent chance of meeting the stranger and his thuggish companions along the same road.

"Let's wait and see if they take the valley road. Then we'll know if it's safe to get you home."

"We're going to do no such thing!" Anjell snapped determinedly, though still holding her voice to a harsh whisper. "Why, if they're *all* looking for you—and I think they are—they'll probably split up at the fork."

The road remained concealed behind the curve of cliffs, or the heavy canopy of the forest, for much of its length along the climb up the Dermaathof. If the strangers took this route, Rudy wouldn't know it until they emerged a few hundred paces from the ridge.

"You can come as far as Dermaat," he said, frustrated—and more than a little afraid. Who were these cloaked pursuers? And why did Anjell have to put herself in such a dangerous situation? With a burning hatred Rudy thought of Garamis. Beyond any doubt that vile nobleman was at the root of all his troubles.

"Let's go," Rudy urged, peering anxiously behind him. His niece, elated with the temporary victory, skipped at the Iceman's side as he started down the winding forest trail. Behind them, he sensed, the mysterious pursuers had already begun to climb the ridge.

— 4 —

"What's that smell?" asked Anjell, her tone a plaintive whine. She had long since ceased to skip, trudging wearily behind her uncle as they came around the last of a seemingly endless series of curves before the village of Dermaat. A creek of the same name flowed through the steep-sided valley. The rolling, darkly forested ridges and gorges of the Wilderhof rose beyond, a bleak and forbidding barrier to the east.

"I don't know," Rudy replied curtly. The stench, like spoiled meat, had grown stronger as they entered the lower reaches of the valley. Now he was forced to breathe through his mouth in order to avoid gagging.

He, too, was tired. More significantly, he didn't know if the cloaked strangers were on their trail or not. He'd looked forward to the chance to rest in the neighboring village, but if the whole place smelled as bad as the outskirts, something was terribly wrong there.

"Does Dermaat *always* stink?" Anjell asked.

"Never before," Rudy replied. He'd been here a dozen times or more, and always in the past had been struck by Dermaat's flowery resemblance to Neshara or any of a half dozen other Halverican towns.

The trees opened up to reveal the village, and immediately Rudy froze, seizing Anjell by the arm so that she couldn't continue forward.

"What?" she demanded.

"The gardens . . . take a look."

Anjell squinted, and then gasped. Nearly all of the flower beds in Dermaat had been stripped of their blossoms—the whole village was in a state of mourning!

A growing sense of foreboding gripped the Iceman, and for a moment he felt an urge to turn and run back to the forest. But that was no solution—he reminded himself, bitterly, that he was already fleeing one nameless threat. He couldn't run away from every unexpected development.

"Wait here," he ordered Anjell.

Slowly he walked into the village. Beside the lack of flowers, he noticed the silence. Any new arrival to a Halverican community could expect to be surrounded by a mob of woofing alphunds; here, not a single one of the big dogs was in sight.

And he saw no people! Dermaat was a small village, but it seemed inconceivable that there weren't a few people about, doing the morning milkings if nothing else.

The slamming of a door behind him sent Rudy into a panicked spin. He didn't remember drawing the blade, but somehow the knife leaped into his hand.

The first thing he saw was Anjell, who had ignored his command and followed several steps behind him. Before he could rebuke her, he saw the source of the slam. The front door of Dermaat House, the village inn, wobbled on its hinges as a man staggered out, stumbling down the steps to sprawl facedown on the paving stones of the walk.

"Jonn!" cried Rudy, recognizing his neighbor from Neshara, remembering that Jonn had been a member of the search party that had gone to the scene of the avalanche. Now Rudy remembered Roggett's remark: Jonn and Pater had gone to Dermaat Valley to see if the neighboring village had observed anything out of the ordinary.

Jonn looked up, his eyes blank and unfocused. Rudy and Anjell rolled him onto his back, shocked by his pallor and ravaged condition. Angry red spots flared across the stricken Iceman's skin, and his cheeks were sunken against his teeth, giving his visage a skull-like appearance. His breath came in rasping, painful gasps. Eyes rolling madly, the man jerked his head spasmodically from side to side.

"Water!" he croaked, his voice cracking.

"Here," Rudy said, quickly unslinging his waterskin. Popping the cork, he held the neck to Jonn's lips.

The ailing Iceman shook his head. *No.* "Water," he repeated. "The water . . ."

"Here—take a drink," urged the younger man.

Abruptly Jonn stiffened, arching his back and trembling as his body was racked by a seizure. His eyes rolled in his head and his feet flailed without purpose—though one heavy boot caught Anjell in the knee and knocked her sprawling.

Rudy struggled to hold his friend down, knowing he was dying, cursing his inability to do anything useful. Anjell crept back, and though there were tears of pain in her eyes, she bit back her sobs as she helped Rudy hold Jonn as still as possible.

In a few moments the convulsion passed, but the stricken man seemed even weaker than before. His eyelids, half-closed, showed only the whites.

"Rudy!"

The urgency in Anjell's voice drew his attention upward to where she gestured. On the side of the Dermaathof he clearly saw the party of cloaked travelers coming around a rocky switchback where the road was temporarily barren of trees. The Hisser gestured downward imperatively; though still miles up the twisting road, the strangers started to jog.

"They've seen us—we've got to get out of here!" Rudy barked, before his attention fell back to the ailing Jonn.

"What about him?" Anjell asked.

He knew there was no way to carry the burly Iceman. Leaving him alone in Dermaat seemed heartless, but what else could they do? The strangers, after all, had been looking for Rudy. Jonn should have nothing to fear from the mysterious travelers.

Even as he attempted to convince himself, Rudy knew that his argument rang hollow. *Everyone*, it seemed, should fear these interlopers—though exactly why this was so, he couldn't say.

"Let's get him back to the inn," he said, gesturing to the nearby door. With Anjell helping, they managed to half-carry, half-drag Jonn back into the coolness of Dermaat House. The great-room was empty, the hearth cold. Laying his friend on a cushioned bench, Rudy was acutely conscious of the threat fast approaching outside.

"Do you want some water?" he asked again.

"Water!" cried Jonn, lurching up to a sitting position. He raised his hands, as if to ward off an attack. Gurgling a painful breath, he thrashed backward and lay still.

Rudy stared in barely comprehending shock. Jonn's eyes were open, yet he saw no gleam, no faint sign of vitality, within them.

"Hurry!" he barked, propelling the wide-eyed Anjell toward the door. Before he followed, he knelt and touched a hand to Jonn's neck; he felt not even the flicker of a pulse.

Rudy followed his niece out the door, quickly dragging her to the side of a large barn across the street. Here, at least, they were safe from observation.

"Let's *go!*" urged Anjell.

"I can't take you with me!" Rudy groaned, slumping against the barn. "I'm going all the way to the Glimmersee!" He didn't even want to think about Galtigor, so far beyond.

"I've *been* there," Anjell protested. "I'll come with you!"

Rudy shook his head. His mind reeled, staggered by one disaster after another. Jonn had not been a close friend, but his death was terribly frightening—all the more so since Rudy had no idea what had killed him. He suspected that it had something to do with the absence of people in Dermaat, and that only suggested an even greater scope of disaster.

"You've got to get back to Neshara—as soon as possible!" he declared.

"But what about—" Anjell gestured to the unseen road until he silenced her with a chopping gesture.

"I've thought about that. Come on!"

He took her hand and together they sprinted from the village onto the road leading down the valley toward the Glimmersee. Without risking a glance overhead, Rudy felt certain that the mysterious pursuers saw his flight, and continued to hasten down the road.

In moments the two had reached the cool shelter of the woods, and here Rudy pulled Anjell off the road, into the thick brush and rocks near the bank of the stream.

Ignoring her squawks of protest, he led her along the shore, retracing his steps to the village—this time, out of sight from above. In a few minutes they came to the back of a mill house which stood very near the bank of the stream.

Scrambling up to the freight door, Rudy pushed on the portal, relieved when it creaked inward. "Come on—we'll hide in here until they've passed. Then I can get you back on the road to Neshara."

Anjell collapsed onto several sacks of grain, her face locked in a tight pout. "I don't *want* to go back!" she spat.

"I didn't ask what you wanted. I'm telling you what's—"

The smashing of the door cut off his words. Rudy whirled to see a hulking form, cloaked in a robe of fur, plunging into the front of the mill house. The wooden door exploded from its hinges in a cascade of splinters as the intruder raised a long, iron-bladed sword.

The fellow was huge, barrel-chested and stout-legged. His garments were identical to those worn by the figures who accompanied the persistent stranger, yet Rudy knew that band of pursuers could not yet have reached the village. The attacker's face was concealed behind a fold of his robe, though dark, hateful eyes glittered savagely from the shadowed depths of his hood. Now those eyes fastened on the young girl before him.

Anjell screamed while Rudy gaped in shock. The brutish attacker lunged forward, looming over the girl, who seemed unable to move. A vivid picture flashed in the Iceman's mind—a vision of his niece torn to bloody bits beneath that cleaving blade.

Rudy dove, his reaction propelled by raw instinct. His shoulder smashed into Anjell's side, silencing her scream as the force of the blow carried her off the grain sacks. Together they tumbled across the chaff-strewn floor, while burlap and wheat flour erupted beneath the smash of the heavy iron-bladed sword.

Bouncing to his feet, Rudy found himself holding his knife, thrusting valiantly at the huge attacker. The blade seemed pathetically inadequate compared to the fearsome weapon wielded by his opponent. That mighty sword hissed through a sideways arc, and Rudy felt the air of its passage as he ducked.

The building shook from the impact as the blade chopped into a sturdy support beam. His enemy grunted in frustration, struggling to release the weapon, and Rudy saw a desperate opportunity. Frantically he thrust with the knife, aiming at the neck—where the cowled hood met the fellow's heavy cloak.

His opponent leaped back with surprising agility, though the tip of the knife blade caught at the fringe of his hood. With a tearing slash, Rudy pulled the concealing garment away—and gagged in shock.

The face that glared venomously at him was that of a misshapen *beast*! A wide mouth gaped, revealing short yellow fangs jutting from an overhanging upper jaw. A blunt, piggish snout separated two glittering, bloodshot eyes, all shadowed by a knobbed forehead. The skin was a wart-covered surface of mottled gray, like leather cured too long in the sun.

Paralyzed by disbelief, Rudy watched mutely as the monster ripped the blade free from the timber. Only then did the Iceman realize his utter peril, diving backward in growing panic as that vicious blade slashed past his chest. Scrambling for cover, Rudy realized that he'd dropped his knife—he didn't even remember when.

"Run!" he cried to Anjell, as the brute plunged after him. "Get out of here!"

Nimbly the girl spun on her heel, dashing out through the splintered door. If more of the beasts lurked outside, there was nothing Rudy could do.

The fanged mouth smacked hungrily as the brute slowed its frantic attack. Deliberately Rudy backed away, forced into a corner. Casting around for some kind of weapon, he saw only a long-handled pitchfork, which he snatched up.

His attacker lunged, and Rudy desperately knocked the sword aside with the tines of his makeshift weapon. The beast pressed ahead and the Iceman fell back, knocked off balance by the force of the monster's attack. Smashing into a heavy beam, Rudy knew that he'd retreated as far as he could.

"Hey—you! Ugly!" challenged a girlish voice. The monster hesitated, and the Iceman felt a surge of panic as he saw Anjell coming back through the door. In her hands she held several rocks, which she released in a sharp barrage at the beast's back. Hulking down, it ignored her, turning its attention back toward the Iceman.

Another shape darkened the door. Rudy, horrified at the prospect of additional monstrous warriors, nearly cried aloud in despair. At the same time the sword-wielder turned with a grunt of surprise, falling back under an unexpected onslaught—and only then did Rudy see the new combatant.

The snow lion pounced through the door in a fluid blur, snarling savagely as it lunged toward the monster's gaping face. Uncoiling like a spring, the shaggy feline smashed heavily into its target, sharp talons hooking through the cloak that covered the monster's chest. Widespread jaws bit its blunt snout, crushing the brute's gape of astonishment. With a strangled howl, the creature toppled backward to the floor, struggling to bring its weapon to bear.

Rudy's heart pounded. He raised the pitchfork, revulsion rising like bile in his throat. He saw the monster's sword come free, the dull edge of the weapon swinging around toward the snow lion's unprotected flank.

The pitchfork chopped downward, the tines puncturing the tough skin of the monster's neck. With a strangled gurgle, it stiffened, and the sword dropped from nerveless, dead fingers. Only then did Rudy sag backward, retching convulsively as he leaned weakly against the wall. He clasped his hands to his chest, feeling the outline of the ice-filled cut even as his belly spasmed.

"A snow lion! *Wow!*" He heard Anjell's squeal of delight, and though he wanted to steer her away from the wretched sight on the floor, he couldn't bring himself to speak. He, too, looked at the animal in amazement. The big feline sat on its haunches, licking that huge tongue across its bristling whiskers, regarding the two humans calmly. Rudy recognized the placid yellow eyes, the smug and self-satisfied smile that he had seen before—this was unquestionably the same animal. When Anjell stepped forward to scratch the shaggy neck, the snow lion settled down with a rumbling purr.

"Let's go—we've got to hurry!" Rudy urged, shaking off his wonder. Carefully he looked out the broken door of the mill house, up the slope of Dermaathof. Though he couldn't see the group who had pursued them from Neshara, he felt certain they were there—and no doubt much closer than before. His original plan began to seem like madness—surely the creatures would sense their presence in the village! Somehow this one monster had located them. Rudy didn't need to stretch his imagination to picture the result if more than one of the beasts should attack.

Only then did Anjell's voice draw his attention up the valley, toward the looming height of Glimmercrown.

"Look there," she said, her tone unusually somber.

Winding along the road that twisted down the valley floor, Rudy saw a great number of cloaked figures, marching steadily in a long column. They were still several miles away, but already he could see dozens of them—with no end to the column in sight.

"Come on," he groaned, taking Anjell by the hand and starting down the valley, away from the oncoming force and past the road leading back to Neshara.

"You're taking me to the Glimmersee?" asked Anjell, as if suspicious that he intended to leave her along the trail.

"As fast as I possibly can," he replied. The snow lion loped at their heels as they raced down the road, once again vanishing into the cool shelter of the trees.

SIX

A Digger of Faerine

There's not a ditch that can be dug that can't be
dammed.
—DIGGERSPEAK PROVERB

— 1 —

When Danri awakened with the hammer beside his pillow for the seventh consecutive morning, he knew that the Madness was nearly upon him.

As on the previous six nights, he'd gone to sleep on his bachelor's pallet after a long, sociable evening of drinking and gambling. The battered hammer—with its centuries-old head of scuffed steel—had been stored in the entryway, just beside the iron-banded front door. Sometime during the night, unremembered now, he'd risen and gone to the tool, carrying it back to bed and placing it precisely beside his head, within a few inches' grasp of his right hand.

He stood with a tingling sense of urgency, certain that the time was very near. It was more than just the exciting discovery of his hammer: for more than a month he'd been eating and drinking far beyond his normal needs, and each night he'd settled for nothing less than twelve hours' sleep. Each night and part of the following day, he corrected himself, realizing that the sun had already slipped past the zenith.

Throughout the eight decades of his life, Danri had never before overslept dawn by more than an hour or so—and each of those occasions had been marked by dire feelings of guilt and irresponsibility. He chuckled wryly as he reflected on the change: here it was early afternoon, and he felt absolutely no remorse for his tardy awakening.

He clumped over to the small, round window. Even without his heavy boots and leather kilt, he walked with a powerful, rolling gait. He stretched, muscles tightening through his shoulders and his long arms, rippling like the lean sinews of a dancer. His legs, by contrast, were short and bowed, gnarled as the trunk of a knotty oak—and just as sturdy. He felt a slight pulling from the bruise on his left shoulder, where a gigant had punched him several days ago. Danri had won that fight, as he'd won all the others in the last few years; still, the big brute had landed some telling punches. Somehow, the digger had developed a reputation that brought gigants down from their aloof heights, looking for Danri because he had roughed up their kinsman or pal. The digger chuckled wryly at a thought: once the Madness claimed him, the gigants could look high and low for their revenge, but they would certainly be disappointed.

Casting open the wooden shutter, he looked across the slate-roofed houses of Shalemont. A cool breeze ruffled his beard, bringing the scents of coal smoke, rock dust, and brewer's yeast—all underlaid by the metallic smell of the up-valley smelting plants. His fellow diggers were already at work, of course. Most of them would be in the depths of the mines, though those blessed with crafts—armorers, minters, stonecarvers, smelters, smiths, and so forth—labored at their shops throughout the town.

Danri wondered if he was looking at Shalemont for the last time. Many of those diggers seized by the Madness vanished forever from the eyes of their families and neighbors, and somewhere deep inside himself, he suspected that he might become one of those.

With that, he decided to spend the day going about the town, seeking his friends and visiting with such of them as he could find. Taking only the time to eat a dozen boiled eggs and a loaf of bread, followed by two quarts of creamy milk, he took up the hammer and left his house.

His first stop found Hakwan Chiseler. The cutter's shop was at the corner down the hill from Danri's house, and he passed through the open door to find Hakwan bent over his wheel, honing the edge of a broad-bladed axe.

"Hay-ah, mate," Danri said. "How 'bout putting an edge on my pick, here." He indicated the chiseled end of his hammerhead, where the point opposite the blunt face tapered into a long, gently curved pick.

"Why, surely," Hakwan agreed, with a ready nod. "Jest set it on the bench there—it'll be a few days before I can do it."

"Umm—hmmm," Danri demurred, gently clearing his throat.

The edge-carver stopped pedaling his wheel, leaning back on his stool to peer upward at Danri. Hakwan scowled curiously, scratching the long gray hairs of his beard as if he sought some explanation in his facial hair.

"You know, I heered somethin' about you—been wakin' up with the hammer, so Kerri tells me."

"Aye—uh," Danri agreed. Kerri, the barmaid at Tailings Pub, had been the first person Danri had told about his premonition. He had figured, correctly, that she would be a lot more efficient than he himself at spreading word through the town.

"How many nights now?" Hakwan wondered.

"Today's the seventh."

"Oh-okay. I'll do yer pick right away." The chiseler took the heavy tool from Danri and started to crank his whetstone. The big wheel of abrasive rock spun slowly on its axle, gaining speed until it rumbled and hummed. Hakwan touched the pick to the stone and a cascade of sparks showered downward. Ignoring the pyrotechnics, the craftsman carefully moved the steel tool back and forth.

"Good steel—I remember honing it for your grandpa once or twice. Ya can always tell digger alloys—if this was human stuff I'd have worn it clean away by now. And even sylvan steel doesn't keep this kind of edge."

Danri sat quietly, enjoying a closeness to Hakwan that he knew he'd miss. Still, it was all he could do to remain seated for the half hour that Hakwan worked. Halfway through the wait, Danri's foot started tapping, as if with a life of its own, and—not wanting to offend his friend—he grimly forced it to stay firmly on the floor.

"Aye-up. There she is—you could pick yer teeth with that," Hakwan said at last, leaning back and admiring the now gleaming tip. "Want me to scuff some burrs off the head, here?" he asked, indicating the opposite end of the tool.

"Reckon I'll wear them off soon enough," Danri grunted, inspecting the sharpened point with keen pleasure. "Thanks." He reached into his belt pouch, seeking a silver coin.

"No charge," Hakwan said breezily. "Jest gimme a thought now and then, when yer in the depths."

Deeply touched, Danri agreed. No digger would willingly clasp a friend in his arms, but he did extend a hand and touch Hakwan on the shoulder before he turned to go. It was a moment of profound closeness for them both, as each wondered if he would ever see the other again.

Danri wandered back into the streets of Shalemont, without any clear sense of destination. His hammer swung easily in his hand, and for a few moments his mind conjured images of dark, Aura-slick rock. His shoulders tensed as he pictured layers of granite tumbling away before the onslaught of his blunt-headed tool. For a moment the compulsion to chop, to dig at solid stone, almost drove him to the mines.

Soon, now—it will begin today.

The streets and alleys of the town formed a maze of stone-walled passages. Smoke from the smelters drifted through the air, carrying the pungent, satisfying tint of productive labor to Danri's nostrils. He came to the laughing course of the Bluerun Creek, where rippling Aura mingled with pure water, sparkling and dancing on its way to the distant sea. Colorful rainbows arced across the stream at several places throughout the village. Made from vaporous Aura, these spectral arches formed bridges with footing every bit as solid as a span built of oak or stone.

Overhead a sleek Auracloud drifted past. Though Danri couldn't see the passengers—since they were on the upper surface of the cloud—he suspected that the vessel carried another party of sylvan or sartor pilgrims to the Eternal Spring. Okay for them, he thought, but he, Danri the digger, would keep his feet on the ground.

Here, in the realm of his people—and in the very shadow of the Watershed—the Aura bubbling from the mountain springs was pure and potent. The massive height of the Source of Three Waters loomed far overhead, and this very stream, Danri knew, flowed from the base of that peak. The humans called the Source "Glimmercrown," and Danri supposed that the minions of Dassadec had their own name for it. To the diggers it was simply the place that gave birth to the three liquids that preserved the sanctity, magic, and order of the Watershed.

Now he wondered how long it would be before he again beheld that soaring peak.

Danri didn't recall crossing the brook, but he found himself at the end of a rainbow bridge, on the bank opposite his house. Blinking in surprise—but not confusion—he started up the winding lane, toward the vast, barren mountainside where the diggers of Shalemont did their mining.

His next stop was Tailings Pub, named for the vast slide of loose stone that spilled, fanlike, across the mountainside below the ancient mines. At one time the pub had been a stone structure on the slope, but it had been buried by rubble centuries ago. Now a long, straight entry corridor, well-shored with heavy timbers, bored through the tailings pile and led to the cavelike confines of the inn, buried deep in the layer of stones.

The ceiling of the entryway arched more than five feet over the floor, providing ample room for any digger to enter the inn without stooping. Danri reached the large, comfortably cool great-room. The chamber was nearly dark, except for a bowl of Aura on each table contributing gentle illumination; Danri's eyes quickly adjusted.

The Tailings was a large establishment, with many booths and cavelike niches set back from the main chamber. A small fire—embers, really—glowed in the fireplace, and the air was tinged with a familiar, pleasant mixture of smoke, soot, rock dust, and ale.

"Danri—hello!" Kerri's cheerful voice pulled him around, and he saw the barmaid flash him a broad wink. A cascade of black curls framed her face, matching the darkness of her large eyes. She had the long arms and broad shoulders of a strapping digger, though the front of her apron strained against the pressure of large breasts. A black leather belt was wrapped around her incongruously tiny waist, above leather breeches that swept outward to curve around her hips and thighs.

Every young male digger in the place, Danri knew, regarded him with a mixture of envy and petulance. He had always enjoyed fostering that ubiquitous jealousy; now, however, it caused him a pang of guilt. Any one of those other men, he realized, would be a better choice for Kerri—after all, they would be here tomorrow.

Then Kerri's eyes dropped to the hammer in his hand, and he saw them mist slightly, before she blinked away the involuntary tears. Sheepishly, he took the hammer back to the entryway, where he placed it on the shelf reserved for digger tools and weapons.

"Sorry," he apologized sincerely as he returned. "I've got no more manners than a human. 'Fraid I don't remember I was carrying it."

Kerri clapped a hand to her face and turned away. His explanation, he saw with regret, only caused her more pain—and why shouldn't it? He rebuked himself, knowing that only a digger on the verge of the Madness would mindlessly carry his hammer where it didn't belong.

He sat at his usual table, near the bar, and Kerri silently brought him a foaming mug of dark bitters. Since the Tailings was mostly empty, her workload was light, and dispiritedly she sat beside him.

Danri found it hard to look at her. His feet abruptly began their involuntary tapping, and the draught before him—normally his favorite—looked bleak and tasteless. He could muster no interest in drinking. Kerri, too, seemed an annoying, extraneous presence, but that was not her fault. At the least, he should try to make his departure as easy as possible for her.

"I heard about your little fracas a few days ago," she said, reaching out to take his broad hand in both of hers. "Did you get hurt? And what did that gigant want?"

"He came down from the ridge, shopping for metal, I think. I met him on the Blue Bridge, and the galoot insisted on crossing first.

'Course, most times a gigant would just let you come across—they don't seem to care about stuff like pride and honor. But this one must of been in a hurry, and he said no. Either that, or he was looking for me."

"Wouldn't be the first one," Kerri observed. "I think they have some kind of reward offered for the gigant that can dump Danri of Shalemont into the water!"

Danri looked at her with a grim chuckle. Even a small gigant, at ten feet tall and a good five hundred pounds, was a mighty opponent for a digger. Yet his quickness and strength had served him well in all his bouts thus far.

"What happened next?"

"Well, I kicked him in the shin, and the gigant picked me right up—was goin' to throw me into the brook, I guess—when I bit him, right on the end of his nose. That ol' gigant, he was so surprised, he dropped me, turned tail, and ran for the highlands!"

Kerri chuckled wryly. "Leave it to you, Danri. I just hope he doesn't have a big clan, all eager to come down here and look for the digger who bit their bro'."

"I don't think he'd find me," Danri said quietly, his words bringing Kerri's laughter to a halt.

For the first time, Danri realized that her laugh sounded very much like the splashing of the Bluerun. The thought caused him a pang of homesickness—and with that reaction he knew that his time was almost here.

Kerri's next words took him by surprise.

"I—um—I have somethin' . . . I *made* somethin' for you." Silently she went to the bar and retrieved an object resembling a wide belt. There was an intricate pattern of beads embroidered on the outside, and when she laid the object on the table he saw that the design formed the silhouette of a mountainous horizon.

"It's the skyline around Shalemont," she said slowly. "I wanted—wanted you to remember us. . . . "

Deeply touched, he took her hand. "I'll *always* remember. Not just the town, but the maid who bid me farewell. Thank you, Kerri." He picked up the gift, impressed by the elegant simplicity of her work.

"It's a waterskin, not just a decoration," she huffed. "You can wrap it around your waist, and use it to carry Aura or water."

"This means more to me than I can say," he declared awkwardly. He pulled the tubular waterskin around his middle and tied it there.

Abruptly Danri rose to his feet, unaware that he had decided to stand until he was looking down at Kerri. He tried not to see the stricken look on her face, but she stood too, and he couldn't look away from her—not now, not when he didn't know if he'd ever see her again.

"Be careful, Danri." She couldn't hold back her tears, but her voice was strong and level. "Take a care where you dig—you don't want to end up in Duloth-Trol or someplace."

"Be well, Kerri," he said, raising a hand to touch her on the cheek.

To his surprise and embarrassment she threw her arms around him and hugged him close, burying her smooth face against the whiskers of his bristling beard. For several seconds she cried, and with each tick of time Danri's agitation increased.

Finally he reached up and gently broke her grip. "You're a special lady," he said awkwardly. It was the warmest thing he'd ever said to anyone in his life, and for a fleeting moment he realized that he was going to miss her.

But the pressure of the Madness was steadily expanding inside him, like a growing reservoir where the waters already lapped over the top of the dam. Nodding gruffly, he turned away and clumped to the door. His hammer beckoned, and when he again held the smooth steel shaft of its hilt he realized that he'd felt virtually undressed without it.

" 'Bye," he said quietly, taking one last look at Kerri's tear-streaked face before marching down the long entry tunnel and again emerging into the sun.

Now he turned toward the heights. A look back at Shalemont showed him only the roofs of the little houses. The bright rainbow bridges stood out in the clear air, and the splashing of the Bluerun carried like distant, haunting music to his ears.

But he felt no compulsion to turn back toward that melodious stream, nor to the town clustered around it. His steps carried him resolutely upward, along the winding gravel road that approached a series of timber-shored tunnel mouths on the mountain.

He would seek one more person, Danri knew—and only because he could find Blaze Smelter on his way. The Madness held him almost fully in its grip now, and it was all Danri could do to avoid turning into the nearest of the mines and following the dark tunnel all the way to its stone-walled terminus.

Yet he suspected that, for him, the Madness had a specific task. He would not randomly select a starting point, any more than would the Madness carry him to a chance destination.

As he climbed past lesser ridges, smoke-belching smelters, and low, rounded summits, the great peak of the Source of Three Waters grew more dominant in his view. Like a jagged, ice-encrusted dagger, it thrust proudly into the sky, soaring above even the nearer summit of Faerimont.

Blaze Smelter was the foreman at the highest smelting house, and it was to this structure that Danri's steps inevitably carried him. Located in a small valley, out of sight of Shalemont and well above the level of the town, the smelting house was a great, stone-walled structure that practically filled the tiny vale. Dozens of mines led into the bedrock in the valley walls above the place, and each of these was connected by a series of steel rails to the smelter itself. The raw ore of the miners was carried by metal carts into the house, where it was burned, boiled, melted, pounded, and chopped until the precious metals of Faerine had been extracted.

As if he'd been expecting Danri, Blaze Smelter emerged from the cavernous doors of the smelting house when his friend approached, falling into step beside him as Danri's steps carried him past the great, clanging factory. Together, in silence, they walked steadily up the trail toward the highest of the mines.

"Good luck, my friend," Blaze offered, after several minutes of hiking.

"And to you. Keep an eye on Kerri, will you?—she's kind of upset."

Blaze chuckled. "It was always *your* eyes she wanted on her, not mine. You sure you want to give me this chance?"

Danri ignored the joke; both of them understood that the Madness was not a question of "want," or even of choice. It was a thing whose time had come.

"I don't know if I'll even be here to take advantage of the opportunity," Blaze said. "I'm due next year to captain the digger garrison up at Taywick Pass. Might be away for a while myself."

Danri nodded; even as he spoke, Blaze seemed to be drifting away from him, becoming harder and harder to understand.

"Been a lot of years for Shalemont, since one of us took on the Madness . . . seems right, though, now that the time has come, that it's you." Blaze spoked plainly, his words touching Danri. "Fact is, the whole town will miss you—but whatever you've got to do, we know it's going to make a fine tale. . . . "

"Tales and legend," Danri replied, embarrassed. "Not that, no . . ." His mind seemed thick, confused, as if it had no place for language. Compelling forces burned in his breast, steadily growing in power, directing him beyond the confines of logic.

"Just have a care—don't be one of these mad diggers who comes up in Dalethica or Duloth-Trol!"

"Hah—you don't believe those old myths, do you? Besides, I'll follow Aura . . . can't get past the Watershed."

"Here—I thought this might come in handy," Blaze said, clearing his throat awkwardly. He swung a coiled line off his shoulder—a rope that Danri hadn't even noticed he carried. The line was slender and supple, woven from a myriad of tiny steelweed strands. Though it was thinner than Danri's little finger, the digger nevertheless knew that the rope would support his weight and a lot more.

"Made it myself," Blaze said. "Soon as I figured out what was going on with you."

"Aye-uh. It's time." Somewhere, from some distant memory, he found the sounds to articulate his sudden knowledge. Absently he took the coils of the rope and looped them over his shoulder. The line settled against the contours of his body, where it wouldn't be in the way.

"That center hole, there—it's got a good flow of Aura comin' out—you might try that."

Blaze's words might have been the distant rumble of thunder for all the meaning they carried to Danri.

Clutching his hammer like a talisman, the digger started toward the mines that gaped like black mouths in the sides of the gray ridge. He didn't choose the center excavation, however—his calling was clear and purposeful.

Danri climbed the winding trail that led to the highest tunnel on the ridge. It was an old, decayed mine, with even the timbers that shored the entrance sagging and rotted. Aurianth only knew in what condition the interior supports might be. Many decades, perhaps centuries, had passed since the last cart of ore had been drawn out of this excavation. Experience had shown the digger engineers that the richer troves lay lower down, the heavier metals having settled deep in the bedrock of these lofty valleys.

But the mine itself was irrelevant. Danri was drawn by the shallow trickle of Aura emerging from the shadowy aperture. Barely a handspan in width, the flowage was too shallow to wet the top of a coin laid flat—indeed, it was more like a slick place on the rocky ground than an actual waterway. Yet the smoothness of that ground, the shallow groove worn there over many years, showed that the liquid of magic had been flowing for a long time.

Hoisting his hammer to his shoulder, Danri stepped into the mine. He never even thought about one last look at the world he left behind.

— 2 —

The next few years passed in a blur. Indeed, for Danri they didn't seem to pass at all—so focused was his life, his quest, that everything pertaining to the surface simply ceased to exist. Since his body required neither food nor sleep, and his environment gave no hint of daylight or darkness, there was nothing by which to mark the passage of time.

He remained aware of four things—his body, his hammer, the stone cocoon encasing him, and the tiny trickle of Aura emerging from the porous foundation of Faerine. Forming a quadrant around reality, these aspects of his universe sustained and challenged him, creating an existence as intense as any life on the Watershed.

Chopping at the granite wall, the tireless digger chiseled a passage through the rock. The tunnel he created was high enough for Danri to stand erect, and wide enough for him to stretch his arms and swing his hammer without striking the walls. The loose debris cleared by his labors he periodically moved to the back of his passageway; the overall length of his rocky shell remained about thirty feet.

Danri was sustained by frequent sips of the Aura trickling constantly through his small, slowly moving cave. That liquid also provided him with illumination; not that it actually glowed, but when Aura was present in a darkened place, diggers, like all creatures of Faerine, could see.

Toughened by his labors, Danri's sinews became like steel, as hard as the rock that surrounded him. His hammer was an extension of his brawny hand and powerful arm, biting into the mountain with inexorable persuasion, frequently chipping free a great slab of rock with a few carefully aimed blows.

As to the course of Danri's digging, that was determined by Aura—he dug away the rocks from which the waters of magic flowed. In this fashion he created a moderately winding passage that gradually approached the heart of the great mountain. He did not leave a usable exit tunnel in his wake because of the need to dispose of the excess rock in the passageway behind him.

Only once in this long, sleepless process did a singular event break the routine of Danri's labors. Near the center of the great mountain, he carved into a loose, rotten shard of rock that crumbled too easily before the blows of his hammer.

Quickly a noxious scent assailed him, and his lungs coughed in reflexive reaction. Darkblood! The poisonous water of Duloth-Trol seeped beneath this mountain as well, and the digger immediately knew that he'd approached dangerously close to a source of this deadly liquid. If it mingled with Aura, a violent explosion powerful enough to shatter rock--and flesh—could result.

Danri instantly turned around in his passage, erecting a barrier over the crumbled stone. He then reexcavated his tunnel, backing up for several hundred feet, laying stone in his wake as surely as any bricklayer to insure a solid and impenetrable wall. During this retreat he noticed another small trickle of Aura emerging from a side wall, and took advantage of it to commence his digging in a new direction.

More time passed, a seamless progression of hours, days, and weeks that carried Danri ever farther through the bedrock of the Watershed. He was surrounded by the mountains that formed the Crown of the World, but his attention was focused on the subtle veins and irregular strata no more than a foot or two from his face.

Eventually he noticed a peculiar alteration in the sound of his sharp blows. His picking, chipping labors against the rock took on a resonance, ringing through his stone-walled capsule like the song of some deep, subterranean god. While this peculiarity triggered no outward sense of urgency in his labors, Danri's mind considered the phenomenon over the course of a hundred, a thousand, ten thousand, blows against the wall.

The resonance gained in strength, too gradually to discern over the course of any series of blows, but obviously enough that it could only have one explanation.

He was approaching some kind of vast open space—a space that was nevertheless still underground, encased in the rock of the Watershed. If he was drawing near the surface, the sound would not resonate in his own chamber, but merely sound increasingly hollow and fragile. In that case he would shortly expect to emerge from the mountain somewhere and let the Madness fall away from him. He would resume life on the surface, trying to understand the destiny to which his Madness had carried him.

But Danri felt with inescapable certainty that the portent of the strange resonance did not indicate that his Madness was nearing its end; rather, he knew that he was approaching some kind of way-station on the timeless journey. Whatever lay before him, his discovery would be important—at least to himself, if not to all diggers.

The changes in the timbre of the noise occurred more quickly, until it seemed that each chiseling smash against the rock must crack a final barrier and reveal to Danri his intermediate goal. Abruptly, a blow of his hammer continued through the wall, and the sheet of rock before his face toppled slowly away from him. He heard it crash and rumble down a steep slope, splintering into many bits of rubble.

In another instant a multitude of splashes rose to his ears, and the tumbling sounds ceased. Leaning forward, Danri blinked in surprise, momentarily startled by the broadness of the vista before him. He had penetrated the wall of a huge cavern. The floor of the chamber was almost entirely covered by still water—a vast, subterranean lake. Illumination from this liquid suffused the entire cave in the dim, glowing fluorescence of a rainbow, so Danri knew immediately that this was not mundane water, but Aura.

Further inspection showed him that the shore of the lake was about fifty feet below the opening he had carved in the wall. A sheer cliff descended for most of that distance, though he could see that just above water level the walls sloped inward, creating a rough, rock-strewn "beach" around the fringe of the Aura.

With a few quick strikes of his chisel, Danri hammered away enough rock to create a solid half-ring of stone, looping like a handle from the bedrock of the mountain. He ran his rope through this ring, doubling the line so that he could draw it free once he reached the bottom. After tugging a few times to make sure that the anchor was solid, he scrambled through the hole in the cavern wall and started to descend.

Paying out his line carefully, he walked backward down the cliff until the soles of his boots settled onto a rounded boulder. Standing once again, he looked around. The still Aura of the subterranean lake stretched into the shadowy distance from this shore, but to either side a thin strand of gravel and rock would allow him to make his way beside the water. He released one end of his rope, hauling in the other until once again he coiled the line into a loose series of loops over his broad shoulder.

Which way to go? He wasted little time in thought; instead, he allowed his feet to choose. No sooner did he have his line stored and his hammer returned to his hand than those feet started carrying him along the shore, to the right.

For the most part the walking was easy, though occasionally he had to scramble over a jumbled pile of boulders, or turn his back to the wall and make his way across a particularly narrow section of the shoreline. As if the lake had been designed to allow circumnavigation, however, there was no place he could see where the waters actually met the base of the cavern wall.

Another thing that struck him about this vast chamber was the incredible, all-encompassing *silence* of the place. It seemed incongruous that, in a place this big, there was not something that would make some noise—a small rivulet of water flowing in, or the trickling of some kind of drainage stream. Like the Madness itself, this place seemed timeless . . . an eternal lake, settled at this level, with neither inlet nor outflow.

As he walked beside the magical water, Danri pondered the nature of Aura, and the unique relationship it bore to him—or to any digger in the grip of the Madness. Though all the creatures of Faerine used Aura—indeed, required it for life—the water of magic was not generally perceived as sustenance. Like sweet wine to humankind, Aura was a delightful supplement to the fruits, breads, juices, and mundane water that nourished creatures of Faerine just as they sustained the humans and animals of Dalethica.

But in a few cases, Aura alone was sufficient to sustain life. A digger in the throes of Madness was the most obvious example—for a time longer than he knew, Danri had had neither food to eat nor water to drink. Other creatures of Faerine, too—the gigants, twissels, sartors, sylves, and even the mighty drackans—all had their own uses for Aura. In special circumstances, it could nurture any of these enchanted creatures just as effectively as it had provided for him these last months, years.

Yet never before had Danri seen so *much* of the precious liquid as now filled the vast lake bed before him. He wondered if this might be the source of Aura for all Faerine—was this a giant reservoir, high in the mountains, from which the water of magic bubbled outward and down, feeding the springs and fountains of the land? Could this be the headwaters of the Eternal Spring itself? But then why couldn't he hear some sound of the water trickling away?

A shape along the shore struck an odd note with Danri, and an instinctive sense of caution brought his hammer up, ready to attack or defend. After a few more steps, he saw that it was no threat—just an object that clearly didn't blend into the jagged rocks of the shoreline.

A boat!

Astonished, Danri halted. He tried to penetrate with his eyes the darkened niches along the rough shoreline, half-suspecting that some sinister oarsman lurked there, preparing to ambush him.

But even before his eyes sought out the shadowy recesses, Danri knew that he was alone in this vast chamber. It was not just the immaculate silence of the place—his certainty came from an abiding sense that he would have *known* if someone else was in here with him.

Carefully, he advanced to the boat, examining the long, narrow craft. The hull was made of wood that had apparently been treated with some kind of lacquer; the planks were slick and free of rot. Untreated wood, he knew, became pulpy and useless after a few years underground, while timbers soaked in creosote—which was the typical digger technique for wood preservation—could last upwards of a century. Yet anything touched by creosote carried a distinctive odor, and Danri could detect no trace of that scent now.

Even a cursory inspection suggested that this seal was more effective than creosote or any other treatment with which he was familiar. It was almost as if a thin sheet of liquid glass had been poured over the wood, completely protecting the timbers against the decomposition wrought by water and time. This boat might have been sitting here for a thousand years.

The skiff was about twenty feet long, with a six-foot beam. It tapered to a point at either end—indeed, nothing seemed to distinguish the bow from the stern. Several rounded rocks supported the hull, indicating that the boat had been pulled out of the water by the last person to use it. At the same time, it was so close to floating free that Danri had to wonder, again, if someone hadn't placed it here in the last few hours. Even though there was no threat of storm or gale in this subterranean lake, what was the likelihood of the water level remaining unchanged for a matter of years?

Danri saw no oars or paddles, but a long pole rested across the seats, and he guessed that this must be the means of locomotion. No matter to him—he had no intention of leaving the solid footing of the shoreline for the tenuous hull of the mysterious boat. With a shrug, he continued past the vessel, following the strand of gravel between the cavern wall and the body of Aura.

In another twenty steps he reached an obstacle. Here the cave wall plummeted straight to the water's edge, merging into the Aura as a sheer, seamless cliff. Leaning outward from the last stretch of shore, Danri saw that the cliff continued for as far as he could see. There was no forward passage here—at least nothing for someone who wasn't prepared to swim.

Of course, like most diggers, Danri *could* swim—but, also like the rest of his folk, he detested immersion in water. He regarded swimming as something one did when the alternative was drowning. Here, of course, he had another choice.

The boat.

A chill shivered along his spine as he realized how fortuitous was the placement of that mysterious craft. With a tinge of resentment, he felt as though someone, somehow, was *forcing* him into the little skiff.

Reluctantly he backtracked along the lakeshore. With a critical eye he studied the narrow hull. Four bench seats, evenly spaced from fore to aft, straddled the keel. With a slight push, he freed the boat from its resting place on the rocks, noticing that it floated with less than a foot of freeboard to either side.

For a moment he considered retracing his steps along the shore to the place where he had entered the vast cavern. Perhaps, if he'd turned *left* there instead of right, he would have found a shoreline fully passable around the lake.

Yet a stubborn sense of purpose prevented him from giving that thought serious consideration. When he'd entered this vast chamber, he had followed his instincts. Now he couldn't turn his back on that intuitive decision.

Muttering a few words—mingling a prayer to Aurianth with a curse against the fate that seemed to compel him over the lake—Danri stepped into the skiff. He'd rather fight a dozen gigants than float on the water, but his course here was too obvious to ignore. The flat-bottomed craft rocked slightly from his weight, but the digger took a wide stance and picked up the long pole. Touching it gently to the rocks on the shoreline, he pushed himself away from the beach.

— 3 —

How deep was the water? For a moment, Danri's mind rippled with apprehension as he pictured a bottomless well beneath him. The pole would be useless as a means of propulsion, and he imagined drifting endlessly across this dark lake—a thought that filled him with panic. Quickly he thrust the end of the long shaft into the Aura.

The tip of the pole clicked against the stone floor of the lake, and he pushed himself back toward the shore, relieved that he'd immersed no more than half the pole before striking bottom. His heart settled back to its stable beat, and he carefully propelled himself parallel to the rocky strand. Poling on the offshore side of the boat, he insured that he wouldn't accidentally push himself too far from shore. The bottom was rough, like a tumble of sharp-edged boulders, and he had no difficulty finding solid niches against which to set his pole.

Soon he came parallel to the sheer cliff that had blocked his passage on dry land. From his vantage on the water, he saw that the barrier extended for a long way—even if he had tried to swim around it, he wasn't certain that he would have had the endurance to reach a passable stretch of shore. Steadily poling, Danri pushed himself beside the cliff, discovering that the water was about fifteen feet deep along this stretch. His eyes drifted over the rock face, studying the jagged outlines of stone formations, the occasional cut and gouge of the narrow cracks that scored the surface in places.

To his left, the dark waters spread to the limits of his vision. Several cone-shaped mounds of stone rose from the surface at irregular intervals—barren islands in the midst of the subterranean lake. Some of these rose into monstrous pillars, narrowing like hourglasses at the waist before spreading outward to vanish into the darkness overhead. These vast columns, Danri suspected, supported the cavern ceiling in several places—otherwise the roof would have caved in long ago.

The digger couldn't see the ceiling or the far walls of the cave, but he estimated that his visibility extended for over a mile. Steadily pushing himself along, he wondered again about this vast expanse of

Aura—why was it here? And who had brought this boat into the cavern? Indeed, how had they gotten it here?

It seemed clear that there must be some access to the surface from someplace in this vast chamber. But was it his destiny to find that exit—or would he continue his digging from some other part of this cave? Danri felt strangely agitated, unsure of how to handle this disruption in the previously unbroken pattern of the Madness.

He pushed the pole against the rocks, feeling the boat glide smoothly forward. The wooden rod broke the surface of the water and drove downward again.

But this time it met no resistance. Gritting his teeth against the sudden onset of disquiet, Danri pushed harder, until he held just the very end of the boatman's pole. Flailing the shaft through the water, he sought vainly for some purchase—but he made contact with nothing. It was as if the bottom of the lake had suddenly plunged away, vanishing into mysterious, murky depths.

A hole! That must be it, he told himself, casting a reassuring glance at the cliff-walled shoreline that remained comfortingly near to his right. He must be floating over a hole in the bottom, and in another few seconds he would again find solid purchase on the sunken rocks. After all, the force of his momentum continued to carry the slender boat forward.

Yet as the craft slowed, Danri probed around with the pole and failed to feel any suggestion of a solid bottom. Finally the skiff came to a serene rest, leaving no ripple of wake. Silently, grimly, Danri probed the waters to all sides.

Nothing. This part of the lake might be a thousand feet deep—even bottomless—for all he could discern.

Scowling, he looked back across the smooth surface. How far had he drifted from the drop-off? He realized with disgust that he didn't know.

Stomping back and forth, the digger circled in the center of the boat as his frustration increased. He longed for the solidity, the security of his tunnel, with the stone walls to all sides, the steady working of his hammer to calm his muscles and sedate his mind. Now his forced inactivity, he felt, would soon drive him mad.

Fixing his gaze upon the cavern wall, Danri tried to find some irregularity, a ledge or a crack, that might give him purchase to climb above the water. Curiously, he could see few details of the rocky face, though he recalled that a few minutes earlier his eyes had noticed each outcrop and stratum.

With the first glimmerings of fear, he understood: he couldn't see any details because the cavern wall was much farther away than it had been a few minutes earlier! Only then did he realize that his narrow craft was moving, borne by some current too subtle to convey any real sense of motion. Drifting slowly away from shore, he had traveled a considerable distance, unaware of his progress.

Muttering an inaudible curse, Danri sat on the nearest of the benches. He laid the pole inside the boat, wondering if he'd ever have the chance to use it again. Yet as he brooded, his mind wrestled with a different understanding of his predicament.

Perhaps, he told himself, it was better to move than to sit hopelessly still. When he started the Madness, he had in a real sense placed himself in the hands of a greater destiny. It was easier to believe that he could serve that destiny by floating on a current rather than sitting motionless in the lake.

His flickering hopes were fanned by the sight of a mountainous island rising from the water in his path. A fringe of stony beach surrounded the massif, which towered upward like a great, conical hill— except that this elevation expanded toward its summit, like the overhanging limbs of a gigantic tree.

The beach enouraged him—if the shoreline continued to slope gently under the water, he might float close enough so that his pole could again strike bottom.

For a long time the massif continued to grow before him. The current veered around the obstacle, carrying the boat and the digger toward the left. Still, as he neared the place, Danri guessed that his course would take him very close to that alluring shore. He began to probe the water with the long pole, holding only the very top of the shaft as he prodded vainly into the depths.

Then a flare of optimism! The rod thunked against solid rock, and Danri pushed and pulled in a frantic effort to draw himself toward the shore. The slender prow glided forward, and soon the water's depth decreased to fifteen feet, then ten and five as he gently pushed toward dry land.

He wasted no time scrambling out of the boat, though he quickly pulled the bow onto the stones behind him, insuring that the skiff wouldn't float away.

Never had he so appreciated the sensation of solid ground under his feet. No matter that he stood on the shore of a nameless island in the midst of an equally nameless lake. Once again his surroundings were made of rock—by Aurianth, he could *dig* his way out of here if it came to that!

Yet with that thought came another, equally certain piece of knowledge: he wouldn't have to excavate his way off this island. He was here because of the same destiny that had compelled him on the Madness, and whatever purpose lay beneath the layer of his awareness, Danri felt certain that it would make itself known.

He did not know, as he paced along the graveled beach, that Nicodareus, Eye of Dassadecc, was turning the capstan on the reservoir of Darkblood—many miles away from here, but still beneath the Crown of the World. The tunnel, bored for over fifty years by kroaks and brutox, came nowhere near this lake, and consequently the deaths of a hundred of those minions passed unknown to the digger—nor did Danri sense the Lord Minion's glee as the foul liquid came in contact with the spring of fresh water.

But the convulsion caused by the meeting of those liquids ripped through the subterranean strata of the Watershed as an irresistable tremor. Danri felt the rumbling beneath his feet before he heard any sound, but even so he wasn't prepared for the resonant boom that shocked his ears, louder than the most deafening clap of thunder.

Air displaced by breaking rock swept against the digger, a strong wind. He saw chunks of stone crack free from the sloping shore of the island, tumbling down toward the water. Darting to the side, he struggled to remain upright. At the same time, he realized that more slabs must be breaking from the ceiling—in a few seconds, this entire lake would pitch and heave with splashing debris.

Seizing the bow of his boat, he pulled, desperately dragging the slender hull over the rocks of the shore, hauling it up the steeply sloping stone of the island. Tremors rumbled through the air, and shards of rock splintered and cracked nearby, but Danri ignored every distraction. When he'd reached this island he'd been half-prepared to abandon the skiff to its fate; now, for some reason, it seemed very important to save the boat.

A surging wave rose from the lake, propelled by the force of a huge section of ceiling that tumbled into the water. The frothing breaker pushed at the skiff, lifting it quickly, driving the prow into the digger's back. Danri fell to the rocks, feeling the Aura wash over him; he clung tightly to the boat as the water receded.

As soon as he could breathe he scrambled to his feet, straining to lift the water-laden skiff still farther away from the surging lake. The hull scraped and bumped over the jagged rocks, but Danri didn't worry about preserving the smooth finish of the planks. Another wave surged upward, and this time the digger anticipated the onslaught. Planting his feet, he grasped the bow tightly—and waited for a beat.

The breaker crashed into the stern, and immediately Danri pulled, driving his short legs against the rocks as he raced the wave up the rocky hill. The boat became momentarily weightless, lifted by the rising water, and the digger took advantage of that fact to scramble for a half-dozen steps. When the wave finally washed over him, he kept a firm grip on the skiff, and in seconds the water spilled away.

This time, however, Danri found it impossible to drag the skiff any farther. Crashes still resonated through the chamber, and the digger collapsed in despair. Perhaps he wouldn't drown, but as more rock broke free from the ceiling he knew that the odds were good he'd soon be crushed to death.

Mist and the bitter dust of shattered rock obscured the air, as thick as a heavy blanket of smoke. Crawling now, relying on instinct to dart out of the way of tumbling rocks the size of his skull, Danri gritted his teeth and wondered what it would be like to die.

Through the haze he saw a shadowy alcove, only a few feet from his face. Scrambling upward, he curled into the scant shelter offered by the small niche. Pieces of gravel stung his skin as larger rocks crashed to the ground outside, but at least he was safe from the debris showering constantly down.

Danri didn't know how long he sheltered in the niche, his world a chaos of noise and convulsion. Finally the cave-in settled, and the digger was surprised to see that the cavern would apparently survive the quake—at least, the roof hadn't broken through to the sky anywhere that he could see.

Then another sense tingled an alarm, shocking him with a sound that seemed incongruous, even impossible. He heard it again, still disbelieving. Yet he knew the sound was a voice, and its plea was simple and direct.

"Help!"

SEVEN

Streams of Hope or Poison

A man can never master a mountain. Upon occasion
mountain masters man; at other times the mortal is
allowed to share the summit's majesty for an eye-blink
of time. But always the mountain remains aloof,
unaffected long after human flesh is gone.
—CREED OF THE CLIMBER

— 1 —

"We should give him a name."

At Anjell's words, the snow lion looked up with interest, long tongue hanging limply from his jowls.

The girl's suggestion, at the same time, brought Rudy out of a trance. Fatigue had numbed his senses into a ritual of pain, one foot plodding after the other as he led his niece down the winding valley road, with the snow lion padding easily behind. They crossed the brook of Dermaat on a narrow bridge, noticing that even over the center of the stream tall evergreens screened out most of the sky. To the right the dark bulk of the Wilderhof massed through the trees, while beyond the stream to their left rose the softer outline of the Dermaathof.

The long, urgent march had even dulled the Iceman's blinding anger—though when he thought of Garamis, his step became more firm, and he automatically checked to see that his knife was loose in its sheath. When he turned to scan the road behind them, his fury was soothed by the sight of the big cat pacing at his heels.

"Why did you help us, big fellow? And why are you following me now? I wish you could talk." He couldn't get answers to his questions, he knew; he could only be grateful for the animal's powerful, comforting presence.

"I'm glad he's with us—but *I* wish we knew what to call him," Anjell pressed. "I wonder where he came from?"

"He found me in the snowslide," Rudy offered, knowing that didn't answer the question. "How about calling him Avalanche?"

Anjell made a face. "How would *you* like to be named after a disaster? No, he needs something important, royal. Like King, maybe. Snow King? Or Killer—no, that's too gory."

"He's a real hero—and he comes from the mountains," Rudy said. "What about naming him after a great Halverican?"

"Dunkar Kalland!" Anjell declared brightly. "Just Kalland, for short. Let's name him for the hero who came from the high ridge just in time for the war!"

"It's a good name," Rudy acknowledged, though his niece's last words caused him a shiver of apprehension. "Hey, Kalland—how do you like your name?"

The big feline blinked his yellow eyes and licked his whiskers, while the tufts on his ears stood straight up.

"He looks thirsty—and so am I," the girl declared.

"Kalland can go down to the stream whenever he wants. As for us, let's get a little farther down the road before we rest."

"I don't want to rest—I want a drink. Give me the waterskin!" Anjell insisted.

"Okay." Rudy shrugged the strap off his shoulder. From habit he hefted the sloshing sack, and his eye fell on the stream. Here the waterway cut right beside the road, below a bank that dropped no more than three feet to a graveled shore.

"Wait—let's take a drink from the stream," he said, "and save what's in the waterskin for now." He wondered if, subconsciously, he just wanted the excuse to rest.

Anjell collapsed on the bank, her feet dangling free for a few moments while Rudy sat beside her. He was troubled by the delay, but he knew that they both needed a few moments off their feet. Kalland stepped down to the water and sniffed; apparently the snow lion wasn't thirsty, since he flopped onto the ground without drinking. He kept his big eyes fastened on the water, bright and unblinking.

Pushing down the bank, Anjell dropped to the streamside shore and knelt beside the sparkling flow. She cupped her hands, raising the liquid to her lips.

Absently, distracted by worry, Rudy looked at the water. The pebbled bottom lay outlined in every detail. Beams of sunlight poked between thickly needled pine boughs, shimmering across the surface. To the Iceman's eye, the liquid looked entirely pure and wholesome.

With a sudden growl, the snow lion pounced at Anjell. The girl cried out, startled, as a big paw lashed out, claws retracted, gently bumping her hands and spilling the water she held back into the stream. Kalland sat upright, purring and looking smug as Rudy leaped to his feet in alarm.

"What are you *doing*?" Anjell demanded of the snow lion, licking at the water that had splashed onto her lip.

The Iceman studied the great feline, then looked at the stream. A shock of pain struck him in the stomach—a burning tear that rippled along the frozen poultice that still scored his chest. With vivid clarity he understood the source of his unease. Frantically he reached out and wiped the drops of liquid off Anjell's face, ignoring her outraged cries.

"The water!" Rudy dropped his voice to a whisper. Anjell's eyes were wide with fright, but she suppressed her furious objections. "There's something wrong with the *stream*!" he hissed.

"How do *you* know?" She studied the sparkling liquid, then turned back to him, her eyes full of challenge. "It looks just fine to me!"

Shaking his head in frustration, Rudy knew that he had no good answer. "I don't understand how I know—or how Kalland knew. But when I look at it, I see . . . poison!"

Dubiously, Anjell looked back at the stream. Suddenly her eyes grew wide. "Jonn . . . back in Dermaat—he said something about the water, didn't he?"

Mutely, Rudy nodded, remembering. "I thought he wanted a

drink—but he was trying to warn us."

"All the people from Dermaat—do you think . . . ?" Anjell's voice trailed away in fear.

Rudy didn't want to think about the question, but he forced himself to face the truth. All the mourning gardens . . . everything *gone.* "Dermaat—the whole town—was killed by this stream," he said in dawning horror.

"That water—did you drink any before Kalland knocked it away?" He spun to study Anjell's face.

"I—I don't know! I don't think I did—but it splashed me. Maybe just a drop. That couldn't hurt me, could it?"

Miserably, Rudy shook his head, knowing that his effort at reassurance was not very convincing. "Here—take a drink from the waterskin. Rinse out your mouth," he instructed.

As Anjell, for once obeying without resistance, spat out several mouthfuls of water, Rudy tried to think. The cloaked figures, he felt sure, remained on their trail—no doubt even now closing the distance on the road back to Dermaat. This stream blocked their passage back to the Dermaathof ridge, and Neshara Valley beyond. Though they might have waded the brook without getting the water in their mouths, Rudy was reluctant even to let the stuff touch their skin; the narrow bridge was nearly a mile behind them, and he didn't dare turn back into the path of their pursuers.

"Are you *sure* you don't see anything wrong with the stream?" he asked.

Squinting studiously, Anjell remained silent for a good half minute, looking up and down the course of the brook. Finally she shrugged in resignation. "Looks just like any other creek to me!"

Rudy tried to picture the beastly threats lurking up the road. He wondered about the numerous figures he'd seen filing down from the heights. Could they *all* be misshapen, monstrous creatures such as the one he'd fought in the mill house? His mind rebelled at the suggestion. He'd spent all his life in Halverica, and never had he even *heard* of such monstrosities. It was inconceivable for a great band of them to suddenly materialize.

Or could they have come from beyond Halverica? That, too,

seemed unimaginable. The mountains north of his country formed a lofty, impenetrable barrier between Dalethica and Duloth-Trol. The Watershed was the great constant of his world—the ridge flanking the Glimmercrown formed the ultimate wall, a barrier to all the realms of humanity.

Yet as fear roiled through his mind, another thought gradually took shape—one that was truly horrifying. Could there be some kind of crack, a breach, in the Watershed? He'd always believed this was impossible—yet it seemed to offer the only plausible explanation for the bizarre occurrences of the last days.

In a flash his thoughts returned to the stream at his feet, and with a gasp of horror he recoiled, pulling Anjell into the road in a desperate effort to get away.

"What are you doing?" she demanded, growing tired of his inexplicable agitation.

"It *is* poison—poison from beyond Dalethica!"

For a moment Anjell looked at her uncle with a scowl of disbelief, but slowly her brow softened into concern. "But . . . *how?*"

Rudy felt the weariness of a night and day of flight, and a rising tide of hopelessness threatened to drag him down right in the middle of the road. But he shook his head stubbornly, groping for an explanation.

"Roggett said something about an earthquake near Dermaat," he told her. "It could be that some part of the Watershed gave way. Somehow, we have a source of Darkblood flowing into Dalethica. It killed Dermaat, and now it's on the way to the Glimmersee—if it hasn't already gotten there!" The grotesque creatures, he believed, must also be connected to this breach, but he didn't give voice to this bleak surmise.

For just a moment he pictured the huge, pristine lake at the foot of this valley. Prosperous and teeming towns lined its shores, while numerous ferries and excursion boats crossed the deep, sheltered waters. The North Shore Wayfarer's Lodge stood near the Glimmersee's outlet. While not actually a town, the lodge had a population of several hundred year-round residents, and was typically the first stop for visitors who came to Halverica from other parts of Dalethica.

The toxic stuff of Duloth-Trol had corrupted a shallow mountain stream and destroyed a tiny hamlet. Was it potent enough to poison that great, deep body of water, inflicting a similar blight on the communities along its shores?

Looking again at the sinister stream, Rudy suspected that it was.

"We should hurry!" Anjell said, beginning to share his disquiet. "I can make it for a while more before we rest," she added.

Glancing at his niece, Rudy sensed the hopelessness of a direct flight down the road. Whatever their determination, fatigue would drag them down within some few miles. The company marching in their tracks, he felt certain, would not be so quick to tire.

"We can't outrun them any longer," he told Anjell. "We've got to try something else."

He looked toward the eastern height, where the rising bulk of the Wilderhof blocked their view of the mountains beyond.

That ridge was a tangle of untracked forests draped around steep, rock-sided gorges. Even worse, it was a place of unexplained terrors and sinister, mysterious inhabitants. It lay close beside Faerine, though of course it was separated by the Watershed from that enchanted realm. An unsettled wilderness, the Wilderhof was avoided by Halvericans and other humans.

Upon further reflection, however, the consequences of staying on the road were all too predictable. He bore no illusions about his ability to take on even a pair of the brutish monsters, if the strangers caught up with him on the road. And, too, there was the matter of the poisoned stream. He wanted to get as far away from it as possible.

Once again he looked toward the tangled wood of the Wilderhof. The slope of the ridge climbed away from them, thickly screened by vegetation—yet at last Rudy knew where they had to go.

"Come on," he told his niece brusquely. He started into the woods, ducking below the overhanging branches of a heavy fir tree while Anjell scrambled to keep up with him. The ground began to rise, and with each upward step Rudy knew that they were leaving Halverica, his home, and all he knew of the world, farther behind.

— 2 —

The woods flanking the Wilderhof proved even more tangled than they had appeared from the road. Too, the slope of the big ridge soared upward with surprising steepness. Rudy stopped to help Anjell across the larger thickets, ignoring the thorns that tore at his hands and arms. He was all too aware, as time passed, that their progress was painfully slow.

"Here—climb onto my back," he gasped, faced with the ascent of a steep rise, perhaps three times his own height.

Anjell wrapped her arms around Rudy's neck while he examined a tree trunk lying obliquely against the short cliff. It looked more secure than the moss-covered rocks, so he pulled himself up the sloping pine, grasping stubs of branches with his hands while balancing on his feet.

He reached the top of the log quickly, but as he scrambled onto the forest floor, fatigue rendered his knees rubbery. Wheezing, and with Anjell still clinging to his back, he leaned forward against a tree, bitterly aware that the terrain continued to rise—though not quite so steeply as the nearby cliff. Kalland scrambled up the log behind him, sharp claws digging into the decayed wood. The snow lion pounced upward and came to rest on the rocky ledge, ears alert and tail lashing as he waited for the humans.

Only then did Rudy realize that Anjell was sobbing. The girl's face was buried in his neck, and though she muffled her cries, her body shuddered from the effort.

Wearily he slumped to the ground, laying Anjell on a patch of soft moss. "We're safe here," he declared, exaggerating considerably. "Let's take some time to rest."

"No," Anjell said softly. "Let's get farther from the road. I can keep going—and you don't have to carry me like a baby, either!"

Rudy smiled, very relieved to hear Anjell return to form. "Okay— and when we do rest, maybe we can find a flatter spot."

"Maybe a cave! Then we'll stay snug even if it rains!"

Rudy had explored numerous caves in his life, and privately reflected that none of them had remotely approached "snug." Still, a cave would be preferable to the open forest floor.

"Look," Anjell informed him, as another branch of hooked thorns snagged his face. The girl stooped forward, bending almost double. "If you get down here, there aren't any thorny branches. It's like paths going every which way!"

Rudy had to duck very low, sometimes even scrambling on all fours, but he found that Anjell was right. The ground was smooth, cushioned with moss and clover, and a series of wide passages curved around the brushy trunks.

They climbed steadily, in silence, for what seemed like a long time, until Rudy saw a shadowy outline through the upslope trees. The ridge slope sheared steeply skyward for a short stretch, and the ancient bedrock had split apart, providing a shallow niche under the cliff wall.

"Here's your cave," Rudy announced, guiding his niece toward the narrow mouth.

"Good," she sighed. "*Now* can I rest?"

"Sure." He didn't add the lie about their being safe, though he desperately wanted to believe it himself. "Here—have some water—but only a few sips. We've got to save what's in the waterskin until we get to a clean stream."

A new fear suddenly shot through him—what if other streams were tainted by the breach in the Watershed? He pictured the pristine Klarbrook as it splashed through Neshara. The thought of his village succumbing to the plague that had swept Dermaat brought bitter dread to his heart. It was too monstrous—nothing less than the end of the world! Certainly Baracan, God of Man, would never allow such a catastrophe. As he tried to convince himself, a nagging voice of doubt suggested that perhaps Baracan could do nothing to prevent it.

He turned his face away from Anjell so she wouldn't see his apprehension, but as he listened to her regular breathing he realized that she had already fallen asleep, her head resting on Kalland's shaggy flank. Rudy lay against the damp rock wall of the shallow cave, and tried, with little success, to convince himself that his fears were exaggerated.

For a time he found release in the growing flame of his hatred.

His mind conjured an image of Garamis, and the multitude of ways the prince might be slain. Any of them would suffice, he decided, as long as he himself could do the killing.

At last, fatigue brought Rudy respite from his bitter rancor and the heart-pounding terrors he'd faced. He could no longer hold his eyes open. Slumping against his uncomfortable backrest, he felt his lids grow heavy, and gradually the frightening realties of his situation faded as he slept.

Several times he awakened, always to full darkness. As he shifted on the rocks, weariness seemed to paralyze every muscle in his body. Anjell slumbered in complete exhaustion, and he took care not to disturb her as he vainly sought a more comfortable position. Yet even on the brutally rough ground he had no difficulty falling back to sleep. It seemed as he drowsed that beautiful music drifted through his dreams. Once, Kalland was gone from the cave when Rudy started into wakefulness. He whistled softly, and the big cat quickly emerged from the impenetrable shadows beneath the nearby trees.

When dawn finally filtered between the trees of the Wilderhof, Rudy woke once more, and this time he knew they had to get moving. He reached over to nudge his niece, and as his hand brushed her cheek a cruel fear swept over him.

Her skin burned under his fingers, smoldering with fever.

"Anjell!" he hissed, terrified. He pressed his other hand to her face, trying without success to deny the dangerous intensity of her temperature. His fear grew to real terror when she didn't respond to her name.

Leaning over the girl, Rudy saw that her face was marred by blemishes—the same red spots he'd seen on Jonn's face before that once-hearty Iceman had died.

"Ma—mama?" Anjell's voice was a plaintive whimper.

"I'm here—it's Rudy," he replied, trying to keep the panic out of his voice. He offered a mute prayer to Baracan—*please* make her well. Even as he knew his plea went unheeded, he remembered—without any apparent connection—that the goddess of Faerine was called Aurianth. Brushing the irrelevant thought aside, he gently cradled Anjell.

"Mama, I don't feel so good," the girl cried. "My head's all hot, and it *hurts*!"

"Don't worry—I'll help you!" he promised desperately.

"Ca—can I have some tea?" she stammered, still not opening her eyes.

Rudy's own eyes misted as he fought to remain calm. How could he help her? This plague had wiped out a whole village, with its herbs and healers, not to mention warm beds and food! He could offer Anjell none of these things.

Yet neither could he just sit here and watch her die.

Shaking off the crushing mantle of hopelessness, Rudy gave the stricken girl several drops of water from his waterskin. Then he poked his head from the mouth of the cave and looked around. Fog filtered through the trees, but though the sun had not yet crested the eastern horizon, the sky overhead was blue and clear. The forest screened his view of the valley, and also blocked any attempt to see farther up the sloping ridge of the Wilderhof. At least, he saw, they seemed to have climbed above the blanket of thorn bushes that had made their early progress so painful.

Rudy's anxiety propelled him into action, though he didn't see how he could do anything useful. He returned to the cave to find Anjell once again slumbering—or unconscious. Either way, he suspected that oblivion was the kindest thing that could happen to her now.

As gently as possible, he cradled the girl in his arms and rose to his feet. She seemed light, waiflike—as if most of her flesh had boiled away from the intensity of her fever. Ducking under the arch of the cave mouth, Rudy passed onto the forest floor, Kalland padding silently behind.

He couldn't return to the valley, and he knew that to stay in this cave only meant slow, inevitable disaster. Instead, he turned toward the uphill slope and began to climb.

Picking his route much more carefully than the day before, Rudy cut back and forth through the trees, avoiding the shelves of cliff that occasionally rose before him—even though these detours often took him far to the side of his desired route.

Steadily he worked his way upward, through a forest like none he'd ever seen. Trees soared into the sky, elegant cones of fir and pine mingling with shimmering groves of silver-leafed aspens. The forest floor was clear of brush, and despite the occasional outcrop of bedrock, the walking was generally easy.

For several hours Anjell never stirred. As the sunlight increased, Rudy saw the angry red spots on her face, observed the tremulous quality of her breathing. He tried to hold her as gently as possible, while his legs functioned automatically, always climbing.

Before noon he reached a rocky knob where the trees had failed to gain purchase. Emerging into full sunlight for the first time that day, he found himself in a grassy meadow, more than halfway up the incline of the Wilderhof. From one side of the clearing, cliffs dropped to the lower shelves of the ridge, offering a vista up and down the valley. Here the demands of the climb forced the Iceman to rest.

Kneeling, he tenderly placed Anjell in the shade of a flowering bush. Her eyelids fluttered briefly and she sighed, rolling restlessly on the ground. Around the crimson blemishes, her skin had grown deathly pallid, forming white rings in stark contrast to the inflammations.

Anguish forced Rudy to look away. The valley of Dermaat was spread below, and to the north he could even see the pristine blue of the Glimmersee peeking between two curving ridges of fir-cloaked highland.

Turning to the south he looked for the village of Dermaat. There, in the shadow of mighty Glimmercrown, he saw the collection of houses and the still-sparkling stream that meandered among them.

He saw no sign of the cloaked figures who'd marched into the village on the previous day. No one moved along the wide lane, and all the doors he could see in the houses and barns of Dermaat were shut. Could that whole force have marched down the road during the night? Hidden in the cave, he would never have seen or heard anything.

Something about the village drew his eye back to Dermaat. The large, squarish block of Dermaat House stood above the lesser cottages. A wispy cloud drifted through the air, and Rudy realized that it was smoke emerging from the inn's chimney. Closer inspection showed him that fires were burning in several other houses. The blazes were made with dry wood, yielding little smoke—but why were they there at all?

The answer, whatever it proved to be, was inevitably ominous. Even if some villagers remained alive—and he had seen no evidence of life when he'd passed through Dermaat—they would not burn mid-morning fires. The day was warm, the breakfast hour long past.

A dark form flickered through the village and Rudy flinched. The shape vanished, then reappeared gliding swiftly across the ground. Only then did the Iceman realize that it was a shadow—actually, a series of wide shadows sweeping along in tight formation.

Instinctively his eyes looked upward, taking in the broad face of Glimmercrown beyond. He saw nothing in the air that could be making such a shadow. The images were far larger than the greatest eagle, yet they seemed vaguely birdlike. Long wings tapered to pointed tips, while a thin snout extended before the shadow like a straight, sharp beak.

Now the dark outlines on the ground rippled across the trees and meadows of the valley forest—swooping straight toward the clearing where Rudy stood. A trio of shapes caused by . . . what?

Desperately he looked upward again. There was nothing in the air—or was there?

The Iceman gasped in fear as at last he saw them: three huge creatures, winging through a fast, swooping glide. Their skin rippled like some silvery reflective material, showing dappled images of the mountainside behind them—an effect that made them nearly invisible. One of the winged beasts soared upward, and as it spread its wings against the blue sky its skin reflected a perfect image of that color. Only with a quick glance at the shadow was Rudy able to follow the course of the diverging monster.

The flying things were far larger than any bird of Dalethica—and his instant, total terror convinced Rudy that they were a grave threat. With the snow lion racing behind, he sprinted to the cover of the bush where he'd left Anjell. Dropping to his knees, he risked a look back at the three creatures. One had swooped below his line of sight. The middle bird-thing came straight on, while the third circled upward, still gaining altitude. Scooping his niece into his arms, Rudy darted into the forest, now cursing the wide spaces between the trees that had earlier seemed so inviting.

A shadow swooped past him and in blind panic he tumbled to the ground, sheltering Anjell and expecting a sharp beak to spear him through the back. He looked up a moment later to see the beast, flying low, turn back toward him, rippling between green and blue as it flew along the upper fringe of the forest. As it closed, the monster's camouflage was less effective, and for the first time Rudy saw the full, unworldly nature of his pursuers.

Short legs, tipped by bristling talons, dangled from the creature's flat belly. The skin was smooth and slick, more like the silvery scales of a fish than the ruffling feathers of any bird. The terrible mouth extended into that sharp, wicked-looking beak, an array of fangs visible along the sides of the maw, emerging from both the top and bottom ridges.

The beak opened and the forest shuddered beneath a sharp, jarring cry—a noise more piercing than anything Rudy had ever heard. He wanted to clap his hands over his ears, to huddle on the ground and await his fate. The creature shrieked again and Rudy sobbed, dropping his head in despair.

Kalland snarled furiously, the sound building to a challenging roar. Head cocked upward, the snow lion darted along the ground, racing from one tree to another, keeping to the shelter offered by the heaviest boughs.

The Iceman saw Anjell's eyes, wide-open and staring at the sky. Her skin looked horrible, but awareness gleamed in her expression— and now, that awareness was stark terror.

"Rudy! Help!" she cried, reaching upward with arms almost too weak to move.

Desperately he picked her up again, hearing the crackling of tree limbs as the flying monster swept the treetops overhead. Stumbling away, Rudy darted between two close-set trunks, and then pushed himself into a lurching run.

Dimly he was aware that the monsters' size was the only thing protecting him now—their wingspread was too huge to allow them to descend into the trees. Yet even as this thought occurred to him, the ground heaved underfoot and he recoiled from a violent, splintering crash.

Staggering backward, Rudy watched a monstrous pine twist free from the soil and topple downward. Lesser trees snapped as the huge monsters flew into them, breaking the trunks. The flyers flapped their wings frantically, going into a lumbering climb as toppling saplings lashed Rudy's skin. The ground heaved convulsively as another forest giant slammed into the turf, bounced upward, and then crashed to lie still. He saw the silvery skin of the monster—now shimmering green with reflected pine boughs—as the terrible thing followed the tree into the opening it had breached.

Blindly Rudy turned, still clutching Anjell. Angry jaws snapped shut behind him with a sharp crack, but he didn't dare look to see how close. He lumbered through the trees, on the brink of falling—but somehow his panic held him up. Anjell sobbed against his shoulder, and all he knew was the desperate need to get her to safety.

More limbs splintered and tore as the bird-monsters threw themselves against the parapets of Rudy's forest bastion. He pressed along the crest of the ridge, away from Dermaat and the Glimmercrown, instinctively turning toward the lowlands. The savage flyers slashed against the trees with complete abandon, smashing three-century-old cedars like kindling.

Shadows soared past to each side, and Rudy slowed his headlong sprint to a more cautious trot. He knew that he could not outrun the creatures, and his panic had finally given way to reason. That sense of logic told him that he should conserve his strength, rather than exhaust himself on fruitless speed.

Passing into a denser thicket, he darted to the side, carefully working from the limbs of one tree to the overhanging shelter of another. The snow lion kept pace, loping along a parallel course a little distance away. Rudy turned again, following the contours of the grove, and for a short time he heard crashing branches some distance away. Briefly he allowed himself to hope that the creatures had lost him.

A shadow flickered past his shelter, and when an ear-splitting shriek echoed through the air, he knew he'd been discovered. The tree beside him swayed to the onslaught of a flyer but Rudy had already leaped away, darting this way and that as he tried to remain one jump ahead of the monstrous beaks and clutching claws.

Abruptly a dark shadow yawned at his feet and he skidded to a halt at the very lip of a deep, steep-sided ravine. Moss-covered rocks fell into the shadows below, offering at best a very treacherous descent. Yet Rudy didn't even see the danger—instead, his mind registered one possibly hopeful fact: the sides of the ravine were no more than eight or ten feet apart. If he could get down, there was no way the huge flyers could come in after him!

Instinctively he dropped into a crouch, and then rolled along the lip of the gorge as the huge form swept past. Sharp talons grasped at a bush only a few inches from his leg, and Rudy squirmed back into the trees before the second monster dove down and stabbed with its hideous beak.

The creatures seemed to sense that the gorge offered him shelter, for they renewed their attacks with fury. All three beasts crashed through the treetops, turning Rudy back from the edge, surrounding him with a tumbling hail of branches. Desperately the Iceman squirmed underneath a low-hanging trunk, pulling Anjell beside him. He found himself at the lip of the ravine, and saw several flat boulders leading into the darkness below.

"Come on!" he hissed. "Hold tight!"

Anjell didn't reply, but she wrapped her arms around his neck and hugged him as he slipped over the lip of the ravine. For a sickening moment his boot slipped across the mossy rock, but then his hands seized a root and he found purchase with his other foot. Heart pounding, he lowered Anjell and himself into the gash of cold, wet rock.

Shadows surrounded them, but it was not as dark in the ravine as it had appeared from above. Kalland pounced downward from rock to rock, finally landing lightly at the bottom. The puffy tail lashed as the snow lion watched Rudy and Anjell descend.

The Iceman made his way down fifteen or twenty feet, until he found the floor—where flowed a clear, splashing stream, no more than a few inches deep. His anxiety about water forgotten, he staggered along the stream bed until he found an overhanging shelf of rock on the bank. Ducking beneath it, he finally collapsed, cradling Anjell on his lap and trying not to gasp and groan as he struggled for breath.

"They can't follow us here," the girl declared. Her voice was a whisper but nevertheless strong and self-assured.

"You're right," Rudy said, barely aware of what Anjell was saying. He was far more interested in *how* she said it.

Wonderingly, he placed a hand to her forehead, breathing a soft sigh of amazement—and relief. "Your fever—it's gone!" he declared.

"I feel *lots* better," the girl said, yawning. "Kinda tired, though."

Hugging her tightly, Rudy looked at Anjell's clear, pink skin. The horrid spots of her rash had vanished with the fever. Weak with relief, he leaned his head back against the rock wall. He palmed his heart, thanking Baracan and all the other gods of men for this miraculous recovery. The dose of poison she'd received must have been too small to be fatal.

But why then had she gotten so terribly sick? It didn't make sense—how could any toxin that had proven so virulent stop just barely short of killing her? Surely there had been no curative benefit to her being hauled like a sack of potatoes on a harrowing flight through the woods. The terror of those interminable minutes, the girl's limp body pressed to his chest, came back to Rudy in vivid detail.

Unworldly shrieks shot through the ravine, echoing from the dank walls, reminding him that the flyers still lurked overhead. He looked up, seeing only a narrow cut of the sky, and as he watched, a rippling flash of color flowed across his vision. Only when the shadow flicked quickly across the ravine floor did he know that he'd actually seen one of the beasts.

"Rudy—what do we do now?" Anjell asked sleepily, turning to make herself more comfortable in his lap.

Her hand came to rest on his chest, and a sudden thought burst upon him. Ignoring her murmured protest, he pulled his tunic to the side and looked for the sliver of ice on his skin.

It was gone.

The icy poultice had completely vanished. And Anjell had been pressed tightly against that spot as Rudy desperately sought refuge.

The connection grew in his mind. He remembered his own weakness upon reaching Neshara—the fatigue that had rendered him nearly comatose for several days. When he'd awakened, he felt fine, and one of the snow-marks had been gone. Now the other had disappeared, and at the same time Anjell had recovered from a potentially fatal disease.

Wonder spread through him with a warm glow. He couldn't explain it, but the results seemed too obvious to question—the ice had *healed* her.

Kalland growled abruptly, the sound rumbling deep in his chest as his woolly hackles rose into a bristling mane.

Anjell pointed a short finger. "Look, Rudy," she whispered. "There's one of those monsters—the two-legged kind, like we saw in Dermaat."

Startled, the Iceman looked up to see a snarling, bestial face silhouetted against the sky. One of the flyers keened, and the land-bound monster snorted belligerently. That creature, Rudy knew, would have no difficulty squeezing into the ravine where he and Anjell were sheltered.

Another horrifying visage came into view—a snakelike head with a flickering, forked tongue. Pale eyes, bright slits of yellow, stared back and forth through the gorge. A dark hood cloaked the reptilian creature's head.

"That's the Hisser!" Anjell gasped. "At least, that's the robe he wore—but he looked like a *man* then!"

As Rudy watched in growing fear, his mind seemed slowed by exhaustion. Would he ever leave the danger behind?

Even as he dismissed the question as unanswerable, he knew that they'd once again have to move. Rising stiffly to his feet, he set Anjell on the ground and saw that she stood steadily, without dizziness or any sign of weakness.

"Come on," he whispered. "Let's move on down the stream—get someplace where they won't be able to find us."

Nodding silently, Anjell followed him as he started along the slick stone floor of the gorge. Kalland kept pace as Rudy looked back once more, just in time to see the first brute cast a long rope down into the ravine. The monster swung onto the rope, starting to climb down, while the Hisser came right behind. Before Rudy ducked out of sight he saw three or four similar creatures poke their snouts over the lip of the gorge, waiting for their chance to follow.

— 3 —

Kalland growled again. The hackles at the snow lion's shoulders bristled angrily, while he kneaded his paws against the sharp rocks of the stream bed. Long, curving claws emerged and retracted as the animal crouched, taut.

"Come on," Rudy commanded, turning his back on the pursuers and starting up the slippery, rough floor of the gorge. Anjell, walking steadily, followed, and with a last warning growl, Kalland bounded after.

The little stream spilled over a series of steplike falls, cascading into pools no more than a foot deep before splashing free on its downward course. These little drop-offs were only a couple of feet high, and Anjell shook off Rudy's assisting hand, asserting that she could climb without difficulty.

A quick glance showed the beast-faced humanoids hastily scrambling down the rope. The first of them dropped to the floor of the ravine, landing on heavy boots and bellowing an inarticulate cry at the humans. The monster stayed well back from the flowing water.

"Hurry!" Rudy cried, scrambling up a higher waterfall and jerking Anjell after him. They trotted along a relatively level stretch of the stream bed as the gorge walls loomed inward. In places Rudy could reach out and touch both sides of the chasm with his outstretched hands.

They hastened around a tight corner. Before them, sunlight sparkled across the water in a wide pool, and Rudy saw in an instant that the basin was too deep to wade through. A rough shoreline surrounded the pool, but passage over that rough terrain would be slow and dangerous. Furthermore, a waterfall nearly twice Rudy's height blocked passage up the gorge, a shimmering curtain of droplets effectively screening the rock wall behind the cascade.

Before he could curse his frustration, Anjell darted past him and broke the surface of the water in a clean dive. He plunged in after her, and in seconds they both scrambled onto the rocks at the base of the waterfall, shivering off the effects of the icy immersion.

"Here!" Anjell cried, pulling him into the shelter of a dripping overhang. He looked back, but all he could see was the glittering sheet of water. Even though they were concealed for the moment, he had the sickening fear that they were trapped.

"Look, Rudy—a cave!" cried Anjell excitedly. She indicated a shadowy passage that seemed to lead into the rock wall behind the waterfall. A quick look showed him that there might be room, barely, for him to pass.

They heard the sharp, angry huff of Kalland's warning roar, and Rudy risked a glance around the screen of water. The snow lion stood in stiff-legged agitation on the other side of the pool, blocking passage up the stream bed. The animal's courage wouldn't stand for long against those wicked swords.

"Kalland!" Rudy hissed.

The snow lion spun, ears pricked upward as his bright eyes sought Rudy. The Iceman, surprising himself, whistled a quick melody. With only a moment's hesitation the big animal threw himself forward, striking the chilly water of the pool with a great splash. Immediately behind Kalland came the first of the inhuman warriors, though the brute stopped at the water's edge—either unwilling to immerse himself or, more likely, waiting for reinforcements, Rudy guessed.

He wasn't going to wait and find out. Kalland plunged through the screening spray while Anjell started into the narrow cave. Fearing pursuit, Rudy backed up as he followed her, holding his long-handled knife and warily eyeing the mouth of their constricted passage.

The snow lion padded behind, pausing frequently to growl in the direction of their pursuers.

"Rudy—it's *big* in here! Big, and dark," declared Anjell, drawing a breath in surprise. The girl's voice was as excited as if she were on a holiday excursion, and Rudy had to suppress an urge to shout at her, to warn her of the seriousness of their situation. After a moment's thought, however, he realized that her enthusiasm was probably just the thing to keep her motivated and moving.

No shadow had yet darkened the mouth of the cave, so he turned to see where they were going. True to Anjell's description, the close-pressing walls of the cave soon swept to the sides, opening into a large, generally circular chamber. No sunlight penetrated from the surface, yet the cavern was diffused with a gentle, vaguely comforting illumination. The light was pale and multihued, glowing in pleasant shades of red and yellow, green, blue, and violet.

For the first time, he realized that not all of the stream water in the gorge outside had spilled over the waterfall beyond the cave. A small flowage trickled across the floor at his feet, and he saw a tiny rivulet spilling down the far wall of the grotto, making its contribution to the brook beyond.

The walls of the circular cavern gleamed with a shimmering beauty, and he saw spires of rock dangling from the ceiling like the ivory tusks of some mythical beast. The far wall of the chamber was wet, and sparkled like a million diamonds set into the stone. Near the center spread a flat, still pool of water—the source of the tiny flowage at his feet.

"I can't see!" Anjell complained, groping forward and stumbling over a large rock—an obstruction Rudy observed quite plainly. Quickly he leaned forward and grasped her arm, preventing her from falling. The girl wrapped her hands around his arm, clutching him fearfully.

A new fear tugged at him. Was blindness some kind of delayed effect of her illness?

"If you can't see, how did you know how big this cave was?" he asked.

"Echoes, silly. You can hear when you take a step. It's not like that little tunnel we came through."

"But you can't see the other side of the cave?"

"I can't even see the ground under my feet! How could I—it's like midnight in here!" Her tone was exasperated, and she glared up at him, at where she thought his face was.

Yet Rudy could still see every feature of Anjell's expression, down to her puckered eyebrows and tight, frowning lips.

"*I* can see," he replied, frustrated. "I'm afraid something's wrong with your eyes."

"How can you see anything?" she demanded. "There's no light in here!"

With dawning awareness of something mysterious, he realized that she was right. The tight entry tunnel twisted and turned so much after the cascade-screened entrance that no daylight could follow them this far into the cave. The walls and ceiling were solid, providing no chink for any external illumination.

"It's the floor—the walls—everything! They're *glowing*! Can't you see it?" he pressed.

Anjell stomped her foot in agitation. "I told you—*no!*" Her tone grew more thoughtful. "Can you see a way out of here?"

"No," he admitted. "But those rocky spires are blocking my view of the far side. Let's go have a look."

"*You* look," she muttered. "Just tell me what you see."

A warning growl from Kalland drew Rudy's eyes back to the entry corridor. Now he saw light flickering there—a surging yellow glow that seemed unnecessarily crude, even offensive, against the pleasant illumination in the cave.

"Torches—those monsters lit torches, and they're coming in after us!" Anjell whispered, frightened.

"Can you see *that* light? From their fires?" Rudy asked, confusion delaying the onset of panic.

"Of course! Can't you?"

"That's not the point!" he hissed. "Come on!"

He pulled her across the wide grotto, circling around the pool in the center. At the far side he led her behind a screening pile of boulders. Kalland followed, crouching beside them. "Wait here!" Rudy ordered in a low but urgent tone.

"What are you—?"

He cut her off with a gentle hand placed over her mouth. Her wide-staring eyes, like a blind person's, darted back and forth, never focusing on his face, though he could still see hers quite clearly.

"Kalland—you stay here, too!" Rudy commanded, his voice barely audible. Amazingly, the snow lion dropped his head to his forepaws in obedience.

Quietly Rudy crept around toward the other side of the pool, his eyes on the entry tunnel. The torch came into view and he shielded his vision from the glare. The guttering flame struck him as an even greater indignity now that he saw the source of the light itself. *How dare they bring that here!* The outrage welled inside him, surprising him with its virulent intensity. Yet a voice of caution spoke as well, and he pulled himself into the deepest shadows at the edge of the grotto. Having come more than three-quarters of the way around the circular chamber, he was slightly closer to the entrance than he was to Anjell.

The torch was held high in the paw of a tusk-faced brute. The monster, responding to an irritated grunt from behind, raised the flickering brand to light the way for two of its fellows who pushed their way through the tight confines of the passage behind. Their boots were wet, but Rudy noticed that the beasts had kept their leather tunics dry, presumably by skirting the pool outside. Only the leader bore a torch. There was no sign of the Hisser; apparently he'd sent a few of his lackeys to explore the cave.

The creatures spoke a few words in a harsh, guttural language. The torch bearer approached the edge of the pool, while the two other brutes split up, each setting out in opposite directions to circle the cave.

As the monster on Rudy's side drew near, the Iceman shrank back against the wall, amazed that the creature's piglike eyes didn't see him. Snorting a wet, profane-sounding epithet, the oaf tripped over a stone and crashed onto its face. Snarling something at the torch bearer, it stood and kicked the offending boulder. The torch was raised, casting more light onto the floor, and the grumbling brute started forward again, drawing closer to Anjell's hiding place.

Rudy watched as the creature circuiting the pool from the opposite side simultaneously advanced on Anjell. Both monsters carried their jagged blades upraised, ready to strike. Rudy knew he had no more than a minute to act.

The torch bearer's eyes followed the progress of its two companions as the creature stepped to the very edge of the pool and cast the light as far as possible without favoring one of its comrades over the other. Rudy crouched some twenty feet from its left shoulder.

Gulping a breath of air, the Iceman felt certain the pounding of his heart would give him away. But he could delay no longer. Advancing in a silent rush, he padded across the cavern floor toward the monster. The knife gleamed in his hand, but he didn't intend to use it—at least, not right away.

The sole of his boot squeaked on the smooth stone surface, and the torch wavered as the beast tilted its head in surprise. With a grunt it started to turn, while a bellow from across the cave confirmed that Rudy's attack had been observed.

With a final lunge he sprang at the whirling humanoid, punching it hard on the left side of its broad chest. The brute tried to bring the torch around in a slash, but Rudy's momentum carried him against its protruding belly. With another punch, he sent the creature toppling into the pool. The torch flew from the monster's flailing hand, hit the surface, and instantly sizzled into cooled charcoal.

Water splashed in a shimmering curtain as the grotesque body struck the pool. Shrill cries of terror foamed upward before the beast sank from sight, leaving jagged, chaotic waves rippling back and forth across the surface of the water.

Rudy looked across the grotto. One of the beasts had nearly reached Anjell, but it had apparently not yet discovered her. Now both of the brutish warriors stared across the pool, faces scowling in wicked fury.

Silently Rudy stepped along the perimeter of the pool, toward the monster nearest to Anjell. His heart soared as the monsters continued to stare mutely at the place where their companion, and the precious light, had disappeared. They obviously couldn't see him.

A tiny voice at the back of Rudy's mind nagged at him—why could *he* see in the darkness that blinded Anjell's human eyes and those of the beastlike intruders? He thrust the mystery aside for the moment.

Gravel crunched under his feet and the nearest monster turned toward the sound. The dangerous blade came up, lashing several times through the air.

Behind the creature, huddled among several rocky spires that jutted upward from the ground, Anjell stared wildly outward. Her chest heaved, and Rudy knew she must be breathing hard. Kalland still crouched in place, but his wide eyes stared unblinkingly at the back of the hulking threat—either by sight or scent, the big cat obviously knew where the enemy was. The other humanoid stumbled and probed its way toward them, drawn by its comrade's grunt of alarm.

"Kalland—get him! Kill!" Rudy commanded, ignoring the sneer of triumph on the nearest brute's face. The monster lunged forward, slashing wildly toward the sound of his voice.

But the snow lion was much faster. Kalland sprang over the intervening spires, burying his claws in the creature's shoulders and bearing it to the ground under his weight. The monster's sword clattered onto the stones as its brawny hands sought vainly to block the wide-stretched jaws drooling on the back of its neck.

Rudy dropped his knife and snatched up the sword, surprised at the weapon's weight. Raising it over his head, he dashed around the pair of combatants, shuddering involuntarily as he heard the twisting, the ultimate *snap!* of bone.

The monster's cries immediately stilled, and in the sudden quiet the remaining pursuer paused, a look of mingled fury and confusion on its broad-snouted face. Longingly it looked toward the door, but then grimly raised its weapon and started forward. By standing absolutely still, Rudy remained undetected as the creature stalked past, a few paces away.

Swinging the blade downward with all of his strength, Rudy sprang forward and hacked at the back of the brute's neck. The blade bit deeply, but the creature stunned him, snarling and spinning about with shocking alacrity. The sheer force of the maneuver almost ripped the blade from Rudy's hands, but he clung tightly and was jerked to the side before he pulled the weapon free.

His movement proved fortuitous as the beast hacked savagely through the space where Rudy had stood a moment earlier. Reacting instinctively, the Iceman stabbed with his own weapon, this time into the monster's throat.

The brute gagged and staggered backward, still blindly flailing. Rudy waited for a moment, stepping quietly to the side before lifting the blade for one desperate, slashing blow.

As if he swung an axe against the trunk of a sturdy tree, he drove the weapon through a wide arc. The beast heard the blade whistle in the air, and started to bring its own sword up, but the whirling strike came too fast.

The Iceman's sword chopped into the flesh below the brute's left ear, and—again like an axe against a tree—gouged into tough resistance. But the weight of the blade was sufficient to carry it deep, and with a gurgling growl the monster staggered to its knees before sprawling face-first in a growing pool of black blood. That dark liquid, Rudy noticed, spread like an impenetrable shadow across the glowing stones, dousing the light as effectively as thick clouds screen the sparkling stars.

"Rudy! You got them all?" Anjell asked, her tone full of wonder and her eyes shining. She stumbled from her hiding place, and as he reached her she wrapped her arms around his waist.

A rock tumbled free from the cave wall nearby. Then a small cascade of stones clattered onto the floor. Only then did Rudy notice a resonant pounding. More debris rolled down, and with a groan of despair he feared that the grotto was about to collapse.

EIGHT
Kianna Kyswyllis

The awareness of men, limited by a life span more
worthy of insects than sentient beings, is insignificant
compared to the glories of Faerine. Song and
sculpture, dance and poetry—these are the gifts of
Aurianth. Yet of far more consequence than the lack of
artistic sensibility is short-lived humankind's greatest,
and most dangerous, weakness: its inability to
remember, and to fear, threats that have lain dormant
for more than a few generations.
—TALLY OF LIVES BY WYSTEERIN HALLOWAYN,
THE SYLVAN BARD

— 1 —

Danri scrambled out of his shallow cave, numb with disbelief. Did his
mind play tricks with him? Had the long months of darkness finally
driven him insane?

"Help!"

The cry was repeated, seeming to rise from the still-surging waters
of the subterranean lake. The tone shrilled, swelling with panic—and
too high-pitched to be either a digger or a gigant.

"Who's there?" he called. "Where are you?"

"Help! I can't swi—!" The words faded into a bubbling gurgle,
and Danri desperately scanned the wave-racked surface of Aura.

The boat still remained where he had left it. Though it had collected a layer of debris, and several good-sized rocks had landed right
inside, the planks didn't seem damaged—at least, not in Danri's hasty
inspection. He started to push the craft downward, surprised to see
that the stern was resting very near water level. Enough rubble had

tumbled into the lake to raise the surface a good twenty feet or more above the previous water line.

Though no more debris fell, the surface of Aura tossed and pitched from the residue of the landslide. Danri peered through the waves, seeking some sign of whoever had cried for help.

There! He saw a hand flash and then vanish behind the crest of a surging wave. Fixing the place, the digger pushed the boat off the island, thrusting as hard as he could in an effort to carry it through the rough water, toward the drowning person.

"Hang on!" he shouted. "I'm coming!"

Snatching up the boatman's pole, he drove it against the shoreline, propelling himself as hard as he could. Ignoring the fact that once again he moved into deep water, he focused all his energies on the need to save a life.

He saw hands, and he caught a brief glimpse of a white, terror-stricken face as a wave heaved upward. Then the body vanished beneath the whitecaps. Frantically Danri drove the pole into the water, finding just enough length to strike the bottom one last time.

A wave rolled back from the sloping shore of the island, giving the boat an additional surge in the direction of the flailing figure. Danri scrambled into the bow, still clutching the end of the long shaft. He extended the pole toward the place where the stranded swimmer had disappeared.

"Here! Grab the pole!" he shouted at the water, hoping his words might carry into the depths.

Once again a hand flashed, and Danri thrust the pole. He saw tiny fingers curl around the end of the wooden shaft, and then a second flailing limb emerged from the water. White-knuckled fists gripped at the rod, and when the hold was firm, the digger hauled back.

Again that pale face flashed above the water, an open mouth gasping a desperate lungful of air—but then another wave surged underneath the skiff. Danri toppled backward, barely maintaining his grip on the pole. When he scrambled back to his feet he saw that the two hands still gripped the lifesaving rod, though the face had again vanished.

Heaving desperately, he pulled the pole hand over hand, dragging the person through the water toward the boat, reassured by the tight grip of those two fists. A final pull brought the figure up to the side of the boat, and Danri dropped the wooden rod, reaching down to seize the wrists of the castaway. His broad fingers gripped tightly, even as he was surprised by the frail, almost childlike arms in his grip. With a straining heave, the digger toppled, collapsing into the boat as he brought a sputtering, girlish figure out of the water.

The swimmer flopped onto his chest, groaning and squirming. Danri heard the boatman's pole roll across the gunwale, and though he grasped desperately with both hands, he couldn't catch the shaft before it splashed into the water.

He darted to the gunwale, unceremoniously dumping the half-drowned person in the bottom of the boat, grabbing the end of the pole just before it floated out of his reach. Only after he had nearly tumbled into the water making his frantic retrieval did he finally clamber back inside the boat, catch his breath, and take a look at his passenger.

Wide green eyes stared back at him, out of a round, feminine face. So bright were those orbs that when long-lashed lids momentarily blinked, Danri felt as though a sudden shadow had passed across his vision. Golden hair, darkened by wetness and dangling in limp strands, framed the waiflike visage.

The small body, clad in a sodden gown that clung to the frail torso and outlined skinny, almost sticklike limbs, shivered—whether from cold or fear Danri couldn't tell. The stranger was no more than three feet tall, though she looked considerably smaller as she huddled on the bench. She resembled a human, he thought, though it seemed beyond possibility that a child of Dalethica could have survived a plunge into this deep chamber of Aura.

Then the digger noticed the frail membranes flexing behind the girl's shoulders, and in a blink of recognition he understood—she was not a human, but a twissel. The race of fairies inhabited the lower valleys of Faerine, removed from the digger domains, but Danri had seen a few of them in his life. Of course, he'd never spoken to one—twissels, like their neighbors, the sartors, had invariably struck him as immature and childish.

"What are you doing here?" he demanded, more harshly than he intended. As those green eyes welled with tears, he immediately regretted his tone.

"Don't mind me," he apologized gruffly. "I'm just surprised to find you here, that's all. After all, you could've been killed—easily!"

Still those wide eyes stared. The mouth opened into a wide O, but no sound came out.

"I'm Danri. I'm a digger—guess you probably know that by lookin' at me, don't ya?"

Mutely the twissel nodded.

"What's yer name? Can ya tell me that much?"

"K–K–Kianna. Kianna Kyswyllis." The voice was soft, tremulous.

"Why, that's a pretty name. Now, how'd you come to get yerself down here?"

"I–I don't know!"

The quivering tones threatened to become a wail, and Danri raised a placating hand. "I won't hurt you—you're safe, now."

"Th-thanks—for saving me. I guess diggers make me a little nervous. Oh, but you're not as bad as gigants! And I don't know *what* I'd do if I ever met a human! It's just—well, thanks, anyway."

"I'm not too fond of gigants myself. And I guess we don't have to worry much about running into humans—there hasn't been a human man or woman in Faerine for about a thousand years. But tell me— what happened?"

"I came to High Faerine to visit the Eternal Spring," she began.

Danri nodded. The Eternal Spring, sometimes known as the Source of Aura, was a sacred place for all Faerine—a fountain of magical water that was reputedly the purest Aura in all Faerine. Most inhabitants of the enchanted realms tried to visit the spring at least once in a lifetime. Though for the most part diggers and gigants, twissels, sylves, and sartors kept to themselves, in the valley of the Source all creatures of Faerine were welcomed in peace and fellowship. The Eternal Spring was a center of music and art, a place where the free spirits of Faerine grew to their most creative heights.

"I was in the grove, picking allfruit for dinner," the twissel explained, her tone more level. "When suddenly the ground started to shake—the air, too. It was bouncing me up and down, and I was afraid. I grabbed onto the tree, and I thought I'd be safe."

"How long ago was this?" the digger probed.

Kianna shrugged. "I guess I don't know. It seems like just this evening, 'cause I haven't been to sleep or anything. But it all happened so fast—everything got so *dark*—that I really don't know. But I think it was just a little while ago."

"That figures." Danri well-remembered the temblor that had shaken this cavern, causing him to fear that the entire mountain range would collapse on his head. "The ground shook down here, too."

"Well, like I said, I held on to that tree. Allfruit was pounding to the ground everywhere, and big bumps came up in some parts of the field. In other places the dirt just fell away, making big holes—trees, and rocks, and even a whole family of gigants, just disappeared." Kianna began to shiver again, and for a moment her eyes closed as she tried to block out the horrific memory.

"I thought I was safe, because the trembling started to slow down. Everyone was crying and screaming, and some people were hurt, and it was just the most horrible thing. All I could do was hold on to that tree."

"Must've been *some* shocker," Danri muttered, half to himself. Though legends of ancient earthquakes had been a part of his education, there hadn't been a major convulsion in his lifetime—or in the lifetime of anyone he knew. What in all the Watershed had triggered this tumultuous upheaval now?

With a stab of concern, he wondered if Shalemont had suffered. Of course, digger buildings were solid, but even so, a few roofs might have collapsed. In growing apprehension, he thought of the mines—how many of the long, dark shafts had caved in? And how many diggers had perished immediately, or been trapped in the depths?

Vaguely uneasy, he realized that this was the first he'd thought of Shalemont in a long time. Did that mean the Madness was fading? He noticed, too, that talking to Kianna was easy, though when the Madness had first closed in, he couldn't even carry on a conversation with Blaze Smelter.

"Just when I thought it was over," Kianna continued, "another bump came. It shook the tree I was clinging to—it seemed to come from right below me. I looked down, and I saw all the ground there tumbling away, down into this huge hole that suddenly appeared. The whole tree fell! And then more dirt fell in on top of me!"

"How did you get down here?" asked Danri, amazed that the twissel hadn't been killed.

"There was a lot of Aura flowing underground, from the bottom of the spring. It just carried me right along. Then the water sank through a hole, like a big drain, and I went down with it. I fell for a long time—I would have flown away, except my wings were too wet—and the next thing I knew I smashed into this lake."

For the first time Kianna looked at Danri as if she were really seeing him. With a delicate hand she pushed the wet strands of hair back from her face.

"I guess you saved my life," she declared, as if the fact had just occurred to her.

"I guess I did," Danri agreed bluntly. "In all likelihood, you would still be down there somewhere."

He gestured into the lake, noticing that the turbulence of the water continued to settle in the wake of the convulsion.

"Well, I don't mean to be ungrateful," the fairy said, pouting at his gesture and his tone. "But what are *you* doing down here? This doesn't look like the kind of place a person would visit for fun."

Danri didn't reply. He wasn't about to go into the tale of his Madness for the benefit of some flighty twissel, even if she was the first person he'd seen in . . . How long had he been under the ground? It didn't matter—he had the greater concern of his destiny to worry about.

He looked across the lake, wondering where that destiny would next lead. It had brought him safely through the bedrock, along a trickling vein of Aura for more months than he cared to think about. Then to this cavern, and along the shore—even provided this boat!—so that he could get on with the pressing business of his quest.

A chilling thought occurred to him: what if that destiny was no more than this, to bring him to a place where he could rescue a fairy? What if *she* was the person whom Fate held in such high esteem—

what if Danri was a mere tool in the furtherance of *her* destiny?

He recalled the current that had carried him to this island, the position he'd been in—in all the expanse of this vast lake, he'd been within a few dozen feet of Kianna Kyswyllis.

"No!" he barked, surprising both of them by speaking aloud.

"No, what?" she demanded.

"I was just thinking," he replied gruffly, more and more irritated by her presence.

"You didn't tell me—what *are* you doing floating around in this lake? How do you make this boat go, anyway? I don't see any paddles, or sails."

"I float with the current," Danri replied.

"And where's the current taking you?"

"It's taking—it's taking me to my *destiny*!" In a huff, the digger turned toward the bow, haughtily inspecting the water before them. Or was it the stern? He realized in chagrin that he had no idea where they were going, or even which end of the skiff led the way.

But something the fairy had said tugged at his mind, and finally he realized what it was. Pausing to listen, he heard the trilling sound of water splashing, and easily imagined a plume of shimmering Aura spilling into the lake from somewhere overhead. Indeed, as he looked into the distance, he saw the place—a column of white spray pouring through an aperture in the roof, tumbling straight down to meet the waters of the lake. A series of spreading circles rippled away from the base of the waterfall.

"That wasn't there before," Danri announced. "This lake was as quiet as a winter frog pond."

"Well, it's not anymore," Kianna declared. "Though I suppose you know all about that—you seem to know about everything else!"

The twissel shrugged her shoulders, flexing her gossamer wings. With a flutter, she shook droplets of water from each of the silky membranes, and within a few moments they had fully dried. Already bored, she looked around the inside of the boat, and then across the settling waters beyond. She hummed a tiny tune, the melody ringing like tinkling bells on the air.

"Where are we going?" she asked, then grimaced. "Pardon me—

I should say, Where is your destiny? That *is* where you said we're going, isn't it?"

"Yes!" huffed Danri. But this time his shoulders slumped in resignation. "I-I don't know *exactly* where we're going. But we do seem to be moving." He indicated the towering block of the island, which had been within a hundred yards of them when he'd pulled Kianna from the water. Now it had shrunk considerably, providing proof that they were making some kind of progress.

"I see—and the waterfall, that's getting farther away too," Kianna agreed. Danri felt a small surge of gratitude for the fact that she hadn't teased him about his lack of a proper destination.

For a time they drifted in silence. Though the ceiling of the vast chamber remained lost in darkness, Danri saw that the many of the islandlike supporting pillars remained intact—enough, obviously, to prevent the destruction of the lake. In places, piles of loose rubble jutted upward from the waters, and he assumed that debris from the earthquake had created these new mounds. Their appearance confirmed that, in many places at least, the bottom of the lake was not terribly far underwater.

"I've never known a digger before," Kianna announced shyly, breaking the long period of silence. "We don't see many of your folk down in the Glades."

"Guess the same could be said for twissels, up in Shalemont," Danri agreed.

"It's funny, isn't it? Faerine is so crowded with different kinds of people, but we all keep to ourselves so much. I wonder why?"

Probably because we can't stand to listen to each other prattle on. Danri suppressed the thought before it became speech, but he smiled privately, certain that he'd put his finger on the truth.

"Just like to stay among our own kind, I guess," he speculated lamely.

"Well, *nobody* likes gigants much," the fairy continued, as if Danri hadn't spoken. "I can see why we don't mix with *them*—they're almost as rude and crude as humans! But what about diggers? How come you never come down from the heights?"

"Diggers are hill people. We used to live in all the high places of

Faerine—'course, that was before the gigants drove us down from the mountain. May Aurianth curse their ancestors and their children!"

"But didn't the gigants move onto the mountainsides when the drackans took over the peaks?" Kianna asked in wide-eyed innocence.

"Then a curse on the drackans, too!" muttered the digger.

"But they only went to the mountaintops because nobody wanted them in the lowlands," the twissel pointed out, continuing the debate far beyond the point of Danri's limited interest.

"And then there's the watchers at Taywick Pass, and the Darkenheight," she continued. "Where *all* the peoples of Faerine send warriors! How come we manage to get along in those garrisons, but no place else."

" 'Cause those are places where all Faerine is menaced," Danri countered, logically. "At Taywick, the mountains are so low that the humans might be able to find their way over the Watershed. And Darkenheight is even more of a threat— Sure, the pass is higher there, but all the minions of the Sleepstealer wait on the other side." He turned and spat into the lake, cleansing his tongue of Dassadec's name.

"But how come, if we can get along when we have a warlike reason to do it, we can't do it *all* the time?"

"How am *I* supposed to know why we're not all friends?" demanded the digger. "Maybe we just like our own kind better than anybody else!"

"You know, I think you might be on to something there." If the fairy had taken any note of his outrage, she didn't let on with her voice. "After all, when you live as long as we do in Faerine, you have to pick your neighbors pretty carefully. It's not like humans, who only have to put up with themselves for fifty or sixty years, mostly. I mean, you diggers live for three centuries or more, don't you?"

"If we don't get talked to death first, yeah," Danri replied. As with his anger, the sarcasm seemed lost on the pensive twissel.

"Same with us, and sartors too. Sylves and gigants, they live twice that long or something, don't they? And drackans—my Flowerwarden says they *never* die!"

"They die," Danri asserted grimly. "My father killed one—a brown drackan."

"Killed a *drackan?*" Kianna's eyes widened almost enough to cover the top of her face. "*Why?*"

"Because otherwise the drackan would have killed him! Why do you think?" sputtered the digger.

As the twissel's mouth opened, Danri continued—as much to keep her silent as from any desire to explain. "The drackan thought it was master of the mountain, but my father was a MineFinder. He knew there was a host of metals under there—but they had to get rid of the drackan first. Brown drackans *never* let you dig up their mountain."

"I should think not. Why couldn't you just find another mountain?"

"We don't *choose* where the metal will be—we just dig it up!"

"Well, it would make a lot more sense if—"

"*Quiet!*" Danri hissed, suddenly tensing as he sensed a change.

"What?" demanded Kianna.

At least she fell silent after claiming the last word. Yet instead of the vast quietude of the massive chamber—the stillness that had surrounded them before—a distant, hissing sound washed through the air. It seemed to come from all around, and as Danri concentrated, the sibilant sound took on a throatier rumble, like a boom of power. Pulsating through the air, through the Aura, the force was something they felt as much as heard.

Steadily the distant pounding increased in volume. A chaotic swelling of noise, it bore no single tone or imprint. Instead, it was a mixture of all sounds—humming, booming, swishing, thumping, all blending into a crescendo of unstoppable power.

"We're going faster, I think . . ." Kianna hesitantly observed. She pointed to a stony pillar jutting from the water a hundred paces from their skiff. Grimly, Danri watched the obstacle sweep past, quickly receding into the distance.

He looked before them, and for the first time since picking up Kianna he saw the shoreline and steeply ascending wall of the great cavern. It was more than a mile away, but they were gliding steadily toward it, carried by an increasingly speedy current.

"It's a waterfall," the digger muttered, as the sound at last took form and identity for him.

"Well, of course," Kianna replied. "I thought you *knew* that! That's where all the water is going."

"All the water—and everything that's floating on the water, if we don't do something quick!"

"You mean, like fly away?" Kianna's wings, fully dried now, buzzed out from her shoulders, vanishing into a silky blur. Slowly she rose from the seat, hovering over the boat. She looked questioningly at Danri, then frowned. "Oh, dear. No wings."

Danri had never actually seen anyone fly before, and he gaped at Kianna for instant. Then he clapped his jaw shut furiously, and turned to scowl at the cavern wall before them.

"How can there be a waterfall?" he demanded. "The cliff goes *up*!"

His eyes disputed his assertion. He gradually discerned a long, vertical crack in the cavern wall, darkened by shadows far beyond the pale lighting in the cavern. As the boat swept steadily closer, he realized that what had at first seemed a narrow aperture was probably a gorge at least a hundred feet wide. There could be no question that the current was carrying them steadily toward that point.

"Do you have a rope?" asked the twissel.

"What? Yes, of course!" Without further question Danri uncoiled the rope on his shoulder.

"Give me the end—*hurry!*"

He threw a loop to Kianna who, still hovering, caught it with a quick grab. "Now, hold on!" she called.

The twissel lashed the line around her waist while Danri sat on a bench, bracing his feet against the hull and gripping the rope.

Kianna darted away, flying against the current. The line pulled taut and she stopped abruptly. Wings buzzing, she kicked like a swimmer at the air—but the weight of the boat pulled her back. The twissel's face grew red, her cheeks bulging as she gasped for air, but still Danri felt only the slightest slowing in their steady progress.

"Better stop," he called. "No point in exhausting yourself so that you can't fly out of here."

Kianna buzzed back to the boat and settled onto a bench. "Thanks a lot!" she huffed.

"What do you mean? What could I—?"

"Like I'd fly away and leave you here. What kind of friend do you think I am?"

Again Danri was stunned, perhaps even more so than when he'd seen her fly. "Well, I just thought—that is—I guess—I didn't know."

He couldn't say—didn't want to admit—that if their situations had been reversed, he would be saying a regretful farewell right about now. "But there's no sense in *both* of us getting killed," he argued, returning to his natural pragmatism. "You can escape—you *should!*"

"Maybe we can both escape!" Kianna pointed out. "Who said you're doomed? I thought diggers were supposed to be tough?"

"I *am* tough!" shouted Danri, his head once again spinning from the convolutions of the conversation. He was about to bellow that crashing over a waterfall meant certain death to anyone, when a voice in the back of his mind rebuked him.

"Can you fly ahead—see what the water does when it goes through that crack?" he asked.

"Sure!" In a flash, Kianna darted away, leaving a considerably chagrined digger to consider, regretfully, the ease with which he'd been about to surrender. What about his destiny?

Angrily he scowled at the looming cavern wall, as if he hoped to alter its shape merely by the force of his belligerence. Instead, he saw details of ledges and outcrops on the rocky surface, the whole sloping toward him to create an unclimbable series of overhangs.

The boat bobbed and pitched now, as the current seized him full in its grip. With surprising speed, Kianna darted back to him and sat on the gunwale to catch her breath. "Well, it goes down pretty steep once it goes through the crack. But it's not exactly a waterfall—more like rapids down the side of a mountain, or a big stairway, if you get my meaning."

Danri did, all too clearly. His heart struggled with his mind, refusing to yield to a seemingly inevitable fate.

"How far does it go?" he asked, striving for some glimmer of hope.

"As far as I could see," Kianna admitted, dousing that faint spark. The thunder of the cascade pounded around them, forcing them to shout. Now the overhanging dome of the ceiling was visible overhead, appearing to roll past like a steadily descending bank of windswept cloud. The walls of the narrow gorge had separated into two distinct cliffs.

Danri felt, uncannily, as though he himself were not moving. Instead, he imagined the mouth of some monstrous beast lunging outward, gulping a massive amount of Aura, and incidentally swallowing the boat and its two occupants into its uncaring maw.

— 2 —

The prow of the skiff toppled forward and Danri planted his feet, gripping the pole like a tightrope walker. The stone walls, sheer and slick with mist, flashed past as the boat momentarily soared through space. It plunged, pointed bow first, into the deep water at the base of the first drop-off, and Danri pitched forward, cracking his chin on the gunwale. Dropping the pole, hoping it remained inside the boat, he grasped a bench with both hands as the little craft pitched and bucked before once again flying into the air.

The skiff pounded against a rock, Danri flying across the hull and barely grasping another bench to avoid a tumble into the raging torrent. His hammer, lashed to his waist, bounced sharply and painfully off his knee. He couldn't see Kianna—but then, with the spray lashing at his eyes, he couldn't see much of anything.

If raw chaos had a sound, Danri thought, this must be it. His eardrums vibrated in his skull, shuddering under the relentless onslaught of thunder. Cascades swept over steplike ridges, crushing into shallow, stone-bound bowls, foaming and surging onward and down.

Water flooded into the boat, washing across the digger and pulling the vessel around, sideways, to the plunging current. Danri could only hold on as the boat caught on a pair of jutting boulders, then capsized and broke free. Still clinging to the bench, Danri rode under the hull, until once again the sickening sensation of free fall gripped him as he plunged over another step on the seemingly endless waterfall.

This time the crash tore him free from the boat, but when he surfaced, the craft had righted itself, the gunwale floating right past his face. Desperately, Danri grabbed at it, pulling himself over the edge and sprawling on the sloshing floor of the boat. The skiff proved surprisingly buoyant, considering that it was full of water.

Blinking back the spray, he saw a figure dart through the air overhead, and was relieved to see that Kianna had taken wing. The twissel's courage impressed him—even though she wasn't trapped by the current, he feared that the thick spray and chaotic tumble of the river could readily drag her into the stream.

Again the boat tipped, though this time it rocketed down a steep chute instead of toppling over the lip of a precipice. Boulders rose before Danri's face, only to vanish as the onrushing waters carried the skiff to one side or the other of the obstacle. Spray continued to sting his eyes, but he kept them open, desperately seeking some sign that this nightmare would soon be over.

A whirlpool caught the vessel in an eddy, and for a few moments it spun lazily through a series of circles. Danri clutched the bench and the gunwale, gasping for breath, trying to see what perils lay ahead.

A seemingly endless series of frothing, plunging steps marked the further course of the stream. He heard deeper, harder noises amid the pounding water, like the clashing of a hammer against stone, and recognized the sound of huge rocks tumbling down the riverbed. Not surprising, he told himself—the force of this water cutting and gouging this channel must erode even the bedrock of the mountains with savage force.

The skiff poked its nose out of the eddy and immediately the current snatched at the little craft, carrying the boat and its grim passenger over another series of drops, plunging ever deeper along the course of the raging subterranean stream. Since there was nothing he could do to steer, Danri continued to cling for his life, cursing the fate that sometimes turned him backwards, but unwilling to take the risk of releasing his hold long enough to spin around in the narrow craft.

The boat lurched to a halt, tilting to the side and swinging about, beam broadside to the stream. A gout of water showered over the digger's head, filling the skiff and momentarily jamming it between a pair of rocks. Danri looked downstream, shocked to see that the stream disappeared from view just beyond the two rocks that held him up.

"Danri! Hold on!" Kianna shrilled, even louder than the thunder of the stream.

"I'm doin' my best!" he retorted, strangely heartened at the sound of Kianna's voice.

"There's another waterfall—a *big* one! Look out!"

The digger teetered at the brink of the falls, clinging to a sharp ledge of rock as the boat pulled at his feet. He cast a single glimpse over his shoulder, saw only a bottomless well of plunging Aura, sharp, jagged rocks—and certain death if he followed the current.

The skiff jerked away but Danri maintained his hold. Frantically kicking his feet, squirming upward, he pulled himself onto a narrow perch and watched as the narrow boat vanished into the surging torrent. His feet slipped, and he toppled from the rock into a deep, pooling eddy, immediately feeling the current tugging him back toward the drop-off.

Clawing his way through churning Aura, Danri struggled to reach the surface. He was surrounded by light—a pale, gentle illumination that nevertheless seemed deadly confining. He feared it would be the last thing he knew in his life. Though his hammer, in his belt, weighed him down, he never considered dropping it.

Then his hands broke from the water, followed by his arms and head. The digger kicked with his feet, lifting his face from the swirling liquid and drawing in a great gulp of air—air that was thick with mist, but as invigorating as any breath he'd ever taken.

He felt tiny fingers grasping his shoulders, pulling upward, and with Kianna's help he kicked himself free of the water, finally collapsing on a shelf of stone. He gasped for breath, too weak for a moment even to raise his head.

"That was *close!*" the fairy announced, shaking her head and spreading a showering cascade of Auradrops. "But it sure was a ride, wasn't it?"

"On a one-way trip," Danri groused. "And it's not so the waterfall was any worse than being stuck here on this ledge. I know *I* don't see any way off!"

"Do all diggers look on the dark side every minute of the day?"

demanded Kianna, stomping her tiny foot.

"What do you suggest?" he shot back. "I grow wings and fly out of here?"

"Well, no—twissels fly. What do diggers do?"

He was about to ignore her, when he recognized the possibility. "We . . . well, we dig, of course. And if there's even the faintest seepage of Aura through the rocks, I could tunnel along its flow. That just *might* lead us somewhere useful."

"It couldn't be too much worse than this," Kianna pointed out with unarguable logic. "And I bet there's Aura seeping through all kinds of springs in this rock. After all, this river wasn't here a little while ago—the water must have soaked into these rocks for centuries. I wonder where this river came from, anyway."

Danri bit back a sarcastic reply as the answer came to him. "The earthquake. It broke open that crack in the wall, and the water started draining out."

He remembered the vast stillness of the upper lake, when he'd first encountered it. The quiet had surrounded him as he embarked in the long skiff, and the current that had carried him away from shore had been gentle, barely noticeable.

Then, after the chamber had been rocked by convulsion, the flowage had swept him along. The raging torrent of the falls, he felt certain, was something he would have heard previously—if it had existed before the quake.

"But how long will it run? Where does it go?" she demanded.

"Good questions," the digger replied. "But not as good as 'What do we do, now?' "

"What's that noise? Hey! Here's a crack where some Aura's coming out," the twissel observed, hovering to one edge of their narrow perch. "Maybe you could start digging?"

"You have good ears," Danri admitted, clumping over for a closer look and finding that she was right.

"Eyes, too," Kianna said smugly. "Why, my mother used to say I'd see Nicodareus himself before— Ulp!" She gasped as Danri clapped a rough palm over her mouth.

The digger looked around the cavern, his eyes wild. "Are you *crazy?*" he hissed. "Saying the name of a Lord Minion out loud! Do you want to get us killed?"

The twissel squirmed out of his grip and confronted him with a condescending glare. "Oh, you don't believe that old superstition, do you?"

"I know what I've heard," Danri snapped back. "And I've heard that speaking their name is what gives them power—that it's like you might as well have invited him in here to visit!"

"That's ridiculous! Why, how do you even know what their names are if you're not allowed to say them?"

"That's different." Why did she find it so hard to grasp simple concepts of logic? "My tutor took us to a sacred mine, surrounded by Aura, when he taught us about the minions. Before we left, he swore us all to silence!"

"Well, if we're not surrounded by Aura now, we never *will* be!" she retorted. "So you've got nothing to worry about."

"I only hope you're right. If not, may Aurianth help us."

"Well, what are you going to do now?" Kianna asked, as Danri continued to inspect the wall.

"This is layered shale," the digger said cautiously. "I can dig here, get us going. But it won't be easy."

"Well, that water was coming down too fast for me to fly back up the river. So I'll come along with you."

"If this leak of Aura flows for a long way through the rocks, I'll be able to excavate a tunnel along its passage. With luck, it will eventually lead us out of the mountain." *If the Madness still lingers, or if my strength doesn't give out . . .*

"Why don't you just dig in a straight line? Wouldn't that be the fastest way out of here?"

"Yes—except that, without the Aura, we'd die within the first week or two."

"*Weeks?*" squeaked Kianna. But she bit her lip, willing to recognize this as their only chance—unless she wanted to fly, alone, up the tumultuous riverbed. That prospect held no appeal for her.

Shrugging, Kianna agreed. She settled down to rest, tucking her wings against her back. Meanwhile, Danri inspected the trickle of Aura and examined the fault lines in the shale.

Finally, setting his feet firmly on the slippery rocks, he raised his hammer and struck the wall.

— 3 —

My seventeenth birthday proved to be the most momentous day of my young life—both tumultuous and terrifying. It was in the morning when Pheathersqyll drew me into his study and appraised me with a strangely emotional expression.

First, he told me that I would be going away, journeying beyond the walls of the Academy for the first time—indeed, *far* beyond. He was sending me to serve in a noble house of Carillonn, hundreds of miles to the east. I was being given as a servant to a high noblewoman of that realm, where I was to learn courtly manners and conventions of ladylike behavior.

Even as I digested this stunning news, Pheathers impassively told me that it was time I learned the second part of the prophecy that continued to guide my life.

> *Your destiny lies in the East,*
> *Where, always, you will serve.*
> *A house high, or low—*
> *   you will serve.*
> *Not matriarch, nor mistress, nor queen . . .*
> *   But in your place shall you rise above them all.*

This was all that Pheathersqyll could tell me; even then he did not know the third and final part of the prophecy. His face blank of emotion—though his eyes were clouded with an uncharacteristic wetness—my teacher and mentor bid me goodbye. At that moment the future yawned as a bleak and hopeless pit, shrouded by ultimate unknowns.

Immediately afterward I met Paderon Zyloth, who would be my

teacher in Carillonn. A high priest of Baracan, Paderon was to show me another side of man, and of mankind. . . .

It was a side I had never seen before.

From: *Recollections*, by Lady Raine of the Three Waters

NINE
Desperate Digging

The higher the wall, the bigger the breach when we
knock it down—and we *will* knock it down!
—DIGGERSPEAK PROVERB

— 1 —

A distant, measured pounding penetrated the bedrock, ringing for
many miles through the strata layered beneath the great ridge of the
Watershed. For a long time the cadence resonated without causing the
creature to awaken from its century-long slumber.

Yet, eventually, the Deep Guardian stirred. A broad and scaly
snout puffed, forcing out a breath of musty air—air stale from more
than one hundred years' confinement in leathery lungs. Claws harder
than tempered steel flexed at the tips of two powerful forelegs. These
were limbs of tough sinew and rock-hard bone, perfectly suited to the
excavation of the hardest rock.

The creature had no eyes; little matter, since it had never been
exposed to light. The body was shaped like a long, tapered wedge, with
a mouth garishly slashing across the full width of the pointed snout.
Rear legs coiled like gnarled tree trunks—limbs intended not for claw-

ing, but for driving the rest of the blunt body forward with inexorable pressure.

A breath rasped inward, replacing the stale air, and slowly the blunt head rose from its pillow of rocks. Now the creature listened, considering the rhythmic beat that thrummed through the ground.

It was a message, an irresistible summons, that could only mean one thing: somewhere, still distant—but clearly within the creature's domain—it would find living meat, food.

Reaching forward, clawing at the solid stone before it, the Deep Guardian began to move.

— 2 —

Once again Danri immersed himself in the rhythms of the digging Madness. At first he had feared that Kianna Kyswyllis would prove a distraction, perhaps even prevent him from attaining the transcendent state required to sustain his labors. His fear proved quite unfounded— in fact, he forgot that she was there.

After chiseling through the cavern wall and then rebuilding a waterproof barrier on the far side, Danri excavated rapidly through the mountain. Traces of Aura trickled through the porous rock, and his tunnel followed the wetness. He had no sense of where he was, at least in relation to the map of Faerine, but as long as he clung to the trail of the magical water, he felt certain that he'd remain true to the course of his destiny.

For a long time after Danri closed the wall behind them and began his burrowing progress through the rock, Kianna chattered on, hurling questions and observations at the digger while he chipped away at the wall or carried rubble to the back of the excavation. He never answered, and gradually she perceived that he did not even hear her. Even when he paused to sip at an Auraslick stone, his attention remained fixed on his task. She readily understood why it was called the Madness.

Yet that Madness did not—could not—possess the twissel as it did the digger. She grew hungry, tired, and bored. She sang every song she knew, including all verses, about a hundred times each. Kianna loved music, but she grew quite sick of these melodies; then, for a time, she hummed tunes of her own invention, until even this grew tedious. Though she, too, sipped the Aura, and found the precious liquid enough to sustain life, she could not thrive on the stuff the way a digger in the Madness could.

At first she tried to help, offering to drag the debris away from Danri's feet. He didn't respond to her suggestions, however, and when she went to help anyway, he came close to stepping on her hands. There was nothing malicious in his manner; it was instead as though he'd forgotten altogether about her presence.

Miserably, Kianna slumped in a corner of the cramped passageway, staying as far back as possible from the flailing digger. After she realized that he would never respond to any of the countless questions and remarks she directed at him, she sulked in silence.

Despite her bored and peevish mood, she found herself watching Danri at work—studying in disbelief the ceaseless tempo, the great force, the rocklike strength of his labors. Gradually her listlessness was, if not replaced, at least accompanied, by a growing sense of awe.

The digger—feet spread into a well-balanced stance, legs bent slightly at the knees—wielded his hammer with precision and apparently tireless strength. Using the chisel end of the tool, he drove a crack along a seam in the rock. Without slowing the pace of his blows, he reversed the hammer and struck with the blunt head, knocking the chunks of rocks free from the wall.

When the pile of loosened debris rose past his knees, Danri set down the hammer and carried the stones to the back of the passage. Kianna was forced to scramble out of his way or she would have been buried, so focused was the digger on his task.

As soon as the rubble was moved, Danri knelt and sipped at the Aura that always trickled across the floor of their enclosure. Then, without any other pause, he picked up his hammer and once again attacked the wall.

It was during one of these brief intervals, as the digger took the time to drink, that Kianna heard the sounds from beyond. She couldn't identify anything in particular, but in the brief respite from Danri's pounding she detected a kind of grinding, steady noise. Kianna didn't get any sense of menace or danger from the vague stridulation—in fact, it was kind of a relief to hear something beyond their little cocoon.

When Danri next paused his hammering, she strained her ears. Even as the digger clumped back and forth, carrying armloads of debris, she heard the sound again. When he stopped to drink, the grinding came clearly into the stillness. The twissel watched Danri to see if he noticed anything, but she was not surprised when he showed no reaction. Instead, he picked up his hammer as he had a hundred times before, and once again started pounding at the wall.

Kianna thought about the sound. She was certain that it had been stronger this time, which meant that its source was probably closer. Were they nearing some underground mining operation, allowing her to hear the labors of the workers? Instinctively she believed that the noise had been too repetitive, too precisely maintained, to result from the uncoordinated efforts of many individuals.

Whatever made the sound was *one* effect—one *creature*.

With that realization her idle curiosity took on a shade of fear. What type of being could make that kind of noise? Why was it coming closer? She told herself that it could be Danri who was closing in on the mysterious sound, not the other way around. After all, there was no way to tell what direction it was coming from. In the stone-walled chamber, the pulsations echoed out of the rock, and even if she pressed her ear to the different walls, ceiling, and floor, she couldn't determine any bearing.

Danri returned to his pounding, once again overshadowing the distant sounds. But now Kianna was too tense to be bored. Instead, she flitted about, anxiously awaiting the next time the digger put down his hammer. As usual, Danri took no notice of the twissel's activities, and she in turn took care to stay away from his worksite.

The next time he halted, the sound was louder still, boring through the stone like some monstrous drill, grinding and crunching the bedrock even more quickly than the tireless digger.

"Danri! Listen! Can't you hear that?" she demanded, as he marched past her with an armload of rubble.

He didn't reply, didn't even look at her. Instead, he dumped the rocks, and returned to gather up another armload. Kianna hovered in front of him until he bumped her, but even then she couldn't get his attention—he simply stepped around her and continued about his business of transferring stones.

When Danri knelt to drink, Kianna seized on a desperate plan to get his attention. She buzzed into the air, darting toward the hammer that lay beside the excavation. As Danri smacked his lips and got to his feet, the fairy reached out and grabbed the tool. Wings buzzing, she flew past the digger as he marched back toward the wall.

The weight of the hammer quickly brought her to the floor, but she settled onto her feet and backed away as Danri turned, blinking in confusion. His eyes fixed on the hammer and he took a step toward her.

"Danri—*listen!*" she cried.

He didn't respond, stepping resolutely forward and reaching for the hammer. He scowled when she dodged to the side, reaching with startling speed to grasp it away from her.

"Oh—you're so *thick!*" wailed Kianna, hurling herself at him and tugging on the steel hammerhead. He turned back to the wall, swinging her around as if she wasn't there—and indeed, as far as he was concerned, she wasn't.

She flew upward and grabbed the hammer on his next backswing. Pulling it away, she tumbled to the rock-strewn floor. Again he turned and marched toward her, the same impassive expression on his face.

"Can't you even get *mad?*" she demanded.

This time she feinted to the right, and when he reached for the hammer, she dove to the left, squeezing behind the digger with a sudden burst of speed.

But the corridor was too narrow, and once he had backed her against the wall he easily grabbed the tool again, raising it without pause. Kianna had to dive toward the floor, zooming toward the back of the cave as hammer blows again smashed into the rock.

Approaching despair, she looked around frantically. The rope around Danri's waist and shoulders caught her eye. She crept closer, pulling one end of the line free when he raised the hammer for another strike. Quickly she uncoiled the rope, swooping up when the digger leaned forward, darting back down when he raised his hand to strike. As she had suspected, he took no notice of her activities.

When she had a sizable portion of the line free, she reached a loop around the digger's legs, laying the coil on the floor. Taking the end of the rope, she braced her feet and pulled.

The line snapped off the floor, tightening around Danri's ankles. Straining hard, Kianna pulled it tight, the closing loop forcing the digger's legs together. With a grunt of surprise he toppled backward.

Before he could react further, the twissel buzzed close, seized the hammer, and swirled out of his reach.

For a few seconds he looked at her blankly, extending a hand toward the hammer. His blank expression slowly tightened, until he squinted at her in confusion that blossomed slowly into rage.

"Danri—*now* listen. Can you hear it?" the twissel asked in exasperation.

For a time she feared that he remained beyond her reach. Then he blinked, his face darkening into a scowl.

"Gi—give me . . . my hammer!" he demanded, his articulation slow and awkward.

"Listen! Something's coming!"

"My hammer!" the digger repeated.

For the first time in her subterranean adventure, Kianna felt as though she was going to cry. Shaking her head angrily, blinking back tears, she stared at the digger fiercely.

"You've got to *listen*! There's something out there, digging. It's coming closer. Can't you hear me? Don't you *understand*?"

Slowly the digger's eyelids lowered, until they half covered his eyes. He stared at the twissel, and she couldn't tell if his expression was crafty, or merely tired. Abruptly Danri shook his head and blinked.

"Why did you take my hammer?" he asked.

Kianna was heartened by the belligerence in his voice—he seemed himself again. Quickly she repeated her warning and Danri listened, squinting in concentration.

The sound rumbled clearly, like a background hiss with a deep and vibrant tone. It was definitely louder than before. Kianna imagined solid rock being churned to gravel and then spilled out of the way; she knew beyond any doubt that something with unspeakable power was forcing its way toward them.

"Aye-uh—I think I hear something." Danri scowled in concentration. Immediately his expression darkened further. "It's pretty faint—I'm amazed you noticed it."

"It sounds plenty loud to me! Maybe my ears work better than yours—remember, on the lake, when I heard the waterfall before you did?"

He nodded. "What do you think it is?"

"It's something dangerous," she replied. "It's coming this way— it *wants* us!"

He looked at her pointedly. "Give me my hammer."

"But—"

"It's our only chance to get away," the digger declared bluntly. "If you're right—if this thing is getting closer—then all I can do is try to dig us out of here."

Wordlessly the twissel handed the implement to Danri. He turned to the wall and began to work, chiseling with renewed fury. His arm thrummed like a drummer's baton, the hammer a blur of gray steel chipping against the wall. Kianna pitched in, dragging the rocks away as they fell at the digger's feet, and this time he took note of her help.

Danri paused only to drink occasionally from the thin film of Aura. During each of these lulls, Kianna perceived the sinister grinding as closer, more imminent. The digger, too, heard it more clearly, and he made each break shorter than the one before. When he returned to his labors, it seemed that renewed energy—or was it desperation?— drove his hammer against the wall.

"It won't work," Kianna said miserably, as the digger paused for one of his brief respites. Rock crunched around them, and it seemed that the source of the noise must be nearly upon them. It had to be something with tremendous destructive power, the twissel realized, in order to destroy this solid granite so quickly.

"We might have a chance," Danri said. "You noticed anything different about *my* hammering?"

"What do you mean?"

"I mean that, for a little while now, the rock has sounded *hollow*!

Like I might be getting close to the surface. Next time I stop, I bet it'll be to take a breath of fresh air!"

Kianna buzzed excitedly off the floor. In truth, she could hear nothing different in the sound of the digger's hammering, but that fact didn't concern her. She didn't believe it was in his nature to tell a lie just to assuage her fears—if he claimed that he heard something, then he did.

The twissel busied herself by dragging several large boulders toward the back of their tunnel. She piled them against the other rubble already collected there, but as she turned around, a tremor shook the pile. Boulders as big as her head toppled free, and she buzzed back just before one of them could crush her foot.

She stared in horror at the rock wall of their little section of tunnel. Before her eyes a jagged crack appeared, shooting like black, malevolent lightning across the gray surface. Was it her imagination, or did the wall bulge outward, as if straining against great pressure.

"Danri! It's *here*!"

The digger didn't take time to look back—instead he smashed at the wall with renewed vigor, pulling great slabs of rock free with his left hand while his right, clutching the hammer, smashed like a maniac's. Now even Kianna could hear the different tone of his blows, as the rock seemed to vibrate like a great drumhead. He must be very close to breaking through.

But the fairy despaired as she looked back. The jagged crack had expanded, sending crooked tributaries branching from floor to ceiling. The central crack slowly widened. It was large enough now that Kianna could have stuck her whole thumb inside—if she totally lost her mind and was for some reason tempted to try.

The flat wall trembled and shook, discharging small cascades of dust and pebbles. Slowly the slab swelled outward, and Kianna instinctively backed away, stopping only when she heard Danri pounding directly behind her.

Without further warning the wall fell in, crumbling into boulders and revealing a dark passageway beyond. No illuminating Aura flowed in this new tunnel, and at first the interior remained cloaked in dark shadows.

Then something moved in there, and Kianna felt the bile in her empty stomach rise up to her throat. She saw two forepaws, each bristling with claws as long as sylvan swords. The skin of the forelegs was slick and scaly, almost like overlapping plates of metal armor.

Those scythelike claws raked at the rock, steadily expanding the hole. Some of the rubble tumbled toward Kianna and Danri, but most was gathered in by the talons, pulled back into the shadows.

Gradually, as the aperture widened, Kianna saw the hideous visage between the two crushing paws. A circular mouth, ringed by teeth like iron chisels, pulsed open and closed, a rictus of hunger. Kianna watched a large chunk of rock, hooked by the saber-like claws. The beast tossed the boulder toward its face, and that horrific mouth gaped wide, then gulped the rocks and snapped shut. Gasping in fright, the twissel watched as the maw flexed and twisted. From inside came the crunching, gravelly sound she'd been hearing for so long.

Now the creature pressed forward, its broad shoulders jamming against the opening, crushing rock as it advanced. Each time a sizable rock fell, the monster paused, sweeping the morsel up and crushing it to pebbles.

"Here we are—almost!" cried Danri, as his hammer smashed away a section of stone. A circle of darkness, no bigger than Kianna's hand, yawned beyond. "I just need another minute or two!"

"It's too late!" Terror put a tremor in Kianna's voice at the same time that it paralyzed her limbs. She desperately wanted to flee, though she knew there was no place to go.

Once again those claws reached forward, as more of the beast squirmed through the narrow opening. The body was long and flexible, like a slug's—except that it was covered all over with a jointed carapace, armored plates tapered toward the back so that they slipped easily past the jagged edges of rock.

Kianna risked a quick glance at the digger. Through the blurring image of his hammer she saw the hole in the wall slowly expanding— though it was still too small even for her head. Danri pounded in a frenzy, but it seemed that he could chip only finger-sized slivers of stone away from the entrance.

Now the monster's shoulders pressed through its opening. Those wicked claws reached outward, flailing through the narrow cave. They didn't seek the fairy directly—instead, they angled toward the noise made by Danri's frenetic digging. Kianna could see no eyes, nor any other sensory organ, on the grotesque head, but it seemed obvious that it could hear.

More of the body came into view, swelling obscenely as it passed through the narrow gap. The twissel wished she had a weapon, even as she knew she wouldn't be able to penetrate those armored plates. Still, she wanted desperately to strike at the beast, to give vent to her fury and her fear.

Stooping quickly, she picked up a chunk of rock and threw it at the monster's face. The boulder smashed into the circular snout and bounced to the floor.

Surprisingly the beast halted. She didn't believe that she could have hurt it seriously—a creature that could chew through miles of bedrock wouldn't be terribly threatened by a thrown stone—but she felt a flare of hope as she watched. The monster groped across the floor in front of it, finally gathering the stone in its long claws. Flipping the rock into its once-again gaping mouth, it paused long enough to masticate the small boulder.

As it started to ooze forward again Kianna was struck by inspiration. She grabbed a larger rock, staggering under the weight as she clutched it in both hands and raised it over her head. Fiercely pitching the makeshift weapon, she once again scored a hit on the probing snout. The creature hesitated, confused by the bombardment, before scooping up the rock, gulping it, and chewing it into little pebbles.

Before it could begin creeping closer, Kianna threw another rock, and followed that with a fourth. She saw that Danri had a larger opening now—perhaps big enough for her to fit through, if she tucked her wings against her back. Still, she knew that the opening would never accommodate the digger's broad shoulders, and if she stopped heaving rocks at the crawling beast, her companion's fate would be assured.

Hastily she picked up another stone, realizing that her supply was almost exhausted. Of course, the back wall of their cave was nothing less than a pile of such ammunition, but the foreparts of the monster's body, bulging into the passageway, effectively blocked her from reaching that arsenal.

Instead she snatched up fist-sized stones, pebbles, and jagged shards of stone—anything that she could reach.

"Just . . . another . . . minute!" Danri gasped, speaking between the staccato pounding of his hammer.

"I don't *have* a minute!" she wailed.

More stones crashed to the floor, broken loose by Danri's hammer, and Kianna snatched these up as soon as they fell, throwing them one by one at the horrific burrower. But now the creature seemed to grasp the nature of her tactic—or perhaps the stones were too small to keep its attention.

Whatever the case, more of its disgusting body oozed into the passageway. Kianna wondered if it crept along like a snake, but finally she saw two massive hind legs. Sinewy muscles rippled, visible even beneath the flexible carapace, and when those legs flexed, the monster surged fully into the narrow tunnel. Turning toward them, it extended the swordlike talons of its forelegs.

Kianna took her last stone, a rounded chunk as big as Danri's head, and smashed it full into the monster's snout. The creature barely slowed; instead it oozed toward her with astonishing quickness. With a low moan, she closed her eyes, devoutly wishing that her life wasn't about to end in such a horrible fashion.

"There!"

She didn't understand Danri's meaning until he grasped her by the scruff of her neck, hurling her through the opening he'd chiseled in the wall.

"Hurry!" she cried, watching those massive claws groping toward the digger's back. Still clutching his hammer, Danri dove after her, rolling across the floor and bouncing to his feet.

The monster oozed forward, but the opening in the rock was too narrow for it to follow—at least, immediately. Quickly those powerful forepaws reached out, saber claws tearing frantically to enlarge the passage.

"Come on!" cried Kianna. "Let's run!"

She grasped Danri's hand, noticing for the first time that he wasn't even looking at their grotesque pursuer. Instead, he was looking past her shoulder, eyes glinting with steely determination—and shock.

Kianna spun around, noticing that they hadn't reached the outside world. Instead, they were in some sort of cave—though not a deep one, judging by the pale illumination spilling around several bends in the passageway. Somewhere beyond, outside probably, she heard a waterfall.

Only then did she see that they weren't alone. Two figures already occupied the cave, and when one of them advanced, the fairy clasped her hand over her mouth in horror. She and Danri were trapped— behind them came the ravenous beast from the depths, while before them they were confronted by another, equally menacing threat.

Humans.

— 3 —

I traveled east, riding a horse in a long caravan of traveling nobles; immediately I understood that my life had changed forever. Pheathersqyll was gone, torn away, and in his place was one for whom I could never feel the same childlike sense of awe and reverence.

Paderon Zyloth . . . he was unquestionably brilliant, eloquent, charismatic—and hopelessly, impossibly dogmatic. The name of Baracan rolled constantly off his tongue, hailed as the source of every bit of good fortune, each benign circumstance that befell the realm.

My old sense of rebelliousness flared to new heights under the strictures of temple and palace life. We spent the winters in Shalloth, where I studied and worked whenever I wasn't sleeping. Summers, at the High Court of Carillonn, were even more tedious, for I was forced to spend many hours doing simple tasks for women who were too lazy—forgive me, too *noble*—to do them for themselves.

In Carillonn—at least, among the nobility—most of the things I knew how to do, and did well, were forbidden activities for females. I was not allowed to practice fighting or acrobatics, nor could I wear trousers, or eat in the kitchen with the stablemen. Music was discouraged; songs and poems raising the name of Aurianth were forbidden outright, and one who so much as thought of the Sleepstealer was expected to perform arduous penance. The only Godstomes allowed for study, naturally, were the *Scroll of Baracan* and the *Codex of the Guardians*; only surreptitiously could I hold on to my tattered *Songs of Aurianth*—even my reading sessions were very secretive affairs.

In those days, it should be noted, Carillonn was indeed the jewel in the crown of humanity. Carillonn's understanding of navigation far exceeded that of the Corsari—who were otherwise the greatest sailors in the world. No warriors of any realm could stand against the One Hundred Knights of Carillonn, bravest horsemen in all the Watershed. Architects used stone for high arches and domes unlike any seen in the history of Dalethica, surpassing even the majesty of Myntar Kosh's pyramids and the serene elegance of Anderan's tall skylines. The artisans, builders, and nobles of the realm achieved heights of elegance and grace undreamed of in more provincial states, while physicians brought plague and other diseases under control.

My mistress, the Duchess of Shalloth, was an elegant lady, mature but unmarried. A great and highly famed beauty, she graciously shared suggestions as to how my own appearance might be enhanced. I served her well, and she never failed to find work for me—yet we had an unspoken understanding that some portion of my duties belonged to Paderon Zyloth. Thus I was "freed" for long hours of study in his temple.

I was certainly exasperating to the priest, with questions that so often rejected his basic life assumptions. I would discuss an appreciation of Aurianth just to provoke his reaction. Paderon desperately wanted to believe—and to convince others—that the Watershed was absolute, that nothing relevant to humanity existed beyond that mountain barrier.

Occasionally I drove him to rages, even brought him to slap me on rare occasions—but never could he drive the "blasphemous" assertions from my mind, nor even keep them from my lips for very long.

In theology as in other disciplines Carillonn claimed a wealth of knowledge—but of this achievement I was skeptical at first, and later scornful. To my eye, raised in the more questioning environment of the west, the blind faith that hailed Baracan and ignored the other gods smacked of folly. It cannot be denied that Paderon and his ilk had an answer for every question, a riddle for every quandary, and a parable for every lesson—but too often these obscure statements were nothing more than self-serving fluff.

How could they claim that Aurianth, font of music and art, prophecy and love, had no effect upon Dalethica? Even more dangerous, in the end, was the zealots' unwillingness to recognize the presence of the Nameless One, Lord of Duloth-Trol. After a thousand years, it is perhaps not unnatural that the generations of man would lose some of their fear.

Yet the cost of forgetfulness can be very, very high.

From: *Recollections*, by Lady Raine of the Three Waters

TEN

Meeting of Worlds

*When confronting a variety of bad choices, one should
strive for the creation of a new option.*
—SCROLL OF BARACAN

— 1 —

Rudy quickly realized that the cavern was not, in fact, collapsing. Instead, only a small section of the wall gave way, crumbling toward Anjell and him in a shower of debris. A steady pounding rang through the air, and he knew that this rhythmic assault was the cause of the small cave-in.

Kalland growled nervously, pacing beside Rudy, hackles raised as he sniffed at the air. Anjell crouched behind the snow lion, a hand laid on the big animal's flank. Nearby, the pool of magical water glimmered in the shadow-shrouded darkness.

Then a slight, feminine figure tumbled from the wall, followed by a stocky, muscular fellow with a face of bristling whiskers. Anjell gasped, and Rudy pushed her behind him, raising the jagged-edged sword he'd claimed from the slain monster. Whoever—or *what*ever—these interlopers were, he sensed menace in their sudden arrival.

The male scrambled to his feet, glaring belligerently. He was well-muscled but dwarfish, much shorter than Rudy—though with his strapping torso and sinewy arms he certainly outweighed the Iceman. Raising a long-shafted hammer over his head, the intruder brandished the tool threateningly.

Only then did Rudy realize that something else still squirmed in that darkened hole. He saw flailing claws, heard rocks torn from the cave wall clatter on the floor. At first he thought that the pair had brought some grotesque beast of burden with them, but when he saw the female look back with distinct horror, he sensed the truth—they were fleeing the monstrous presence in the cave. The two newcomers, the Iceman realized vaguely, saw in the dark as well as he did.

"Move, human—or die!" barked the hammer-wielder. The words were harsh and guttural, but Rudy understood them clearly.

The snow lion sprang forward with a growl, tail lashing in agitation. He crouched before Rudy, protecting him from the bizarre intruder.

"Human?" Rudy echoed, too astonished to get out of the way. "What in the Watershed *are* you?"

For the first time, he noticed the frail wings jutting from the girl's shoulders, and his jaw slackened in astonishment. He looked again at the male, and saw that while the fellow's legs were bowed and gnarled, they did not appear malformed. Indeed, the miner's barrel-chest and long arms indicated strength far beyond Rudy's own.

"Move, damn you!" snarled the digger, taking another step forward.

"Look out!" Rudy cried, horrified at the sluglike brute crawling through the opening in the cave wall. "This way—follow me!" he shouted, turning toward the entrance of their narrow cave.

The winged girl buzzed into the air, hovering beside her companion. Anjell, still blinded by the darkness, stumbled toward the entryway.

"Help her!" he cried to the fairy. "She can't see!" Then he stepped around the stocky miner, raising the heavy sword in the face of the creeping horror, determined to buy enough time for his niece to escape.

For a moment he thought that the bearded intruder would attack him with that massive hammer, but he merely stared in astonishment at Rudy's courageous stance. The Iceman risked a glance back, saw that the fairy had taken Anjell's hand and led her, stumbling, toward the cave entrance.

A thunderous crash rumbled through the air, and once again Rudy shook off the apprehension that the roof was falling in. He heard stones pounding, felt the ground vibrate under his feet—and then he realized that the sounds came from the mouth of the cave.

"No!" he cried, whirling to see a shower of debris cascade downward, filling the outward passage. Anjell and the fairy leaped back just in time to avoid the crush.

"We're trapped!" Rudy shouted. He remembered the stalking monsters waiting outside their cave—had they triggered this collapse in an attempt to trap them?

"Good timing," muttered the dwarflike miner, his tone heavily sarcastic. At least he'd apparently given up any thought of attacking Rudy; instead, he stood at the Iceman's side, watching the approach of the claw-studded burrower.

The grotesque body oozed through the hole in the wall. Rudy's stomach heaved as the form expanded, emerging from the confining passage. Even the hefty sword, a strange and awkward weight in his hands, seemed puny, useless, against this nightmare apparition.

Kalland growled, drawing his legs underneath his muscular body, tail whipping back and forth. "Stay!" Rudy hissed, horrified at the prospect of the heroic animal hurling itself into those rending talons.

The digger took a step backward, and Rudy retreated too, eyes never leaving that armored shape. He saw the circular mouth, sensed that it was ravenous for meat. Claws scratched on the cave floor, scoring deep gouges in the rock, leaving little doubt as to what they would do to flesh.

"What *is* it?"

"Bad news, that's what," muttered his impromptu ally.

With surprising speed the beast whirled away from them, extending the forequarters of its body in a long, arching leap across the pool of Aura. For a moment it looked like a gruesome reptile, slender and serpentine, but then the hind legs followed the rest of the body. It bunched together on the far side of the pool, again hulking upward like a slug. Talons reached, grasping toward Anjell and the fairy.

The winged girl darted away, trying to pull Anjell by her hand, but the human tripped over the rough ground and sprawled headlong with an anguished cry.

"No!" howled Rudy, dashing around the pool, springing into a fighting stance before his niece's still form.

Claws raked toward him from the right and he raised his blade, clumsily bashing the attack aside. His blow left him pathetically open on the left, and the hooked talons of the beast's other forepaw circled around his arm, tugging him toward that steadily expanding mouth. He struggled to break away, crying out in pain as the talons ripped through the skin of his arm. Blood flowed freely as Rudy kicked and squirmed, drawn inexorably closer.

But then the beast paused. Rudy twisted away, sprawling on the ground, too shocked and horrified to move farther, to do anything except stare in disbelief at the monstrous apparition.

The creature pulled its bloody claws to its maw, almost as if it were trying to hook itself in the mouth. One of the crimson talons disappeared into that circular opening, then emerged, sucked clean of blood. For several heartbeats the monster remained still, and Rudy took advantage of the chance to squirm backward, out of the beast's immediate reach.

No one moved or spoke, all four of them watching the horrific burrower as it gradually started to ooze backward. With deliberate care, the grotesque body twisted into a half-circle, forequarters turned to face the hole out of which it had crawled. Almost as if it were reluctant to depart, it inched to that aperture.

The beast forced its head and front legs through the hole, a ripple bulging back along its plated body as more and more squirmed out of sight. It took a very long time for it to disappear, and Rudy wasn't sure he'd drawn a breath in that whole interval.

Finally it was gone. The Iceman heaved a ragged sigh and sat up. His left arm throbbed painfully, and he gingerly lifted it across his lap.

"You're hurt." The fairy made the observation, hovering beside him and slowly settling to the ground. Her eyes, which were naturally large and luminous, now grew even bigger with concern.

"Kianna—he's a *human*!" The comment came from the stocky miner, who still stood with his hammer half-raised, as if he thought he might need it at a moment's notice.

"Here, have a drink of Aura," Kianna urged Rudy, ignoring her companion. She cupped some of the water in her tiny hands, and when the Iceman sipped it, he felt the stinging pain in the arm slowly fade.

"What's going on?" demanded Anjell. "Who are these people? What are they talking about?"

"I'm a twissel," Kianna said shyly. "And that's Danri—he's a digger."

"What are you doing in Faerine?" demanded the digger, again facing Rudy. "Humans are not allowed to pass the Watershed!"

Suddenly Rudy's pain vanished into a distant part of his mind, and he threw back his head and laughed. His laughter only served to irritate the scowling Danri—a reaction that Rudy found rather gratifying.

"Faerine?" he asked incredulously. "Faerine is a whole mountain range away from here. Welcome to Dalethica, friend."

"That's impossible!" the digger asserted quickly. He hesitated, his eyebrows glowering like dark storm clouds. "We followed a stream of Aura all the way here . . . It can't pass the Watershed."

"It did," Rudy replied, growing serious. A suspicion grew in his mind. "Why can you see here, in the dark?"

"Because of the Aura—there's proof!" The digger gestured to the thin stream of liquid spilling from the wall—the spring that formed the pool in the center of the cavern. "That water's magic—pure as any in Faerine."

"It's proof that the Watershed has been breached!" Rudy argued, exasperated with the digger's stubbornness. "If we get out of here, you'll see that you're at the edge of Halverica—with the Glimmersee two dozen miles away! I've lived here all my life, just one canton away. That's not Faerine, that's Dalethica."

For the first time, Danri seemed to doubt himself, clamping his jaw shut and scowling furiously. He tapped his foot in agitated cogitation.

"How did you get rid of that Guardian?" the digger demanded abruptly.

The Iceman shook his head, helpless to answer and frustrated by his lack of knowledge. "I don't know!"

Just like I don't know how I can see in the dark, or how I healed Anjell's wounds . . . Questions bombarded Rudy until he groaned aloud, clapping his hands to his head and turning away from Danri.

Sagging wearily, he looked around the small grotto, noticing the growing stench of death in the air. He saw the bodies of the sword-wielding attackers—slain what seemed like days ago, though it had been only a few minutes before the Faerines' arrival.

Gesturing toward the corpses, he challenged the digger. "And them—they didn't come from Dalethica, either!"

Danri's face, behind his beard, paled as he saw the two ghastly shapes. "Kroaks," he said, his voice a disbelieving whisper.

"They come from Faerine too?"

Now the digger's eyes were grim, and they came to rest on Rudy's with an expression that was almost sympathetic.

"No, not Faerine. Kroaks come from Duloth-Trol—they're minions of the Evil One."

"Rudy—what are you talking about?" Anjell cried, frightened. "I recognize your voice, but I don't understand a word you're saying!"

Unconsciously he changed languages. "What do you mean?"

"Before—when you were talking to these two—I couldn't understand you!" Anjell clung to him, as if he'd returned from a long trip.

"Do you know what she's saying?" he asked Kianna. The words were out of his mouth before he realized that he'd spoken in a different tongue—a language he had never heard before the twissel and the digger had arrived.

The fairy shook her head. "Aurianth help me—I can't understand her."

The strange knowledge he possessed frightened Rudy to his core. What was happening to him? He could see in the dark, speak and comprehend strange words. He had perceived the menace in the waters of Dermaat. How? The explanation, he began to sense, had at least its origin—if not its explanation—in the snowfield that had buried him at the foot of Glimmercrown.

He forced his mind back to the present. "Outside this cave, there's more of those 'kroaks.' And at least one that's not so big, but has a head like a snake's. I think that one made himself look like a man. Also three huge flying things—they're not birds." He described the rippling, silvery skin that had allowed the creatures to vanish so effectively into the sky. "If it hadn't been for their shadows, they would have killed us easily."

"Stalkers—they're the snaky shapeshifters. And terrions," Danri said, with a whistle and a shake of his head. "Both are kinds of minions—even worse than the kroaks. The terrions can cross the Watershed by flying, but they rarely do—like all the minions, they can't go too far from their source of Darkblood."

"We'll have to worry about 'how and why' later. Let's figure out what to do now—how do we get out of here?"

"How many of the kroaks are waiting outside?" asked Danri, absently fingering his hammer.

"I don't know—I saw about six, though there may be more. Three are dead—one of them ended up in the pool."

Danri looked at the Iceman with a trace—a *small* trace, but definite—of respect. A thought seemed to occur to him, but he hesitated. "You fought three of them in here, and they're all dead?"

"Kalland helped," the Iceman explained, scratching the purring snow lion behind his ears. He studied the digger, who squirmed uneasily, shifting his balance from foot to foot.

"What is it—do you have an idea?" Rudy asked.

"No, a question. How can *you* see in the dark? The light of Aura is a blessing only to those of Faerine—as is our language, yet you speak it well." There, again, was that grudging sense of respect in the digger's manner. At the same time, his voice held an undercurrent of suspicion, even accusation—as if Rudy had stolen some precious treasure that he had no right to possess.

"I can't explain it, because I don't really know. I've never seen in the dark before—and until I heard you speak, I certainly didn't know that I understood your language. Maybe, when we have a little more time, you could help *me* understand what's happened to me."

Danri was obviously skeptical, but he stubbornly shook his head—as if to clear away the fog of his doubts. "Well, I don't know about that. What about getting out of here?"

"The cave-in." Rudy pointed. "There must be enough kroaks left out there that they could pry all those rocks free. They probably figure we're trapped in here for good."

"Hah!" Danri was grimly amused. "They don't know there's a digger in here—it'd take more than a few tons of loose boulders to keep me penned up!"

"Did you *dig* your way here, all the way from Faerine?" asked Rudy, suddenly wondering about the fellow's bizarre arrival.

"After a fashion. Fact is, if you're right about this being Dalethica, I should just turn around and dig my way back the way I came. Humans! You're dangerous, violent, unpredictable, and impetuous—worse than gigants, even! We should just get out of here, as fast as possible!"

For some reason the thought of the gruff stranger's retreat caused a rise of panic in Rudy's heart. Despite his cantankerous nature, Danri seemed so competent that his mere presence gave the Iceman a sense of assurance that he'd lacked even after he had slain the three kroaks. He quickly realized that he had a moral ally in the twissel.

"*No*, Danri!" she wailed. "We're so close—let's at least go out and see the sun, breathe some fresh air, before we go back underground. Aurianth knows, we deserve a look at the sky!"

"Rudy, tell them to come out with us. Maybe we can all help each other." Anjell couldn't understand the words, but apparently the tone and inflection of the Faerines' voices were enough for her to comprehend the debate.

"Ah, I gotta see for myself anyway," the digger mumbled. "You seem like an honest enough fellow, but until I get a look at Dalethica, I won't believe I'm there."

"Fair enough," Rudy said, glad for anything that would prolong the digger's presence. He indicated the pile of debris that choked off the cavern entrance. "Do you really think you can dig through that barrier?"

"Aye-uh. No problem at all."

"What about the kroaks and terrions outside?"

"*They* might be a problem." Still, without further hesitation, Danri hefted his hammer and approached the barrier of stone.

— 2 —

Despite his dark-attuned eyes, Rudy couldn't follow the flailing of Danri's hammer, so quickly did the digger assault the rock pile. Chips of stone flew to the sides, and great boulders crumbled into gravel following a few well-placed blows. Soon pale light streamed through the barrier, penetrating from several chinks, and they heard the steady pounding of water from outside.

"A waterfall," Rudy explained. "This cave mouth stands behind it."

"There's a piece of luck," the digger admitted. "Maybe the kroaks won't hear me digging."

In another few minutes Danri had hacked a tunnel all the way to the outside. The passage was a tubular shaft, barely three feet in diameter, but wide enough for each of them to crawl through. A small amount of daylight reached them—enough to allow Anjell to let go of Kianna's hand and walk without tripping or falling into the pool.

"What if they're waiting for us right outside the tunnel? We'd be pretty helpless, crawling out there one after the other," Rudy observed.

"We need to scout the situation," Danri agreed. "Find out where they're waitin'. If we're lucky, like I said, they didn't hear anything from my digging."

"But *how* can we find out where they are?" Rudy flinched at the tremor of fear in his own voice. Why couldn't he be calm and self-assured like this digger?

"I can find out," Kianna offered shyly, whispering to Danri loud enough that Rudy could overhear.

"It's pretty dangerous," the digger countered, shaking his head. "Even if you can fly, kroaks can throw rocks—and those terrions have me pretty worried. As soon as they see you, I'm afraid it—"

"They *won't* see me!" Kianna retorted. She crossed her arms and scowled.

"How can you—*what?*" Danri sputtered, but Rudy didn't notice the digger's agitation—he was too busy looking for Kianna. One moment the fairy hovered in the air before them; the next, she vanished from sight without so much as a sound.

"Where'd she go?" demanded the Iceman.

"I'm still here—but this way they won't see me!" A disembodied voice emerged from the place where Rudy had last seen the twissel.

Straining, Rudy thought he heard the buzzing of those gossamer wings—though perhaps it was merely his imagination.

"You're *invisible!*" Danri declared, his bearded face split by a wide grin. "You know, I'd heard that some of the sartors and twissels could do that—but I never quite believed it!"

"Well, we can—though it's awfully tiring, and I can't do it for long. Maybe I should get out there and have a look."

"Yes—by all means, do that!" the digger agreed. "Just be quiet!"

Whether or not Kianna had remained to hear all of Danri's instructions they couldn't tell, for she made no reply.

"Rudy—where did she go?" Anjell's tremulous question reminded Rudy that, to his niece, this whole experience must be especially bizarre and frightening. Remembering that she hadn't understood anything they had discussed, he briefly explained the plan to her.

"You mean, she went out to look for those—what did you call them?" Her tone was hushed, full of concern.

"Kroaks. Yes, but she should be safe since they can't see her any more than we could—I hope."

"She—she's *magic!*" breathed the girl. "Rudy—what's going on? Magic is supposed to stay in Faerine, isn't it?"

"Just like those kroaks—and the flyers, the terrions—are supposed to stay in Duloth-Trol. Something's wrong with the Watershed—it's not keeping the lands divided like it should."

"And you?" Anjell's voice took on a tone of awe. "You're turning into something magic, too! Aren't you?"

The blunt certainty implicit in her question forced the truth upon him. "Yes—yes, I think I am."

A shadow darkened the tunnel toward the waterfall, and Rudy flinched. Some deeply abiding instinct compelled him to snatch up the sword, even before he knew what he was doing.

"Oof!" Kianna exclaimed, gliding into the cavern and settling to sit on a small rock. Her wings drooped, and for a moment she lowered her head, gasping for breath.

"What did you see?" demanded Danri impatiently.

"Four . . . kroaks!" she panted. "And one stalker."

"What about the terrions? Did you get a look?" pressed the digger.

"No . . . no sign of them. I went up to the treetops and looked around—I think they're gone."

"Where were the kroaks?" Rudy asked, as Kianna recovered her breath.

"They were all gathered around a fire, at the shore of the stream and a little downhill from here. They've stuck some poor animal—a big one, with two branches coming out of its head—on a spit, and now they're roasting it."

"A stag," Rudy murmured, with a pang of despair. The mighty creatures were rare, this high in the mountains; he had always admired their grace and serene dignity. The killing of one by kroaks was a horrible desecration.

"It was *really* big," Kianna went on. "And it had claw marks on its back, like maybe the terrion caught it."

"Figures," Danri said. "Kroaks'd be too slow and dumb to bring any wild animal down themselves."

"A stag will feed a lot of them," Rudy observed. "Maybe they're planning to stay out there for a long time."

"You'd never know by their rations," Danri said grimly. "Kroaks—any kind of minion, for that matter—don't eat. All they need is Darkblood, and some water, and they can survive."

"Why would they kill the stag then?" the Iceman demanded.

"Sheer cruelty. Probably the poor thing didn't die till they had the fire going for a while. That's what'll happen when minions get bored—they'll even torture and kill each other, if no other enemy shows himself."

"How do you know so much about these . . . minions?" Rudy challenged. "You claim to be from Faerine, yet you speak as though you know Duloth-Trol."

"I don't—not personally," Danri said, with a shrug that indicated he took no offense. "But some of my folk have made it into the Sleep-stealer's realm, and from them—those that returned, anyway—we've learned a lot about the place. Not that anyone would *want* to go there—but sometimes, it's been necessary."

"So the Watershed doesn't prevent diggers from crossing?" Rudy asked in surprise.

"Within limits, it does. You probably know that there are a few gaps over the Watershed—between Faerine and the rest of the world."

"I know of Taywick Pass, where the mountains aren't terribly high," Rudy acknowledged. "But that's supposedly guarded by ava-lanche traps and quicksand—there's no way across."

"It's just as well you think that. Plus, I don't think any human could find the way through. There's another pass far to the south, called the Darkenheight—that's guarded the same way, except that beyond it lie the tar flats of Duloth-Trol. But aren't we getting a little bit ahead of our immediate problem? Or do you think I'm some kind of minion spy?"

"No—of course not."

"So now we need a plan. How to get rid of these kroaks so that we can get out of here—whichever way we choose to go," he added meaningfully.

"How can the two of us defeat five?" Rudy asked. "Of course, there's Kalland—he's a match for one."

"I'd guess," Danri said, eyeing the huge snow lion critically. Kal-land raised his eyebrows to return the look, though his head remained cradled comfortably on his forepaws. When Rudy spoke, the animal turned to look at the Iceman.

"The gorge is narrow, and shadowed. Plus the waterfall makes enough noise to conceal our approach. How about if we wait until night—then, at least, some of them might be asleep, and we can sneak up on the rest without being seen."

"Minions don't sleep, any more than they eat," Danri said. "But goin' out there in the dark might be a good idea anyway. Specially with the Aura flowing through the gorge—that'll give us some chance to see."

"But it doesn't help them!" Rudy agreed, remembering the blindness of the three kroaks whose torch had been extinguished.

"I can help, too!" Kianna declared. "They *certainly* won't see me sneak up behind them!"

"Good," Danri declared. "We'll go after sunset."

Rudy picked up the heavy sword, swinging it awkwardly.

"Here," Danri said, not unsympathetically. "Let me show you a thing or two about how to hold that."

— 3 —

The bonfire blazed high, flames crackling far over the heads of the blunt-faced kroaks. They must have uprooted entire trees, Rudy thought, in order to build such a huge fire. The four brutish warriors gathered in a ring, sitting well back from the blistering heat; at one side of the mountainous pile of coals, hulking low in his dark-colored robe, squatted the Hisser.

"Good—they're as stupid as we could hope," Danri whispered, crouching back in the shadows of the gorge floor. When Rudy raised his eyebrows in a mute question, the digger explained. "They can't see too well in the dark to begin with—and by staring into that fire, they destroy whatever night vision they have."

The Iceman and the digger carefully advanced along the slick, rocky ground. The walls of the gorge rose steeply to either side; they had already checked for a way out, but the only path required them to go past the minions and their raging bonfire.

Rudy held the sword he'd claimed from the dead kroak. Thanks to Danri's quick instructions, he kept the blade low, ready to flick toward the right or left at an instant's notice. He could use both hands to add extra force to a blow, and quickly reverse the single sharp edge if he needed to parry an attack from above. Still, he felt nothing like a warrior, and the thought that, outnumbered, he now moved forward to make an audacious attack against a brutal foe caused him considerable agitation.

Kalland padded silently behind them, his great tail lashing back and forth in the shadows. Above the snow lion hovered Kianna, awkwardly carrying Rudy's knife in both of her hands. She would remain visible for as long as possible, though she had already shown them that, as long as she held it, the knife disappeared when she did.

Though the flow of Aura from the cave was considerably diluted by the time it trickled out here and mingled with the flow from the waterfall, the enchanted liquid still cast the base of the gorge in a pale luminescence. Overhead, a myriad of stars twinkled in the heavens, but they were too remote to shed meaningful light and there was no hint of a moon.

Silently Danri gestured to the right, indicating the side of the gorge Rudy should follow. Hefting his hammer with ease, as if he approached a stubborn piece of rock that stood in his way, the digger crept forward. The Iceman feared that the pounding of his heart would give them away, but raucous laughter from the kroaks assured him that they felt secure from any threat.

Gesturing to Kianna, Danri clapped a hand over his eyes. She nodded, and blinked out of sight. According to the plan, she would fly well above the encamped kroaks and prepare to attack them from behind. Counting off two dozen beats, Danri nodded to Rudy and leaped out from the shadows. In deadly silence he rushed toward the chortling minions.

Rudy dashed behind him, quickly overtaking the digger. With a low growl, Kalland flew past, charging in a series of leaps that flowed smoothly into a lightning rush.

A shout of alarm rose from the far side of the fire, as one of the dull-witted brutes saw movement in the shadows. Kalland, an apparition of snarling jaws and sharp, slashing talons, exploded from the night to bear a screaming kroak to earth. Another kroak rose up before Rudy; already the shock of the attack had passed, and the monster snatched up a sword identical to the Iceman's.

Sliding to a halt, the Iceman struck at the kroak's neck—but his wild blow was deflected by the deft parry of the monster. The beast crouched and Rudy instinctively leaped back, saving himself from a swing that whooshed past his chest. He retreated again, and the kroak blinked, staring savagely into the shadows beyond the fire.

A howling kroak leaped toward Kalland, upraised blade held in both hands, aiming a blow at the snow lion's unprotected neck. Short legs churning madly, Danri rushed into the fray, crushing the monster's knee with his hammer. As the kroak tumbled, shrieking, the digger struck a blow against the sloping forehead. The monster was dead as it struck the ground.

Rudy hacked against a rain of blows as his intended victim took the offensive. The kroak rushed forward, forcing the Iceman along the rough, slick floor of the gorge. Stumbling, Rudy dropped to one knee; only a desperate two-handed parry, the blade held over his head, saved him from a blow that would have split his skull down the middle.

The kroak pressed its advantage, raising the wicked sword for another blow. Desperately Rudy kicked, but his other foot slipped on the wet rocks and he tumbled to his back. Only when he heard it clanging across the stones did he realize that he had dropped his sword.

Nearby, Danri drove the stalker and a kroak back from the fire, but the pair of minions held the digger's full attention. Kalland grappled with another of the beasts, brute and snow lion rolling back and forth between the gorge wall and the pile of blazing logs. The snarls and growls arising from the melee sent chills along Rudy's spine, as much because he couldn't tell them apart as from their inherent ferocity. He knew he would get no succor from that quarter.

The looming kroak seemed to sense his despair, for the beast hesitated a moment, the light of cruelty flaring in its tiny bloodshot eyes. It slowed the course of the jagged blade, dipping it casually to torment the helpless human—

—Until a howl of agony burst from the monster's lips. When the kroak spun in panic, Rudy saw the hilt of a knife jutting from its burly shoulder, and recognized it as the weapon he had given to the twissel. In another instant Kianna popped into sight, flung by the force of the kroak's turn, smashing her back against the gorge wall. She shrieked in pain as her wings crumpled; then, without another sound, the twissel dropped limply to the ground.

The cruel injury inflamed Rudy. With a bestial snarl of his own, he snatched up the blade he had dropped, chopping savagely into the back of the kroak's leg. The monster spun as it stumbled heavily; this time it was the minion flailing desperately to parry an attack.

Rudy feinted with a sideways slash, watching his enemy's blade block frantically. As soon as the kroak committed, the Iceman halted his swing, cocked his arms back, and then drove the sword in higher. The edge caught just below the creature's chin, hacking through gristly flesh. With a gurgling moan the monster collapsed, dropping its blade and clasping both hands to the crooked gash in its throat.

Black, oily blood bubbled between its fingers, and Rudy stared in horrified fascination as the piglike eyes slowly glazed over. Abruptly the kroak toppled onto its face and lay still.

Beyond the corpse, Kalland howled sharply, and Rudy saw the kroak on the ground pushing the snow lion back toward the crackling fire. Leaping over the body, the Iceman raised his blade and chopped against the monster's wrist, drawing a bark of pain and causing the kroak to squirm backward, releasing Kalland as it struggled to rise. The bulging belly was smeared with black blood—the snow lion's talons and fangs had already inflicted serious damage.

The brute clawed for the sword that it had been unable to draw while wrestling Kalland, but now a kind of battle haze had settled into Rudy's mind. He leaped and stabbed at the same time, driving the tip of his blade against the kroak's belly with all his strength. The steel edge cut into that deceptively tough membrane, hurting the monster but not sinking deep enough for serious injury. Still, the kroak stumbled back, and before it fully drew its sword Rudy chopped again, a hard blow that rendered the monster's left arm useless.

A howl of pain from behind told Rudy that Danri had scored a solid blow, but he didn't dare turn and look. Instead, he pressed against his wounded target, while the kroak bashed wildly with the heavy sword. The beast had no difficulty wielding the weapon with one hand, but it was distracted by Kalland—who rose from the ground and now crept forward, hackles raised, at Rudy's side.

Desperately the kroak swung, driving Rudy back a step. Kalland ducked from the hissing blade, and the monster apparently decided this was the best chance it was likely to get. Throwing down the sword, it spun and pounded along the gorge floor, racing away from the battle.

"Get him!" Rudy called, though Kalland had already sprung. The snow lion leaped twenty feet to land on the fleeing kroak's back. With a hideous shriek the monster went down, and this time those fanged jaws closed about the hardened skin at the nape of the creature's neck.

Rudy turned away as the screams rose to a hideous level, drawn out for a long time before a loud *snap!* brought the shrieks to an instant, fatal halt. Kalland shook the heavy corpse for good measure, though the powerful snow lion could only raise the head and some of the torso off the ground.

With a loud cry, inarticulate but unmistakably triumphant, Danri whirled against the last of the minions—the grotesquely hissing stalker. The reptilian form crouched, pinned against the wall, flailing with a slender, long-bladed sword. The creature dodged and swerved like a dancer, its skin rippling through shades ranging from scarlet to green. The slitted eyes that had so unsettled Anjell now flashed with panic— when they fastened for a moment on Rudy, the Iceman shuddered under their seductive, swirling gleam. Stumbling in confusion, Rudy didn't even feel his sword drop from his nerveless fingers.

The monster turned toward the digger, fastening that hypnotic glare on Danri's face. The Faerine warrior hesitated, shaking his head. With a sigh of apparent exhaustion, the digger slouched in place, swinging the hammer loosely toward the ground. He staggered, tearing his eyes away with visible effort.

Then with a blink and a curse, Danri raised his weapon and attacked. The Hisser tried to block the blunt head of the digger's hammer, but the nimble Faerine swiftly reversed the weapon, driving the pointed pick through the stalker's temple, piercing the hateful brain. Soundlessly the monster collapsed, leaving the gorge in a silence so sudden, so complete, that Rudy staggered dizzily.

Only then did he hear Anjell.

"That's all right—you'll be okay," she said soothingly, holding Kianna's trembling body around the shoulders. "That was *real* brave, the way you stuck that kroak. You saved Uncle Rudy's life."

"What are you doing here?" the Iceman demanded, appalled to

see Anjell among the litter of corpses and blood. "I told you to—"

"I know what you told me," she replied tartly. "But I got scared back there, all by myself! What if one of them had come back that way? I figured it was safer out here with all—"

"You *figured*?" Rudy sputtered. "You disobeyed me! You're just luck—"

"Here now, 'Uncle Rudy,' " Danri said—with a definite twinkle in his eye. "Why don't we leave the lass alone for now—she's not done any harm that I can see. Matter of fact, kind of looks like the twissel could use a bit of comfortin'."

Sheepishly, Rudy nodded, realizing that in his explosion at Anjell he had begun to tremble all over. "I guess it's the fight—it's got me taut as a rope with a two-ton load."

"Just think how you'd feel if we'd lost," the digger replied, and this time there was no humor in his tone. With a shudder, Rudy realized how close they had come to defeat.

"Thanks, Kianna," he said quietly. "Anjell's right—you saved my life."

Sniffling, she looked up at him, and he was stunned by the pain in her eyes. "I've never hit anyone before," she said with a tremor. "I don't like it!"

"Come on—kind of a grim place to stand around and talk," Danri said. "Let's get out of this gorge and have a look around. We'd best get goin' before the buddies of these fellas come along to relieve 'em."

"There's a place leading up the wall not too far away," Rudy said. He quickly led them to the staggered series of steplike rocks. The Iceman scrambled up first, then stepped carefully through the woods, finding only bushes and trees. "It's clear—come on up," he whispered hoarsely.

Anjell came next, helping the battered Kianna. Rudy reached down and gave them both a lift up to ground level. In a few seconds Danri had clambered up behind them. They stood still in the darkened forest, allowing their eyes to adjust to the lack of Auralight.

"You know—the stars are the same as in Faerine," Danri observed quietly, looking upward.

"Does that mean you admit that you're in Dalethica?" Rudy asked.

"I guess I've been prepared for that ever since I saw the kroaks. *Something* is terribly wrong with the Waterhshed—it seems almost like an afterthought that I followed a spring of Aura right out of Faerine."

"You're n-not going to try and *dig* your way back, are you?" Kianna Kyswyllis asked fretfully.

Danri sighed. "Even if I wanted to, I don't think I could. You see, the Madness has passed—it was already fading when we were chased by the Guardian. I think only that threat let me go on as long as I did. I can still dig, but I'd need food, and fresh air, and sleep—just like anyone else underground. Nope, little one, I guess we'll have to get back home the old-fashioned way—by walkin'."

"You mean, over the Taywick Pass?" Rudy asked. "Or is there some secret passage you diggers know about?"

"Taywick's the only place I know," he said. " 'Less you can tell me another one."

Rudy shook his head.

"What's *your* plan?" Danri asked. "How'd you get mixed up with minions anyway?"

"It's a long story." Rudy felt the familiar chill when he remembered Garamis—again hatred surged, and he vowed grimly that he would see the prince's dead body at his feet. He touched the writ of the Palefee, tucked in his belt, determined to secure his family's future even as he obtained revenge.

But there was still the problem of Anjell. He wouldn't consider the idea of taking her all the way to Galtigor with him, yet what kind of danger might he bring to Neshara if he were to return there?

"We're on the slope of the Wilderhof here," Rudy said. "If we can make our way through the hills, moving north, we'll come to the Glimmersee. I know that there's at least one ferry stop somewhere below. We can go that far together." Perhaps he could meet someone he knew there, someone he could trust to get Anjell safely back to her home. This hope was desperate, at best; but how else could he insure that he himself didn't return home to bring menace on the village?

"Very well," said Danri. "It's the four of us, and the big lion—or is it a blunt-nosed wolf?"

"A little of both," Rudy explained. "But, yes, Kalland is coming along."

"Tell me, then—which way to the Glimmersee?"

ELEVEN
Lords of Galtigor

Those rare specimens, human and Faerine, who swear
fealty to the Sleepstealer must do so with absolute
obedience. Love, guilt, thirst, hunger—even
conscience itself—shall be subsumed in the name of
devotion to Dassadec.
—TOME OF VILE COMPULSIONS

— 1 —

Nicodareus once again stood on the dais, centered in the great throne
room of Agath-Trol, where he communed with his master. Unlike the
previous occasion, he did so alone.

Reaper, he knew, was far in the west. The great wyrm had gathered tens of thousands of minions to his banner, the teeming horde
massed along the Dry Basin, ready for an advance into Dalethica
through that deep and forlorn desert. On the slopes below Darkenheight Pass, Phalthak was in the process of assembling an equivalent
force. This army, too, would be ready to march upon the Sleepstealer's
command.

You, my Eye—you have the most delicate task. Dassadec's words
reached Nicodareus as the Lord Minion sat on the throne atop the
towering obsidian pillar.

*Two factors led to my defeat—my temporary defeat—in the Four
Century War. One of these was the stubborn defense of Halverica. This*

tactic we have already negated, by the breach excavated beneath the Crown of the World.

"True, Great Lord," Nicodareus agreed humbly. "The tunnel will lead our troops straight into the center of the enemy's rear. This time there will be no last stand at the Glimmersee." The Lord Minion shrugged, remembering even after ten centuries that horrible expanse of water, lurking like an ominous presence off the dark army's flank.

The second, continued Dassadec, *was the entry of the Faerines— allied with the humans. The combined force in the end proved more than even my Lord Minions could match.*

"Though I pledge we tried," Nicodareus said. He looked uneasily at the two splintered pillars flanking the trio of thrones for the living lords. Before the Four Century War, the Lord Minions had numbered five.

I know this—else you would not have survived since, Dassadec intoned bluntly. *But that is enough of history—now listen while I tell you how we shall remove the threat of Faerine. . . .*

— 2 —

Five days later Nicodareus paced at the prow of the *Dreadcloud,* tense and ready. Plunging through stormy overcast, the great sky-ship cruised almost within spitting distance of the high crest of the Watershed—though that mountainous barrier remained screened from normal vision by scudding tarclouds. The Eye of Dassadec, however, suffered not at all from this flimsy obfuscation—from this vantage Nicodareus found that his Sight could reach, unimpeded, into much of Dalethica.

Abruptly he stiffened, as he saw several stone-skinned figures standing atop the ridge, studying the *Dreadcloud* through the misty sky. Guardians! Even across the vast distance Nicodareus felt a quiver of discomfort, and he stalked behind one of the towering batteries until the watching creatures had been left safely behind.

A harsh cry shrilled through the ragged clouds, as Slasher wheeled on a high current, downwind of the great battlecloud. Nicodareus felt a twinge of regret mingling with his unease—once again, he would be forced to leave the mighty terrion behind. While Nicodareus could disguise himself, the soaring minion could not—Slasher would be an unnecessary encumbrance as the Eye undertook the second journey allowed by the Power of Three. This time he would fly in the body of a condor, soaring over wild lands as he made his way toward the destination commanded by the Sleepstealer.

Again he carried a gift for the human prince—a precious treasure, from the very deepest vaults of Dassadec. The bundle was already wrapped at his waist; now, having passed the Guardians, the Lord Minion was ready to depart.

Captain Direfang cleared his throat, softly, behind the Lord Minion's shoulder, and Nicodareus turned his head slightly toward the brutox.

"The lower ridges, your lordship. They lie several miles off the starboard bow. There's quite a wide gap there—no need to hurry, of course."

The Lord Minion nodded. The captain of the *Dreadcloud* had brought him to a low section of the mountains of the Watershed, to spare Nicodareus the discomfort and cold of a lofty flight. Perhaps the brutox even knew of the Lord Minion's aversion to the Guardians; if so, Direfang was shrewd enough not to mention it.

"There is a hurry, after all," replied the Eye of Dassadec. "It's time I was going."

His wings sprouted feathers even as he leaned forward and tumbled from the parapet of the cloud's forward battery. In another second he rode the currents of mountain wind.

— 3 —

Prince Garamis stood atop the wooden spire, the crest of the highest tower in his father's sprawling palace. Below him spread the vast, bustling metropolis of Landrun. People thronged the streets, all of them staring upward, cheering and exhorting—calling to *him*.

Abruptly, Takian and Boric stood beside Garamis. The round face of the youngest brother gaped guilelessly from Garamis to Takian, as if he waited for some kind of announcement. Takian sneered at them both, and Garamis felt a certain menace in that uncharacteristic expression.

The tenor of the crowd changed, the cries growing deeper. The anger of the populace, sensed the eldest brother, was directed at Takian—after all, it had been his appearance that brought about the vocal displeasure. In the clarity of that realization, Garamis knew what to do.

Suddenly Takian was falling, tumbling soundlessly through the air, his face locked in an expression of sheer horror—an expression Garamis found compelling, even erotic. He continued to watch, thinking that his brother was taking a very long time to reach the ground.

Ten thousand voices rose from the streets, once again swelling into a chorus of triumphant praise. The noise rang through the air, and still Takian fell, still his face twisted into that terribly exciting look of terror.

Boric laughed and clapped his hands, and Garamis felt a warm glow of pleasure—it was good to make Boric happy. But why didn't Takian hit the ground? It seemed as if he was taking far too long to fall.

"Die!" Garamis shouted, his voice roaring from the tower, drowning out the sounds of the multitude. He stared wildly, leaning far out from the parapet, compelling his brother with all the power of his mind, demanding that Takian's body smash into the ground and shatter into lifeless flesh.

Takian looked upward from his tumbling position in the air. Though he was far away, Garamis could see his face clearly—his brother was frightened and confused, but not angry. Why wasn't he enraged? And why did it take him so long to hit the ground?

Finally Takian did just that. The twisted horror on his face exploded outward in a shower of blood and gore. The body struck the hardened dirt of the courtyard and plunged right through the ground, vanishing into the dark depths of the world. As Garamis watched breathlessly, grass sprouted from the sod around the gaping hole where Takian had disappeared. The greenery knit together, forming a dense blanket over the hole, as if it were solid turf.

But Garamis knew that it wasn't. Even as the voices of his people reached a new crescendo, washing around him, lifting him up, buoying him with might, power, and confidence, the prince recognized the menace in that concealed opening.

The place where Takian had disappeared might look like an ordinary patch of sod, yet Garamis recognized it as a trap—a deadly pitfall that would forever remain in the grounds of the palace. No planking could cover it; no amount of fill would rise to the level of the surrounding courtyard. Truly, he could not dispose of his brother so easily—in fact, it was dangerous even to try.

He was seized by an irrational fear: despite the fact that he knew about the pit, would take great pains to avoid it—would not in fact visit this part of the palace again in his life—that pit would continue to menace him. One day, when Garamis was an old man, his brother's death long behind him, he might forget. He could venture into that portion of the royal grounds, and unknowingly step where his brother had died.

When he did, he, Garamis, would perish in the same place, in the same terrible pit where his brother lay waiting, watching . . . laughing.

Yet still, behind Garamis, Boric clapped his hands. He chuckled and laughed and smiled.

It was nice to make Boric happy.

— 4 —

Garamis sat up in the broad bed, chill sweat making his face and hands clammy. A *dream!* But no—Takian was *dead!* Garamis had watched him die, had seen him vanish into the ground, disappearing forever!

As he shook his head, clearing the cobwebs of sleep away, the prince realized that his brother's death had in fact been a dream—but a dream that was terribly vivid, starkly terrifying in its realistic detail.

Only once before had Garamis had a dream like that. Then the images of sleep had lingered with crystal clarity in his mind, and when he thought about the meaning, he recognized it as a summons to meet with Nicodareus. Instinctively the prince had understood where he was supposed to go, and when he was due to arrive. He had performed well, he knew—Nicodareus, and through him Dassadec, had been pleased.

But what was the meaning of this dream? It summoned him to no meeting, so far as he could tell—nor did it make any demands upon him for service.

Or did it?

Again he remembered the terror on Takian's face, the long time it had taken him to hit the ground. Slowly, he began to understand.

Garamis licked his dry lips. He remembered the sweet nectar Nicodareus had drawn from his palm, the dark stuff that had flowed into the prince, pulsing with an energy beyond anything Garamis had ever known. He was desperately thirsty for another taste of that Darkblood; the knowledge that there was none to be had brought bitter tears to his eyes, and cast an evil pall over the upcoming day.

This was a thing that was becoming habitual, he realized. Every morning, upon awakening, Garamis' thoughts turned toward that potent liquid—before he even thought about getting out of bed. When would he have the chance to taste it again? He muttered a silent prayer to Dassadec, to any of his immortal children who might be listening—please, *please* let it be very soon!

Roughly he tried to shake away the craving, succeeding only partially. Still, he found enough strength to rise. Clapping his hands, he summoned his dressing maidens. Two young girls scurried fearfully into his chambers, bringing silken robes, soft moccasins, and a selection of capes and belts. Barely thirteen, the two girls kept their eyes averted, knowing that—sometimes—the lord would use young female servants in ways that did not involve his toilette. They did not understand what fate lay in store for them—he never used any one girl more than once—but they were smart enough to fear it, Garamis thought with a wry chuckle.

For today, at least, the maidens needn't worry about his baser urges. The only lust raging within him craved a thing no human could supply. In irritation he slapped the girls away, throwing clothes haphazardly over his wiry, well-muscled body.

His thoughts returned to the dream. Had he guessed at its meaning, at the implicit command buried there? He felt certain that he had. What remained was for him to act—and before he could act, he needed a plan.

For a brief moment the prince took his immaculate sword down from the wall. Sliding the weapon from its golden scabbard, he admired the pure, ink-black blade. Sliding a finger along the edge, watching his own crimson blood well in the cut, he wondered at the killing power there—and his own immunity. A week earlier he had cut one of his dressing maidens—a tiny slit in her arm, no more. Within minutes she was dying in an agony so excruciating that the prince was forced to leave the room until she expired.

Garamis considered the power of Darkflight, which he had kept secret from even his trusted captains. Now, as on many other occasions, he wanted to use that power, to blink swiftly to the places he wanted to go, even to work violence—such as against Takian—and then swiftly vanish. Yet the risks were too great; as always, he forced the desire aside.

Stalking into the paneled halls of the palace, Garamis tried to think. He realized immediately that the timing of the plan was impor- tant—and perhaps fortunate. Since the emissary from Carillonn was due in several weeks, most of his usual ceremonial duties had been canceled, and the prince's time was his own.

"Hi, Garam!" The delighted voice pulled at him from behind and Garamis slowed.

"Good morning, Boric."

"What a *great* day!" babbled his brother, looking around in won- der at the palace hall—as if he had never seen it before.

"Perhaps it will be," Garamis said quietly, causing Boric to look at him uncomprehendingly. "Have you seen Takian yet?"

"He was going to go hunting," Boric said, his face sagging into a pout. "I asked him to take me, but he said no. He always says no."

"Next time I hunt, *I'll* take you," Garamis offered, clapping Boric on one of his rounded shoulders.

"I'd rather go to the war," Boric suggested, with a shy, hopeful smile. "Could you take me to a battle sometime?"

"You know, Boric, maybe I will," the older prince replied. He remembered his dream: it was nice to make Boric happy.

"Come and eat breakfast now, Garam." The younger brother tugged at his arm, pulling him toward the dining hall.

Roughly Garamis shook his head. The thought of mortal food, mundane drink, sickened him. How could he desire any sustenance other than that exquisite Darkblood?

"How come you never eat with us anymore?"

"I'm just not hungry. But you go—you know, I think the cooks were doing some syrup rolls this morning."

Beaming, the younger prince wandered off to look for some sweet bread. Garamis left the palace proper and started across the courtyard to exercise Cyric. His mind returned to Takian.

"Hsst! My lord Garamis!" The voice, whispered from the shadows beside the stable, drew the prince's attention to a huddled figure, cloaked in rags. The beggar squatted against the wall, scabrous skin showing at his wrists and ankles. Though he held his face down, Garamis saw that his mouth was masked by a matted brown beard.

"How dare you address me!" snapped the prince, shocked at the man's impudence. He drew back a foot for a sharp kick, when the beggar lifted his face—and Garamis saw his eyes.

"My—my lord!" gasped the nobleman, staggering at the sight of those flaming emberlike orbs. The prince's rudeness came back to him in a flash, and he wondered weakly if he was about to die. "I—I had no idea!" he managed to stammer, starting to drop to one knee.

"Stand, fool!" Nicodareus commanded, and Garamis—jerking like a marionette—halted his gesture of obeisance. "I will follow you into the stables," the Lord Minion hissed.

Guiltily the prince looked around, relieved to see that none of the stableworkers were near. Trying to assume his normal posture of arrogance, he swaggered through the open doors and marched toward Cyric's stall. The black war horse snorted a greeting while Garamis looked through the nearby stalls, insuring that no one else was present.

He turned back to the door, only to see that Nicodareus—still in the guise of a beggar—had crept up behind him. Garamis froze, terrified for his life and at the same time exalted by his master's presence. In his mind he licked that drop of Darkblood from the Lord Minion's palm, remembered the ecstasy, the explosive pleasure of that first taste.

"I bear a command—from the Sleepstealer," Nicodareus declared. His voice carried its full, rumbling weight—though it emerged incongruously from this frail and wasted body. "For fifty years your people have played with war—now it is time to commence that conflict in earnest."

Garamis thrilled to a sense of relief and exhilaration—here was a command he knew how to obey. "Name my enemy, lord—not a single realm of Dalethica can stand against the might of my sword!"

"Splendid—but your enemy is not man. Dassadec commands that you take the masses of your army, and wage war against Faerine."

"Faerine?" Garamis gaped stupidly, then felt the lash of a sharp claw across his face. He cursed himself for his ignorance. "It shall be as you command, master. But how does my army cross the Watershed? The only low place in the mountains is Taywick Pass—and doom awaits any man who goes there!"

"You are mistaken. The Wards of Taywick seem deadly, but they are illusions only. An army that is not fooled by those illusory effects will be able to fall on the accursed Faerines by surprise, routing the tribes one after the other."

"And how can these illusions be defeated?"

"You have obtained the means yourself—the Ice of Three Waters, claimed from the Glimmercrown, will negate the Taywick illusions. You need only carry the block in the midst of your army, and your men shall see the ground as it really is, not as the treacherous Faerines have disguised it. The magical illusions and enchanted traps will disappear before its scouring light."

Garamis' heart pounded at the thought of the victory that could be won. "Give me the command—I will start the march tomorrow!"

"Your enthusiasm is commendable," the Lord Minion noted dryly. "But Dassadec does not work haphazardly. There must be a plan, a scheme that will enable the peoples of Dalethica to recognize the threat posed by the Faerines."

"Yes, of course—a plan!" exclaimed Garamis, though he had no idea what such a plan might be.

"You have men—warriors—you can trust?"

"An army, lord—thousands of men who wear the Black Mantle! And my Redsteel Guards, my elites, each of whom has sworn his life to my service."

"Let the Guards be the ones," the Lord Minion decided. "When I have departed, you will look under the straw at the back of Cyric's stall. There you will find six arrows—*sylvan* arrows."

Awestruck, the prince could only nod. The feathered shafts and steel arrowheads made by the sylves were the deadliest missiles in all the Watershed, reputedly accurate at ranges approaching a mile. They were clearly identified by the curved grooves spiraling along the silver shafts.

"These arrows must be used in a fashion that will cause public outrage to rise, directed—naturally—against the sylves. Human nature being what it is, this fury will easily spread to hatred directed at *all* Faerines."

"My warriors are to take these arrows, make the attack?" Garamis deduced. "But where will they find a proper target?" A glimmering hope was born in his mind—Takian! Surely an assassination, blamed upon the sylves of Faerine, would inflame all the folk of Dalethica. Yet once again Nicodareus had his own plan.

"Conveniently, your victim is even now on her way to Landrun. You will find it quite a pity that she will never make it. . . . "

"The Duchess of Shalloth!" gasped Garamis, astonished—and titillated—by the bold nature of the plan.

"You are quick to grasp the potential, but heed me well: you will attack from ambush. You cannot be discovered. Leave the arrows in the victims, and blame will fall where it should."

"I'll meet with the captain of my riders immediately," the prince announced. "The lady shall not live to set foot in Landrun!"

— 5 —

Garamis rode Cyric down to the drill fields below the city wall. Hundreds of men, all wearing the uniform of the Black Mantles, marched to and fro, blocks of bristling pikes or precise ranks of steady swordsmen. The prince reined in on a low rise, observing with pleasure the training of his personal regiments.

A line of heavy infantry formed beside the pikemen, and even from the distance the prince could hear the taunts exchanged between the troops of the two formations. Abruptly men broke ranks from each unit, clashing with fists, swords, and knives in a violent melee. Officers waded in and, using the flats of their swords, beat the troops apart—but not before several men crumpled to the ground. Several of these writhed and screamed; others lay still on the trampled grass.

By the time they were finished, Captain Wilfriz had noticed the prince. The burly commander rode over to his lord, shaking his head in disgust.

"Two men killed—a dozen wounded," he groused. "These are *warriors*, my prince! It's waste to keep them in training."

"Two lives . . . a small price to pay for maintaining the readiness of my best men. And trust me, Wilfriz, they will not be wasted."

"Where's the campaign? Orders went out yesterday, to bring the rest of the Black Mantles into Landrun. We need to be marching these men back to the battlefield, not crowding them into barracks."

"Patience, my good captain—only for a little longer. It so happens that I have a plan." Garamis proceeded, quietly, to discuss the proposed ambush, as well as the intent of the upcoming offensive.

"But Faerine?" questioned Wilfriz.

"Aye—a *new* enemy, with treasures beyond belief awaiting the victorious invader! You have only to obey, and you will be rich beyond your dreams!"

Wilfriz listened earnestly to the prince's commands. His initial reservations were overcome by the knowledge that Garamis himself would accompany the mission.

"I have spies in the North Shore Wayfarer's Lodge," the prince added. "They will let me know about the duchess's schedule. I've heard that she's already taken to the road—we should get word shortly of her whereabouts."

"How will we strike her down so that we're not identified?" asked the captain.

Garamis withdrew the bundle of precious missiles. "You've heard of the arrows made by the sylves of Faerine—I have six of them. We will leave them in the victims; when they are found, the weapons themselves will identify the offending parties."

The captain's eyes widened as his fingers stroked the long shafts, made of a silver too pure for any Dalethica alloy. The spiraling grooves might have been scored with a needle, so narrow were they, while the heads were wickedly sharp razors of hard steel. White feathers, tiny and narrow, were fletched on the missiles' tails. Certainly Wilfriz wondered how his master had come by such rare and potent weapons; with equal certainty, he knew better than to ask.

"Summon the Redsteel Guards to stand by their horses," the prince commanded. "Await me in the stables—when I give the command, I'll want to ride within a few minutes."

"Aye, lordship. You desire all of the riders for this task?"

"Half should be sufficient. Leave two dozen of the Redsteels behind to supervise the training of the line companies."

Wilfriz went to marshal his men, while Garamis decided that the time had come to speak to Takian. He found his brother in the palace gardens, on a high knoll overlooking the river and the sprawling city below.

A thought flitted through Garamis' mind—a quick stab, a push off the bluff, and how many of his problems would be solved? He forced the thought aside, knowing people had seen him enter the garden. He must have the discipline to stick to his plan.

"Greetings, my brother," Garamis offered, coming up behind Takian, who seemed to be lost in thought.

"Oh, hello, Garam. You know, I was thinking about the people of the west," Takian remarked, with a shake of his head. "Do you know that in Myntar Kosh the women are not allowed to eat in the same room with the men? They have a whole array of strange customs, and not a single foodstuff that is fit for the human palate!"

Takian, of the golden hair and the fair skin, smiled at his brother, and Garamis wondered if the other man's eyes concealed the same kind of bitter hatred and resentment that he himself felt. If so, the elder prince hoped that he could do as effective a job of masking his feelings as did Takian.

"I've always thought it was more important to learn about places closer to home."

"Oh, it is. But even Carillonn is such a crossroads, I met people from places I'd never even *heard* of! Did you know that there's a *Southern* Zanthilat? They've got animals there—big, shaggy things—that can cross the desert for two or three weeks without a drink of water! And forests with birds so colorful they'd blind you—I know, I saw some of the feathers!"

"Interesting," replied Garamis absently. "I must visit Carillonn myself, sometime. Shalloth in particular, I think. Tell me, Tak—did you see the Castle of Shalloth?"

The younger prince flushed. "Yes—yes, I did."

Garamis smiled knowingly. "The duchess, incidentally, must have begun her journey by now, has she not?"

"Yes, but it will take her a while. She's taking the highland route, to avoid the battlegrounds. A wise precaution, I thought, even with the truce. She'll cross the River Ariak, near Glimmersee, in a fortnight or so."

"Sooner—I have heard from a, er, merchant, that she will reach the North Shore Wayfarer's Lodge within the next few days. Even if she stays there for a while, she should be here soon."

"I warn you, Garamis," Takian announced with a good-natured chuckle. "This woman is the most beautiful creature I have ever seen! I intend to give this suit every bit of my attention. Don't think that because you're the elder the duchess will automatically swoon for you."

"Yes . . ." Garamis had no care for the woman's appearance or desirability—she merely represented an important tool in his master's design. It amused him that his brother spoke as if he expected to find in her womanhood the key to his life's meaning!

But Takian was laughing. *Does he mock me?* The question flared like a white flame in Garamis' mind, and even when he realized that there was only nonmalicious humor in his brother's laugh, his rage continued to burn.

"When she reaches the city, we shall have to commence our duel in earnest," Takian declared, still chuckling.

But his brother wasn't listening. Instead, Garamis' mind wandered its own trails, developing an idea that began to grow into a full-fledged plan. *Yes*—he was beginning to see the solution to all his problems. He chose his next words very carefully.

"Perhaps our encounters with the duchess shall wait until she reaches the palace—though who's to say that my first meeting with her must occur within the walls of Landrun? I take the hunting trail tomorrow in search of a trophy stag." Garamis flashed his brother a sly look. "Though if I should meet the duchess and her entourage, it would only be proper for me to introduce myself."

Garamis smiled tightly as he saw Takian consider his words. The younger prince scowled at him, as if he thought he could penetrate the veil of his mind. "Steal an unfair advantage, would you?" Takian accused, some of the good nature fading from his voice.

"What's unfair? Surely we both have an equal chance—we both can ride the forests of Galtigor where we please. If I am fortunate enough to steal a kiss before she sees you again, that would be your poor fortune."

"Indeed," Takian replied thoughtfully, after a long silence. "Perhaps I, myself, shall give some thought to a hunt."

Garamis' smile grew broad as he watched Takian leave the garden and start for the palace. A little later, in the courtyard, he learned that Takian had announced his intention to ride from the city; he was expected to be gone for several weeks.

The prince knew that it was time to put the rest of his plan into motion. He went to look for Wilfriz, caressing the sleek outlines of the sylvan arrows beneath his cloak.

— 6 —

As my years in Shalloth passed, I learned to bite my tongue in the face of Paderon Zyloth's bigotry. My devotions to Aurianth were silent, private rituals, performed in the dark of my own chambers, while the rest of the great castle slumbered around me.

I was an effective servant for my lady, probably because of the patience I had learned under Pheathersqÿll. The rules of courtly behavior were easy to learn—at least, I never made the same mistake twice—and I adopted the comfortable mask of following them with apparent willingness.

Yet during all this time, my sense of loss never lightened. The first prophecy of my life snatched me from my dreams; the second carried me from Pheathersqyll. I began to dread the third and final foretelling, though I had no idea from what quarter it would come.

Indeed, though the first and second auguries had been given to me by my teacher, I could not conceive of the third originating from that source—now that Paderon Zyloth was entrusted with my education. Not a week went by that he didn't discount the very notion of a god-given prophecy as arcane mysticism.

At the same time, I sensed that he held real affection for me. And nothing in my life surprised me as much as the discovery that his fondness for me was, increasingly, returned.

From: *Recollections,* by Lady Raine of the Three Waters

TWELVE

Glimmersee

One must be alert, ready and willing at all times to act,
and act decisively, in the defense of order—for chaos
needs only the tiniest toehold to set in motion the
ultimate collapse.
—SCROLL OF BARACAN

— 1 —

Rudy whistled in amazement as the companions came around the pine-frosted ridge to find the full expanse of the Glimmersee sparkling before them. Framed by sun-speckled sky and snow-crested summits, the azure waters beckoned with a color so rich, so vibrant, that it rendered everything else a muted gray.

The snow lion pricked up his ears, purring at the Iceman's birdlike notes. Kalland nudged the broad wedge of his head against Rudy, who could only laugh and scratch the tufts of the shaggy mane.

"I've seen the 'See before," he admitted. "But never like this."

"Isn't it *beautiful*," Kianna sang, her voice full of the musical lilt it had acquired in the last few days—as soon as they had been out of danger, surrounded by the comfortable wilds. "I've never even imagined anything like this before! Oh, let's go down to it! Can we swim?"

Anjell looked at the fairy with an arched eyebrow. "Only if you don't mind blue toes," she said in clear, if halting, Faerine.

"That's a big lot of water," Danri admitted, frankly awed. "There's nothing like it in Faerine."

Four days in the Wilderhof had carried them through myriad pastoral beauties, but the huge lake had been concealed by encircling ridges until now. Barely two miles away—and two thousand feet below—it sparkled like an expanse of precious stones. The shadow of a lone cloud scudded across the surface, heightening the contrast of the pristine water and sky.

"I guess I was right about our path," Rudy suggested immodestly, pointing to a large building and several smaller structures clustered on the nearby lakeshore. "There's the ferry station. We'll be able to get passage there."

He paused, the unspoken dilemma surging to the forefront of his mind. Garamis! The Iceman's most important goal was to force the murderous prince to pay for the wrongs done to House Appenfell—a debt that must be satisfied in gold, and then in blood. He carried the writ of the Palefee; details of the confrontation he would work out later, when he had learned more about his enemy.

Indeed, the entire realm of Galtigor was to a great extent a vast unknown to Rudy. Yet Garamis certainly couldn't know that the Iceman was still alive, and consequently Rudy should be able to spend some time making a plan. His confidence never wavered, at least as far as he himself was concerned.

But there was Anjell. . . .

Kalland pounced after a rabbit that darted back and forth through the flowered meadow, and the companions took the occasion to flop onto soft grass and admire the view. The snow lion, licking traces of rabbit fur from his whiskers, trotted over and sprawled lazily beside them.

Anjell, who had remained quiet for most of the day, scratched the big animal's belly and refused to meet Rudy's eyes. Though she and the twissel had spent much of the previous days chattering away in an ongoing language lesson, today the girl had restricted her remarks to a few wry observations. The Iceman understood why—she was worried about the decision her uncle would be forced to make in the next few hours.

"It's pretty, isn't it, Anj?" Rudy asked gently.

His niece was silent for several seconds. Finally she turned to him with a frown. "Are you going to send me home?"

Rudy sighed, knowing there was only one real option. "I'm *taking* you home," he said. "I'm not going on to Galtigor until you're safe under your mother's roof."

The girl's eyes welled with tears. "But you *can't*! It's all my fault you have to turn around and go back—and it's not fair! Keep going to Galtigor—but let me come with you!"

"I can't, Anj," he said quietly. "It's just too dangerous." Over the last few days, this fact had become glaringly clear to the Iceman. His simmering fury kept his own determination strong, but he couldn't subject his young niece to that kind of threat.

"There's danger in Halverica too," the girl declared, apparently reading his thoughts.

"In Dermaat, yes—but not Neshara."

"We don't really know that, do we?" she pressed mercilessly.

"Stop it! Would you wish disaster on your own house?" Rudy snapped.

"Of course not—but what I said is true. There could be minions all over the place, looking for you! What if they find out that I was with you all this time? Then they'll want to find me, won't they?"

"That's not going to happen! And you can't come with me—you might get hurt, or worse! I can't have you in the way—"

"Rudgar Appenfell!" Anjell declared, sitting upright and planting her tiny fists on her hips. "I can *help!* And I won't get in the way—I promise!"

"I know you'd try, Anj—but what could you do? There's just—"

"What could I *do?*" She looked at him, appalled at his lack of imagination. "Why, I have ideas! I can think of things! Like, what about disguises?"

The other three regarded Anjell curiously.

"Did you think two Faerines could just march down there and get on a ferry, and nobody would raise an eyebrow?" She confronted her uncle with the question.

"Well, I was figurin' we'd kind of try to avoid people," Danri said.

"You can't," Anjell said bluntly.

"She's right," Rudy admitted. "Even if we didn't take the ferry—and that would mean a fifty-mile walk along the shore—we'd have to pass through towns. No, we'll meet people all right."

"Why, word would spread across Halverica and Galtigor and everywhere else!" the girl declared. "Some people would probably think we're being invaded! Others would say that Danri and Kianna are spies. *I* know that's not true, but still people would say it!"

"But . . . *disguises?*" The digger was skeptical.

"Sure." Anjell took off her shawl and gestured to Kianna. "Here, stand up straight. Now, just wrap this around your shoulders—that doesn't hurt your wings, does it? Now look—she's a human girl!"

"Y'know, she could pass for your sister," Danri admitted with a chuckle. The digger gestured to his own short, bowed legs. "But I daresay mine's a little harder."

"Hmmm." Anjell thought for a moment before reaching into a nearby thicket of small trees and shrubs. Quickly she pulled out a gnarled but reasonably straight stick, breaking it off to leave an open wedge near the top. Placing this wedge under her armpit, the girl leaned on the stick and hopped awkwardly. "Carry this with you. When we meet people, just lean on it and limp a little. Nobody will think twice about it."

"I'm supposed to be a *cripple?*" the digger blustered.

"Sure." Kianna Kyswillis thought that was a great idea. "I'm going to be a human, too! You can be my old grandpa!"

"Hmph!" Danri protested, but not too forcefully. The digger's eyes narrowed as he concluded that the girl's suggestion was a wise one. He turned back to Rudy. "What do you know about this Galtigor place? It's on the way to Taywick Pass, you say?"

"After a fashion—I know the White Range, where Taywick is, forms one of the boundaries. As to how much I know. . . . " Sheepishly the Iceman shrugged his shoulders. "Well, I've heard Galtigor's got the biggest army of any realm in Dalethica. The same family has ruled there for centuries, I think—though there's been some violence between rival heirs and such. For Halvericans, Galtigor is a place that buys our cheese and wine—and, occasionally, sends a young nobleman this way who's looking to climb a mountain. The palace is in Landrun, and that's a long way from here; it may be that your route to the pass won't take you that far into the lowlands."

"We'll see," Danri said, apparently in no hurry to strike off on his own—a fact that continued to cause the Iceman some relief.

"Look—there's the ferry." Rudy pointed to a white, triangular sail a dozen miles or so up the lake. "Let's get down to the shore before it reaches the station."

"Does that mean I'm coming with you?" Anjell demanded.

"Yes," Rudy sighed. "I guess it does."

Anjell squealed and gave the giggling Kianna a hug. Even Kalland purred and stretched, sensing the girl's joy. Tail high, the snow lion trotted behind the companions, down toward the green and grassy shore.

— 2 —

Rudy and his companions stood in the bow of the *Glimmer*, before the tall mast and billowing sail. The sleek cross-lake ferry knifed through waters so powerfully blue that they verged on indigo or purple. A crisp wind from the west pressed the elegant sailboat to starboard, and the ferryman and his crew held steady on a fast course directly toward the North Shore Wayfarer's Lodge.

Before them, still a few miles away, rambling wooden chalets sprawled across the verdant hillside, framed by rising, pine-covered hills beyond. The deep, pristine waters of the Glimmersee provided a sparkling highlight to the immaculate structures, colorful gardens, and manicured lawns of the fabled inn.

With a backward glance, Rudy wondered about the captain, Rolf Ferryman— Did he notice anything terribly odd about a young Iceman traveling with two girls and an elderly cripple? As if sensing Rudy's thoughts, Danri snorted angrily, hoisting his crutch, ready to toss it into the lake. The digger's face remained locked in a glowering stare, daring anyone to speak to him.

Hiding his amused grin, Rudy leaned out from the rail until he could see around the sail. In the stern, grizzled Rolf—who not only captained but owned the sleek vessel—scratched Kalland behind the ears. Upon their arrival at the ferry dock, in fact, the big snow lion had attracted more attention than his companions. Since embarkation, the weathered sailor had continually fed the animal scraps of fish and other tasty morsels; Kalland, no doubt appreciating the man's good taste, had pestered Rolf for treats during the entire twenty-hour voyage.

The other passengers—perhaps two dozen in number—sat inside the deep hull of the *Glimmer*, sheltered from the wind, while Rolf's two crewmen braided rope in the stern.

"Be there pretty soon," Danri declared, indicating the sprawling lakeshore inn. "Can't say I'll be disappointed to set foot onto dry land. Being cooped up with all these humans makes me edgy."

"I don't know that it'll be much better in the lodge," Rudy cautioned. "There'll be even more of us about."

"Aye-uh—but at least we'll have a room, with a door!" A new concern darkened the digger's brow. "We *will* have a room, won't we? And it *will* have a door?"

"Of course," the Iceman assured him, assuming that those basic amenties could be taken for granted in the great lodge at the edge of Halverica. "The North Shore Wayfarer's Lodge is like a small town in itself."

"Why isn't there a town here?" wondered the digger. "It's quite a crossroads, isn't it?"

"I don't know why. This was the scene of a huge battle—the deciding fight of the Sleepstealer War, a thousand years ago. Ever since then, it's been a sort of hallowed place."

"I remember hearing about that fight," Danri said. "A goodly number of diggers and gigants shed their blood there, to stop the army of minions."

"I didn't know that. I thought this was where all humankind finally united to stand firm against evil."

"Well, that's true enough. It don't surprise me that human legend would leave out a few little details 'bout us Faerines."

Rudy felt a twinge of unreasonable guilt—as if he bore the responsibility for mankind's forgetfulness. For a moment, looking at the lodge, he wished they could end their journey here, spend days or weeks on that hillside, among the gardens and halls he saw in such clear detail. As he looked at the blue waters—so clear he could see fish twenty feet under the surface—he felt a strange sense of melancholy. The great lodge by the shore was farther from home than he'd ever been before, and his worries about Neshara, combined with his fear that he might never see his home again, darkened his spirits like a heavy storm cloud.

Neither the pastoral trek through the wilderness nor the smooth sail across the 'See had allowed Rudy to shed the feeling of disquiet and menace that seemed to lurk just behind his shoulder. His mind leapt back and forth between imaginary pursuers, or ambushers, or treacherous lords. At the same time, his secret determination to kill Garamis had burned as hot as ever, waking him early every morning and driving him to coax every ounce of haste out of his companions.

He wondered uneasily about the pollution of Dermaat Creek. After hearing Rudy's description of events, Danri had speculated that the minions of the Sleepstealer would stay in Dermaat for the time being. He told Rudy that the minions needed a nearby source of Darkblood, which the Iceman realized must be the trickle of inky liquid he'd seen at the foot of the Glimmercrown. Though a band of the minions had traveled as far as Neshara, he remembered that they had hastened back to Dermaat and its nourishing fountain.

Furthermore, the digger had suggested that the tiny spring of Aura on the Wilderhof—which eventually spilled into Dermaat Creek—would provide enough of the enchanted liquid to dilute the trace amounts of Darkblood polluting the creek. When mingled with a great amount of water, Danri claimed, Darkblood and Aura could cancel each other's effects, nullifying the violent convulsion that would result if the two potent liquids met without the soothing medium of mundane water.

Unconsciously the Iceman touched his bulging waterskin, thinking of the amazing liquid within. Before departing their cave, both he and Danri had filled their water sacks with pure Aura. Already Rudy had seen the liquid's potent healing power, as his wounds from the Deep Guardian—and Kianna's from the battle with the minions—had immediately vanished after drinking of it. The digger told him that, in Faerine, the fluid of magic had many uses.

As the North Shore Wayfarer's Lodge grew to fill Rudy's vision, Rolf had to make only a slight correction to bring them toward the mouth of the sheltered harbor. That tiny anchorage was encircled by a breakwater of piled boulders, backed by two wings of the lodge that reached out like loose wooden sleeves to embrace the marina and its flotilla of small vessels.

Though the lodge itself seemed as big as a small village, Rudy saw that it was in fact one massive, sprawling building, made of wood and fieldstone. Here and there, flower boxes, vines, and tall, sculpted pines broke up the view to the structure, but as they sailed past, the Iceman saw that behind these screens covered breezeways or low-ceilinged hallways connected the various wings.

In a dozen different places wooden stairways descended from the hilltop of the dock-lined shore of the harbor. Everywhere the wood gleamed, and tulips and geraniums in a riot of colors practically shouted from the gaps between the walkways and steps. Wide plazas offered views overlooking the lake at several elevations on the rolling hillside; at each site there blossomed a multitude of silk and canvas awnings, dyed in colors to rival the gardens.

Several armed men strolled along the dock, and Rudy felt a start of anger as he saw that they wore black—just as Prince Garamis had worn. Could these be that nobleman's warriors? In a flash of excited anticipation he wondered: could Garamis himself still be here?

Of course not—but the thought brought a pounding to the Iceman's heart, and his fingers itched toward the captured kroak sword that was hidden in the bundle of his bedroll. Forcing himself to take several deep breaths, he tried to calm the trembling of his hands. He heard a gentle humming behind him and smiled—for once the music of the twissel was a pleasant distraction.

"Shhh," he reminded Kianna gently. Her music was more beautiful, more melodious than any human could have made, and as such—sadly—it tended to weaken her disguise. The twissel blushed and bit her lip, silent again.

With barely a nudge the *Glimmer* eased gently into her berth at the foot of one of the steep stairways. Shoremen slid a gangplank into place near the stern, and passengers quickly began to debark. Rudy and his companions waited until nearly everyone had left the boat before going back to the tiller. Kalland's tail stood tall as the snow lion stretched and yawned.

Rolf Ferryman raised a friendly hand, and cast Rudy a wink. "You have a care lad, now—I mean it!" he whispered, as the Iceman lingered at the rail.

"I will," Rudy promised, touched.

Anjell, Danri, and Kianna had already gone ashore, and Kalland bounded down the gangplank. With a last "thank you" to the boatman, Rudy picked up his light bundle and followed his companions toward the lodge.

— 3 —

Lady Bristyn Duftrall's hindquarters were as sore as any portion of her anatomy had ever been in all her twenty-five years of life. Though Snowcloud, her gentle mare, had been selected for her easy gait and smooth disposition, and the softest saddle available in all Carillonn cushioned the ride, the Duchess of Shalloth was not used to spending *any* amount of time on horseback. Now, after two weeks, each day of which had involved many miles of sidesaddle riding, she was ready to order the mare butchered and fed to scavenging hounds, while she demanded for herself the respite of a feathered mattress for at least the next three days.

Still, she was a woman of principle and duty, performing a mission commanded by the King of Carillonn himself, so she gritted her teeth and persevered. At the very least, however, she vowed to rest at this accursed lodge until her aching bones had a chance to recover. Frustrated, she pushed strands of golden hair back from her forehead. Her tresses were usually a source of great pride, but now she knew they were little more than a bedraggled tangle, mercifully concealed by her hood.

She tried to avoid the real cause of her brooding, but she could not. Each step of the road, each hour and day of travel, brought her closer to the fate that, throughout her life, she had been determined to avoid. During her "diplomatic" mission, she was to select one of the princes as her husband. The king had not actually commanded her to do so, yet even before receiving the monarch's vague suggestions she understood the stakes: her wedding to Galtigor would stop fifty years of war. For such an achievement she had no choice but to proceed—her duchy and her kingdom would benefit by lives and treasure saved, land preserved from Galtigor's annexation, and the many attendant advantages of peace. All this, she understood, was good and necessary.

But when those gains were measured against Bristyn's happiness, her freedom—her very *life*—they made for scant consolation. "I wield all this power—and I'm *trapped*!" she whispered to herself bitterly, through clenched teeth.

As if he sensed her discomfort, Paderon Zyloth urged his horse into a trot, pulling beside the lady while they approached the open gates of the North Shore Wayfarer's Lodge. The priest's blue robe, symbol of his station, somehow remained clean even after days on the trail. The appointed advisor of Lady Bristyn's late father, the duke, Paderon had proved himself adept at handling the independent and stubborn members of the Duftrall family; he was also the only person courageous enough to approach Bristyn when, as now, she was in one of her moods.

"Nothing like a hot meal—perhaps a warm bath—to take one's mind off the tribulations of the trail, eh what, my dear?" Paderon Zyloth chuckled, a sound that had come to irritate Bristyn mightily in the last fortnight. The priest patted his ample stomach, as if he could already feel the warmth of said meal.

"This is probably one of those places where all they eat is sausage and cheese," she replied sourly. "And I'm sure it'll take me three hours to get a tub filled—and then it will be lukewarm, at best!"

"Now, you can't expect that every realm of Dalethica dines on rare roast beef or rack of lamb at every meal. In Shalloth—as in all Carillonn—we have it pretty good."

Bristyn didn't want to hear how good she had it. She knew that the mines in her duchy produced most of the gold and silver in the kingdom of Carillonn, that Shalloth's forests were the favored hunting grounds of all Carillonn's royalty. Many times had the king himself been a guest of her father in the splendid ducal castle—a structure exceeded in grandeur only by the king's palace in High Carillonn.

Paderon smiled, with that tolerant avuncular expression that made her want to smack him. But of course she could never do that—while she might pout or even scream, physical assault definitely exceeded the boundaries of ladylike behavior.

Still, the elder's round face made a tempting target, with the crinkles of skin extending outward from his beaming smile almost as if they were put there as an aid to someone who wanted to bash him in the mouth. Mopping a pudgy hand through the stringy brown hair that, barely, covered his rounded pate, Paderon chuckled again. "Baracan be praised—at least it was a smooth trail today. And we're almost there!" he added, as if she couldn't see the buildings sprawling across the wide hilltop before them.

"This is the last stop before Galtigor—I should like to stay here awhile," the duchess declared.

Paderon cleared his throat awkwardly. "Perhaps we could remain for two nights instead of one. However, you know the need for success is desperate. . . . "

"Yes—I know! But how can I make haste? I'm certain the other brother of House Larriac is just as pompous, every bit as arrogant, as Prince Takian!"

"You—you seemed to like young Takian, at the summer court last year," Paderon reminded her.

"As a courtier, he was smooth enough—but as a husband?" snapped Bristyn. "I think he was nice to me only because *he* wants to be the one who seals the peace!"

"Now, Briss—perhaps you're wrong about him—he seemed like quite a decent fellow to me."

The duchess glowered in silence while the looming arch over the entrance to the lodge grew tall before them. Turning in his saddle, the priest called to the young woman riding a short distance behind. "Raine—you'll probably find a soulmate here, in the innkeeper himself!"

"You know him?" the duchess inquired, as Paderon slowed their pace to allow Raine to come up on his other side. "Indeed—Awnro Lyrifell is the greatest bard I've ever heard. Quite a rake he was, in his younger days. He would sing all manner of bawdy songs."

"An interesting choice for *your* friend," Bristyn remarked wryly.

"Oh, you know—I can be quite broad-minded when I wish to be. Though for appearance' sake, I make those times rare." The priest chuckled, his laugh a deep rumble.

"I must say—your mood is even lighter than usual," the duchess declared sourly. "I never thought you had such deep affection for horses!"

Paderon only laughed louder. Captain Matheral, riding from the gate of the lodge, waved the party forward. The burly knight and five of his men had arrived several hours earlier and checked the lodge for any sign of danger or treachery, leaving six watchful riders as escort for Bristyn, Paderon, and the duchess's maid, Raine. Now they waved the banner of Carillonn—a golden drackan embroidered on a field of blue—as a sign that all was well.

Bristyn Duftrall sighed, wishing that her father were alive to offer his counsel. Indeed, if the fever had spared him last winter, the Duke of Shalloth would have accompanied his daughter on this journey.

"Raine," she called to her servant, who veered her horse closer to the duchess. "When we arrive in our rooms I shall desire an immediate bath. Then I want you to find me a saddle softer than this one—I don't care how much it costs."

"I'm sure one of the men could visit the stables and leather shops," Paderon suggested, as the party rode beneath the overhanging bar of the gate. Captain Matheral led them toward the stables.

"No—I want Raine to do it. She always seems to find what I want."

"Yes, lady, of course," pledged the servant, dipping her head. Unlike the duchess, Raine wore leather breeches and rode astride her mount, rather than sidesaddle. The maid's dark hair was cut short, almost boyishly, and her large eyes seemed to absorb Bristyn's meanings, understanding them even through the sometimes-misleading filter of her words.

"We're going to stay here at least a day, Raine. Put on a gown, tonight, won't you?"

"Of course, Your Grace."

"And Raine, when we ride into Landrun, I want you to dress like a proper maid."

"Certainly, lady."

The riders entered the courtyard of the inn at an easy walk. A man cloaked in a voluminous robe that concealed his limbs and torso stepped lightly down from the porch. The fellow's long beard curled into an upward point, and his long hair fell far below his shoulders. With a wide smile he swept off his many-feathered hat and bowed.

"Greetings, noble guests—and welcome to the cozy comfort of my humble inn!"

The innkeeper placed his hat back on his head and hastened toward them from the main building.

"Awnro Lyrifell—it's splendid to see you again, my good man!" Paderon surprised Bristyn by sliding from his horse like a youngster to embrace the hearty, gray-bearded fellow.

"May I present the Duchess Bristyn Duftrall of Shalloth. She travels on a mission for His Majesty, the king! And lady, this is an old friend of mine. I must warn you that he's not a proper devout—indeed, I've forgiven him a blaspheme or two over the years—but I can assure you that his hospitality is warm, genuine, and total. Once he was wandering minstrel, and now he runs the grandest inn in all Dalethica!"

"I'm just lucky," Awnro said modestly, bowing deeply and offering Bristyn a smile that—despite her sternest intentions—seemed to break up her foul mood like a wind dispersing an early morning fog.

"Descriptions of your beauty have preceded you, Your Grace—

but they have left me miserably unprepared for the delightful curve of your cheek, the graceful arch of your neck. And those eyes! Baracan stand aside—you are a vision of gorgeous Aurianth herself!"

"Awnro!" gasped Paderon. Raine smiled momentarily and then blanked her expression.

"Please," Bristyn demurred, allowing her lips to curl with the hint of a smile. She, like the priest, was faintly shocked at the comparison to the Goddess of Magic; at the same time it was impossible to take offense at Awnro's words.

"Ah—and a smile men would die for! Your Grace, you honor us with your presence, and I hope that you have a most comfortable stay," he added graciously.

"Thank you," she replied sincerely. "This ride has just about finished me."

"Perhaps a hot bath, followed by a dinner of roast beef and potato bread?" Awnro suggested. "When I saw you coming up the hill, I took the liberty of having your tub filled—if it's too hot, one of the serving girls can add a dipper or two of cold water."

Bristyn, somehow, found the fortitude to smile. Awnro clapped his hands, and a liveried servant snapped to attention behind. "Take the duchess and her companions to their rooms—and see that they are not disturbed."

The manservant offered Bristyn a stool and a hand, and she stepped regally down from Snowcloud. "This way, Your Grace," he said, indicating a private passageway off the stables.

"Splendid," murmured the duchess. "Oh, and Raine—don't forget about that saddle. When you find it, come and let me know."

Then, with a wave of her dainty hand, the duchess swept through the doorway and disappeared inside the magnificent inn.

THIRTEEN

The North Shore Wayfarer's Lodge

Mortal lives—even those of Faerines—must eventually
reach a conclusion. Only through the legacies of song
and poetry, of theatre, dance, or legend created and
performed for the peoples of the land, does an
individual achieve a measure of immortality.
—TALLY OF LIVES

— 1 —

" 'Ere you go, lords," said the floppy-haired youth, showing Rudy and
his companions the two adjoining rooms in a back hallway of the inn.
"Um, I suppose you been told—animals have to stay in the stable?"

"Yes—I'll take him there as soon as my sisters and my grandfa-
ther are settled," Rudy promised.

The fellow gave Kalland a friendly pat. "If it was up to me, he
could stay—but I guess some of the guests get frightened of animals.
They don't allow dogs inside the lodge, either." With a wave, the youth
trotted away.

"Ooh—a real bed!" Anjell squealed, sprawling on the thin mattress that she and Kianna would share.

"Hmph!" snorted Danri, tapping the floor and the walls with his
crutch. "Can't say I think too much of sleeping in a wooden box! But
at least it's got a door!" The digger shut that portal, threw down his
crutch, and stretched.

"Just think of it as a cave that's above the ground!" Kianna teased. She peeled off the overshirt of her disguise, letting cramped wings flex and flutter. A song rose from her lips, faintly murmured, with a sound that Rudy found very soothing. Reasoning that no one could hear them through the walls, he didn't remind her of the indiscretion.

"Caves're made of *stone*!" Danri argued, but as he, too, tested the mattress it seemed likely that the digger would overcome his reservations quite easily. "I guess, after a night spent in a boat, anything would be an improvement—except maybe a gigant dungeon," he allowed gruffly.

"Why don't you all get some rest?" Rudy suggested. "Dinner isn't for a few hours yet. I'll get Kalland a spot in the stable, and be back in a few minutes." He slung the waterskin off his shoulder, acutely conscious of the precious liquid within, and set it underneath the small bundle of their extra clothes.

With the snow lion trotting at his heels, Rudy crossed the courtyard of the sprawling inn. Despite his fatigue and worries about home, the North Shore Wayfarer's Lodge excited and intrigued the Iceman.

Across the yard he saw several horsemen in training, zigzagging around barrels on the sleek golden chargers that Rudy knew were the trademark mounts of the Thutan riders. Thute was terribly far away—even beyond Myntar Kosh—and yet here were a half-dozen of their famed horsemen, whirling through maneuvers only a hundred paces away from him! Swords clashed and a curse rang through the air as two of the magnificent horses collided, sending one rider tumbling to the dirt. Unfazed, the man bounced to his feet and sprang back into his saddle, ready to continue the mock duel.

A tall wagon, drawn by eight oxen, jangled and clanked up the hill. From the dusky color of its driver, and the rich, exotic scents that wafted toward Rudy on the wind, he guessed that this must be a spice merchant from distant Zanthilat. He had heard, when they'd entered the great-room of the inn on the way to their rooms, that even a royal lady of Carillonn was staying here! Of course, her apartments would be in the elegant wings overlooking the lake—there was little chance of seeing her mingling with the commoners in the courtyard.

As Kalland padded along, people pointed and stared at the big cat. A couple of brave children came forward and skipped beside the placid animal, who seemed to accept the attention as his due. At the same time, Kalland showed no undue interest in the horses, goats, and pigs that grazed around the wide common. Rudy took delight in all the exotic sights, even as he remained mystified as to why the mountain feline had elected to remain with his human companions.

A nearby door burst open and two hulking warriors swaggered into the courtyard. Like the men on the dock they wore the black mantles of Galtigor, and Rudy was surprised at the flush of anger that swept through him. He watched the pair squabble over a bottle of whiskey, one of them snatching it away from his companion and gulping down a long draught. Arguing profanely, the other grabbed it back, cursing his companion's greed.

Turning his back in disgust, Rudy entered the stable door behind a lad whose short, dark hair blew wildly in the wind. Only when the youth spoke, asking the stablemaster something about a saddler, did the Iceman realize that he was standing behind a young woman. Embarrassed, he stepped back, though he caught a fascinating glimpse of alert, deep eyes as she turned and made her way out to follow the man's directions.

"Well—I'm busy here. What is it?" The stablemaster's gruff voice pulled Rudy's attention away from the departing woman. Stammering, he asked about a stall for the snow lion.

"All full up here," the fellow barked. "The saddle shop has some extra stalls. Take the stairs down behind the stables, and you can't miss it."

Elated, Rudy hastened after the woman. Now that he had seen her face, she didn't seem so boyish from behind—not as he looked at the narrowing of her waist and the outward curve of her breeches with an appreciation for her true shape. And she was going to the saddle shop as well!

Desperately, Rudy wished that he had the courage to step forward and talk to her, but his feet—perhaps anticipating his tongue's imminent failure—held him back. Instead, he stayed several steps behind as she descended to the lakefront and followed the dock to a shambling wing of the inn. Though the place was smaller than the main stables,

Rudy saw mounds of straw and plenty of empty stalls through the open door.

The gray-haired saddler was pounding leather on a form, and he looked up as the young woman approached. Rudy held back, reluctant to pry, though he overheard her asking about some kind of special saddle. The Iceman, with Kalland trotting after, looked through the stalls, deciding that any one of them would make a comfortable pen for Kalland. "It's just for a day or two, big fellow," he assured the snow lion, who nevertheless regarded him suspiciously.

Rudy emerged from the stalls as two large shadows darkened the door. He recognized the warriors of Galtigor he'd seen in the court-yard. A vague sense of disquiet struck him and he paused in the narrow alcove, watching warily. The young woman was describing the type of saddle she needed, while the weathered leatherworker nodded his head understandingly.

"Out of the way, boy—we've got a man's problem!" declared one of the warriors, roughly shoving the woman. He swaggered toward the saddler. "We need a strap for—"

"Hey, Karro, look here!" interrupted his companion, his face twisting into a crooked grin. "This's no boy!"

"Now—*that's* the thing for a man's problem!" exclaimed the first warrior, with a gap-toothed, leering grin at the young woman.

The Iceman's heart pounded. He saw the woman's eyes—those dark pools that had so drawn his attention—flash from one warrior to the other. Even through his own tension Rudy thought that she showed a surprising lack of fear.

When one of the warriors grabbed her wrist the saddler barked an objection, and the other man knocked the elderly fellow backwards with his fist. The old man collapsed on the floor, his face white with fright.

"Bitch!" The warrior holding the woman cursed as her foot caught him in the groin. She twisted away as he doubled over, but his companion seized her by the shoulders and tackled her, bearing down upon her with all his weight.

"Stop it!" Rudy dove from the shadowy doorway, driving his shoulder into the leering warrior's flank. The man rolled sideways, shouting furiously, but the Iceman straddled him, punching him with both fists.

Kalland snarled and leaped, holding the second warrior at bay, while the woman scrambled to her feet. Rudy continued to flail until the man twisted and kicked, sending the Iceman flying onto his back. Gasping, he sat up, helpless as his opponent drew a long dagger and lunged. Rudy tried to squirm away, but he was too slow; he could only watch in horror as the blade whipped toward his face.

A *crack* of bone was the next sound. The woman flashed past Rudy's face, her foot driving into the wrist of the Galtigor's knife hand. Howling in pain, the man dropped the weapon and she delivered another sharp kick, this one full into his face. The fellow toppled and lay still amid the straw and tools of the shop.

The second warrior, still grasping his crotch and staring into Kalland's growling maw, backed slowly out the door.

Rudy's vision cleared enough to see the woman extending a hand, which he gratefully took. Her face was creased into a tiny smile, and though he failed to see anything funny, he thought again that she looked beautiful.

Suddenly, as she met his gaze, her eyes widened in shock and she gasped audibly. Clapping a hand to her mouth, the woman spun away; then, blinking in confusion, she turned back to Rudy. He felt her eyes on his face, squirming inwardly from the intensity of her look.

"Um, thanks. Are you all right?" he asked, dusting the straw from his hair and tunic.

"Yes, I am—but thank you for your help," she said, before turning to assist the elderly saddler. Even as she did, the woman's eyes remained on the Iceman—and he felt fully exposed to that penetrating gaze.

"Thugs and ruffians!" declared the old craftsman. "In the old days that wouldn't happen—now these bullies of Galtigor think they're lords wherever they go!"

"I hope not," the woman said with a thin smile. "I'm on my way to Galtigor—I'd like to think they're not *all* like these two."

"You beware—that's a bad place!" the old man warned.

"The saddle will be ready the day after tomorrow?" she asked, smoothly changing the subject.

"Aye—but come first thing tomorrow to see if it's what you—er, your mistress—wants."

"That will be perfect." With a nod of thanks to the saddler, she turned and walked to the door, where she paused. Once again her eyes met Rudy's, and as she vanished outside she seemed to be shaking her head in disbelief.

Rudy's hopes had flamed again when he learned that she was journeying to the same place he was. Then he realized that he hadn't even learned her name, and he darted through the door in her wake.

"I'm Rudy Appenfell," he said quickly, catching up with her as Kalland trotted behind. "I'm going to Galtigor, too."

Her eyebrows rose, but he couldn't tell if her expression was one of amusement or interest. "My name is Raine," she replied.

"Raine what?"

"Just 'Raine.' " For the first time he detected a hint of melancholy in her manner. "You might say, 'Raine serving the House of Duftrall,' I suppose. But that's not *my* family."

Rudy couldn't think of a reply, but he stumbled along next to her until she spoke again. "That was courageous of you, coming to my aid in there."

"Well, I couldn't let them . . ." He trailed off, embarrassed.

"Oh, *I* wouldn't have let them, either," Raine replied. "But I appreciate your heroics, nonetheless."

At first he was about to dispute her assertion, but when he remembered her swift kicks, the confident manner in which she'd first confronted the thugs, he began to wonder if maybe she *would* have been able to protect herself. Yet he had no regrets for getting involved.

"Will you have dinner in the lodge tonight? Perhaps, that is— could I meet you in the hall?"

Raine shook her head, he thought, with real regret. "My mistress will need me, I'm certain—she always needs me. In fact, I'm on a mission for her now."

She stopped and looked at him, and he felt those brown eyes

embrace him. Perhaps she liked what she saw; in any event, her expression grew pensive, even sad. "But I'll remember you, Rudy Appenfell—and perhaps our paths may cross again."

"They will," Rudy declared, uncertain how he knew this. Raine turned with a wave, disappearing into the private wing of the lodge, and the Iceman remembered that he still hadn't arranged for Kalland's stall. With a long sigh, he turned back toward the saddler's shop.

— 2 —

Dinner was a splendid affair, with plenty of meat, bread, cheese, and potatoes. Rudy and his companions ate in the large common hall, where several hundred boisterous guests had gathered to partake of the meal. Sturdy wenches moved among the tables, replenishing food and bearing mugs of cold milk or foaming beer.

After the meal, Awnro Lyrifell came onto the small stage. The owner of the lodge bore a small lute in his hands, and before he spoke, several delicate notes rose from the instrument's strings.

"Greetings, guests of old," he began, "and to those who visit us for the first time. We are honored tonight by the presence of Lady Bristyn Duftrall, the Duchess of Shalloth—and her entourage."

Rudy looked across the room and up toward a small gallery adjoining the main balcony, realizing that the formerly empty gallery now held several figures. The foremost of these was a dazzlingly beautiful woman, with sheer golden hair coiled about her shoulders and several brilliant diamonds sparkling at her ears and throat. Then his breath caught as he saw a slight figure behind the duchess. Raine's short hair was neatly waved, adorned with a gleaming silver comb that contrasted with her dark locks and the dusky skin of her bared shoulders.

"Of course!" he muttered, drawing a surprised look from Anjell. He hadn't recognized the name of Duftrall because he hadn't known the duchess's full name, but it made perfect sense. Raine was a handmaiden to that noblewoman, who Rudy remembered was embarked on a mission to Galtigor.

"*Shhh!*" Anjell hissed, as Awnro continued to speak.

". . . dancers and musicians who will rival the muses of Faerine!"
he boasted. Rudy heard Danri's ill-concealed snort of contempt. "But
first, I would like to explain a bit of the history of our lodge, in order
to put the performances into perspective."

"Bring on the dancers!" cried a rambunctious drunk near the
front, but he was hushed by his companions as Awnro smiled toler-
antly.

"The dancers—in fact, *all* the performers—will re-create pieces
of our story for you. But first, you need the framework of the past."
As Awnro Lyrifell spoke, his fingers darted over the strings of his lute,
bringing notes sweet or sad to complement the feeling he conveyed
with his words. He did not sing so much as state, yet the overall effect
was decidedly musical.

"You are seated in a place won by blood and steel, won at a time
when Dalethica faced its greatest threat. Though these events occurred
a thousand years ago, it is our sacred task to preserve the memory of
their glory and their pain—and to pray that such times never come
again."

The notes of his lute dropped into a minor chord, wafting with
heartbreaking purity through the still air of the crowded room. Rudy
strained to hear every word, every sound.

"Though the world of our tale is ten centuries gone, the glories
and terrors of that age shall ever be remembered—for in remembrance,
the heroes never die. And in our knowledge and readiness, may we
hold the darkness at bay against its return.

"The stage is set thus: after eons of life, he of the Unspoken
Name, the Dark Lord who dwells beyond the Watershed, at last sent
his minions against the hosts of men. They rumbled across the Great
Basin, striking across the dry wastes, first into western realms . . . and
everywhere in their path, came Death.

"And now, my good man," Awnro concluded, with a wink at the
drunk in the front row. "The dancers!"

Rudy watched, his mouth gaping, as shrouded figures moved onto
the stage. They did not dance—at least, not by his definition of the
word—yet they stunned him with their formidable presence; the deliberate pace of their movements was evocative of an army on the

march. Though no more than a dozen figures hulked and clomped across the stage, they might have been ten or a hundred times that many, for all the awesome might projected by the costumes, their bodies, and their movements.

"Look!" whispered Anjell, gripping Rudy's arm in a thrill of terror. "Those are *kroaks!*"

Astonishingly, though the dancers were unquestionably human, with the aid of their billowing capes and a few masks, they had indeed brought those tusked and hulking minions to life on the stage. "And there's one just like the Hisser!" Anjell gasped, entranced by the spectacle.

Rudy felt a rekindling of his own fear, and had to forcibly remind himself that he was watching a performance. Around him, people clapped and cheered, and he wanted to grasp them by the shoulders and shout at them. Knowing that he was probably the only man in this room—perhaps in all Dalethica—to have actually seen a real-life kroak, Rudy felt a growing sense of loneliness. *Why me?* he wondered in anguish.

"And the minions of the Dark Lord marched across the world." Awnro's voice emerged from the shadows, accompanied by the mournful strains of the lute. "The beasts of Duloth-Trol dragged their wagons full of Darkblood, slowly spreading the pollution of their master's nectar into places where good water had once flowed. And wherever humankind tried to stand against them, men died—and still the flood came on."

More dancers emerged, dressed in a variety of armaments—bronze shoulder-plates, leather jerkins, and helmets. They carried different weapons: spears, small wooden bucklers, and curving swords of wood that had been painted to look like rusty iron. These newcomers, the human warriors, tried to stand before the inexorable press of minions.

"In Myntar Kosh, the archers of the Sun Lord made a valiant stand!"

Three men, shirtless, wearing leather breeches and quivers, pantomimed a volley of arrows, and though the leading minions fell, those in the rear danced over their fallen comrades. The slain ones rose again, and soon the mass had washed over the archers; indeed, when the monsters passed, Rudy could see no sign of the bowmen, though he couldn't imagine how they'd gotten off the stage.

"The riders of Thute came forth, with lance and chariot—and the spearmen of Tiber stood at their flank!"

More dancers appeared, and though there were no horses on the stage, Rudy clearly saw the tactics of the Thutan cavalry, as three riders swept in with lances couched. One by one they were dragged to the ground, and the Tiberian spearmen were scattered almost as an afterthought.

"And at last the minions reached the great heartland of Dalethica, where Carillonn stood—as it still stands today. Even then, Carillonn was a place of bold knights, of learned scholars and musical bards. High King Danathal reigned there, and his wisdom and might were praised across the land. The fierce sailors of Corsari joined him, Carillonn's own enemies becoming allies to face the greater foe."

Painted Corsari, bearing crooked scimitars and small metal hooks, crept onto the stage. It was the knights of Carillonn who, garbed in gleaming armor that crinkled like parchment, charged and momentarily drove the horde of minions back. The sailors hacked against the flank, and for a painful moment, equilibrium seemed to reign.

Yet, watching the tension of the dancers, Rudy saw that the press of the minions would be too great. One by one, the Corsari fell, and then all but two of the knights. As the cloaked minions surged, the two remaining knights backed slowly toward the edge of the stage. Leaving them alone, the minions danced on.

"Now the eastern realms felt the threat of the Dark Lord's tread; Galtigor, Falteran, and even distant Andaran quailed before the unstoppable onslaught."

More fighters, armed with sword, spear, and bow, stood fast for brief, heroic moments before the swirling force of the Sleepstealer's minions swept them aside.

"Indeed, good listeners—at that point in the history of the Watershed, it seemed that the tide of evil would sweep our ancestors away. Fouling the wells and streams, damming the rivers wherever they trod, the minions used Darkblood to destroy our water, and to give them nourishment—but they did even worse than this!"

"Worse?" groaned Anjell softly. "How?" Rudy saw that her eyes were wet with tears.

"For now the ranks of the minions began to swell, not with other minions, but with new allies—allies whose nature should bring to us all a measure of shame!"

"Shame!" The cry thundered from a chorus somewhere offstage, striking the audience like a physical blow. The clapping and cheering of the crowd immediately died, replaced by a stunned silence.

The dancers garbed as human fighters—those who had been slain in the first part of the show—now came back on stage, with weapons raised. Yet instead of battling the minions, these traitors were now in league with the dark horde, pressing forward with sword, spear, horse, and scimitar against the two knights of Carillonn—the only two warriors who still battled against the tide of evil.

"Despairing and wretched in their misery, many of the folk of Dalethica turned to the Dark Banner for salvation and glory. The numbers of the Black Host swelled, until they counted a score, fifty, a hundred, for each brave man who stood against them! And still they came, until it seemed that no corner of Dalethica would remain untouched."

The two knights battled bravely, struggling to hold the minions and their human allies at bay. But the numbers were too great, and though he knew it was only play-acting, Rudy couldn't suppress the feeling that the two valiant warriors were in terrible danger. Even when fighters representing Galtigor and Falteran joined the line, it didn't seem possible that they could survive.

"Hold!" Awnro's cry, accompanied by a jarring chord from his lute, brought the dancers to a halt. "Before our tale can continue, we must narrow the setting, and incorporate some new players!"

The performers remained frozen in tableaux, while the innkeeper-bard's eyes swept the crowd. Quickly they fell upon Rudy.

"Young man—come here." Though the Iceman sat well back from the stage, he knew immediately that he was the target of Awnro's summons. Feeling a strange sense of exhilaration, he rose to his feet and made his way between the long tables to the stage.

"Our scene is now the shore of a beautiful lake—the Glimmersee. Imagine if you can, that we are gathered atop this very hill. But no lodge stands here, only trees; no banners wave—there is only the grass, swaying like dancers in the breeze."

A few performers at the front of the stage began to mimic the swaying of grass with their hands and arms.

"It is to this place that High King Danathal journeys. He travels with an escort of a hundred knights—half of what survives of his once-elite army."

One of the knights broke from the tableau and came to stand behind Rudy.

"The folk of the mountains have sheltered behind their lake, throughout four centuries of warfare, as one after another of the human realms yields to the inhuman invader. But the Halvericans, under the rulership of their Council of Queens, had forsworn war—except as a means of defending their own realm. These matriarchs had ruled the mountain cantons since the raising of the Watershed. Always they dwelled in peace and prosperity—though of course they had never before faced a threat so dire as the one that now wracked the land!

"And so the council appointed a High Queen, the matriarch who would meet King Danathal, and hear his pleas. But hold our tale for a moment—we need another player!"

Once again Awnro's eyes scanned the crowd, this time looking at those seated on the upper level. He passed over the main balcony and studied the smaller gallery, where sat the duchess and her party. He raised a hand and swept through a gracious bow.

"If Your Grace would be kind enough . . . ?" He gestured toward the gallery.

For a moment Lady Bristyn Duftrall stared in disbelief, before finding her voice. When she spoke, her tone was icy. "I hardly think—"

"Forgive me!" exclaimed Awnro. "But I was asking permission for your maidservant to join us—the charming damsel to your right. If she may?"

Rudy stared in astonishment at Raine. She met his gaze and he thought she was going to stand, but then her eyes flicked toward the duchess and she hesitated.

"May the lady join us, Your Grace?" Awnro asked again, with a bow so deep it verged on mockery. The duchess, her face flushing, nodded curtly.

Raine rose, disappearing at the rear of the gallery and then reappearing on the wide stairway that descended to the main floor. Hurrying forward as the crowd began to rumble, she stepped up to the stage and took Awnro's hand. Her eyes remained fixed on Rudy with an intensity he found almost painful; at the same time, he was aware that a shimmering red silk gown swept downward from her breasts and her narrow waist, swirling gracefully as she walked.

"Now, face each other—here," Awnro directed, smoothly escorting Raine around to Rudy. "You are the High Queen of the mountain folk—and you, sir, are the High King of Carillonn. War growls at your heels, and this woman holds the only safe ground in all Dalethica!"

Immediately the frozen tableaux melted into action, as the minions surged toward those few human warriors who still stood. The horde closed in on Rudy and Raine from three sides, while the edge of the stage dropped toward the audience on the fourth.

"The fate of humankind rests on your words! Make your plea!" Awnro cried to Rudy, his voice rising along with the swelling chords of his lute.

The Iceman stood in place, paralyzed by indecision. A knight fell, swallowed by his dark-robed foes so completely that he seemed to have been devoured. Rudy's tongue caught in his throat; his breath escaped him, leaving him incapable of speech. Suddenly his position felt deadly serious, as if the fate of the world *did* rest on his shoulders. No, he told himself—this was a play, mere entertainment. If he didn't know what to say, Awnro would surely give him lines.

Another human fighter fell, and the minions pressed close.

Still the innkeeper said nothing. The great hall had fallen silent. Awnro's eyes fixed upon Rudy with a glare like a madman's, shining and penetrating at the same time. When the Iceman looked at Raine, he sensed a plea there—*she* wanted him to break the silence.

"Please . . . I—we—need your help." He stammered at first, but his voice grew strong. "The Nameless One is doom to us all—divided we perish alone! Give us shelter, aid, strength—for only if we unite can we hold. Together let us triumph!"

"You are welcome to our realm—you and all of your people who need help. None shall be turned away, as long as we live. And all the strength we possess, we share."

As she spoke, Rudy saw the battlefield around him—there was a field of mud where once there had been grass. Smoke obscured the waters, but he knew they were no longer blue. Along the shore the Glimmersee was dyed red, while farther out the lake was murky with the debris of wrecked ships and burning fire rafts. He stared into Raine's eyes, and saw the agony of many thousands of grieving widows; in his own arms he felt the weakness caused by too many years of war—and the war was *real*!

Tears flowed down Raine's cheeks, and Rudy's too. He reached out and took a step forward—she, too, raised her arms. When they fell together, clasped in a firm embrace, he felt as though he had been drawn out of the darkness, raised through the skies by the hand of Baracan himself—or was it Aurianth?

Far, far below, the minions of the Sleepstealer streamed away in full retreat.

— 3 —

"I've *never* seen anything like that!" Anjell exclaimed, bouncing on the bed in one of their tiny rooms. "You were *great!*"

"But why was that other lady so angry?" inquired Kianna. "She practically dragged Raine out of there when you were done!"

"I don't know why," Rudy admitted. In fact, he remembered the end of the performance only hazily—so vivid was the imagined scene on the lakeshore battlefield, he had remained in a daze since stumbling back to the room with his companions.

"She was fuming about somethin'," Danri declared. "Just as well you weren't standin' in her way."

"I think she just likes to be the center of attention," Anjell stated. "It bugged her that everyone was clapping for her servant girl."

"She's not a girl!" Rudy snapped, surprising them all with his vehemence.

"Well, our Iceman enjoyed his little stint as an actor," declared Danri with a broad wink at the others.

"The arts of Aurianth are not reserved just for Faerines," Kianna said. "You did a great job! I even understood the story!" she added proudly, demonstrating her command of the human tongue.

"You know, even that priest—the one with the duchess, who clucked his tongue all the time—even *he* seemed impressed," Anjell remarked. "He was staring, pretty mad at first. I don't think he liked all the music and stuff. But by the end of the play he was just looking at the stage, kind of in awe. He even stayed in his seat watching, after everybody else had left!"

Shaking off their laughter, Rudy went through the doorway into the small chamber where he and Danri would sleep. The mattress was comfortable enough to carry him swiftly toward slumber, though when his eyes closed, the image of Raine filled his mind, and he held sleep at bay for a surprisingly long time.

He awakened just after dawn while his companions still slept. Immediately he thought of Raine, and the performance. Without wondering why, he left the room and made his way down to the lakeshore, where the mists still swirled through the air, screening the dock and flowing around the saddler's shop.

The leatherworker hadn't raised his shutters or unlocked his door yet, but that didn't matter. Rudy's heart pounded as he saw Raine sitting on the edge of the pier, waiting for the shop to open.

She looked up, and a startled expression flitted across her face, before she smiled quietly. He sat beside her. "I'm glad I found you before you start for Galtigor."

"I am, too," she said. "I'm sorry I had to depart so abruptly last night."

"Why do you let her treat you like that?"

She tossed her head, shaking off the question, and he didn't pursue the matter. Instead, he spoke of something else that had been on his mind.

"There's a prince in Galtigor called Garamis. I believe that he intends to meet, perhaps to woo, your mistress. I know him—he's an evil man. Can you warn the duchess?"

Raine's eyes had grown wide as he spoke, but again she shook her head. "I doubt she'd believe me. But why do you warn me?"

"I'm worried. I wish you weren't going there—it's not safe!"

"It frightens me, that you would say that."

"Do you believe every stranger you meet?" he asked lightly, dismayed at the thought that he had disturbed her.

"No," Raine declared firmly. She took Rudy's hands and stared into his eyes. "It's because it's *you!*"

"Why?" he asked, mystified.

"Because—because I've *dreamed* about you! Every night, when I was a little girl—you were there while I slept, in my mind. That's why it was such a shock to meet you yesterday!"

"What did I do in your dreams?" he asked, awestruck. His hands were trembling, but he gripped her tightly. He wanted to know the answer.

"You—you *warned* me. Or you protected me, somehow. Or I helped you. It always varied."

"I want to do all those things," he pledged. "Will you let me?"

"My life is not my own," she said, abruptly rising. Rudy saw that the saddler had opened his door. "But I *will* tell the duchess what you've said. Perhaps I can make her listen."

Rudy had his doubts, but it seemed that he could hope for nothing more.

FOURTEEN
A Cloud over the Forest

A mountain storm is born of many ingredients—earth
and sky, warmth and wetness, season and sunrise.
When these elements attain the proper alignment, the
result can be unlimited power, or absolute chaos.
—CREED OF THE CLIMBER

— 1 —

The Iceman spent much of the day writing a letter to Dara and the family, explaining in as much detail as possible about his mission to Galtigor—and about the danger lurking in Dermaat, and how that menace had thwarted his intention of returning Anjell to Neshara. Working at a small table on one of the high verandas, with the sweep of the Halverican peaks shimmering across the lake, he found it hard to believe that he would be leaving the highlands behind.

At the same time he noticed a change in his own determination. Previously he had been willing to sacrifice everything in his quest for vengeance; his own survival was a secondary concern. Now, with Anjell along, he made a grim, private vow—a promise that he would return her to Neshara. To do that, he would have to stay alive.

The letter completed, Rudy wandered through the teeming halls and patios, hoping to encounter Raine. She was nowhere to be found, however. A check of the stables showed that Kalland was bored, but not uncomfortable, and after the Iceman took the cat out for some exercise it was time for the evening meal.

Rudy was further disappointed when they went to dinner and he discovered that the duchess and her party were eating in their rooms. Still, the extra day of rest was beneficial to himself and his fellow travelers, the companions all slept soundly on their second night at the Wayfarer's Lodge.

Word gossiped its way through the inn while Rudy and his companions ate breakfast the following morning: the duchess and her party would depart in the early afternoon. Since the Iceman and his companions were still a little footsore, they decided to postpone their own departure until later in the day. Anjell wanted to see the duchess ride past, and Rudy couldn't hide his own enthusiasm for the idea.

His missive to his family completed and sealed, the Iceman decided to give it to Awnro Lyrifell personally for posting. As he took up the parchment from the table beside his bed, his eyes fell on his waterskin, bulging with Aura and untapped since the heights of the Wilderhof. He felt a pang of peculiar, fundamental thirst. Picking up the skin, he uncorked it and took a small swig, feeling the wetness cool his mouth and trickle down his throat. It tasted no different from ordinary water, yet he realized that the momentary thirst had immediately been quenched.

Passing through the halls, he found the innkeeper on the high patio, where lunch was being served above a splendid view of the lake, the mountains, and sunny skies. Perhaps the air was exceptionally clear today; in any event, Rudy had never seen a more spectacular view. He paused for a moment to admire the summit of Glimmercrown, soaring high above the snow-swept massifs of the Wilderhof.

The bewhiskered bard sensed the young man's approach, and turned from a table of silk-garbed Tiberians. "Ah, my young Iceman— that was a splendid performance you gave us all, two night's past!"

Rudy stammered his thanks, embarrassed that he couldn't remember more about the experience. "Um, I was wondering if you could see that this gets sent to Neshara. You see, I have to leave today—"

"You, too, journey to Galtigor?" asked the innkeeper, raising his eyebrows.

"Yes—but not with her," Rudy replied, before he thought about the words.

Awnro smiled wistfully. "Come, walk with me. There is a high balcony on the other side of the lodge. From there you will get a good look at the road to Galtigor. And yes, I will see that your letter sails on the next ferry."

They climbed a wooden tower that squatted like a watchpost at the northern end of the great hall. From the outside it did not look terribly high, perhaps because of the huge building beside it; but as he emerged onto the small wooden platform at the top Rudy could see for many miles.

"Galtigor—a flat contrast to Halverica, as you can see," Awnro pointed out. Indeed, the land sloped gradually away from this range of hills at the Glimmersee's outlet. In the middle distance it flattened out, vanishing into a haze marked only by different shades of green. "An hour down the northern road, you cross the Ariak on the ferry; everything beyond is Galtigor."

"I've never been out of the mountains before," Rudy admitted.

Awnro gave him an amused look, his expression plainly declaring that the innkeeper wasn't surprised by this piece of knowledge. "You should understand that all the contrasts are not necessarily found between different realms. Often the greatest of opposites can be found within a single place—even a single house!"

"What do you mean?" asked Rudy, sensing that the bard awaited his signal to say more.

"Take Galtigor, for instance. The lord who visited Neshara—did you meet him?"

"Aye—well do I remember Prince Garamis."

"Well, he is typical of one side of the Galtigor people. They can be boors and bullies, and they don't care whose feet they trample on when it comes to getting what they want."

"That would describe the man I know," Rudy agreed readily.

"But he has a brother, Prince Takian, with whom I am also acquainted. And Takian is to Garamis as day is to night. Takian—who also embodies many of the traits of his folk—is a man of boundless energy and great, creative determination. He is loyal to his friends, and courageous in defense of himself and those he protects. Yet he is not a bully."

"Why are you telling me this?" Rudy was forced to ask aloud. He remembered the writing tutor of his youth, old Umma Krauz, and felt again as if he listened to a lesson of mystifying, but important, purpose.

Here Awnro drew a deep breath, expelling it in a long, slow sigh. "I wish I knew—but I don't. However, I do know this, Iceman: for you, Galtigor is trouble and danger. It will serve you to understand that not everyone there need be your enemy—though you will have a sufficiency of foes, I suspect."

"Tell me, then, how you know so much about this?" Rudy pressed.

"I have not always been a humble innkeeper," Awnro said—with a smile acknowledging that not *everyone* might think he was terribly humble. "Before I came to live in this place, I traveled the length and breadth of Dalethica, my lute in my hands. The wit of my speech and the sweetness of my tune were the only things between myself and starvation, but fortunately they served me well."

"You made enough money to buy this inn?" the Iceman asked in surprise.

"The North Shore Wayfarer's Lodge is not a thing that is bought and sold," Awnro explained carefully. "Though it always needs a care-taker, the inn stands long after each temporary master here turns to dust. I was fortunate enough to be chosen to be the caretaker, for such time as Aurianth grants."

"Aurianth? But Baracan is the God of Man!"

"Ah, but the muses—bards and sculptors, dancers and poets—all save a prayer for the mistress of Faerine. It is she, you know, who grants the power of art."

Awnro stopped speaking long enough to point. "Look, there's a sight!"

The Duchess of Shalloth's party trotted around the great hall, making its regal path toward the gate. Hundreds of folk gathered in the yard, waving and gawking as the sixteen beautiful horses, and their elegant riders, swept closer.

An armored knight, bareheaded, rode at the head. He bore a tall staff, atop which trailed a blue banner emblazoned with the coiled image of an emerald-colored drackan. Three pairs of riders followed him in neat ranks.

Next came the duchess herself, regally sidesaddle atop a smooth-pacing white mare. She was resplendent in blue satin that served as a vibrant backdrop for her golden hair, silver jewelry—winking and sparkling with diamonds—and pale, flawless skin. The older man, in the flowing azure regalia of a high priest, rode beside Bristyn.

Behind the pair came Raine, dressed in leather riding clothes, without adornment for hair or skin. Rudy saw her eyes flick upward, and he wondered for a fleeting instant if she had seen him. Then he felt a warm pulse in his heart, and he knew that she had. He waved slowly, though she didn't look again.

Six more armored knights, ranked in pairs, brought up the rear of the procession. Soon the column passed beneath the arch before the inn's courtyard, and Rudy watched as they trotted down the road and vanished into the shade of the forest beyond.

Knowing that he should join his companions so that they could get started too, he nevertheless allowed his eyes to drift across the vista of the lowlands, into the vanishing haze of Galtigor.

Abruptly a jolt of pain shot through his body, spreading outward from his eyes. He stared in shock, not seeing anything that might alarm him—yet at the same time understanding that terrible danger lurked out there, with deadly purpose and killing power.

And the danger was close—an imminent threat that Rudy sensed would shed blood before the sun had set.

— 2 —

"Even if you're right, we'll never catch 'em," Danri declared bluntly. "Us on foot and them riding those big horses—they'll pull farther away with every step."

The digger stalked about the small room, while Anjell and Kianna sat on the narrow bed and Rudy stared out the window. Every fiber of the Iceman's being urged him onto the road, desperately hastening to warn Raine and the duchess about the threat he had seen in the distance.

But even if they caught up to the riders, what he could say to them that would not make him sound like a madman? "I tell you, I *know* there's something terrible out there!" he repeated.

"I believe you," Danri said soothingly. Rudy had told him about the sip of Aura he'd taken, and this seemed to confirm for the digger that the Iceman's intuition was probably accurate. "But that doesn't change the fact—unless you want to steal some horses?"

For a moment Rudy actually gave it some thought; he discarded it more because the stables at the lodge were too well-guarded than from any inherent misgivings about right and wrong. After all, it was a matter of life and death.

He turned back to the window in time to see five horsemen gallop out the gate of the inn's compound. They wore the black and red of Garamis's warriors, and raced along the King's Highway to Galtigor, in the wake of the duchess and her party. Rudy spun back to his companions in growing agitation.

"I'm going to get Kalland," he declared. "Then we'll get started—we have to *try*!"

"There might be a way," Kianna, speaking for the first time, interjected hesitantly. Rudy realized that, throughout their conversation, she hadn't hummed a note.

"Well?" demanded Danri.

"I could go ahead—flying, I mean. I think I could catch up to those horses, unless they're running really fast."

"I hardly think the duchess is one for a gallop," Rudy remarked, remembering Bristyn's aloof, sidesaddle posture.

"Well, maybe I can catch up and warn her," Kianne said.

"But *flying*?" Anjell asked, her small forehead creased into a frown of concern. "You can't do that and remain disguised! What if someone sees you?"

"I—I could make myself invisible if anyone comes along. I saw the road this morning—there weren't many people on it. Probably nobody would see me. And besides, there doesn't seem to be any other way."

Rudy hesitated. He imagined Kianna's fright, and powerfully admired her bravery, but he didn't want to send her into danger by herself. Yet she was right—there seemed to be no other way they could raise the alarm. Reluctantly he agreed to her plan.

"When you find them, try to get to Raine—she's the one who came onto the stage with me two nights ago. Tell her about the danger, and see if *she* can talk the duchess into turning around. If not, you'll have to show yourself to the lady, and hope that you can make her believe!"

"And we'll be coming along behind, just as fast as we can!" Anjell pledged. She turned to scowl at Rudy. "Well, I thought you were going to get Kalland. We can't get going until you do!"

Humbly, realizing that Kianna's courage gave them a chance of success, and with his niece's nagging reminding him of his own duty, Rudy turned toward the door.

Before he could leave, Kianna blinked out of sight. The puffing of wind through the opened window was the only sign of her departure.

— 3 —

Garamis led his Redsteel Guards southward along the King's Highway, disguising his identity even in the land his father ruled. At each village Wilfriz quietly investigated, ascertaining that Takian had come this way during the previous day. The younger prince was accompanied only by two bodyguards, Garamis learned with grim satisfaction—and his claim that he had gone hunting was a patent fabrication. Clearly, Takian rode the South Highway with one purpose: he intended to meet the Duchess of Shalloth before she arrived at Landrun, perhaps even at the very border of Galtigor.

Nothing could have suited Garamis better.

During the ride the elder prince was joined by one of his spies who had been posted at the North Shore Wayfarer's Lodge. The fellow told Garamis of the duchess's arrival there, and the fact that she was likely to stay for at least a day or two.

"She's easy to spot—she rides a white horse, and seems to dress always in white or blue. Quite a looker, too! Golden hair, fills out her gown real nice—"

"Never mind about that!" snapped the prince. "How many men do we still have in place at the lodge?"

"Blaric's the captain, and he has four others to help him. They'll start out after her as soon as she leaves."

"Good." Garamis had long understood the importance of alert observation, which meant maintaining a large network of spies. Once again he was rewarded.

Each night the party of more than two dozen Redsteel Guards stayed at a large inn, where Garamis remained concealed by a heavy cloak and hood. Fortunately the highway inns were all commodious establishments, since they often sheltered large mercantile caravans. The riders took their meals in their rooms, and the Guards—whose well-earned reputation for brutality was widely known—were given a wide berth by the rural citizens of Galtigor.

As the party neared the River Ariak, which marked the border of the kingdom, Garamis urged his men to a faster pace. They rode into the morning of the sixth day, since the prince suspected that Takian would meet the duchess very shortly. When that happened, Garamis and the Redsteel Guards would be near at hand. Wilfriz rode out front, with the prince and the other twenty riders holding well back, loping easily along with the knowledge that Takian couldn't be far ahead.

For the hundredth time, the Prince of Galtigor reflected that he had been granted the opportunity to carry out a perfect scheme. He couldn't disobey the command to make the Duchess of Shalloth the target of his deadly intent, yet Takian's advance meeting with her provided the ideal means of slaying his ultimate enemy in the same attack, as he complied with Nicodareus' dictates. And his brother's murder would only make the "Faerine ambush" that much more outrageous! Plus, it would allay any suspicions the King of Carillonn might have held regarding the true nature of the woman's assassins.

Garamis looked up to see Wilfriz galloping back toward him. The captain of the riders reined in beside his prince, his ruddy face flushed with excitement. "We've caught sight of Takian. Not more than a mile ahead of us—you can see him as we come over this rise."

"I'll trust your eyes—and yours alone," Garamis declared. "We'll wait back here, out of sight, until he's moved over the next horizon."

"Very well, my prince!" Wilfriz saluted, putting the spurs to his lathered horse as he raced back up the gentle divide. Garamis and the other riders came along more slowly.

The prince touched his quiver, reassuring himself that the deadly sylvan arrows were still there. He felt the curving grooves along each shaft, trying to picture the flight of a missile so lethal that it could soar for a mile and then unerringly strike its target. It was his intention to give one arrow each to six of his men, entrusting them with a single lethal volley.

The riders loped over several more of the low hills, and always Wilfriz kept the younger prince and his two bodyguards in sight. Finally, late in the day, the captain came pounding back with urgent news.

"Over the next hill, Your Highness! They approach a band of horsemen—and those riders bear the banner of the golden drackan!"

"The duchess!" cried Garamis jubilantly. "Did you see someone wearing a blue gown, or white, riding a white mare?"

"Aye—that would be her. She's in blue, today. And, my prince, there's a sheltered clearing at the hilltop—we can observe them without being seen," the scout informed him.

Soon the Redsteel Guards had gathered in the shade of several towering evergreens. By peering between the branches, Garamis got a clear view down the road. A mile away, Takian dismounted, approaching the duchess and her party on foot. His brother was ever the non-aggressor, Garamis sneered—no danger that someone would mistake *Takian* for a threat!

"They should be along here in a few minutes," the prince said, whispering even though their targets remained a good distance away. He called his six best bowmen forward, and gave to each of them one of the grooved shafts.

"I want you to shoot them when they're in the road, about half a mile from here." He gave one man orders to shoot at Takian, who was easily identifiable by his golden mantle. Another was instructed to shoot at the duchess, who was distinguished by her blue gown and rode the white horse.

"Sight the head of the arrow over the target, as you would a normal shot. Don't worry about the range. As long as the victim is in view—and you aim carefully—you'll hit."

If any of the men wondered how their lord had come to possess such exotic weaponry, they were wise enough to hold their tongues.

"After you shoot we'll need enough time to clear away from here without being seen. We'll ride along the trails through the woods for a mile or two, then set up an ambush. If any of the guards catch up to us, we'll make sure they can't take back descriptions—or anything else."

"Without more arrows?" asked Wilfriz.

"It won't matter. We'll simply make certain that none of them get away. A stab from a sylvan sword will look pretty much like a wound from this!" He tapped the hilt of his own weapon.

Then he turned back to the road, watching his brother approach the Carillonn party. The ambush was set, all the pieces in place.

Now they had only to wait.

— 4 —

The wind shrieked in Kianna's ears and stung her eyes. Never had she flown so fast, or for so long. Fortunately, the road was mostly empty, so for the most part she didn't have to go through the effort of making herself invisible. When she came to a great river, she vanished for the time it took to fly across. Shortly after, she met a farmer's wagon rumbling toward the ferry crossing and the North Shore Wayfarer's Lodge with milk and eggs; she blinked out of sight long enough to buzz past the farmer, drawing only a confused nicker from the fellow's stolid horse.

A little later she encountered a long merchants' caravan, at least a dozen wagons together with a train of mules, and some two dozen burly drivers and freightmen. Frightened by the mass of humans, she darted off the road and hid in the trees until the creaking vehicles and the cursing men had meandered past. As soon as they were out of sight, she buzzed back into the roadway and darted toward the north.

She caught up to five riders whom she had not noticed depart the lodge—though they must have done so after the duchess's party. They wore the black and red mantles that Rudy had pointed out to her, marking them as men of Galtigor. Holding her breath in fear, Kianna disappeared *and* left the roadway, buzzing through the woods until she had safely outdistanced the horsemen—who seemed to be proceeding at a surprisingly lackadaisical pace.

The sun had drifted far toward the western horizon before she found her quarry. She immediately recognized the silver shoulder-plates of Bristyn's escorts, but as she buzzed closer a growing sense of disquiet took hold of her. Blinking into invisibility, she hovered under the tree limbs that overhung the road, and tried to think of what to do next.

She could see Raine, riding behind the duchess near the center of the column. To reach her, she would have to fly past half the armored riders—and she realized with despair that this was something she just couldn't do.

These huge, hairy men, clad in metal armor and bearing an assortment of swords, spears, knives, bows, and arrows, absolutely *terrified* her. Even invisible, she felt very vulnerable as she watched them from a hundred paces away. The thought of flying right beside them required more courage than she had.

Miserably, Kianna hovered and bobbed along, keeping the riders in sight, trying to figure out what to do. The column rode down a long, straight hillside, and the fairy saw a stone bridge over a narrow stream ahead of them.

Then she noticed something else—on the far side of the bridge, three riders approached, apparently headed for a meeting with the duchess's entourage. The trio seemed to be some sort of lord and two servants, judging by the way the plainly dressed pair hung back from the golden-robed leader. While she watched, that eminent rider halted his horse, dismounting at the stone bridge and holding a hand up in a gesture of welcome—or warning.

Were these men the threat Rudy had perceived? The thought made Kianna's heart pound, but somehow she didn't think so. After all, the duchess had a dozen men to protect her; any attack by a mere trio seemed foredoomed to failure.

Then Kianna thought she saw her chance: the riders from Carillonn reined in, and began to dismount. Breathlessly, the twissel clutched a pine bough, watching for her chance.

Several of the duchess's men advanced toward the trio on the bridge, while a stout, elderly fellow—the priest, she had heard him called—escorted Bristyn into the shelter of the forest beside the road. Raine accompanied them, while several of the bodyguards took up positions on the road.

Stealthily Kianna buzzed among the higher branches of the trees. She was too tired to remain invisible, counting instead on the thick foliage to provide concealment. Soon she came to a small grotto, where the stream waters eddied into a pool surrounded by smooth stones and thickly leafed bushes. Settling to a branch, the fairy looked down—directly onto the head of the Duchess of Shalloth.

"Honestly—why all this concern over three men!" the noblewoman was complaining.

"Matheral is checking things, just to make sure there's no trick," the priest explained. Kianna thought he seemed impatient with the duchess, as if his mind was on other things.

Abruptly the stout man cleared his throat, obviously ill at ease as he addressed Raine.

"I—er, I have difficulty admitting that I may have been wrong . . . wrong about very many things. When you stood on that stage two nights ago, reciting the parts of history, I was at first outraged—it seemed a frivolous mockery of true suffering."

"It *was* frivolous!" Bristyn snapped, but the priest continued as if he hadn't heard.

"As the song went on, it seemed as though I was touched by the art, by the music . . . by a force I couldn't understand. I began to see things I have ever ignored. Is it possible, Raine, that all my life has been a waste?"

"What kind of a question—" The duchess started to object, then bit her tongue as her maidservant interrupted.

"It has *not* been a waste," Raine said softly, calmly. "You have risen to great heights of knowledge, in an area where few can excel."

"But I have ignored so much! Prophecies! They contain the wisdom of Aurianth, and I refused to acknowledge it, refused to believe— until I was touched by the muse."

"Prophecy?" Raine stiffened. "What about a prophecy?"

"Enough," sighed the duchess. "Continue your discussion on the road—I wish to rest, now. Paderon, you can leave me for now—Raine will remain."

"Very well, Your Grace." The priest looked as though he wanted to say something else to Raine; instead, he turned to Bristyn. "I must insist that I remain near. These are the woods of Galtigor, remember."

"Oh, Paderon," Bristyn said, with barely concealed exasperation. "Stop looking for trouble behind every tree."

"Very well, my dear—but please, be careful!" With that warning, the blue-cloaked priest withdrew, disappearing through the trees leading toward the road.

"What kind of concerns are those?" demanded the duchess peevishly. "No—I don't want to know. But here we sit in the woods, like little ducklings sheltered by their mother! Three men ride up to us— and he's convinced it's an ambush. Though I have to admit, I don't mind the chance to rest. Help me with these, won't you, Raine?" Bristyn still wore her heavy riding gloves, and she extended her hands so that the maidservant could pull them off. "That's *much* better!" She ran her fingers through her long golden hair, tilting her head back toward the sky.

Her eyes met those of Kianna Kyswillis before the fairy could become invisible or move. Bristyn gasped and rubbed her eyes. "There's a *girl* up there!" she cried.

Instantly, the twissel flew off with a startled squeak, buzzing around the tree before coming to ground at the edge of the little grotto.

"What kind of girl are you?" demanded the duchess, rising to her feet and planting her fists on her hips—once again a figure of authority.

Kianna was terribly frightened by the frowning human, and for a moment she trembled too hard to speak. When she answered, she spoke to Raine, who gaped silently beside her mistress.

"I—I'm a friend of Rudy's!" she stammered.

"Who? Speak to me, child!" insisted the duchess.

But Kianna couldn't force herself to face that stern countenance. "Rudy sent me to warn you—he said there's danger on this road. You have to stop! Or something *terrible* will happen!"

Bristyn's glare turned on her maidservant. "Who is 'Rudy'? I take it the name is familiar to you."

"Yes, Your Grace. He was the man who came to the stage with me, two nights past—the Halverican. I also . . . encountered him at the leatherworker's, when I went to obtain your new saddle." She told her mistress of the events in that lakeside stable, when the two Galtigor thugs had threatened her—going so far as to slightly exaggerate Rudy's role in coming to her rescue.

"Why would he send us a warning? Is he smitten with you—so much that he would resort to deceit in order to delay our mission?"

"No, Your Grace!" Raine insisted. Kianna was impressed by the manner in which the servant girl came to Rudy's defense. "That is— he seemed a very honorable young man. But more than that—there was a manner about him, things that he *knew*—" Raine shook her head in frustration. "It—it's hard to explain!"

"Rudy is special!" the twissel interjected, her indignation giving her the boldness to speak directly to Lady Bristyn. "He was buried in the ice for two weeks—ice of Aura, from Faerine. And he lived! And now he can . . . well, he sort of *sees* things. Like when he looked down this road, after you left. He saw something really, *really* bad!"

"What did he see?" asked the duchess, still frowning.

"He couldn't say *what*—just that it was so bad that it could probably kill you!"

Raine's face grew pale. "Those three men—you don't suppose?"

"Just three?" snapped the duchess. "No, I *don't* suppose they are a team of assassins!"

"But what if there are more than three?" pressed the servant. "What if these three were a decoy, a ploy to stop us here? How do we know a whole army isn't concealed in these woods?"

For a moment Kianna thought that the duchess was going to lose her temper—her face grew flushed, and her jaw clenched as she stared angrily at the woods, as if *daring* any lurking ambushers to attack. Finally she sighed and something within her seemed to relax. She turned to look at Raine.

"Would you trust this young man?"

"Your Grace—there is something I hesitate to tell you, but I must. When I was a little girl, I dreamed about a man—a tall, brown-haired man. He was a protector, a friend. In those days my life was so regimented that he was also a breath of adventure and freedom, a friend who always made me feel safe. I haven't dreamed of him for many years. But, lady—*Rudy is that man*!"

The duchess raised her eyebrows, her expression not unsympathetic. "You know, I had a feeling about him myself—when I saw him on the stage of the inn. It was as if he were something more than a player—like he *became* the king when he stood there and made his plea." For the first time, the duchess smiled—her mouth a thin, tight line of amusement. She addressed Raine. "Even you, my girl, took on an aura of nobility on that stage. Perhaps I shall need to watch that you don't have designs on my position!"

Raine shook her head in shock. "Oh, *no*, Your Grace! Never think—"

The duchess raised a placating hand. "I'm speaking in jest, of course. But the fact is this—we have a message from . . ." Her voice trailed off and she looked at Kianna appraisingly. "What *are* you? And how do you come to be involved in all this?"

Kianna's heart sank—the last thing she wanted was to talk about herself. But she could see no way around it.

"My name is Kianna, and I'm a twissel, from Faerine, of course. I came here with Danri—he's a digger—and since we can't dig our way back under the mountains, we're going to Taywick Pass so we can go home. And Rudy and Anjell are going to Galtigor, which is pretty much the same direction, so we're all traveling together."

"A cozy arrangement, if a trifle unusual," said the duchess with a trace of amusement. "Does this mean that you will continue on to Galtigor, while I myself am to be deterred by your warning?"

"No! Yes! I don't know!" wailed the twissel. "Can't we get out of here and talk about it later?"

"Your Grace," said Raine, quietly persuasive. "There *is* real danger here! Rudy knows! Let's ride back at least until we meet him and his companions—perhaps they can tell us more."

"I can just imagine Captain Matheral's reaction. Of course, I can order him to turn us about—and he'll do it. But I shudder to picture what he'll be thinking!"

"Perhaps we should ride, just the two of us," Raine suggested. "After all, Matheral is meeting those men from Galtigor—we don't want them to overhear our plans."

"Can you two sneak off like that?" asked Kianna, surprised.

Raine outlined her plan to the duchess. "Matheral's put two men to guard the back road. We can reach them through the woods. You and Kianna stay out of sight while I tell them that you need to see them, offer to hold their horses. As soon as they head back here, we can mount up and ride."

"But what about Snowcloud? You mean, I should ride a different horse?" demanded Bristyn, who was beginning to seem, to Kianna, like quite a temperamental person.

"Your Grace, you'll have to! It's a matter of life and death. We'll slit your gown so you can mount the saddle. If you want, as soon as we can stop again, I'll sew it into a pair of leggings. But don't you see—we have to go, and do it now! There's no way to get Snowcloud, without announcing to everyone out there what it is we're doing!"

Bristyn turned away, stalking to the edge of the stream and glaring at the surrounding forest as if she expected to cow the very woods with her look. But after a moment she turned back, her blue gown swirling around her legs.

"Very well. We'll go—but make the cut in my petticoats. I'll tie up my dress. And promise you'll sew the leggings as soon as possible."

"Of course, mistress."

Raine produced a short knife from her belt, and carefully sliced two long cuts through the white silk of the duchess's undergarments. Meanwhile, Kianna helped the noblewoman hold the gown out of the way, and then secure it around her waist with a strip of cloth.

"*Now* can we go?" pleaded Kianna. "This way—you can get up to the road along a deer trail, and no one will see you!"

The two women followed the twissel, who walked along the path, glad of the chance to give her wings a rest. True to her word, they soon reached the bank at the edge of the road. Two dozen paces farther down the highway stood two of Carillonn's knights, each holding loosely to the reins of a sleek war horse.

"Work your way through the woods," Raine urged, gesturing Kianna and the duchess toward the fringe of forest out of sight of the road.

As soon as the pair had moved off, the maidservant stepped from the trees, skipping gracefully down the steep bank. "Hello Oskar, Parric. Her Grace is down by the stream, there—she asked if you could give her a hand with a piece of wood she's found. I think she'd like to save it."

With a sigh of resignation, the bigger guard turned toward his comrade. "I'll go—you keep an eye on the road."

"It's big," Raine put in quickly. "I think she needs both of you. But I'll stay here and watch your horses for you."

Grumbling, the two warriors started along the trail. As soon as they had slipped out of sight, Bristyn slid down to the roadway. She rubbed her buttocks. "I'm not going to like this," she warned, with a look at the knight's stiff war saddle.

Nevertheless, she seized the pommel and—using Raine's cupped hands as a stepping stool—lifted herself up and straddled the horse. Her legs, under the stark white of the rent petticoat, were too short to reach the stirrups, and Raine made a hasty adjustment.

"Hurry!" hissed Kianna, still watching from the underbrush. She looked back toward the stream, but there was no sign of any activity on the stretch of road she could see.

Abruptly a rough hand fell on her shoulder, pulling her around as she squeaked in dismay. She found herself staring into the bloodshot eyes of a huge, bearded human—a warrior! But this was not an armorclad rider of Carillonn who had sneaked through the woods. She saw the black mantle, trimmed in red, draped over his shoulders, and remembered Rudy's description of Galtigor's thugs. At the same time she recalled the riders she had seen on the road—they had been following the duchess!

Kianna saw three more of the fellows, moving past the man who had grabbed her, lunging toward the women in the road.

"Run!" cried the twissel frantically. "Get away—!"

Her voice pierced the quiet of the woods before terminating in a strangled gasp, as the warrior clapped a rough palm over her mouth.

The last thing the fairy heard, before dizziness and fear overcame her, was the pounding of two horses, thundering along the road, followed by the cursing of the thugs who had leaped, too late, into the track.

Then her world faded away, into a blackness that was as menacing as the brutal men around her.

— 5 —

"Your Highness," hissed one of Garamis' men who had been posted to watch Takian's meeting with the duchess.

"Did they start along the road? Stand to your arrows, men!" ordered the prince, pushing through the trees to the side of his lookout.

"They're stopped—they've dismounted by the stream down there."

"What?" Garamis looked to where the man pointed, seeing the white horse, already riderless, beside his brother's mount. Cursing, he settled back to rethink his plan. Should they wait here, hoping to remain unobserved until the group set out again? Or should they try to force the affair?

The forest floor was relatively open, free of underbrush but frequently interrupted by the thick boles of towering trees. It seemed to the prince that they would be able to work their way forward, staying off the road, until they got fairly close to the duchess and Takian. A volley from the woods could prove quick and deadly—if they could get a good line of fire.

Or should they wait here, concealed and ready for a perfect ambush? Patience, Garamis told himself—they will make splendid targets coming up this hill. Sooner or later he would get the chance to kill.

But the prince was not a man who could easily sit and wait when action beckoned. "I'll be right back," he whispered, before slipping through the ring of trees. When he was safely out of sight of his men, he drew the Sword of Darkblood and pointed at a clearing in the forest ahead.

"Nicodareus!" he hissed. A wind surged through the trees, rustling leaves, but before the swirling foliage settled, Garamis had traveled to the small clearing. Again he used the power of Darkflight, and again, until he reached the crest of a boulder pile overlooking the road. Peering through a gap in several neatly spaced rocks, the prince found that he could see quite well. Takian and his men stood some distance away, talking casually with several of the Carillonn knights; Garamis smiled cruelly at the thought of exactly how short-lived this peace mission would be.

Quickly he traveled back to the company. Detailing five men to hold the horses away from the road, Garamis and the other Redsteel Guards began to work their way stealthily through the woods. For a painfully long time they crept over a carpet of evergreen needles, pine cones, and brittle branches; their pace seemed agonizingly slow to the prince, who longed to unleash again the power of Darkflight.

Eventually they reached the clump of rocks. Garamis and his archers climbed this outcrop, settling behind some flat-topped boulders. Once again they got a clear view of the road.

"Still, we can't see their picnic spot from here—they're down in front of us somewhere," Wilfriz declared, peering between two rocks. "But we can see the road in both directions. Should be able to get a clean shot."

Garamis carefully observed the roadway around the stone bridge. As before, several knights of Carillonn stood there with their horses, along with Takian and his two bodyguards. There was no sign of the duchess.

Shouts of alarm rang from the woods, and two knights stumbled onto the road, gesturing and shouting to their companions.

"Get ready!" spat Garamis, sliding to the side so his archers could take the best vantages. He could still see the far half of the road, though the tops of trees concealed the nearer side. Swiftly the men drew back their arrows, sighting along the grooved shafts.

"There they go!" hissed another man, as several more knights raced out of the woods. The men on the road mounted their horses, several knights galloping along the road—*away* from the Redsteel archers!

"Shoot! *Shoot*! There's Takian—and look!" Garamis pointed farther down the column of riders, where a figure in swirling blue struggled to control the white horse.

Six missiles soared into the air, arcing toward the targets with an eerie, mournful wail. The first arrow struck Takian full between the shoulders, and the prince collapsed, motionless, across the withers of his horse.

Two more of the deadly shafts dropped Takian's bodyguards, and another pair claimed knights of Carillonn. The last arrow moaned toward blue silk, striking its target full in the back, driving the suddenly limp body to earth.

Ten knights of Carillonn milled on the road. Their captain, bearing the green-drackan standard, stared upward—though Garamis and his men had already ducked down behind the concealing shelf of stones.

"Come on—back to the others," the prince barked, leading his men down from the rocky knoll.

"Wait—look!" hissed Wilfriz, still observing from his sheltered niche.

The killings done, Garamis wanted only to be out of there, but he bit back his impatience and crept to his guardsman's side. He saw the backs of the galloping knights, who inexplicably left their dead in the roadway as they hastily backtracked along the road. Takian's terrified horse, the motionless rider still slumped in the saddle, thundered after the other horsemen.

"Impossible!" spat Wilfriz. "I've never seen the knights of Carillonn rout from a fight—and here they haven't even seen the foe!"

"The terror of the sudden attack turns the will to fight into the need for flight," the prince announced. He, too, was amazed by the knights' cowardice, but he wasn't about to question his luck.

Wilfriz looked skeptical, but knew better than to argue with his prince. They led the Redsteel Guards around the rocky promontory and approached the bodies, after Wilfriz sent several men to search through the surrounding woods.

Garamis' elation lasted only until he reached the roadway and stood over the corpse in blue silk. Furiously he turned and lashed his bowman across the face.

"It's not the duchess—you killed some blithering *priest*!" Garamis, his face flushed with rage, gestured toward the blue-cloaked body on the ground. The sylvan arrow jutted from the unfortunate fellow's back, having pierced straight through to the heart.

The prince slapped the archer again with his heavy gauntlet, knocking the cringing fellow to the ground. "And what of Takian?" he hissed, confronting another of his archers.

"Th—the arrow took him the same way!" declared the trembling warrior. "Right through the back! But his feet were locked in the stirrups—his body stayed on the horse as it ran up the road."

"That might not be so bad," mused the prince. "If the steed carries my beloved brother's corpse all the way to the ferry station, then the alarm will be raised that much sooner."

Wilfriz returned from an inspection of the four bodies that lay slightly farther down the road. In accordance with the Prince's instructions, he had not touched or disturbed them; part of the plan required that they should be discovered with the arrows jutting from them, just as they were slain.

"Counting the prince, all six were kills," he declared. "But still, why did the rest of them keep running?"

"They ran because there was nothing for them here, you imbecile!" snapped Garamis. "They ran because they were chasing their lady duchess—because *she* had already started down this road!"

"Here—what's this?" cried one of the men, gesturing toward the woods.

A warrior of Galtigor stepped out, dragging the squirming figure of a little girl. The prince recognized Blaric, his spy recently stationed in the North Shore Wayfarer's Lodge. Only on closer inspection did Garamis notice the prisoner's shoulders—the girl had wings!

"Caught this one with the duchess—helping her to get away, she was," Blaric explained.

"You fool!" snarled Wilfriz. "Why take the girl when you could have had the *real* prey?"

"The duchess was already mounted and racing away. I was lucky to get this one!" replied the spy belligerently.

"Peace, my good captains," Garamis said, with a chuckle of amusement that quickly grew to a disbelieving laugh. Already the results of this ambush had begun to seem very bright indeed.

"This situation can work to our advantage. Remember that, given the circumstances of our attack, it may serve very well to have as a prisoner one who can *prove* that these attackers came from Faerine!"

FIFTEEN

The King's Highway

When a man creatively employs his resources,
applying every ounce of ingenuity to a task, it is
possible to surmount any obstacle.
—CREED OF THE CLIMBER

— 1 —

Late afternoon found Rudy, Danri, and Anjell on the north bank of
the River Ariak, hastening along the wide roadway. The rest they'd
taken at the North Shore Wayfarer's Lodge gave them the endurance
to continue past sunset; worries about Kianna overwhelmed any urge
to stop. The companions were further aided by the full moon that arced
upward from the east, casting even the tree-shaded sections of the road
with enough light for travel.

"I hope that scatterbrained fairy remembered what she was supposed to do!" groused Danri, stomping easily along with his crutch
resting on his shoulder.

"Of course she will!" Anjell declared. "I just hope she gets there
in time."

"And that they believe her," added Rudy. He vividly remembered
the stubbornness of Lady Bristyn Duftrall, and feared that the woman's
recalcitrance would prove to be the twissel's biggest obstacle.

Kalland, pacing slightly before them, suddenly paused and pricked up his ears. A soft growl rumbled in his throat, as his attention fixed upon the roadway before them. Danri quickly dropped his crutch to the road, hobbling forward as the companions came around a gentle bend.

A small encampment occupied a clearing beside the road. A dozen horses grazed beside the camp, which consisted of several large wooden shacks. Three men, bearing swords and wearing steel helmets, lolled beside the road, but ambled forward as the trio approached.

"What's yer business in Galtigor?" demanded one, scowling suspiciously at Danri. "Ya don't look like any kind of merchants to me!"

Rudy's heart pounded, and his throat grew dry. "Well—we're not!" he blurted, feeling foolish. Why hadn't he anticipated a border post? Now their lack of preparation threatened imminent disaster.

"That much is obvious," sneered the guard. "But what kind of business are you about? Or are you spies?" he suggested unpleasantly.

"Listen, you little—" The digger's temper ran away with him, and Rudy's hand edged nervously toward his sword.

"Oh, Grandpa!" Anjell said suddenly. Her voice seemed very loud, perhaps because Danri, his eyes bulging in surprise, immediately ceased speaking. "We'll never get to Aunt Sadie's if you have to stop and argue with everyone we meet!"

"Aunt Sadie?" The guard directed his question at Rudy.

"Um, my sister," he said.

"She married a woodsman," Anjell continued without pause for breath. "And we're just now getting to visit her! *If* we ever get there," she added, with a pout at Danri.

The guard laughed. "Get along, then," he said, strolling back to his fellows.

"Good job, little one," Rudy whispered, patting his niece on the shoulder.

Breathing deeply, the companions continued on, with Kalland padding along in the lead. Full nightfall had settled over the woods, but the moonlight was strong, and the trees had been trimmed well back from the wide highway. Another hour passed before Kalland once again growled an alarm.

"I hear horses!" Anjell announced, her voice low.

"Coming this way," Rudy agreed. "Let's get back in the trees—right next to the road."

Quickly the companions took shelter—Danri, Anjell, and Kalland vanished into the forest, while the Iceman stood right at the bank of the dirt highway, crouching beside the trunk of a sturdy pine as he listened to the approaching hoofbeats.

He wondered what to do. Was this Raine returning along the road—or some stranger, in a hurry to reach the lodge? Or, even worse, some ally of Garamis' on a sinister mission? If Rudy just strolled into the road and ordered the riders to halt, would he expose himself and his companions to terrible danger?

After a moment's thought he hefted his waterskin off his hip and quickly uncorked it. He took a quick swallow, feeling the Aura course through his system, refreshing and invigorating him. His senses tingled with new alertness.

A conviction grew: this *was* Raine coming toward him, and he felt her fear. He stepped into the road without delay, trotting to a bright patch of moonlight so he would more readily be seen. Looking toward the north, he saw nothing for several moments, though the hoofbeats grew steadily louder. Then two shadowy forms came into view, thundering rapidly closer.

Rudy raised his hands, waving them slowly, hoping that the riders would see him. The pair of horses pounded closer, until one uttered a whinny of surprise. The slight-figured rider drew back, hard, on the reins, and both steeds skidded to a halt, snorting and gasping. The Iceman felt a flaring of joy as he saw Raine staring down at him, wide-eyed and out of breath.

"Rudy!" she cried, as he stepped to her side.

"The noted actor," added the duchess wryly, as she studied him appraisingly.

In the ensuing silence Rudy suddenly realized that the night was far from quiet—he heard many more hooves pounding on the road, some distance behind the duchess and her servant.

"You're pursued!" he whispered.

"You don't say!" snapped Bristyn Duftrall, as Raine took Rudy's hand and squeezed it.

"Come on—get off the road here. You can hide in the shadows till they ride past. Let's go!"

Raine smoothly dismounted, taking the reins of the noblewoman's horse after helping Bristyn down, while Rudy took the bridle of Raine's mount. The Iceman looked around, suddenly frightened.

"Where's Kianna?" he asked.

Raine, her eyes shining with tears, turned to look at him before she vanished into the sheltering woods, and the stricken expression on her face sent a shiver of terror through the Iceman. Numbly he stumbled after, casting a last look down the road—but seeing no sign of the twissel. The sounds of pursuit grew louder, and he hastily led the balking horses underneath the low-hanging boughs in the woods.

"Where is Kianna?" Anjell was demanding as Rudy reached the companions in a small clearing among the trees.

"Shhhh!" he hissed, suppressing his own concern as he wrapped his niece in his arms. They listened, barely breathing, as a large band of horsemen drew close. For several moments they thundered past, the ground shaking underfoot, until the sounds faded along the road leading back to the North Shore Wayfarer's Lodge.

"Who were they?" Danri asked, when they again dared to speak.

"My bodyguards, I think," the duchess replied. "Though there were men of Galtigor with them as well—an advance party of three men that met us on the road. I thought it best that they not find out where we had gone. At least, until we know more about what's going on," she added, with a pointed look at Rudy.

"What about Kianna?" he insisted. "I'm assuming that she found you."

"Yes, she did," Raine said. She stepped to Rudy and took both of his hands. "She warned us to come back, that danger lurked on the road. We were on the point of starting out—she was coming with us—when some men of Galtigor jumped out of the woods and grabbed her. They tried to get the duchess as well—it was all we could do to get away."

Rudy's heart sank as he imagined the fairy's terror. "Did they harm her?" he asked.

"Not that we could see—I think she was taken captive."

"That's bad enough," Danri noted. "The discovery of a twissel in Dalethica is going to attract a whole lot of attention—none of it good!"

"We'll have to rescue her," Anjell said bluntly. "Let's get going!"

"You're right—we do," Rudy agreed. "But let's take a minute to make some plans."

"Tell me about this danger," said the duchess. "Did the fairy warn us of the ambushers, only to get captured herself?"

"I'm afraid so," Rudy admitted. He described the feeling that had possessed him atop the lodge's tower. He didn't mention his taste of Aura, however, fearing that it would only serve to confuse things further. He also related his knowledge of Garamis' agents at the lodge, and the fact that the five men had ridden off shortly after the duchess.

"What about these three riders that met you?" Rudy asked. "Did they wear black mantles, with red trim?"

"I couldn't really see. Paderon rushed me into the woods before they could get close—he's always worrying about something or other. But I saw that one of them wore a golden cape, while the other two had mantlets of gold," Bristyn said. "The men who came out of the woods and grabbed Kianna—*they* wore black and red, though. What does the color mean?"

Rudy related how the factions of Garamis and Takian differed as he had heard it from Awnro. "It could be that the three men were emissaries of Takian; the ambushers, then, were the men of Garamis."

"Prince Takian—of course. I met him in Carillonn, this past year. He was an . . . interesting man. One of two studhorses fighting over the mare," Bristyn declared sharply, surprising Rudy with the bitterness of her tone.

"His brother is a scoundrel," the Iceman replied grimly. "I can't speak for Takian, but I know Garamis to be a murderous dog!"

"We've got to go after Kianna!" Anjell urged again, tugging at Rudy's sleeve.

"The lass is right," Danri agreed. "We can plan as we walk—for all we know, they're taking her farther from here with every minute."

"I know," the Iceman agreed, despairing. "I should have gone after you myself," he said to Raine. "It was foolish to let—"

"Without a horse you would not have caught us—and she did." Raine spoke bluntly. "Don't blame yourself for your companion's courage."

Rudy looked at Raine, his eyes growing hard. "You're right," he said slowly, determinedly. "Let's get her back."

The grim, frightened travelers made their way back to the road. "Why don't you ride for a time?" Raine suggested to Rudy. "I've been on horseback for hours—the walk will do me good."

Rudy shook his head. "I can go for miles, yet. But perhaps you could pull Anjell up behind you. Or Danri—"

With a firm shake of his head, the digger squelched any notions of mounting him on a horse. "Guess my legs have carried me this far from Faerine—won't hurt to use 'em a little longer."

Raine helped Bristyn mount, then lifted Anjell up to the back of her own horse. "I'll just stretch my legs a bit—then I'll ride too," the maidservant explained. Rudy felt a measure of gratitude as she fell into step beside him, the pair of them and Kalland leading the two horses at a fast walk down the road while Danri brought up the rear.

The Iceman's mind reeled with terrifying images of Kianna's fate, and he unconsciously increased their pace to a near trot. Only after several minutes of jogging along did he realize how fast they were moving, but when he started to slow down, Raine—loping in a long, graceful stride—pulled ahead and he again picked up his own speed. His endurance had been honed by years of hard work in the high country; he was surprised and impressed to notice that the woman matched his pace without even breathing hard. Danri, too, huffed along tirelessly, his short legs pumping with machinelike regularity.

Something moved through the darkness ahead of them and they came to a quick halt, senses tingling in alarm.

"Wait here!" Rudy hissed, before ducking to the shadowy shoulder of the road and cautiously advancing to investigate. He felt, rather than heard, Raine padding silently behind him; his instruction to the contrary, he was glad of the company.

Soon he made out the form of a tall war horse. The steed ambled slowly toward them, and Rudy relaxed slightly when he got close enough to see that there was no silhouette of a rider atop the animal. Then, in another few steps, he discerned a shapeless bundle slung across the horse's back. Cautiously he and Raine drew nearer, as the horse stopped and nickered softly.

"It's a man!" Raine whispered. "But he's hurt—or dead."

"Look." Rudy pointed to the long shaft of an arrow that jutted upward from the fellow's back. Taking hold of the horse's bridle, he held it still long enough to look at the man's face, to feel for a pulse in the neck.

"He's still alive—I think," he said, his fingertips detecting only the faintest flicker.

"Who is he?" asked Bristyn, as she, Anjell, and Danri drew up.

"Not one of Garamis's men," Rudy declared, realizing that the fellow's mantle was too light-colored to be black. Squinting in the dusky light, he made out a few more details. "He wears gold—could this be one of the men who met your party on the road?"

"These look like the same clothes," Raine remembered. "I, too, went into the woods before they joined us. But this looks like the one who seemed to be their leader."

"Let's get him down—see if we can do anything for him," Rudy urged. He was desperately anxious to resume their search for Kianna, but compassion dictated they try to do *something* for the man. At the same time, something told him that this man, if he could talk, might have some knowledge of the fairy.

"He's so *cold*," Raine said, as they eased the unconscious man out of his saddle.

"He wouldn't have lasted long if we hadn't found him," Rudy agreed, as Danri came up to help them lower the fellow to the ground.

"Careful of that arrow—we've got to lay him on his side," the Iceman instructed. Gently they set the barely breathing figure down.

The digger gave a low whistle of surprise. "Take a look at this arrow—the grooved shaft, the golden feathering. There's only one folk in all the Watershed who make arrows like this. The sylves."

"You don't think a band of sylves came all the way from Faerine—?" The thought seemed hopelessly implausible to Rudy.

" 'Course not," Danri said. "Sylves're too high and mighty to get worked up about about human affairs, any way you shake it out. No, I think this is something even *worse* than that."

"What could be worse?" Rudy demanded, still trying to shake off the notion of Dalethica facing an invasion of sylvan warriors. "War between Faerine and Dalethica would be disastrous—nothing could help the Sleepstealer more!"

"Right. And I'm tellin' you that no sylves came into Galtigor just to stir up trouble. What this means is that someone wants you humans to *believe* that's what happened."

"Why?" cried the exasperated duchess, who'd been shaking her head back and forth as the conversation progressed. "Why not just . . . ?" Her voice trailed off, as explanations apparently began to occur to her.

"Exactly," Danri grunted. "Like Rudy said, war between our two lands would play perfectly into the hands of the Sleepstealer—at least, if he has a plan that he himself intends to put into motion. And from what we know of the breach in the Watershed, up in Halverica, that's beginning to seem more likely than ever."

"So this arrow was shot by an agent out of Duloth-Trol?" exclaimed Rudy skeptically. "I thought you said they couldn't travel far from a source of Darkblood!"

"They can't—at least, not the *minions*."

"Who else would serve—?" Rudy paused, a chill filtering slowly along his spine. "Garamis!"

"What about this man?" Anjell snapped, tired of the debate. "Are we going to help him?"

"Can we remove the arrow?" Rudy asked, not very optimistically.

Raine reached out and touched the shaft, drawing a weak groan of protest from the unconscious man.

"Let me see that," Bristyn offered, coming to kneel down beside the still form. "That face!" she declared. "I've seen it before."

"Where?" Rudy asked.

The duchess sat back on her haunches, her face sagging in disbelief. "This isn't one of Takian's men—it's Prince Takian himself!"

Raine leaned close for a look at the moonlit face. "It is," she agreed wonderingly.

"Someone tried to kill him—an assassination?"

"Makes Garamis seem even more likely, doesn't it?" Danri observed grimly.

Rudy could only agree, though the monstrous nature of the crime brought a flaring of outrage that made him tremble. The deaths of his own brothers, he knew, also rested at the feet of the elder prince of Galtigor. The Iceman felt the embers of his hatred growing into a burning fury. "He's a *monster*!" he spat, his rage tempering his voice into a husky whisper.

"And he's got Kianna!" Anjell declared tremulously.

"Hold him still," the duchess commanded. "I'll try to get this arrow out."

"You—?" Rudy was skeptical of Bristyn's ability to do anything so practical. "Perhaps it would be better if—"

"My lady has considerable training in the healing arts," Raine cut in.

"Or did you think I sat around in the palace all day, giving orders to my servants?" snapped the duchess, locking her fiery eyes on Rudy's face.

"I-I'm sorry," he stammered. The Iceman and Danri gripped Takian's shoulders, as Bristyn gingerly worked the shaft back and forth.

"It's lodged against his shoulder blade," the duchess declared. The wounded man groaned and thrashed, but she finally pulled the bloody missile free. Handing the arrow to Raine, Bristyn tore a strip off her ragged petticoat and used it to stem the flow of blood trickling from the wound.

"Can you lift him—gently—high enough that I can wrap this around his chest?" she asked. Danri and the Iceman carefully propped the prince up while Bristyn took longer strips and, aided by Raine, tightly bandaged the wound.

"What can we do about him?" Rudy asked. He indicated the woods surrounding them—they hadn't passed so much as a farmstead in hours. "Should we split up—some of us stay here with him? I've got to go after Kianna!"

"Me too," Danri declared. "There *is* another thing we could try." The digger indicated the waterskin hanging at Rudy's side, and the Iceman remembered that he carried a supply of the enchanted Aura.

"Do you think it would help him?" he wondered.

"In Faerine it does—when someone's hurt by accident or violence, Aura is often enough to bring them back to health."

Rudy remembered Anjell's terrifying bout of fever, how he'd held her to his chest, against the sliver of Aura ice, and how, when she'd recovered, he found the ice had melted. Now he pulled the waterskin from his shoulder and gently trickled a few drops onto the wounded man's cracked lips.

Takian showed no reaction. Carefully, Rudy slid the neck of the waterskin into the prince's mouth, and squeezed out a little more of the magical liquid. This time Takian groaned and moved slightly, licking the precious stuff with his tongue. Almost immediately the Iceman noticed an increase in the strength of the man's breathing.

"I know we have to move quickly," Danri said. "But it's full dark now, and we could end up moving right past 'em in the middle of the night. Plus we'd have to split up—if we don't want to leave Takian here alone. On the other hand, if we let this fellow rest overnight, he might be strong enough to travel in the morning. And don't you think we could all make better time if we wait until dawn?"

Rudy looked down the road, wondering how far away Kianna was. He tried—unsuccessfully, he felt certain—to imagine her terror. Yet he knew that Danri was right, and slowly, reluctantly, he nodded his head. They found a small clearing in the woods, sheltered on all sides by dense trees. Not daring to risk a fire, the companions opened up their bedrolls and made themselves as comfortable as possible.

Only as he was about to fall asleep, his head on a pile of moldy leaves, did it occur to Rudy that the digger had asked for his decision, deferring to him as if he expected the Iceman to be some kind of leader.

— 2 —

The horse stank worse than anything Kianna had ever smelled before—
yet even so, she pressed her face hard into the animal's lathered shoulder, hoping to blot out cruel reality by burying herself in sensory
misery. She found some slim comfort in sharing the plight of this big,
dumb steed. Like herself, she reflected in a rare moment of semi-calm,
the horse was a captive of humankind.

The man who rode this horse seemed like an especially monstrous
example of the breed. He was huge and fierce-looking, almost like an
angry gigant, except that his body and breath smelled far worse than
any Faerine's possibly could. His hands were rough, and the ropes he
had used to bind and gag her cut into the skin of her face, her arms,
and her legs. Her wings were crumpled painfully against her back,
looped in many additional coils of rope.

She whispered a desperate prayer to Aurianth—not so much for
assistance, as for the strength to bear her travails. She wanted to sing
a song, or at least to hum a little melody, but it seemed that her throat
was too dry for music.

For a long time they rode through the moonlit night. Kianna saw
enough to realize that the horsemen were following narrow forest
tracks, not the wide highway she had traveled before. This fact increased her despair—how would her friends find her in the maze of
woodland trails?

She had no doubt that they would follow. Indeed, she had full confidence in Danri and Rudy's ability to get her out of this mess, once they
found her. But it was this latter concern that threatened to prove her un-
doing—that, and the fact that these ruffians rode fast horses, and were
more than willing to push their mounts to the limits of endurance.

At the earliest hour of dawn the file of horsemen trotted into a
clearing in the midst of the forest. The leader, a man with foxlike black
whiskers, dismounted and came over to the horse that still bore Kianna's bound body.

As he approached, the twissel felt the presence of powerful, paralyzing evil. Reaching out a hand, the human seized her hair and twisted her head so that she was forced to stare into his face.

"Tell me, little girl—why do you arrive now? Are you destined to help me?" His voice was a sneering assault against her ears, and she could only quiver helplessly.

"Here—I see the rope has got your tongue." He reached out, steel gleaming in the dim light, and Kianna whimpered as his knife touched her cheek. The blade turned out, and the ropes fell away from her face—but her skin burned from the cold touch of the metal, and she stared at him with wide, terror-stricken eyes.

"Why don't you speak?" he demanded, seizing her arms and pulling her roughly off the horse.

"Perhaps she doesn't understand the human tongue, my prince," suggested the red-bearded rider whose horse had carried the captured fairy.

"Bah—I have no need of her words!" snapped the prince. He pushed and pulled at her, turning her around and tugging at her wings. She suppressed her cries of pain as he twisted her.

"A rather pretty little girl, after all the rest," her captor observed. His voice rasped, as if his throat had gone dry, and these words scared her far more than did his brutal inspection.

"No sign of pursuit, my liege," another man announced, coming into the clearing along the path they had followed. "I followed the men for some distance. I saw your broth—that is, Prince Takian's horse, following in the wake of the Carillonn guard. The rider was motionless, an arrow sticking from his back."

"Very well." Suddenly the prince was tense and nervous again. Kianna felt a wave of relief—at least his attentions were no longer focused on her. "We ride on immediately. I want to reach the square of Birchglen by late this afternoon. That's where I intend to 'learn' of the treacherous ambush directed against my brother and the Duchess of Carillonn!"

"And the prisoner . . . ?" asked the rider who had carried Kianna this far.

"Throw her back over your horse," the prince dictated. "We ride at once."

The twissel's face was again pressed to the horse's flank. Miserably, Kianna tried to think of a song, of some thread of music, that might lighten her despair.

But she couldn't remember a single note.

— 3 —

Prince Takian was awake, sitting up and leaning against a mossy stump when Rudy came to check on his condition. The pale blue of dawn's arrival barely filtered through to the floor of Galtigor's sweeping forest. The duchess knelt beside him, retying the bandage across his chest with a fresh strip from her petticoat. Seeing her noble leg bared—and kneeling in the mud—the Iceman was surprised at the extent of the woman's dedication to her patient.

Then he looked at the patient and his surprise became astonishment. The prince's cheeks were flushed with vitality, and his blue eyes danced with a fire that had been all but extinguished the night before.

"I'm glad to see you're better," said the Iceman. "The Duchess of Carillonn has saved your life."

"That she has," Takian replied, taking Bristyn's hand in his own, forcing her to stop tying the bandage and look into his eyes. "It's nothing less than a miracle. I shall *always* be grateful—and I only hope that I have the chance to prove my gratitude."

The duchess looked away, flustered, and the prince extended a hand to Rudy as the Iceman sat. "I understand that you, too, have offered me healing—though my lady is most mysterious about its nature."

"The true kindness has been hers. I only gave you drink, and held you still as she removed the arrow. How does it feel now—does the wound immobilize you?"

"That's the strange thing," the prince said wonderingly. "I'm not even sore! My chain mail deflected the arrowhead, I think, saving my heart—but I know it plunged deep into my back. There should be some kind of wound there!"

Those blue eyes drilled into Rudy, causing him to squirm under the inspection—as if the handsome prince would peer into the hidden corners of his mind. Rays of the rising sun probed through the trees, and when they fell upon Takian his blond hair shone like spun gold.

"You should rest," Bristyn urged. "We can talk later." She rose, and gestured Rudy to do likewise.

"No," Takian declared. "I'm fit—and I'm going after these assassins!" To prove his point he climbed to his feet, and though he winced slightly as he stretched his arms over his head, he moved with grace and coordination.

"They have a . . . companion of ours," Rudy explained. "I believe they'll try to take her back to the city."

"To what city?" demanded the prince. "Aren't these mountain bandits? Or rogues from Falteran?" He looked at the duchess, suddenly appalled. "Not Carillonn . . . not your own—"

"Of course not!" snapped Bristyn, her face whitening.

"It was Garamis—the men of the Black Mantle," Rudy declared bluntly. "They'll be taking Kianna to Landrun, I'm sure."

Takian looked shocked. "What lies are these? Do you seek to turn me against my brother, against my realm?" he demanded.

"It's too late for us to make your brother into your enemy," Rudy said quietly, meeting the prince's suspicious gaze.

Takian's eyes narrowed as he scrutinized each person in the little group—from Rudy to Anjell to Danri, Raine, and finally Bristyn. "Why did you ride away when my men and I first met your party? Did you, too, distrust me?" he asked.

"None of us distrusted *you*. But we—were warned, by Kianna," the duchess declared in a burst. "She said that Rudy knew that terrible danger waited for us along the trail. When you showed up, we naturally feared that something was wrong."

"As it was," Takian muttered. He looked again at the arrow. "But how would Garamis . . ."

Rudy began to speak, calmly and without emotion so that his words would carry their maximum weight. He told Takian about the ascent of the Glimmercrown, of the black blade his brother bore, of the butchery and blasphemy Garamis had committed in a sacred place—and, lastly, of the murders that had left bloody scars on the Appenfell family.

The prince remained impassive during the tale, except that the color that had returned to his features slowly drained away. At last he slumped against the tree trunk, as weak as when he had been pierced by the arrow—but this time the wound penetrated his spirit.

"I hate what you've told me," Takian admitted. "But I believe it. I've ignored too many things about Garamis, for too long. Now it seems that my brother has sunk to the lowest depths of treachery and betrayal."

"Betrayal—not just of you, but of all your people," Rudy pointed out.

"If this is true—and I've already told you I believe that it is," the prince continued, "then it's not safe for me to show myself in my own realm. The men of the Black Mantle are everywhere, and certainly any one of them would long to conclude the matter their leader has begun."

"Nor can my lady afford to be identified," Raine noted, with a meaningful look at the duchess. "The same assassins are a dire threat to you, as well."

"What can we do?" cried Bristyn, clenching her hands into fists. "Go back to Carillonn and let the war go on?"

"We can try to stop Garamis," Rudy declared. "He's got Kianna—and the first thing I need to do is rescue her. Perhaps the duchess should return at least to the North Shore Wayfarer's Lodge—"

"No!" snapped Bristyn Duftrall. "The fairy—Kianna—risked her life to protect me! Do you think I would abandon her to her fate?"

No, Rudy thought, even as he looked at her in surprise. Perhaps he had underestimated her.

"I can disguise myself," Takian said. "Bootblack on my hair, and an old cloak—I'm certain I won't be recognized. After all, everyone knows me as 'the Prince of the Golden Hair.' "

"And my disguise has worked this far," Danri added. "I'm coming with you for the rest of the way."

"As are Raine and myself," declared the duchess. "In disguise, as well."

Looking at the duchess, her undergarments rent by the need for bandages, her skin and hair dirty from the night spent on the ground, Rudy suspected that little further disguise would be needed. At the same time, he was grateful for her courage—and desperately glad that Raine would remain with them as well.

"It's only my jewels that might give me away," Bristyn noted, a trace of wistfulness in her tone. She pulled several rings off her fingers, tucking them into her beltpurse. Then she reached up to undo the clasp of her sparkling necklace, a chain of diamond-studded silver links supporting a golden-drackan pendant.

"I heard Rudy call you 'Big Fellow.' Is that your name?" she said to Kalland, who rested nearby. The snow lion raised his head expectantly as she held out the ornate piece of jewelry. "Perhaps you'll carry this for me?"

The shaggy animal bounced to his feet and ambled slowly over to the duchess. His throat rumbled with purrs as she wrapped the gem-studded collar around his neck. Though it mostly vanished into a wealth of tawny fur, an occasional diamond glittered from the mass of mane.

It took Takian only a few minutes to get a tin of black polish out of his saddlebags and darken his hair. When he threw a travel-stained cloak over his shoulders, he looked nothing like the royal figure he'd been on the previous day. Soon the group was on the road, Danri and Rudy on foot while Anjell rode behind Raine.

In a short time they approached the stone bridge over the stream where the ambush had occurred. Several ragged bundles lay beside the road, and Bristyn gasped, choking into a sob as they reached these bodies.

"Paderon!" she cried, jumping from her horse and stumbling to the limp figure of the blue-robed priest.

"No!" Raine's voice, dry with horror, rasped in her throat as she, too, raced toward the corpse.

The digger, Rudy, and Anjell approached more slowly, reluctant to intrude on the women's grief. The Iceman laid a hand on Raine's shoulder as the maid and her mistress embraced, weeping.

"Shot with arrows—though the missiles have already been re-moved," Danri observed grimly.

"Probably for the evidence—there've been travelers along here since the attack," Takian noted. "No doubt half of Galtigor is con-vinced by now that we're being invaded by sylves."

The duchess sobbed wretchedly over the dead man. "It should have been *me*! He was holding my horse, wearing the same color as me! Oh, Paderon—*why?*"

"We've got to move," Rudy said, more harshly than he intended. He was surprised when Bristyn rose to her feet and stumbled back to her horse. "You go on—I'll stay and bury him," she declared, pulling a silver knife—more like an ornate letter opener than a weapon—from her saddlebag. "Raine—help me."

The maidservant had already folded the priest's robe over his face. She knelt for a moment, eyes closed, her lips moving in silent prayer. When the duchess came back, Raine took the ornamental blade and started to scrape at the ground.

"By all the gods!" Danri groaned. "We can't split up—they won't last half a day!"

Resigned to helping, Rudy took his ice axe and Danri raised his pick-hammer. Together they chopped a shallow grave. The Iceman was aware of the women's silent gratitude, even as he felt time slipping past. With each heartbeat, Kianna was getting farther away—but Danri was right: they couldn't let their small company be divided still further.

Finally they laid the priest in the grave, and marked it with a plank of wood and several white stones. When they resumed their march, they walked at a trot, trying to make up as much time as they could.

By late afternoon they came to an expanse of cultivated land carved from the forest, and just beyond they saw the cluster of build-ings signifying a small town. With Danri, Takian, and Bristyn mounted and cloaked, the companions approached the village over an arched stone bridge. A great throng of people had gathered in the market square, and as the companions joined the crowd they observed several men standing on a platform before the village inn.

"Kingswall is threatened!" cried one burly fellow, bedecked in gold chains and velvet robes—obviously the burgmeister. "The enemy has come from beyond the Watershed—and now it lurks in our woods! We have the arrows—proof positive of sylvan treachery!"

He indicated another man, well-dressed and plump, who stood beside him. "This noble merchant, on the road back home from a long caravan, reports he has seen the bodies, cruelly left beside the road. And fleet-riding Wallace"—the burgmeister pointed to another fellow, dusty from the trail—"returns from the north, with news that Prince Garamis is raising an army to seek vengeance! Well, my good citizens of Kingswall—it is time to stand up and fight for our town and our forest! I lead a contingent to Landrun at first light tomorrow! Do you ride with me?"

"Aye! We ride!" Cries rose from the crowd, united in hatred. Rudy cringed inwardly from the force of the people's fury—what fools they were! But he did not deceive himself—their foolishness could make them a very deadly force indeed.

Leaving Anjell and his disguised companions in the courtyard of the inn, Rudy went inside with Raine. Paying out a few of their precious coins, they arranged for two small rooms, determined to get themselves out of sight and to try to rest until the dawn.

— 4 —

Nicodareus sank into the pool of steaming, bubbling Darkblood, immersing himself to the tips of his curling horns. The infusion of power felt good, right—and much needed. Two journeys across the Watershed, he knew, had sapped the reserves of his power.

Of course, the Lord Minion felt nothing so crude as fatigue—his muscles were as powerful as ever, and if necessary, he could have traveled for many days in response to his master's commands. Instead, his malaise was more a spiritual problem, as if the very stuff of his soul had been sapped by too much time away from the sustaining mire of Duloth-Trol.

Now, as the Darkblood soaked and soothed his skin, Nicodareus felt a slow restoration of his might. For uncounted hours and days he lay fully immersed, tended only by the brutox that regularly spilled more of the inky liquid into their master's great vat. Gradually the fire returned to the Lord Minion's soul, building into a seething inferno of hatred, once again ready to explode across the land.

Remaining fully submerged, Nicodareus extended his Sight across the world. From this center of power he could view even places across the Watershed, hundreds of miles away. He observed the actions of his human tool, and was pleased by the progress of Garamis' plans. War between Faerine and Dalethica was imminent; and this was as Dassadec desired, so Nicodareus was pleased.

He allowed himself to seek out and observe his fellow Lord Minions. Reaper, the Talon of Dassadec, had gathered a mighty host of minions on the western flats of Duloth-Trol. Kroaks in the tens of thousands, countless brutox, great flights of terrions, and stealthy, insidious stalkers all assembled in vast encampments. The mighty wyrm prowled among them, his awesome presence binding the creatures to their master in life and death. The horde awaited only Dassadec's command, Nicodareus knew, before it would unleash an invasion such as Dalethica had not seen in a thousand years.

To the east, Phalthak—the multiheaded Fang of the Sleep-stealer—seethed and chortled, his snake-necks twitching this way and that as if he felt the Eye of Dassadec in its surreptitious observation. Phalthak had gathered a much smaller force than had Reaper, for the forbidding slopes of the Darkenheight Pass effectively precluded a large army from entering Faerine. Yet the Fang of Dassadec numbered a great multitude of terrions among his army, as well as full companies of brutox that had long practiced scaling steep slopes and crossing high mountains. Phalthak, too, would be ready to strike when the master gave his command.

The only threat Nicodareus could see—and at first it was a minor one, but vexing—was the persistent survival of the young Iceman. As the days passed, the Lord Minion began to sense a danger in that human that exceeded any reasonable assessment of his power. He had survived the minions in Halverica, and now he seemed determined to create difficulties for the Prince of Galtigor.

He was a problem, Nicodareus knew, that he himself would have to address—obviously, there was no other solution. Though he had already spent much time on the far side of the Watershed, his tasks there were not yet completed. He had one final use remaining of the Power of Three; that journey would at last give him the chance to kill.

Gradually the Lord Minion emerged from the pool of Darkblood. His skin glowing with an ebony sheen, he rose to his full height as he stalked toward his chambers, secure in the heart of Agath-Trol, near the great throne room itself. Eager brutox, sparks showering from their trembling fingers, stood alert, waiting for their master's commands.

"I embark on another journey," he announced, picturing the long flight to Galtigor with a sense of growing anticipation—not because of the journey itself, but because of the killing that would follow when he arrived. To insure the success of his mission, he had resolved that he would not travel alone.

"I shall depart with the sunset, and I desire a companion for the journey," he declared, his voice rumbling with potent authority. He turned to one trembling brutox.

"Summon Slasher. This time my terrion flies beside me," he declared, before starting for the ramparts of the fortress's mighty towers.

— 5 —

Paderon Zyloth's death was like a great earthquake, tearing away the solid ground of my existence and leaving me at the brink of a perilous, growing chasm. For the first time in my life the protective framework of strictures and prophecies, the steadiness provided by a mentor and teacher, were gone—leaving in their place naught but blood-soaked tragedy and impenetrable enigma.

Even my mistress ceased to require me, at least to the level she had before. Part of this effect was necessitated by disguise, for as we traveled through Galtigor, any difference in class revealed between us could have proved a threat to her anonymity.

But even more than these essential changes, Bristyn Duftrall—like myself—found herself at a great branching in her life; and I believe she discovered herself wanting.

It was a strange procession along that King's Highway of Galtigor. I had met, and was becoming friends with, the man who had visited my girlhood dreams. At the same time, we traveled through an enemy country, often camping in the forest, constantly on the alert for the men of the Black Mantle. Periods of almost giddy discovery would be followed by moments of terror, as we were forced to cower in the hedges while companies of armed men rode or marched past.

Our strange group was propelled by many things, it seemed. Most obviously, it was a quest of rescue; some were also driven by a desire for vengeance, restitution—even escape across the Watershed. We all worked, traveled, talked, and prayed together.

And yet, we still didn't know—hadn't even guessed at—that goal for which we strived.

From: *Recollections*, by Lady Raine of the Three Waters

SIXTEEN

Shadows in the Sky

An enemy's ability to cope with your actions is
invariably based upon his previous experience. Strike
him in a way he has never before imagined, and he
will be utterly paralyzed.
—TOME OF VILE COMPULSIONS

— 1 —

For days Garamis and his Redsteel Guards galloped beneath the canopy
of trees, pausing only for a few short hours of rest during the nights.
They followed forest paths well off the King's Highway, racing from
one tiny village to another on the long route to Landrun. By the third
day, the prince was delighted to learn that word of Faerine treachery
had preceded him even in these remote locations.

The mute twissel remained bound securely, strapped to the withers of Wilfriz's mount. At every village or roadside inn, Garamis
dragged her off the horse and displayed the twissel to anyone who
would look: proof positive that the Faerines had begun a treacherous
invasion.

"My brother slain by assassins—the Duchess of Carillonn has
disappeared!" The Prince's appeal was short, direct, and apparently
incontrovertible. "I summon all brave men of Galtigor to assemble
beneath my banner, gathering at my father's palace in Landrun! Join

me—soon we march against Faerine!"

Garamis counted it sublime good fortune that had brought the twissel into his hands, and every time they showed her to a group of his countrymen, he got further proof. Indeed, the fairy's presence, coupled with the nobleman's lurid tale of ambush and assassination, inflamed the passions of the humans—on several occasions the Redsteel Guards actually had to protect the twissel from furious mobs.

The prince's efforts were further aided by the reports, begun by the merchants who had first stumbled upon the ambush, of the sylvan arrows. Garamis himself said nothing about these unique weapons, allowing the rumors to build under their own momentum. The combination of those imaginative stories and the presence of the twissel were enough to lay aside any doubts among his people.

When she wasn't being displayed like a captive animal, the fairy remained securely bound and gagged. Garamis had considered cutting off her wings, as a further measure to prevent escape, but decided that those gossamer membranes were too important—they provided the best evidence of her true nature. He spent no time wondering what had brought her to Dalethica—it was enough that her presence fit in so perfectly with his plans.

Following their winding trek through the woodlands, the company of Redsteel Guards approached Landrun. The captive, after more than a week's captivity, showed signs of pallor and malnutrition—but even if she died right now, her presence had proven of incalculable value. Every day more men had joined the procession, bearing swords, shields, and spears, swearing to avenge the treacherous attack. The night before they reached the city, the prince returned to the King's Highway to stay at the Inn of Two Wells, twenty miles south of Landrun. His entourage filled the courtyard and every surrounding pasture with the tents and bonfires of a large encampment.

Hundreds of men jostled and shoved, seeking a look at the terrified fairy in the midst of their drinking and carousing. The fires and ribald songs lasted well past midnight, and dawn found a trickle of additional recruits—mostly men from distant farmsteads—reaching the inn in time to join the final march to Landrun.

The growing mob passed through the city gates late in the day.

A throng of the prince's countrymen lined the streets—and this time there was nothing hollow about the cheers. Men surged down adjacent lanes, pledging their allegiance. Garamis appointed several of his Red-steel Guards to organize these recruits, and more companies were hastily formed.

The prince saw groups of armed men gathering in front of taverns, irregular units assembling in the city plazas. Everywhere curses against sylvan evildoers rang through the air. Blacksmiths' hammers clanged as war horses were shod, while armorers honed and polished weapons for the anticipated campaign.

The prince entrusted his captive to Wilfriz as they ascended the winding road to the hilltop palace. "Take her to the hightower," he instructed. "I want her chained on the balcony, where the whole city can see her."

"Aye, my lord," agreed the captain, who still bore the miserable twissel across the withers of his horse. She hadn't spoken a word during her long, rough ride—but as Garamis had predicted, her very appearance was enough to inflame the ancient prejudices of his people.

Garamis went to find his father, locating him in the formal gardens overlooking the vast curve of the river. King Larriac looked at his elder son with tears in his eyes, causing the prince to stop, startled. Garamis had never before noticed the lines etched into his father's face—certainly they had never been so deep. And when had his body become so frail? The king's face seemed almost wasted of flesh; the hair on his scalp and his chin was sparse and stringy. Boric was with his father, sitting happily on a bench, watching a pair of redbirds.

"Garam!" cried the youngest prince, rushing forward to embrace his brother in a firm hug. "You're back! And you brought Takian with you, I bet! Didn't you?"

There was something frantic in Boric's eyes as he looked over Garamis' shoulder, expecting their other sibling to march boldly into view. In the king's eyes Garamis saw that word of Takian's presumed fate had already reached the city.

"They said Takian got shot!" Boric exclaimed, shaking his head in steadfast denial. "But he didn't, did he? You tell 'em—he *didn't*!"

Garamis remembered his dream, the one in which Takian had

fallen away from the lofty tower—the place where Wilfriz, even now, was taking the fairy. In the dream Boric had laughed and clapped his hands with delight. Now, of course, Boric wasn't laughing, and somehow that fact seemed more distressing to the prince than the reality of his other brother's murder.

"Dear Bor—I'm afraid he did. You'll have to be brave, like a warrior. He would have wanted that."

Boric, with a gasp that expanded into a howl of anguish, stumbled away, collapsing onto a bench and crying piteously—his grief as unrestrained as a child's.

"They said his body was never found," King Larriac declared numbly.

"That's true," Garamis agreed, cautiously. In fact, this remained the most disturbing development in his plan. "But we can't hold on to that for hope—he was struck by one of the sylvan arrows, and each of those missiles claimed the life of its target. Father, it was an attack of monstrous treachery—but I promise you it shall be avenged!"

The prince stood silent for a moment, expecting his father to endorse the cry for vengeance. Instead, King Larriac shambled over to the bench where Boric sat crying. The monarch sat down and laid a gentle hand on his son's shoulder. Then Larriac's own chest shook with a racking sob, and he bent to embrace Boric.

Garamis was appalled. In disgust he spun on his heel and stalked from the garden. His father, obviously, had grown too old for the affairs of leadership. How could he let himself wallow in grief, when such a definite course of action beckoned? Even in death, it seemed, Takian was not about to let his elder brother have the freedom of his father's attention!

The prince found Terral in the throne room, organizing the assignments of daily work; the advisor looked up from his ledger as Garamis strode toward him.

"Yes, Your Highness?" Terral inquired deferentially.

"I want the banners of war flying from every flagpole in the city!" the prince demanded. "Get the word out—every able-bodied man is to report immediately. I will muster the greatest army Galtigor has ever seen—and it will march against Taywick Pass before the week is out!"

— 2 —

"This is the Inn of Two Wells," Takian said, as the companions turned into a narrow lane off the Landrun Road. "It's a popular wayside, a short day's ride from Landrun. I've stayed here myself, but I don't think anyone's likely to recognize me now."

Rudy smiled thinly in agreement. "Even if they haven't heard you've been eaten by wolves."

"Indeed." Takian chuckled grimly. "I wonder if our little fiction has reached my brother yet—if the rumormongers are on the job, it should be soon."

"Whatever they've heard, no one's going to want to talk to you," the Iceman pointed out.

For the last fortnight, as the companions had traveled through Galtigor, Prince Takian's disguise had grown more and more complete. The formerly fair-haired nobleman now sported a mane of boot-polish black, and a similarly colored stubble covered his cheeks and chin. His garments were trail-worn and mud-stained, displaying none of the grandeur of his station. In addition, the prince had adopted a stooped posture, and a stuttering manner of speech that seemed to instantly unsettle any strangers who so much as stopped to ask directions.

The Duchess of Shalloth had also discarded or disguised her noble status. Vanity had compelled her to keep a pair of diamond rings, but her plain woolen shawl and darkened hair—the latter also dyed with Takian's bootblack—altered her appearance quite completely. Additionally, the inky stuff in her hair continually smudged her cheeks and hands, forcing her to remain grimy.

Now the footsore Bristyn Duftrall limped along, leading her patient gelding by the reins—because her buttocks were too sore for her to ride. Yet she had surprised her companions during this long, hard trek: since the burial of Paderon Zyloth she had almost ceased to complain about her personal discomfort. She remained aloof, and sometimes asked Raine to tend to her hair, or gather her food on the many occasions when they had camped in the woods. Yet she carried her own bedroll and ignored her obvious pain, keeping up with the others in determined, stubborn silence.

Raine quietly offered to take the gelding's bridle; with a sigh, the duchess handed it over. Like her mistress, the maidservant had been changed by the priest's death. It seemed to Rudy that she had lost some of her self-assurance; that she was afraid in a way she hadn't been before. The Iceman knew, without understanding why, that it wasn't Garamis and his Redsteel Guards that frightened her.

"Why is it called the Inn of Two Wells?" Anjell asked, stepping easily beside her uncle. The days of walking had hardened the girl's muscles until she could keep pace without difficulty or complaint. Now she almost skipped at the prospect of coming to a new inn.

"Th-there are two big cisterns along the st-stream behind it," Takian explained, wheezing in his masquerade voice. "It's said that they draw . . . pure water up out of the ground—and from one of them the water is quite hot, perfectly suited for a bath. The water comes from springs, up there on the hill across the stream. Kirkith Phleet, the innkeeper, has an arrangement of pipes and valves that allows him to draw from whichever well he wants."

"Sounds clever," Danri agreed, limping on his crutch. "We Faerines use springs like that too. All of us but the gigants, who're just too stupid."

"How come you hate gigants so much, Danri?" Anjell asked.

"Just have good taste, I guess," the digger replied, with a spit into the ditch.

The prince chuckled a laugh which rattled into a convincingly gasping cough as they entered the courtyard. "My brothers and I came to this inn many times when we were young—happier times, those."

"Brothers?" Anjell asked. "I thought your only brother was Garamis."

The prince's eyes grew unusually soft. "Boric is my other brother—you'd like him, I think. He enjoys children—likes to play games and such. In some ways, he *is* a child."

"He sounds quite nice," the girl said politely.

They came in sight of a large, sprawling establishment of weathered wood, the second story of which was surrounded on three sides by balconies. A scenic stream meandered through a channel just beyond and below the inn, and several large culverts were visible at the far side of the waterway—the drainpipes of the wells, Rudy guessed. A spacious stable stood off to one side.

The companions entered the great-room and sat down, except for Raine and Rudy, who wandered to the bar and inquired after the innkeeper. A large man with a bulbous red nose and tiny, bloodshot eyes came waddling out of the back room. He stank of whiskey, and swayed slightly as he stood before them.

"A pair of rooms, three or four per room? Yes, we can do that—you'll be on the second floor, toward the back. That will be two coppers for each room; four total. If you make it six, you can all have dinner as well. Seven and that big dog can stay inside with you."

"Seven it is," Rudy said with casual friendliness, ignoring the misidentification of Kalland. "We'll be wanting a good meal in our bellies when we start for Landrun in the morning." He had found that, by offering tidbits of knowledge about himself and his companions, most of the people he met would be glad to provide him with reams of information about local goings-on.

"That's a full day's march—but no trouble if you get a start while the sun's low in the east. By the by, I'm Kirkith Phleet—yer host. What'll ye be drinkin'?"

"How about a pitcher of ale—and another of milk?" Rudy said.

"Ye ain't goin' to mix 'em, are ye?" Kirkith asked, squinting as he inspected the companions.

"No!" Rudy assured him.

"Have a seat, then—they'll be right over."

Apparently business was slow enough that Kirkith didn't have a barmaid on duty; in any event, the innkeeper brought their pitchers himself. He studied Rudy with an appraising eye.

"Goin' to Landrun to join the prince's army?" he inquired.

"Um, yes—after I attend to my family's care," the Iceman replied. He wanted to insure that he had an excuse to remain with his companions in case Kirkith pressed him to pledge some kind of early enlistment.

"That'll be a grand campaign. I just been to the city myself. There's new companies marching hither and yon outside the walls; mounted knights and lords crowding the streets—each of 'em ready to prove his honor at the drop of a hat. I seen veteran troops of the Carillonn wars, carousing through Landrun. Looked like they been drinkin' for a week, some of 'em!"

"Has the prince announced his plan of campaign?" Rudy asked. "How can any human army strike at Faerine?"

"He's goin' right for Taywick Pass—and here's the best part: Prince Garamis has gained a talisman from the highest mountain in the Watershed. It's ice, a block made from the three waters of the world. Says that with that chunk of frost, his army'll be able to march right through Taywick. All those barriers're just magical illusions anyway—everybody knows that!"

"How does he know of this ice's powers?" asked Takian tensely.

"How do I know?" Kirkith, looking cross, took a swig from a small flask he kept in his apron pocket. "Maybe a little fairy told him," he said, with a rude wink.

The innkeeper went on to explain that any traces of doubt were eliminated by the presence of the captured Faerine "assassin." Though Rudy's cheeks flushed from anger when he heard the tale, the innkeeper was too engrossed in the telling to notice. The twissel, Kirkith Phleet explained, was now displayed on a balcony, perched high on a tower in the palace so that she was visible from the great market square beyond and below the outer curtain walls. Twin iron brackets secured her tiny ankles to heavy chains that were anchored to rings set into the stone.

Kirkith muttered, disappointedly, that "all she does is sit there," but when Rudy probed casually, the innkeeper stated that she did not appear bruised or battered.

"Just enough to have her there, where everyone can see, I guess. Best recruiting picture the prince could hope for. Though he'll prob'ly dump her in the river when it's time to move out. Sure wish I could go."

"In the army, you mean?" Rudy probed.

"Yeah. I got a bad knee, cut up in the Carillonn wars. Keeps me pretty close to the inn, 'less I get a wagon ride to the city." Kirkith nodded to them and then crossed back to the bar to tend to the needs of other customers.

"Not much of a limp for someone with a bad knee," Anjell observed tartly. "Am I glad he's gone," she added with a shudder.

"Me, too," Rudy agreed. He gestured to the drinks on the table. "Let's finish these up and get some rest before dinner."

— 3 —

The two great, winged forms sailed through dawnlit skies, soaring in a long glide from the crest of the Watershed. Centuries earlier, Nicodareus had found the body of the terrion to be his favorite tool, when he wanted to go to the effort of flying under his own power. Now, with mighty Slasher rushing through the air beyond his wingtip, the power of flight felt like the greatest of all gifts.

His Sight had probed before him at sunset, locating the essence of the man from Halverica in a wooden building beside a stream. The image beckoned with powerful allure, and the Lord Minion and Slasher had flown closer throughout the night. Although the Sight of Nicodareus did not provide him with physical details of appearance, the soul of this man was a thing so strong, so vivid, that the Lord Minion knew his victim would be easy to identify.

The structure where he stayed had gradually resolved into a clear image, and its location was burned indelibly into the Eye of Dassadec's mind. Even through the overcast, Nicodareus knew that it was near. Now, at last, came the time to descend.

The gray clouds still concealed the two great flyers, and Nicodareus was grateful—the fewer people who witnessed this attack, the better. Of those in the immediate vicinity, of course, he would make sure there were no survivors. But it was better if local farmers and woodsmen couldn't provide details about the brutal onslaught. Let the humans speculate, he thought with a grim chuckle—the destruction would no doubt be blamed on some predatory assault from Faerine.

With a croak of pure, savage hate, the Lord Minion tipped his wings and increased the speed of his dive.

— 4 —

Rudy woke with a sense of panic, throwing back his blanket and leaping out of bed before he remembered where he was. The drab walls of the Inn of Two Wells looked so much like the other places where he and his companions had stayed previously that he had to shake his head and force himself to sit before full recollection returned.

His surroundings established, Rudy's thoughts immediately jumped to Kianna. How did she fare? He could only hope that her terror had rendered her numb to pain and discomfort—for the thousandth time he rebuked himself for allowing her to embark on the mission to warn Bristyn Duftrall. The fact that the twissel's courage had saved the life of the duchess, and quite possibly Raine's life as well, did little to assuage the Iceman's sense of guilt.

Rudy stepped to the window of their cramped, dingy room, staring into the treetops that stretched away to the north. Since that first night in Galtigor, camping beside the road, he had been awed and amazed by the forests of this land. Mile upon mile of woods, mingled with lake and stream and marsh, stretched to all horizons. Some of the trees were hardwood, while others were evergreens of pine, fir, and cedar. Often patches had been cleared for farmsteads, and the villages frequently stood in the midst of wide pastures, but the roadways linking these steadings seemed to meander beneath an eternal archway of branches and leaves.

Rudy strained to penetrate that tangled wood, to see his goal or to learn some hint of the future. He had told none of his companions of his intention to kill Garamis, but since the capture of Kianna, that obsession had flared with renewed fury. Too many had died because of the Prince of Galtigor's cruelty, ambition, and greed. He, Rudgar Appenfell, would put an end to it!

He reminded himself that the previous tragedies, miserable though they were, paled in comparison to the cataclysm that could result from the prince's intended war. Danri had assured Rudy that Taywick Pass was watched and garrisoned by a small force of Faerines, but its defense rested primarily upon the barriers of magic. These illusions distorted the appearance of the terrain and sky, so that any human venturing there immediately became confused and lost.

The digger had grimly added that if the pass were in fact breached, the pastoral vales of Faerine would prove easy pickings for the conquering humans. The suggestion that the Ice of Three Waters would negate the pitfalls on the pass was too frightening to be ignored.

Traces of dawn mist glided among the trees while a breeze whispered through the branches like a chorus of ghosts, as if daring Rudy to enter their sanctum. He watched the meandering stream, noting again the two large pipes leading underground from the bank of the brook. The Iceman felt a chill that was unrelated to the cool dawn, but as he reached to close the shutter he hesitated.

No—there are no ghosts there, he told himself.

At the same time, there was *something*.

He knew this even before he noticed the tickling of thirst, scratching at the back of his throat like the craving for water, but just a little different. Unaware of what he was doing, he reached for the half-full waterskin of Aura that lay beside his bed, drawing it to his lips for a drink.

As the liquid washed across his tongue and quenched the dryness in his throat, Rudy felt the same tingle of delight he remembered from the North Shore Wayfarer's Lodge, when he had drunk the stuff of Faerine. This time the sensation passed in a matter of moments, and his attention was again drawn to the window and the woods beyond, to the north.

He saw a vague and disturbing menace there, but it was—for the moment at least—a passive thing, lurking in Landrun, a score of miles away, not directed at Rudy or his companions. With a shudder that was partly revulsion, partly awe at his own awareness, he realized that some vague sense of his had reached out and touched Lord Garamis. The prince was far away, and his attentions were focused elsewhere.

But why the sense of thirst? Uneasily, Rudy looked back and forth across the trees. Something was wrong about this forest, but it remained a vague thing, undefinable but certainly a threat.

The window of his room faced to the north, toward their destination. With growing disquiet he began to sense that the danger was not terribly distant—instead, perhaps Rudy was looking in the wrong direction.

In one movement he reached the door and threw it open. Crossing the hall, he knocked—softly, but with urgency—against the door of the room where the women slept.

"Who is it?" The voice, sleepily irritated, belonged to Bristyn.

"It's Rudy—let me in! Hurry!" Even though he whispered, she must have sensed his growing fear, for the door quickly opened. The duchess, ruffled by sleep, wrapped a cotton gown around herself and frowned at him. "The window!" he cried, leaping past her and throwing open the shutter.

The awareness of evil lurking in the southern sky knocked him backwards a full step and set his heart hammering in his ribs. Desperately he forced himself to scan the sky, trying to penetrate the clouds that brightened with the rusty light of dawn.

Whatever he sensed was a far more powerful entity, an infinitely greater threat, than the ambushers who had awaited Raine and the duchess along the road. It darkened the sky like a massive storm cloud, seething like an unworldly cyclone as it swept inexorably closer.

Yet when he pushed his sight, really tried to *see*, he understood that the approaching menace was a more precise thing than a nebulous storm; that the whirling vapors he sensed were closer to the creature's presence than its actual body. Furiously he probed, staring into that steely sky and tearing away the layers of cloud with his mind.

He saw a pair of long, slender wings, and he recognized a terrion. The ceature, rippling in the dark colors of the clouds, was plainly visible to him, soaring from Duloth-Trol, riding its power and its speed on some mission across the Watershed. The terrion was coming to attack them, he knew, but this knowledge seemed of vague, almost inconsequential importance. But how could that be?

In a shocking instant he understood—the terrion was a mere servant to the real menace, the darkness that swept through the clouds and spread its foul aura across a hundred miles of forest.

"Wake up!" he shouted, caring no longer that his voice rang through the whole slumbering inn.

Anjell screamed and sat up, while Raine sprang from her own bed and came to the window. In a moment Danri and Takian appeared at the door, while further commotion arose in the hallway.

"Something's coming—fast!" he cried. His hands flexed, and he realized that he'd left his sword in his own room. At the same time he sensed how utterly useless a steel edge would be against the menace that swept closer by the second.

"Grab everything—get your weapons and hurry downstairs," he called, as the others hastened into action. Rudy darted across the hall, snatched up his sword and slung the waterskin over his shoulder. Danri and Takian armed themselves with haste, the prince fixing Rudy with a penetrating gaze.

"We're going to be attacked," the Iceman blurted. "By something huge—and horrible!"

"Did you see it?"

"No—not exactly. But I know it's coming. And I don't think we should be upstairs when it arrives."

"That's good enough for me," Danri said to the prince. "I think the kid knows what he's talking about."

Without further hesitation, Takian buckled his sword belt and followed Rudy into the hall. At the top of the stairs they ran into Kirkith, who scowled suspiciously as the digger sprinted from the room.

"What's the commo—hey! What kind of cripple *are* you?" he asked, glowering at the digger's back.

"I don't have time to explain—but there's danger on the way. You should get everyone into the cellar. I'll try to protect them." Even as Rudy spoke, he wondered how he could possibly do anything. Then another fact struck him hard, tingling with frightful reality: they had precious little time.

"Let's go!" he cried, leaping down the stairs, through the great-room, and throwing open the front door of the inn.

He saw them, winging below the overcast, swooping toward the

building from the south. At first he thought they were two terrions—
a black one in the fore, and back of it, another, of rusty gray—a color
to perfectly match the clouds—flying in tight formation.

His attention focused on the black terrion, and he realized that
this was the creature he had sensed through the mists of the dawn. It
only *looked* like a terrion; in truth, it was something far more potent
and awful.

The real terrion squawked, the fearful cry ringing over the forests
of Galtigor, a harbinger of horror unlike anything heard here for a
thousand years. It trailed after the leader, soaring toward the front
porch of the inn, where Rudy stood momentarily paralyzed. Kalland
pressed forward beside the Iceman, mane bristling, chest rumbling with
deep growls.

As it dove, the black terrion's eyes bored into the Iceman, and
Rudy felt as though he were looking into an infernal furnace of hatred.
Two spots of red glowed like fire, searing him with their vitriol, convincing him beyond any doubt that this creature had come specifically
for *him*.

The monster changed shape as it swept closer, the long, tapered
wings shrinking into broader, batlike membranes. The body lost its
avian sleekness, metamorphosing into a distorted form of humanoid
arms and legs, with the wings expanding like black sails from the shoulder blades. The face caught Rudy's full attention—curved white fangs
dripping in a wide-stretched maw, framing a blood-red tongue. Those
fiery eyes continued to burn as they flickered across the mortals at the
front of the inn. This was the visage of an inhuman monster, cruel
beyond measure, so much more terrible than a kroak or terrion as to
clearly establish this mighty being as the master of those lesser minions.

"I come for you, Iceman," declared the beast, in a voice that
rumbled more deeply than Kalland's most savage roar. "Only your
blood will slake my thirst!"

"Back!" cried Danri, seizing Rudy by the belt and hauling him
into the great-room. Takian slammed the front door shut and dropped
the heavy beam across it, though the barrier would barely be a nuisance
to the monstrous attacker.

Other people spilled into the great-room, stumbling down the stairs in the confusion of abruptly ended sleep. Kirkith had apparently taken the warning seriously, for he lunged behind the bar and threw open the heavy door to his cellar, calling to everyone who would listen to seek shelter there. A fat merchant pushed past the innkeeper, tumbling down into the darkness, while the cook and several maids hastened after.

Raine raced across the room to the fireplace, where several woodsmen had left their unstrung bows the night before. Rudy saw that she carried the sylvan arrow they had removed from Prince Takian's wound. Now the woman snatched up a heavy, double-curved bow, bending the wood and slipping the string taut in one smooth gesture. She nocked the missile and stepped to Rudy's side as the Iceman waited inside the front door. Danri, clutching his hammer, and Prince Takian with his slender rapier drawn, flanked them.

Rudy felt the approach of the horror as if he could see through the heavy door. It swooped lower, dropping its head toward the portal like a charging ram. The Iceman felt the image of those powerful, curving horns, and instinctively raised his sword in a desperate parry.

The dark figure struck the front of the inn with cruel force, splintering the wall and smashing the door inward. Pieces of broken lumber crashed into Rudy, knocking him onto his back. The door itself landed on his chest and for a moment the Iceman lay stunned beneath the heavy wood.

He heard a roar, an explosion of sound as deep and ominous as the avalanche that had swept down on him from the Glimmercrown, and he knew that the great black creature had entered the inn. Screams arose from near the cellar door, the shrill tenor of the cries clearly indicating that several people had been badly hurt.

Struggling to breathe, driving the crushing weight off his chest, Rudy scrambled to the side, emerging into a scene of chaos and rubble. The entire front wall of the inn was gone, leaving splintered beams and broken plaster to frame a view of the overcast sky beyond. The terrion settled to the ground outside, wicked beak lashing through the gap in the wall, driving Rudy backward.

Inside the shambles of the room, the dark-winged humanoid loomed over Danri, and the digger frantically dove away, barely avoiding the talon-studded paw that swiped at his foot. With a leap and a sharp blow of his hammer, the nimble Faerine twisted backward. Prince Takian darted in, distracting the monster for the second Danri needed.

Raine stood alone in the center of the room, the sylvan arrow pulled back to her cheek, the arrowhead centered on the looming monstrosity. She did not shoot, and at first Rudy feared that terror had paralyzed her. But her dark eyes flashed with awareness and determination—though she was afraid, that fear did not hold her in thrall.

In an instant he understood—she had but one of the potent missiles, and she seemed to sense even an enchanted weapon such as the arrow of Faerine would be little more than a pinprick to this creature. Instead, she lowered the weapon and darted quickly to the side, seeking a way around the horror.

But the monster sensed her intention, lowering vicious claws to block Raine's escape, feinting a murderous slash to hold Takian and Danri at bay. The floorboards trembled as it took a menacing step toward the woman.

Rudy acted without thinking, lunging with the sword he had claimed, so long ago, from the dead kroak. Chopping with all the strength in his lanky body, he slashed at the back of the hulking monster's legs. The weapon struck that shiny black skin—and bounced away without leaving so much as a cut. Hacking again in mindless rage, Rudy shouted in fury, as terror for Raine choked away any sense of his own safety.

The monster spun, with a thundering roar that exploded through the room, driving the Iceman backward like a blow across the face. Raine, still carrying the bow and arrow, ducked past and raced out through the shattered wall. Takian charged again, courageously facing death as Bristyn Duftrall, towing Anjell by the hand, sprinted past on the other side of the monster. Rudy felt a sick sense of relief as the brute spun back to him; at least there was a chance that his friends might escape with their lives.

The Iceman looked into the burning eyes and knew that he faced a creature whose power so dwarfed his own as to render him insignificant. He saw the hands, with their awful claws, reach forward to rend him, and he knew that he was about to die. But he didn't reckon on the courage of the digger from Shalemont.

Danri lunged at the creature's back, the spiked end of his hammer driving toward the sinewy thigh. He struck with brutal force and the beast emitted an inhuman scream—more fury than pain, perhaps, but the distraction saved Rudy's life. The Iceman tumbled beneath the broken timbers of the wall, sprawling into the dust of the courtyard and desperately scrambling to his feet.

The monster turned away from him in murderous pursuit of the courageous digger. Danri scrambled behind the bar, ducking out of sight as the creature's brutal fists came crushing down onto the hard-wood surface. Splinters flew as the top shattered, collapsing to the floor, but there was no sign of the digger.

Kirkith Phleet took that moment to break from the cellar, stumbling toward the rear door of the inn with a terrified backward glance. In an instant the beast reached out, seizing the innkeeper by the scruff of his neck.

"Are you—?" The rumbling voice began with a question as the furious eyes flashed into Phleet's sweating, horrified face. "No—you are not the one I seek." With a crushing squeeze of that powerful hand, the creature broke the stout innkeeper's neck, casting the limp body to the floor as it turned back to the companions.

Anjell's scream brought Rudy's attention around, and he whirled to see the massive terrion, its fang-studded beak gaping, drop like a stone toward the companions huddled before the ruined inn. Kalland sprang upward, his powerful leap carrying him into the air over the girl's head. The snow lion's claws raked across the terrion's belly and the huge flyer shrieked and veered away.

The courageous animal dropped back to the ground and leaped again as the monster made another pass. This time the terrion's claws darted outward, seizing the snow lion and shaking the animal like a tiny doll. Veering sideways, the creature chopped with its beak and then dropped Kalland to the ground. The snow lion tumbled into the weeds beside the stream and lay still; the terrion swept back toward Anjell.

The Iceman raised his sword, racing to his niece's side as a sense of utter hopelessness tried to drag him down. He didn't think he could save her—at best, he could sacrifice his own life in her defense.

Beside him, Raine raised the bow, once again drawing the sylvan arrow back to her cheek. With a smooth gesture she aimed and shot, sending the sleek missile soaring into the overcast sky, toward the rippling form of the mirror-skinned terrion.

The arrow flew straight into that gaping maw, and the terrion's scream, which built toward a killing pitch, abruptly faded into a shrieking gurgle. Rudy pulled Anjell out of the way as the creature smashed heavily into the ground before them. It lay still, dead.

The bellow of rage from within the inn exploded with more force than any previous outburst. Danri and Takian, still clutching their weapons, came tumbling through the gap in the wall, and the massive, stalking figure of the beast came after.

"To the water!" shouted the digger, pointing toward the nearby stream.

Instantly Rudy seized on the chance—certainly no part of the buildings or forest would shelter them from this horrendous onslaught. The cisterns of the Two Wells! Pulling Anjell by the hand, he raced to the edge of the stream. They dove in together, as Bristyn, Takian, and Raine jumped beside them. Even the digger didn't hesitate, plunging down the bank and immersing himself just a short reach in front of the lunging monstrosity.

Surprisingly, the creature halted at the water's edge, howling its fury at them with inarticulate snarls and barks. Wading across the stream, the companions thrashed toward the nearest tunnellike opening. Wings spread, the monster took to the air as Anjell reached the mouth of the pipe.

A trickle of water spilled from the broad-mouthed culvert, but there was space to breathe at the top. The Iceman hurled his niece into the opening, roughly pushing Bristyn and Raine afterward. Behind him Takian and Danri faced the swooping horror.

"Go!" cried the digger, and Rudy instantly obeyed. He heard Danri splashing behind—but when the Iceman looked back, all he saw were those horrific ember-eyes, fixed on him with an intensity that sent daggers of icy terror through the Iceman's body.

Finally Rudy twisted around a bend in the pipe, following the sound of Anjell's sobs deeper into the cistern pipe. He was immediately surrounded by darkness and a strong current; as he pressed forward, he barely noticed the numbing cold.

— 5 —

Matheral of the Hundred Knights slowed his foaming charger to an easy walk, ducking under another set of low-hanging limbs--and cursing the fate that had condemned him to a life of hunting through interminable forest. Yet, as captain of Duchess Bristyn's personal bodyguards, he could only continue to search diligently for some sign of her fate.

The trail he followed now was barely more than a game-track— but he didn't dare lead his small company back to the well-traveled King's Highway of Galtigor.

"This is madness!" he muttered, too quietly for his men to hear. Nine knights filed silently behind their captain, trusting to Matheral the business of deciding what to do. But he didn't even know if the truce between Carillonn and Galtigor was still intact! Palming his heart in an unconscious return to childhood training, Matheral continued to look around.

He thought back to the fateful attack, wondering for the thousandth time if he could have done anything to prevent it. Matheral had seen the arrows kill Paderon Zyloth, Prince Takian, and four brave guards. It was not hard to guess that the lady Bristyn had been the actual target of the arrow that killed the priest.

Just before the arrows streaked outward, his men had reported that Bristyn and Raine had taken two horses and galloped away. Had they known about the attack? He trusted the duchess implicitly, yet why had she not given him the chance to do his job?

Then the two women had simply disappeared. In nearly a fortnight of searching, he had found not a single clue as to their whereabouts. His quest had taken the company all the way back to the Wayfarer's lodge, where his hopes were dashed when he found that the pair had not returned that far. Since then, he and his knights had been probing through the wooded country of Galtigor, trying to avoid detection even as they sought further information about their headstrong mistress.

At least, Matheral found one thin straw of hope to help him believe that she was alive: if she had been slain by the assassins who made the first abortive attempt, those murderers would want to spread word of their bloody deed. Thus the knight tried to take as good news the fact that nobody knew anything about the duchess.

And then there was the other strange thing about that tragic, violent afternoon. As Paderon Zyloth lay on the ground, mortally pierced, he had seized Matheral's hand. Gasping, bleeding from the mouth, the priest had pressed a parchment into the knight's grip—with a grunted plea for Matheral to see that it was delivered.

A message from a dying man was a charge that no knight could ignore. The words had been hastily scrawled in the Olde Script, so Math couldn't have read the brief scroll had he wanted to. But the mystery did not stop there. Math would not have been mystified if the priest had asked him to give the message to the duchess—something about the emissary, perhaps—or even return to Carillonn and carry some urgent word to the king.

Instead, Paderon Zyloth's desperate missive, scrawled the morning of his last day of life, was to be delivered not to some nobleman or ambassador, but to Bristyn's Duftrall's maidservant, Raine.

SEVENTEEN
Like Rats on the Run

It was not merely to separate the Three Waters that the
gods created the Watershed. Well do the immortals
understand: the intermixing of the triad's peoples is a
menace as great as the mingling of the fluids that
define the separate realms.
—Codex of the Guardians

— 1 —

Somewhere in the flowing trough, Rudy lost his sword. He crawled on
his belly through a narrow connecting tunnel, finally joining his companions as they huddled in a large cistern, where the water rose almost
to his chin. Now, with Anjell's shivering body clutched to his chest,
he felt no compulsion to go back and look for the weapon. Of what
use was a sword against the kind of enemy that now assaulted them?

"Is anybody hurt—badly?" The voice was Duchess Bristyn Duftrall's, surprisingly steady against the rippling background noise of their
small movements and the flowing water outside.

Nobody replied. A sense of briefly delayed disaster dragged Rudy's spirits down—what did it matter if one of them had a broken leg,
or a punctured lung? An intact body merely seemed to promise the
chance to die fighting.

"Kalland!" Anjell sobbed. "He saved me!"

"I know," Rudy said, pulling her close. His mind recoiled from the image of the loyal snow lion leaping at the terrion.

"Is—is he dead?"

"I'm afraid he is, Anj." It was not easy for Rudy to speak, but somehow he got the words out as he cradled the crying girl. A hand reached out, touching his arm and then sliding down to enclose his clenched fist. It was Raine, and for a moment the desire to live flared up in him like an unstoppable force. They *had* to escape, to get away. . . .

Then despair closed in. How could they evade a beast like this—a thing that could stalk them across the miles, and find them in a lonely inn—though it could only have flown from distant Duloth-Trol? And it had come for *him*! He knew that, beyond any doubt; had sensed it in the creature's probing, fiery eyes, even before the creature spoke and confirmed that knowledge.

Yet at the same time he had a curious realization: though it had come seeking Rudy, it had not been entirely sure of his identity once the fight began.

Something sloshed through the water, crawling out of the drainpipe to join them in the cistern. Too numb to feel any alarm, the Iceman realized that he had known it was Danri since he'd first heard the sounds in the water. Another sense that he now possessed, which he could neither explain nor put to any practical use.

"I looked around—*felt* around, more like, 'cuz it stays pretty dark in here," Danri said. "But there are at least three of these big drainpipes, each leading to a different part of the river bank. 'Course, Lord Ugly's probably walking around out there, checking each one of 'em."

"Rudy? What *was* it—that thing Danri called Lord Ugly?" Anjell's voice, free of tremor, whispered against her uncle's chest.

"I don't know, Anj," he replied, shaking his head miserably. "But we're safe . . ." He couldn't finish the lie.

"That could only be a Lord Minion—spawn of the Nameless One himself," Danri said, awkwardly clearing his throat. His reluctance to speak on the topic tightened his voice. "There are three of them, supposedly. Once there were five, but two were killed during the Sleepstealer War. They're the generals of the minions, subordinate only to the . . . the Evil One, himself."

"It came for me . . . but *why?*" Rudy asked.

"Because of who you are, son," the digger replied enigmatically. "Or should I say, because of *what* you are?"

Rudy stiffened. "Why do you say that?"

"Because it's true." This time it was Raine who spoke, and her voice was calm and sympathetic even as her words drove into Rudy like merciless spears. "I knew it the first time I met you—and you've proved it since. You're something *more* than a human—something that embodies Faerine as well as Dalethica."

Rudy thought it strange to hear this truth so bluntly; at the same time, it was almost a relief to have it expressed by somebody else.

"And perhaps even a part of Duloth-Trol," he admitted slowly. He told them of the tiny tear on his tunic, after he had awakened in the avalanche. "It looked like I'd been stuck straight through with a sword, but of course I wasn't injured, so I didn't think that could explain it. Yet if Garamis truly bears a sword of Darkblood, and he drove it through my heart, could not some essence of the blade remain within me?"

In Rudy's own ears his words sounded horrifying, yet no longer did he fear this truth. Instead, he felt as though crucial pieces in the jigsaw puzzle of his life were falling into place. His overall emotion remained a numb sense of acceptance.

"Aye-uh. The Deep Guardian, do you remember?" Danri suggested. "It pursued us until it came to you; then it turned and crawled away, like there was nothing to worry it any longer?"

"What about it?"

"The Guardians, Deep and High, have as their sacred task the protection of the Watershed. They are charged with separating the world, insuring that all creatures remain in the realms where they belong. It pursued Kianna and me because we were crossing the boundary. When it touched you, it found something that was not of *one* Watershed, but included parts of all three. There was no threat there, so it turned away."

"And the High Guardians, those who attacked Garamis on the Glimmercrown—" Rudy recalled. "They sought to prevent him from reaching the summit, and breaching the sanctity of the three Water-sheds."

"What you say is true . . . all of it," Raine said suddenly, her voice hushed. Rudy squeezed her hand, silently urging her to explain, but she said nothing more.

"Is any of this going to get us out of here?" asked Lady Bristyn, not unkindly. "We've got to do something before we all freeze to death."

For the first time, Rudy noticed that Anjell's teeth were chattering. Raine shivered beside him, and he pulled her close too, the three of them drawing heat from each other. The Iceman took a deep breath. He knew what he had to say, and once spoken, the words would set his life on an irrevocable course.

"I have to go out there—alone," he said. "We know that this 'Lord Minion' is looking for me. Perhaps I can escape, lead it in some different direction. Even if I can't, it shouldn't have any reason to wait around for the rest of you, afterwards. . . . "

"Nope." Danri dismissed his suggestion so abruptly—and firmly—that Rudy couldn't muster the words to object. "It's a brave notion, lad, and I know you'd do it. But it might not even work—how do we know that it wouldn't want the rest of us out of sheer spite, or 'cuz we helped you?"

"Well, but—"

"Danri's right," Raine whispered. "There has to be a better way—a way that gives us *all* a chance."

"We could try to attack that thing, that Lord Minion—take it by surprise." Takian spoke boldly. "If Rudy, the digger, and I sneaked out of here, we might be—"

"No," the Iceman said quietly, but in a tone that silenced the prince's arguments.

"Rudy?" Anjell asked. He was terribly alarmed by the drowsiness of her voice; even through her shivering, she seemed ready to drop into sleep. "That Lord Minion *did* come for you—but how come it could fly across all of Dalethica and know just where to find you, and then not know who you were when it got here? I know it's magic and all, but it just doesn't make any sense to me."

"Me either," he sighed, rocking Anjell back and forth, his back rolling against the chill cistern wall.

"What if it perceived you, somehow—could find you easily, wherever you were—until you did something that made it lose you?" Danri made the suggestion slowly, as if mulling over the idea in his head while he spoke.

"What did I do to cause that?" Rudy challenged.

"You had that waterskin in your hand when you came in our room," Raine remembered. "Did you drink from it?"

Rudy sat upright, energized by the memory. "The *Aura!*" he whispered. "I took a drink right before the monster reached the inn!"

"And after you drank the Aura, the Lord Minion lost track of you. It knew where to find you, because it was so close, but it lost the actual sense of where you were!" Danri concluded.

"Do you think that could work for *all* of us?" Bristyn wondered.

"Can't say for sure. We all know there's something different about our young Iceman here—but maybe a taste of Aura will mask *anyone* from Lord Ugly."

"We'll have to experiment," Raine declared. "I'll go."

Rudy was about to object, but the pressure of her hand over his grew firm and he bit back his words. "All right. Let's go together— see if he senses us."

"I think that I should go." Prince Takian spoke, his voice emerging from the darkness like he was a great distance away. "It is my brother who is in league with this fiend, I'm certain. The quest for vengeance is mine."

"There's plenty of right to vengeance against Garamis of Galtigor," Rudy declared. "You make your claim as a brother he betrayed— I tell you I've lost three brothers to him! But that doesn't matter— now it's not vengeance we seek, it's escape!"

"Very well." The prince's voice echoed in the darkness. "But, by Baracan—I *hate* it! We're trapped in my own kingdom, attacked from all sides and I'm as much a fugitive as anyone!"

In the darkness Rudy passed the skin of Aura to Raine and heard her take a swallow. Taking it back, he took another sip himself—there was no telling how long the screening effect would last. Then he gently passed Anjell to the duchess, who took the girl on her lap. Finally he gave the waterskin to Danri. "There's enough for each of you to have a drink—if this works."

"Don't forget, I have a sackful of Aura too," Danri said, sloshing his belt pack.

"I haven't forgotten," Rudy replied. "But something tells me we should save that—we might need it in the future."

"Why don't we drink before you leave?" Anjell wondered. "That way, if he's using magic to tell that the rest of us are still down here, he won't know."

"Makes sense," Danri agreed, and the duchess and prince quickly assented. Rudy waited while they each drank the water of magic.

The Iceman brushed a kiss across Anjell's cheek, and clasped the digger's hand. He felt Raine crouching at his side, before he turned his head to the drainpipe and crawled out of the cistern. Raine stayed right behind him, and when they reached the branching channel, he turned left—simply because that was opposite the direction they'd come.

They crawled in silence, fearing the Lord Minion could hear them even over the steady wash of the waters. Rudy felt a side passage open up after a few minutes, but he passed that one by. Shortly, another chute led upward, and this one he followed. Though the surface below him was slick and wet, the steep drain currently had no flowing water in it. The passage continued for a surprisingly long way, until the pair came to a narrower pipe, also empty of water. Looking up this passage, Rudy detected a grayish haze—enough light to convince him that the pipe led to daylight beyond.

Raine tapped him on the heel and he paused as she slipped up beside him. He placed his ear beside her face, waiting to hear what she wanted—then he felt the kiss of her lips against his cheek, and she scooted by, preceding him up the tight passageway.

Only the need for silence prevented him from thrashing after her, so desperately did he fear for her safety. Somehow he managed to move carefully, and in a few minutes he saw her emerge from the tile pipe onto a stony surface. In seconds he followed, finding that they had reached a hilltop near the inn. Quickly he crawled after

Raine, who had taken shelter in the woods.

Through the grove they saw the Inn of Two Wells, now a mass of splintered beams, broken shingles, and scattered debris. Crows squawked and bickered, probing among the ruins, while vultures circled overhead, grim evidence of the fate meted out to the unfortunate victims trapped inside. Even the floor had been ripped up, and no sounds emerged from the cellar. With a shiver of horror, Rudy remembered the dozens of people who had sought shelter there.

A moving figure stalked around the wreckage, and the Lord Minion came into view. The monster stared at the stream, freezing in place as if it had entered some kind of trance. Apparently it could not find what it sought, for the black head shook angrily, the leathery, batlike wings stretching in agitation.

Stalking to the dead terrion, the beast turned its face to the sky and uttered a fierce, yet mournful roar. Was there grief in that sound? Rudy couldn't be sure, though the most powerful current was pure rage.

The creature spun on its heel, staring through the woods, eyes drifting across the hilltop where Rudy and Raine lay—but it never hesitated, even looked right past their hiding place. The snarling of the beast's frustration rumbled in the distance.

Rudy blinked, wondering if his eyes played tricks as the image of the monster wavered, changed. No, his vision was fine—it was the beast itself that altered. The hulking form shrank in size, stooping forward and apparently shriveling away. Only the wings remained large, spreading, sprouting black, glistening feathers. In another moment the monster was gone entirely; in its place squatted a large, bald-skulled vulture—a larger cousin of the scavengers wheeling over the ruined inn.

Astounded at the transformation, the Iceman watched breathlessly as the hulking, unnatural condor spread its wings, groping at the wind until it slowly drew itself into the air. Rudy stared after it until the vulture became a speck in the sky, and finally disappeared.

Only then did he realize it had flown north, toward Landrun.

— 2 —

All but consumed by his own rage, Nicodareus used the vestiges of his strength to carry himself through the sky. His body, his senses, were stretched to the breaking point—he was desperate to get back to the nourishing Darkblood of Duloth-Trol. But he had another task to perform before he returned there. Most galling of all, it was a task necessitated by his own failure.

Failure! He, Nicodareus, had *failed*! Somehow the Iceman had eluded him, had vanished from his Sight as effectively as if he had ceased to exist! Moments before the Lord Minion had reached the inn, something had blanketed the man's essence. A shriek of fury from the vulture's beak was the only outward display of his rage—and even that burst of energy caused him pain.

Apparently the Power of Three had limits that the Lord Minion had not fully understood. This final time that he used the power, the surroundings of Dalethica weighed heavily against him since he had first crossed the Watershed. His endurance, which had never flagged before, was not equal to a prolonged immersion in this accursed place of pure water—he needed the Darkblood, the liquid that was the stuff of his master's life.

Now, against the background of that pain, he resolved to find the human who was his master's tool—the Prince of Galtigor, who had been committed to evil by the taste of Darkblood. It galled him beyond measure that the help of this mortal was required; yet his own endurance was all but gone.

The Eye of Dassadec had no other choice.

— 3 —

King Larriac of Galtigor lay in state on a marble bier within his great throne room. Garamis, alone with his father's remains, paced back and forth across the polished wooden planks of the floor. The

Sword of Darkblood tugged the bejeweled scabbard downward at the prince's waist, like an anxious hound pulling at a leash.

Every so often he whirled and fixed his eyes upon the corpse, as if his accusations might extend over the gulf between life and death. But soon afterward he slumped in resignation, and then resumed his pacing.

The monarch had expired peacefully, in his sleep—without the violence and struggle that had marked so much of his life. Yet somehow, still, Garamis felt betrayed by his father. The greatest campaign in the history of Galtigor stood on the brink of inception, and by all rights the prince should have had the king's eyes upon him as he rode off to glory.

Takian! It was *still* Takian's fault. His brother had reached out from the grave to deprive him of their father's praise and high regard. Garamis had heard a rumor claiming that his brother's corpse had been devoured by wolves—he deeply regretted not being present to observe the feast.

Still, the army would be ready to march in a matter of days. Garamis' mind turned to the legions of footmen, the companies of cavalry and archers, the plain strewn with tents beyond the city walls. Every hour more men marched into Landrun, flocking to his banner like bees to nectar—or flies to carrion, he imagined with a grim, dry laugh.

At least his father had lived to see Garamis address Takian's death with a proper sense of familial vengeance. In truth, the Faerines *would* pay for the affront to House Larriac. In Garamis' own mind the true facts of his brother's death were lost to him, reduced to scrap buried in the trunk of his life's recollections. For so many days had he been calling for vengeance against the Faerines that he himself had come to believe it was justified.

Abruptly he paused, muscles tightening as if wires suddenly drew them taut. He looked around the throne room, into the paneled corners and shadowy alcoves, and he saw nothing.

But still, Garamis knew.

He was here.

Immediately the prince fell to his knees, raising his hands to his father's bier and turning his face to the ceiling. "Welcome, master!" he cried.

Nicodareus approached from behind, but Garamis did not dare turn until he felt the taloned hand come to rest on his shoulder. Then, reverently, the prince prostrated himself on the floor, daring to reach out and touch those broad, padded feet.

"Rise, princeling—or should I say 'king'?" rumbled the deep voice.

Garamis climbed to his feet. "My coronation occurs after my victory in Faerine. Know that I have obeyed your commands, Mighty One—the army shall march within the week!"

"You serve me well." The praise sent shivers of pleasure through the prince's body. He felt a powerful thirst in his throat, forcing it to the back of his mind. "But we shall need to make haste."

The note of concern in the Lord Minion's voice could not be ignored. "Is something wrong, master?"

"The young Iceman who climbed the mountain with you— he lives. And he is a threat to you," Nicodareus declared. "As we speak, he makes his way to the city, determined to put an end to your plans."

"But I killed him—stabbed him through the heart!" babbled the prince, immediately fearing the punishment for failure. Surprisingly, Nicodareus made no hostile move.

"I believe you," declared the Lord Minion. "There is unusual menace in him—he has even evaded my Sight. And he is close. He may well reach the city by nightfall."

"Then we'll set men at the gates, watch the waterfront! Surely he won't get through the guards!"

"You will do all this, but I suspect that he will get through. I do not know what his plans are, but I know the best way to counter them."

"Speak, and I obey!"

"Your army must march with the dawn, striking out for Taywick Pass before he has time to disrupt your preparations."

"But—" Garamis caught himself. "Yes, lord—we set out at sunrise. The regiments that have yet to form can trail to the rear, catching up along the road."

"It is good that you understand."

Garamis grew weak as he watched Nicodareus lift his hand. If it were to reach out and tear his head from his shoulders, the prince would have died happily, knowing that he had succeeded in pleasing his master.

Yet the Lord Minion made no such move. Instead, sensing the prince's thirst, knowing that he was the only one who could slake it, Nicodareus thrust a claw through the skin of his palm. Darkblood—pure, black, and malevolent—welled there, and with a sublime sense of reward Garamis knelt before his master and drank.

— 4 —

"The cotton barges pull up here," Takian said, pointing to a spit extending into the broad river. "Often they offload outside the city and save a lot of tariffs. Plus, it's easier for the oxen to haul them back upriver from here—the channel between here and Landrun is fast and narrow, so the upstream hauling fees are high."

"But how will this get us past the gates?" asked Rudy skeptically. He trusted the prince's notion that they needed to enter Landrun surreptitiously, but he didn't like the way the plan was shaping up. The river before him was huge, flat, and placid, like a lake—as different from the mountainous streams of his homeland as he could imagine. And once they committed to Takian's plan, they were trapped, helpless to regroup if something went wrong.

"I told you—once we sneak on board, we can hide among the bales until we draw up to the pier. Then, when we're next to the docks, we'll drop overboard and swim. The waterfront is too long for all of it to be patrolled, and I know a few shadowy places where we should be able to dry out without being noticed."

"Let's get on with it, then," Danri grumbled, his tone sharp. "Maybe you want to talk about it all night—but personally, I think Kianna's getting kind of lonely for us."

Rudy lowered his head, ashamed. "Lead on," he said to Takian.

The prince, his bootblack-darkened hair slick in the light of sunset, led the companions down the steep, brushy bank. Several large barges were lashed to the long pier below them, but the only sailors in sight lounged listlessly at the far end of the wharf. A few freight wagons, heavily laden and hitched to teams of patient horses, waited in the yard beyond the docks.

This was a ferry crossing as well as a cargo landing, though for now the giant capstan that controlled the ferry sat idle, four oxen listlessly chewing their cud as they awaited the command to begin their eternal circle. The ferryboat, hooked to its cable, was currently across the river. There a few passengers filed past a similar mechanism.

Movement stirred at the near end of the dock, as several sailors clambered over one of the barges. They lashed down bales of cotton, filling in the gaps where a portion of their cargo had just been offloaded to the wagons. The barge-captain stood by the shoreline, ready to cast off when his crew was finished.

Takian scuttled behind the shelter of a stack of barrels, darting across the dock and pouncing silently to the deck of the broad, flat rivercraft. In short order, Rudy and Anjell, Danri, Raine, and Bristyn followed. The Iceman turned to help the others, and was once again impressed by Raine's fluid movements. The woman landed silently as a cat, and helped the Duchess of Shalloth into the shadows of tarpaulin-covered bale. Soon all the companions had wedged into firm hiding places, buried between the bundles of cotton and the canvas sheets stretched across them.

Within a few moments the barge began to move, bobbing along in the current of the great Black Eel River. True to Takian's word, the flowage picked up speed until the great flatboat bounced and pitched along; somehow the boatmen kept the bow pointed downstream. The rapid current made for a tense ride, but in the end this proved fortunate—none of the three crewmen had the time to look around as the barge surged the final distance to Landrun. Without speaking, the companions remained huddled among the bales, fully concealed for the duration of the journey.

Sometime after full darkness they heard shouts, and the clanking of metal tools. An object thudded into the hull of the barge, and slowly

the craft left the natural pace of the current, responding more stubbornly to the pressure of towlines pulling toward the dock.

"Halt out there!" The call cracked through the darkness. Rudy
sneaked a look from beneath the tarp and saw a company of men at
the dockside holding blazing torches aloft. "Stand by for an inspection!"

"Hey, what?" The captain's tone was belligerent. "We never had
no inspection before!"

"You will now—orders of Prince Garamis! Now, lower that plank
and let us aboard!"

"Bah—you waste my time! But come ahead." Cursing fluently,
the captain ordered his men to set out the gangplank.

The Iceman's heart pounded with fear, but Takian had already
reacted. He took Anjell by the hand, and the others slipped behind as
he worked his way noiselessly to the offshore side of the barge. Rudy
heard the gangplank drop to the opposite side of the hull, followed by
the tread of heavy boots—but then Takian, still holding Anjell,
dropped over the side. The others followed, swimming silently as dark
waters closed over their heads. The current carried them along the side
of the rivercraft, and then past the flatboat and down the wharf of
Landrun.

Another barge, already inspected and unloaded, stood hard by the
pier, and Takian led them into the shadows beneath this boat's stern.
Here they found a ladder leading up toward the dock and emerged
onto a deserted stretch of the waterfront. Everywhere Rudy saw dilap-
idated buildings; the stench of rotting fish surrounded them.

But there were no guards here. With a growing sense of relief,
the Iceman followed the prince across the pier, between two buildings,
and into the shadowy security of a narrow alley. Sill nothing stirred
nearby, though he heard the shouts and laughter of many men in some
of the surrounding buildings.

"If I never go swimming again as long as I live, it'll *still* be a
hundred years too soon!" growled Danri, shaking himself like a water-
logged hound. "But let's go, now—where's this tower?"

"Up there," gestured Takian, and Rudy looked up, toward the

palace of Galtigor. He drew a deep breath, more encouraged than he had been for many days. For the first time he began to believe that, perhaps, they might succeed.

— 5 —

The great head rose from a pillow of mud, black nostrils sniffing the air. Sore muscles . . . pain everywhere. For a time the wounded animal licked the gaping slash in his flank, cleaning dirt and dried blood from the wound.

Broad feet, velvet paws, limped across the ground, over to the muddy pool. The wide, blunt nose tilted upward, seeking—vainly— that wondrous, secret smell.

Vividly he remembered the first sweet touch of that odor. It had drawn him to the man buried in snow, and for many days it had bound him to that man with a tie deeper than any the animal had ever known.

Now that scent was gone; he had only a body racked by pain, a mind swollen with despair. Still limping awkwardly, the animal hobbled toward the road. He remembered that, for many days, the man had been traveling along the highway. Grimly plodding, the snow lion started toward the north.

— 6 —

The tower atop the hill rose beyond the palace wall, soaring into the night sky, lower tiers illuminated by flaring torchlight while the highest reaches vanished into shadow. Rudy tried to imagine the palace grounds, teeming with troops and sentries, lit by enough fires and torches to send this rosy glow into the sky.

The royal enclave occupied the top of a steep-sided bluff, surrounded on three sides by a curl of the Black Eel River. The companions remained at the foot of that bluff, where along a narrow strip of waterfront merchants and tavern keepers had carved out miniature domains. The bluffside overhead was not a cliff—indeed, it was criss-

crossed by steeply climbing streets and ramshackle buildings perched
with one end often hanging into space—but it looked like a steep and
twisting climb.

"That's the tower where Kianna's supposed to be?" Rudy asked,
after staring for several moments into the darkness overhead. The companions stood at the fringe of the quiet street along the Landrun riv-
erfront; sounds of raucous celebration emerged from nearby inns, and
several groups of men had trooped past in the last few minutes, but at
the moment nobody was in sight.

"She'll be at the very top—that balcony is lost in shadows. Besides, Kirkith said she's facing the marketplace—that's on the opposite
side of the tower," Takian explained.

The sounds from the nearest inn reached a crescendo of shouts
and curses, until the door burst open and a man tumbled out to collapse, motionless, in the street. Rudy couldn't tell if the fellow was
alive or dead, nor did he feel any urge to try and find out.

"Why is it so lively tonight?" asked Bristyn, stepping into the
roadway enough to look at the tower.

"Ssst!" Anjell whispered. "Here come some more of those apes!"

They ducked into the shelter of a doorless, sagging shed, barely
avoiding detection by the armored men who came swaggering down
the center of the street.

"Good eye," Rudy whispered to his niece, as the fellows thumped
past. "These guys look like they mean business."

Indeed, the band of eight men marched in a precise formation.
Their metal armor gleamed, reflecting small traces of lamplight from
nearby windows. The warriors displayed a steady, firm tread that was
clear proof they hadn't been imbibing the way many of their
fellows had.

The small company pulled up before a ramshackle inn several
doors down from the companions' hiding place. Weapons snapped to
their shoulders, two burly sergeants-at-arms tromped up to the door.

"Everybody out!" one bellowed, loud enough for Rudy to hear
the words clearly. An immediate chorus of objections arose from the
raucous crowd, but the fellow didn't let that slow him up.

"New orders, men. We make an early march tomorrow. Now, get

to your beds—and remember, you'll thank me for this warning when dawn rolls around!"

The objections swelled in a chorus of outrage, but even through that roar Rudy heard the rest of the detail march through the door of the inn. The curses turned to howls of pain and quickly a stream of drunken men sprouted from the place. They staggered into the street, weaving this way and that, arguing among themselves every step of the way. Several fistfights erupted as various comrades disputed the shortest routes back to their companies.

"Back—as far as you can!" Takian hissed, drawing the companions deeper into the shadowy shed. "Now, stay still!"

They drew past all manner of stinking refuse, until they reached a wall of rotted planks. Here they concealed themselves in the corners—and none too soon, as several of the rousted revelers tumbled into their shed—"gonna have a lil' nap; set here fer a minit"—and sprawled out of sight of the road.

They heard the detail trooping down the street, clearing out one tavern after another, and for a long time the street was filled with rowdy, disgruntled men. Rudy felt the seconds tick by with each beat of his heart, and the thought that they were so close to Kianna nearly drove him into action. Several times Raine placed a hand upon the Iceman's shoulder, with soothing and restraining effect.

Finally Takian's wisdom began to grow apparent. As the last of the men tottered away, or collapsed into slumber, the street became very still. Slowly, cautiously, the companions emerged from hiding, stepping over the snoring forms of the several men who had stumbled into the shed.

"Now it should be safe," Takian whispered. "As long as we stick to the back streets, keep our eyes open, and don't make any noise."

The prince led them around a dark corner and along a narrow lane. Darkened buildings—shacks, mostly, with a few balconied houses of three or four stories among them—pressed close to either side, tilting so far forward that the stars were reduced to a narrow strip between the ramshackle eaves. The surface was mud, and the grade quickly developed into a steep ascent.

Somehow the companions blundered along, helping each other

when one of them fell. Takian, in the lead, seemed able to locate the obstacles that would make a noise if stumbled into—woodpiles, loops of metal chains, empty kettles, and slumbering drunks. Silently the prince ushered his companions around these hurdles, and then glided smoothly to the fore, self-assuredly selecting a route within a labyrinth of twisting lanes and narrow cross streets.

The path was made doubly difficult because it climbed so sharply upward, switching back and forth along streets that angled across the hillside in steep, diagonal sections. Though lost in the maze of build- ings, Rudy knew that they must be ascending the bluff facing the river, and he approved of Takian's tactic—after all, the tower that was Kian- na's prison stood at the very top of this elevation.

Finally they turned into a street somewhat wider than the twisting lanes. The avenue ran along the crest of the bluff, and on the other side of the road a wooden palisade rose upward to a height of perhaps thirty feet. This solid fence ran to the right and left as far as they could see, though it curved away from them in both directions. In some places the wall rose directly from the road's edge, but in others it swung back a little way, allowing brush and shrubbery to thrive at its foot.

"The palace of my fathers," Takian said softly, and Rudy won- dered why he didn't hear more bitterness in the man's tone.

"How do you propose we get through that?" Danri demanded, his sour tone hissing through the dark.

"I can climb it," Rudy said unhesitatingly. The grooves between the wooden pales looked very much like the channels in some of the stony cliffs he'd climbed as a youth.

"I'll come with you," Raine offered, before anyone else responded.

Rudy was about to suggest that he go alone, but the underlying confidence in Raine's tone changed his mind. "Good," he said. "Let's get across the street—we can find shelter at the foot of the wall."

"Wait!" Takian warned, raising a cautionary hand and pointing along the avenue. Several voices were audible there, growing louder by the second. Rudy pulled Anjell into the darkened gutter before a nar- row shack; the other companions melted into the shadows nearby.

A group of men-at-arms meandered toward them. Their manner was relaxed but sober; apparently these were some of the sergeants who'd put in a long shift rousting their charges out of the taverns. Now they talked quietly as they drew closer to the companions.

". . . start out so quick? Even Prince Garamis, I thought, would wait till all the companies was ready," one guard observed, clearly mystified.

"Who can hold *him* back?" another challenged.

"I think it's what happened at the Inn of Two Wells, just this morning—that makes it urgent. I heard it was sylves. They burned the place, butchered everyone!"

"Sylves and a drackan, I heard."

"Ah, no drackan. It's sylves, I tell you—and how much of the army do you think it'll take to rout a bunch of dancing fairies and singing sylves?"

"That's fer sure," chimed in the first speaker. "Why, I just hope the Redsteel Guards leave a few a them magicks fer the rest of us!"

The men chorused agreement.

"Mighta been cuz of the king, that Garamis wants to go so quick." The first speaker ventured his opinion; apparently, he was a respected authority, because the others fell silent as he spoke. "Who'd a figured he'd up an' die like that—not two days after he hears about Takian getting shot by sylves!"

Rudy plainly heard the gasp from the nearby alcove where the prince was hiding. Tensely the Iceman watched the warriors to see if any of them had detected the sound, but they tromped on in ignorance.

". . . only hope that stuff works to get us through Taywick Pass," groused a stoop-shouldered guard. "Don't know that I like the thought of marching to war with some kind of magic battering ram!"

"A block of ice, he says! All I can say is I hope we get some chilly weather for the march!"

A chorus of assenting grumbles confirmed that this fear was shared by all the warriors. By now they had moved beyond the companions' hiding place, but Rudy had heard enough to confirm Kirkith Phleet's information.

The Iceman's thoughts turned to a more immediate concern as Prince Takian, taut as a wire, emerged from his hiding place. He stepped into the road as if he would go after the sergeants, but Rudy laid a gently restraining hand on his arm.

"My father . . ." The prince's voice twisted in pain, and for a moment the Iceman wondered if he would pull away. But Takian drew a deep breath and turned to Rudy; in his eyes was a glint of fury beyond any rage the Iceman had ever seen. "It is yet another thing for which Garamis must make an accounting."

Takian turned toward the high wall. "I called this the palace of my fathers. No more—now it is held by my brother, and I brand him a traitor. When next I meet him, I will make his kingdom my own."

EIGHTEEN
Tower of Terror

Darkblood is sweet nectar, font of the Sleepstealer's
faith. As such, it is crucial to the sustenance of might;
conversely, its absence causes weakness and,
ultimately, failure.
—TOME OF VILE COMPULSIONS

— 1 —

Takian led the companions across the street and into the shadows at
the foot of the wall. They quickly found a dense cluster of lilac bushes,
where they could shelter well-screened from the road.

"Do you *really* think you can climb this?" Danri asked, looking
at both Raine and Rudy.

The Iceman nodded, and it was the duchess who spoke for her
maidservant. "I know Raine can scamper up walls smoother than this—
I don't know how she does it, but I've seen it happen."

"Here." Danri passed the loops of his rope to Raine. "When you
get to the top, drop this down—the rest of us will come after you."

Rough-hewn logs separated by narrow gaps formed the palisade.
Apparently the wall was thicker than the one ring of stakes, however,
since they could see only darkness when they peered through the gaps.
As Rudy stepped back, looking for a good place to start, he saw Raine
reach upward and quickly pull herself off the ground. Hand over hand,

with steady movements, she rose up the wall.

Quickly the Iceman wedged his boot between two logs, reaching up to find a handhold. His second foot found purchase and he grabbed at the wood above him, pulling himself higher—until a splinter punctured his skin, lancing pain through his hand. Grunting, he let go and slipped the three feet to the ground.

He looked up to see Raine disappear over the top of the wall. Shaking his head ruefully, he waited for her to drop the line, which he then climbed hand over hand until he joined her atop the wall. Twin ramparts ran along the palisade, flanking a walkway perhaps six feet wide. There was a drop of about twenty feet to the courtyard of the palace.

He flushed, wanting very much to impress this woman and feeling as though he had failed miserably. When she met his gaze and touched a finger to his lips, however, his trivial concern melted away in a gentle wave of relief. He looked over the wall, his first examination of the palace of Galtigor.

The torches and lanterns he had pictured earlier sparkled here and there against the darkness of the huge courtyard, but the massive wash of light had been for the most part extinguished. Rudy braced the rope for his companions while he studied the royal residence. The buildings were tall and squarish, with none of the sleek elegance that characterized the North Shore Wayfarer's Lodge. Many were surrounded by battlements, and all were enclosed by this wooden curtain wall.

Nearby rose the great tower, its surface a mottled pattern of gigantic fieldstones. Now, with most of the lanterns gone, the entire structure was cloaked in shadow. The top of the spire extended so far up into the night sky that Rudy could only locate it by seeking the dark outline against the stars.

He turned his attention back to the rope, as he and Raine hauled upward to help the gasping Bristyn over the top. Next came Takian, climbing with strong hand-over-hand movements, while Anjell, with her arms wrapped around the prince's neck and her eyes tightly shut, held on until the pair had joined their companions on the narrow walk. Danri came quickly behind, and didn't even pause to catch his breath before he threw the line over the other side of the wall. "The sooner we get down into the shadows again, the safer I'll feel," he admitted.

In short order they completed the descent, until only Raine and Rudy remained on the wall. "Why don't you go first," she offered with a slight smile. "I'll drop the rope down and follow."

Chagrined, he did as she suggested. As soon as his feet touched the ground in the courtyard, the rope coiled down over his shoulders. Shortly thereafter Raine descended the line, dropping free six feet off the ground to land lightly beside the others.

"We need to make a plan," Takian whispered, his voice a rustle barely louder than the breeze. "Kianna's sure to be locked up, and the keys will be with the guards at the tower door, down at ground level."

"Don't need the keys," Raine said with a firm shake of her head. "I'll take care of the locks."

Rudy stared at her—in astonishment, but not doubt. How, he wondered again, had this woman acquired so many extraordinary skills?

"Do you think you can climb the tower?" Takian pressed.

"Yes," Raine replied without hesitation.

"That tower, at least, is *stone*," Rudy pointed out in a whisper. "I've had more practice climbing rock than climbing trees! I'm coming with you!"

"I'm glad," she whispered, giving his hand a squeeze.

"The guard walks up and down the stairs every hour or two— but other than that, the tower should be empty," Takian whispered, once again leading the way along a roundabout path beneath the shelter of many broad oak trees. Beside them ran a dense hedge, and some-where beyond the leafy barrier Rudy heard water splashing.

"Hi!" The curious voice broke through the darkness from the rear of the party. Takian had already vanished in the shadows ahead as Rudy whirled, appalled to see a large, round-shouldered fellow ambling out of the garden, waving.

"Hello," Anjell said, her voice a rasping whisper.

"Oh—are we being quiet?" The newcomer's voice dropped to match the girl's.

"Yes," Anjell whispered back. "We have a secret."

"I *like* secrets!" the fellow declared, enthusiastically bobbing his head as he crouched beside the girl. Though he was the size of a man, there was a childlike quality in his stooping posture and conspiratorial excitement. "My brother Garamis told me a secret—but I can't tell you."

"You're—you're *Garamis'* brother?" she gasped.

"Yup—I'm Boric. Who are you?"

"I'm . . . Anjell." She stood very still, keeping her eyes on Boric. Rudy, beneath the shadows of a nearby tree, sensed her straining not to look at him.

"My brother's going to take me to the war!" Boric announced proudly.

"Oh—that's too bad," the girl blurted.

"No—it's gonna be fun!"

She stomped her foot, her voice firm but quiet. "War's *not* fun—and don't let your brother try to tell you it is! And you be careful if he takes you there."

"Oh." Taken aback, but still friendly, Boric nodded his head. "Okay, I will."

"I—I have to go! Let's keep our secret, okay? See you later, Boric," Anjell stammered, before scampering around the tree where Rudy waited. Only when he took her hand again did the Iceman notice his heart pounding like a drum. At least the young prince didn't try to follow them.

They approached the foot of the great tower without further incident—indeed, they didn't see a guard within their portion of the grounds. Here the stone wall rose steeply upward, without a door or any other feature along its base; they observed it from behind the trunk of a large oak some twenty paces away.

"The tower gate is on the other side. There'll be a couple of guards at the gate, but they shouldn't have cause to come around here. The prisoner will be on the balcony on the far side of the tower, where she can be seen from the marketplace of the city."

"Can we climb right to that balcony?" Rudy wondered.

"There are several lower galleries extending all the way around the tower. Once you reach those, it'll be easier to slip inside and go up the interior stairs. Then, when Kianna's freed, she can fly down to us and you can come down the same way you went up."

Above them the Iceman could barely make out the dark outlines of the lower balconies, circling the tower about midway up. Certainly the lowest of these was an easier objective than the top of the tower.

He and Raine made their way cautiously to the wall, while the others remained in the shadows beneath the tree. The Iceman found niches, toeholds, and cracks that gave purchase to fingers and toes as he lifted himself carefully from the ground. Raine proceeded steadily upward beside him. On the rough fieldstone, he could keep pace with the woman—though he certainly didn't outdistance her. He had a startling fear once: that she purposely slowed her own pace. Quickly he discarded the notion—he didn't want to know if it was the truth.

For long minutes they labored in silence, carefully ascending the rough surface. Footing was treacherous, handholds precarious knobs that offered only a desperate fingertip grip. Once the Iceman heard Raine's foot slip, and his heart nearly exploded in panic; only when he sensed the measured pace of her breathing, still on the wall beside him, did he settle down and resume the climb. They moved slowly, carefully, in the darkness—thankful that the shadows screened them from anyone who might look upward from the ground.

As when Rudy climbed a mountain face, the drop below ceased to exist in his mind; he measured progress only by the extent of wall remaining above. The courtyard sprawled wide, and though he didn't dare turn his head to look, Rudy saw flickering spots of light from the corners of his eyes. What if one of those wandering guards stumbled upon the companions below? Disaster, he knew—but this fear, too, he forced from his mind.

Finally his upward-reaching hand met a surprising shape, and he realized that it was the spindle of a railing, leaning slightly out from the tower wall. The first balcony! With palpable relief he pulled himself over the barrier, and soon Raine collapsed beside him, breathing deeply on the smoothness of a flat floor. They lay still for several minutes, hearing a solitary guard trudge up a stairway. Shortly they heard him go past again, descending.

"We can go inside from here," Rudy remembered. "How does a stairway sound to you?"

Nodding, the woman got to her feet. Unconsciously he took her hand as they stepped through the shadowy, doorless entryway leading to the interior of the tower.

They paused for several moments to allow their eyes to adjust to the nearly total darkness within. Rudy vaguely discerned a series of steps, spiraling upward to his right, and he led Raine in a cautious ascent. Passing several other platforms, and seeing stars or the city stretching beyond, they knew that these were additional balconies. Yet they continued upward as fast as possible, since Kianna was supposed to be at the very top.

Finally they reached a floor where the stairway ended. A ladder ascended to a trapdoor in the ceiling, which presumably opened onto the roof of the tower. Three balconies led outward from this floor, and Rudy took a moment to orient himself.

"This way." He nodded toward the gallery that looked out on the city proper.

Cautiously they stepped through the open door. The balcony extended for some distance to each side, but was only a few steps wide from doorway to outer railing. Squarely in the center was a heavy stone pillar, and Rudy stepped around that barrier scarcely daring to breathe.

Kianna Kyswillis lay motionless on the far side of the pillar. Chains held her arms to her sides, while additional brackets secured her feet. At first Rudy feared that she was dead; the rasping, hoarse sounds of her breath at last told him that she slept.

Raine knelt beside the twissel and pulled a series of shiny wire probes from her pouch. Feverishly she worked one of these devices into the lock securing Kianna's foot.

The fairy opened her eyes, blinking in confusion—and then cowering backward in fright.

"Kianna—it's me, Rudy. We're here to help you," he whispered, aching at the sight of her fear. "You'll be safe, now—we'll get you out of here."

"I—I found the duchess, Rudy," the twissel said through chapped lips. "I warned her!"

"I know you did," he managed to say, before his throat tightened, cutting off any further attempt at speech. The Iceman hugged the fairy, shocked at the frailty of her trembling body. He tried to hold her still while Raine twisted her pick into the lock.

The *snap!* of a releasing latch signaled the woman's first success. Immediately she started on the other foot bracket, probing and twisting. That lock, too, released its clasp—and far more quickly than had the first one.

So intent was Rudy on watching Raine work that at first he didn't notice the sounds of commotion from the palace grounds. When he did, he thought some late-night carousers were still being driven from their revels.

But then he discerned a serious note to the cries—he heard rage there, even hate. The sounds came from below, and as lanterns flickered into light and shouting guards closed in from all sides, he knew beyond any doubt:

His companions on the ground had been discovered.

— 2 —

"Try to get the last lock!" Rudy urged Raine, as the sounds of discovery grew violently louder below. "I'll see if I can help Takian and the others!"

The woman didn't reply except to nod her head curtly while she pressed her wire probe into the lock holding Kianna's wrist. The twissel closed her eyes, trembling, and Rudy gently touched her cheek before he sprang to his feet.

For the first time since coming from the Inn of Two Wells, Rudy felt the loss of his sword. Still, he had his hunting knife; he drew the weapon as he raced from the balcony to the interior of the tower, bounding down the spiraling steps four or five at a time. His dizzying descent soon took him past the level where he and Raine had entered the tower. For a long time he sprinted in circles through the featureless interior, until finally he leapt the last few steps and ran toward the heavy door.

He saw two men-at-arms there, illuminated by a torch that sputtered in a wall sconce. The guards had pulled the iron-strapped door shut, and now glared outward through a small grate. Beyond, Rudy saw flaring torches and heard sounds of rising tumult. The unmistakable clang of steel against steel rang through the night, immediately followed by a shrill cry of pain.

The commotion outside was so loud that, apparently, neither of the guards inside had heard Rudy's mad descent. One reached down and checked the latchbolt, insuring that the door was secured against forceful entry.

The Iceman's knife was a leaden weight in his hand. Suddenly he felt acutely conscious of its killing power—he could rush the guards, perhaps stab them to death before they knew of the menace within the walls of the tower. Couldn't he?

More swords clashed outside, and suddenly a high-pitched voice shot through the darkness, straight to the young Iceman's heart.

"Rudy!" Anjell's scream was full of terror and desperation, and it propelled him to action. He lunged at the two guards, his pounding footsteps swallowed by chaos.

As Rudy brought the blade down, some internal judgment reversed the direction of his weapon. The heavy hilt crashed into the skull of the nearest man-at-arms; the guard slumped to the floor without a sound.

The second whirled in alarm, an expression of shock pasted across his battle-scarred features. The man fumbled for his sword, but as he drew the weapon Rudy brought his shorter blade through a savage swing. The blade caught the guard on the knuckles, knocking his weapon free and forcing him to his knees. The Iceman leveled the tip of the knife toward the lump bobbing in the man's throat.

"Open the door!" Rudy snarled, surprised as the savagery in his own voice.

"I—I can't! My orders—" stammered the guard, his eyes darting wildly around the chamber.

"Now!" shouted the Iceman, drawing the knife back, fully prepared to drive it home.

Fumbling in panic, the fellow seized the latchbolt and drew it aside. Immediately the heavy door burst open and Anjell and Bristyn tumbled through. His niece ran toward him, but when Anjell saw Rudy's weapon and his attention on the guard, she stepped to the side.

Outside, Takian and Danri stood side by side, backs to the open door, holding a press of guards at bay. Torches waved near the back of the crowd, while the men in front thrust with swords at the valiant pair. Even as Rudy stepped forward, he saw Takian stab a man in the chest, while Danri's hammer flashed, crushing the knee of the lunging swordsmen.

"In here!" shouted the Iceman, and his companions took advantage of the twin casualties to step backward, through the narrow tower doorway. "Now, get out!" Rudy ordered the guard who had opened the door.

The man dove headlong into the press of his fellows and the digger quickly slammed the door shut behind him. With a wrenching twist the Iceman thrust home the bolt, giving them at least a temporary measure of security. The door shuddered under the impact of bodies and fists as furious guards threw themselves against it. The pounding thundered in the circular room, but the door seemed quite solid against it.

"Nice work," grunted the digger, with an appraising look at the second man-at-arms, who lay motionless on the floor. Rudy reached down and claimed the man's sword and scabbard. The weapon was lighter than the kroak blade, with a keen edge along both sides of the blade.

"And none too soon," Takian agreed. "I was beginning to get discouraged by the odds. Though I must say, sir," he added to Danri, "I have never seen a hammer wielded with such devastating effect."

"Looked like you knew what to do with that sword, too," Danri replied, before turning to Rudy. "There's six or eight guys out there that aren't going to be doing much of anything for a while."

"What about the two dozen others?" asked Bristyn wryly. "Although it's probably a couple of hundred by now."

Takian winced, but nodded. "You're right—they're coming from all over the palace."

"What happened?" Rudy asked.

"A pair of the fools stumbled onto us." Danri spat disgustedly. "I bonked 'em with my hammer, but not before one got a shout off.

Seems there were men hiding all over the place out there—we're just lucky we didn't walk right into them on our way to the tower. But what about Kianna—did you find her up there?"

"Danri!" The fairy answered the question herself, stepping gingerly forward from the stairway to embrace the digger in a hug that brought a crimson blush creeping upward from his beard. She buried her face in his shoulder as her wings twitched then fluttered tentatively. Raine, following on foot, came down the last steps and joined the companions beside the door.

"Your maidservant knows her way around locks and bolts, as well as walls," Rudy declared to the duchess, taking Raine's hand. "Those apes had Kianna pretty well locked up!"

"It wasn't so bad," declared the fairy, wiping away several tears of delight. She embraced an equally teary Anjell while she spoke bravely. "Of course, I missed you all. And there were some times I wondered if you'd be able to find me—not that I ever doubted that you'd try. But it sure is good to see you all! What happened since you lost me? How did you get here—I rode on the back of a really smelly horse! Where's Kalland? And who are you?" she asked Takian.

"A Prince of Galtigor," he replied with a rueful smile. "Welcome to my palace. But I'm afraid we've got a few problems to deal with before we commence a proper reception."

The pounding against the door abruptly ceased, but Rudy suspected it was likely to be a short respite while their attackers looked for something heavy enough to batter it down.

"Is he dead?" Danri asked, with a look at the motionless guard.

"I—I don't think so. I didn't stab him—I hit him on the head."

"Whatever works," the digger grunted, kneeling beside the guard. With a slice that removed a short piece of his rope and a few quick twists, Danri had the man securely bound.

"Here, help me with this bar," Takian suggested, indicating a heavy beam Rudy hadn't noticed before. The two of them lifted it into place across the door, adding a further measure of security.

"What do we do now?" Bristyn asked Takian. "Can you try and talk sense to those men out there?—after all, *you're* as much their prince as Garamis!"

"Not *these* fellows," Takian replied sourly. "Those who wear the black and red of Garamis have sworn to give their lives for him. Every guard out there is one of his faithful. One shouted my name in that melee—it only drove them to a greater frenzy."

"In other words, we're trapped," the duchess summarized.

"That states it pretty well," Takian agreed with a sigh. "I'm sorry that you've all—"

"None of that!" Danri interjected. "We're in this together, and no point one of us being sorry for the rest. After all, we'd still have come after Kianna—and without you to show us through the city, we probably never would have made it to the palace grounds."

"Danri's right," Rudy declared. "Let's see what we can do about getting out of here."

"If we climb to one of the balconies, we could get a look at the grounds," Raine suggested. "At least we'll see what they're planning to do against us."

"Good idea," the Iceman agreed. After a last check to see that the guard remained securely bound, they trooped up the stairs until they reached the first level of balconies. Looking through the arching portal, they could see that dawn was beginning to color the eastern sky.

"Careful," Takian warned, as Rudy approached the open platform. "My brother commands some very accurate archers. They might be waiting for a target."

The Iceman dropped to his belly and wormed forward until he could see between the spikes of the balcony railing. The courtyard below teemed with men, many carrying flickering brands, though in the growing daylight they began to extinguish their torches. As he watched, the throng parted, and he saw a tall figure cloaked in black stalking through the ranks. Rudy recognized the elder Prince of Galtigor, and his hatred came flooding back with angry force.

"Too bad *we* don't have one of those archers," Rudy muttered, even though Garamis remained out of range for the moment. He saw the prince confer with several men, then march forward again, toward the base of the tower.

As if he knew where they had gone, the prince looked upward, toward the balcony where Rudy and his companions lay concealed.

"My brother!" cried Garamis. "I am delighted to know that you live! Come down here and talk to me!"

Takian snorted in contemptuous amusement.

"It will do you no good to cower within those walls! Deliver yourself to me, and you have my word that your brave companions shall go free! Fail to do so, and every one of you must perish—a tragedy that I dearly wish to avoid!"

Cautiously raising himself up to peer over the railing, Takian shouted to the throng in the courtyard, "You're an assassin—and doubly treacherous, for aims against your own house! Think you that I'm such a fool as to walk into my executioner's arms?"

"Ah, my brother—it *is* you! And no, I don't think you're a fool. But what other choice do you have?"

"We can fight against traitors and villains!" Danri shouted, adding his own voice to the debate. "We can prove wrong those who seek to blame their own crimes on the innocents of Faerine!"

Garamis merely laughed. "You have a very attentive audience, I assure you—men who know where their loyalties lie. Your falsehoods will have no effect on the men of the Black Mantle!"

A cheer from the gathered warriors supported the prince's claim. Wearily, Rudy slumped against the cold stone of the floor. Raine took his hand and he smiled wanly at her, until she nodded toward the far side of the courtyard. "Look," she whispered.

More and more men marched through the gate in the curtain wall. At first Rudy thought they were carrying some sort of provisions, for all of them were heavily laden, but as they drew closer his heart sank. Each new arrival carried an armload of firewood, a bundle of straw, or a heap of kindling.

"Must be planning on a monster of a campfire," Danri muttered, without amusement.

"Can they burn this tower?" Rudy asked softly, his disbelief challenged by growing horror. "It's made of *stone*!"

"The walls are," Danri noted grimly. "But there's plenty of wood inside—the stairs, the floors at each level. Could be that the stones will make a nice chimney."

"Rudy? What are we going to do?" Anjell asked as he squirmed back to the shelter of the tower's interior.

"I don't know," he was forced to admit. He looked at Takian, whose face had grown dark with rage and frustration. "Is there any way out of here—besides the door? Like an underground passage that might get us past the guards?"

The prince shrugged helplessly. "Nothing that I know of. And I presume, if Garamis knew of such a passage, we'd already be seeing visitors coming in that way."

They heard the logs striking the walls and didn't need to look in order to see that the flammable material was being piled around the base of the tower.

"I will turn myself in to him," Takian declared abruptly. The prince rose to his feet and started toward the stairs. "At least, there's a *chance* I can make him stick to his agreement and free the rest of you!"

Rudy sprang after Takian and roughly took his arm, spinning the startled nobleman around to face him. "No!" cried the Iceman. "There's one thing I know: if we trust our lives to Garamis' honor, we only insure our doom! There *has* to be another way!"

"This is your last chance, my brother!" The voice rose from below. "Come down, and I will spare your companions. Remain up there, and you will all perish!"

"I *have* to go," Takian declared. "There is no other way—to stay here means certain death!"

They smelled smoke from the ready torches, wafting upward on the breeze. As if to spite them, the wind had picked up, a strong, steady force blowing from north to south. Rudy looked upward, seeing a few scudding clouds racing toward the unseen mountains, and for a fleeting instant he wished he could ride the wind. Danri, he was surprised to see, stared at the sky and scowled in deep thought, apparently wishing the same thing.

"I agree with the Iceman," Bristyn Duftrall declared, breaking the stalemate between Rudy and Takian. "You gain nothing--neither for yourself, nor for us—by going down there."

"What else can we do?" demanded the Prince of Galtigor, furiously spinning on his heel. "There's *nothing*—"

"Don't say that, just yet," Danri interrupted. He looked at the humans, and his face was pale, more frightened than Rudy had ever seen it. Yet the digger's voice was calm and steady as he spoke. "I have one idea. It'll sound like madness—by the gods, perhaps it *is* madness. But it might be worth a try."

Garamis shouted another warning. Carried upward by the strong wind, wisps of torch smoke gusted past their balcony; when the bonfire was lit, it would quickly fan into an inferno.

"This," said the digger grimly, "is my idea. . . . "

— 3 —

"Behold my brother—traitor not only to Galtigor, but to all of humankind!"

Some distance from the base of the tower, Garamis exhorted his men. The elder prince stood atop one of the wagons that had hauled a load of wood onto the palace grounds. Around him thronged hundreds of men of the Black Mantle. Several had fought Takian, insuring that he had been trapped in the tower—and also providing Garamis with valuable information about Takian's comrades.

"He travels in the company of diggers—he murders his own people in an attempt to rescue the treacherous fairy! But he will not succeed!"

A roar arose from the men. Dawn streaked the sky, growing quickly toward daylight, but everywhere stains of smoke swept above them to cast a pall over the courtyard. A great pile of scrap wood had been laid around the full circle of the tower's base.

"Who won't succeed? *Who*, Garam?"

The Prince spun, startled to see his youngest brother climbing into the bed of the wagon beside him. His face bright with curiosity, Boric stared wonderingly at the mob of men and the torches flaring around the base of the tower.

"Boric, there are spies in the palace," Garamis declared forcefully. "We are going to kill them now."

"Spies from the war?"

The prince nodded curtly, his attention returning to the tower. Words of exhortation choked in his throat, killed by the necessity to keep the truth from Boric.

"I know you're going to the war again," Boric said. "Will you take me with you this time?"

Inspiration flashed. "Yes—this time you'll ride with me. We'll take the hounds, too. In fact, we need to make sure that they're all in the kennels, ready to go. Will you do that for me, Bor?"

"Sure!" Boric, lumbering in his eagerness, raced off to the pens where the great warhounds dwelled. As soon as his brother had traveled beyond the fringe of the crowd, Garamis turned back to the stone-walled tower.

"Let it never be said that Garamis of Galtigor is not merciful! I ask you a final time, my brother—will you surrender yourself?"

Garamis dared the question because he was certain, by now, that Takian wasn't coming out—nor did his brother disappoint him with a reply.

"Light the fires!"

Eagerly the men of the Black Mantle, Redsteel Guards in the lead, surged forward. Dozens of armored men tossed brands onto the dry kindling. Flames licked upward, crackling through the loosely piled tinder, until fiery tendrils spurted twenty and thirty feet into the air. Heat soon drove the men back from the base of the tower, while clouds of dark smoke, carried by the increasingly strong wind, swirled upward and spread to the south in a streaming plume.

Garamis searched, quickly sighting Captain Wilfriz. At his leader's gesture, the warrior pushed his rust-colored stallion through the mass of men. Soon he reached the prince's side, where he dismounted and bowed.

"How do the companies stand?" Garamis inquired.

"I've just come from the camps beyond the city. They're either ready to march, or will be ready within an hour or two."

"Good. Get the first groups on the East Highway now; the rest should fall in as soon as possible. I'll stay here for a little while, then bring the men of the Black Mantle along as soon as I can."

Garamis barked his orders, then paused to observe the very satisfying progress of the fire—the blaze licked upward, eager to burn everything in reach of its fiery fingers. "The Redsteel Guards will accompany my chariot, where the Ice of Three Waters will be carried. Take the road toward Taywick Pass—and see that the leading elements make it as far as the Bannerbrook by tonight."

"Yes, my prince! Am I to assume you will join the camp by nightfall?"

"I'll do my best—or tomorrow, at the latest. In any event, the time for waiting is past. I want the army drawn up before the pass, ready to attack as soon as humanly possible!"

Wilfriz's face was split by a cruel grin. "Yes, lord. I'll see that the advance guard gets on its way immediately."

Wilfriz mounted his war horse and pushed toward the palace gates. Turning back to the tower, Garamis looked upward, and tried to imagine his brother's death.

The heat penetrated the stone walls, igniting the interior of the structure, sending smoke spewing from the lower balconies. The door had burned to an iron gridwork, and much of the tinder around the structure continued to blaze. Flames spurted from the balconies, and the prince smiled as he saw sparks wafting upward on the breeze, settling to the tower's wood-shingled summit—a roof that was increasingly obscured by smoke.

Finally the churning clouds grew too thick to see anything except the occasional tongue of orange-red flame. The fire roared upward, consuming every bit of fuel in its reach. Stones cracked, spitting fragments out of the wall, and from within the building came the sounds of collapsing floors, as wooden beams burned away and unsupported stairways tumbled, adding fuel to the hungry coals below.

Garamis looked across the faces of his men, saw their fierce exhilaration as the blaze consumed their enemies. For a moment, the prince thought, longingly, of Nicodareus—it was too bad the Lord Minion could not be here to observe this triumph.

More embers showered outward, as other interior levels of the tower collapsed. Additional stones cracked and split from the walls, and the great structure began to sag as it lost its interior support.

"Back—get back from there!" Garamis shouted, and the command was taken up by a multitude of sergeants. Slowly, reluctantly, the bloodthirsty men backed away, as the tower trembled at the verge of ruin.

— 4 —

"There are, in Faerine, sages who use Aura to create cloudships that sail through the skies," Danri explained. The companions had climbed through the trapdoor onto the tower's gently sloping roof, and now the digger addressed them—reluctantly, as if he didn't like what he was forced to say.

"It's true!" Kianna agreed readily. "I've seen sylvan masters do it right by the Eternal Spring!"

"Well, if we had a sylvan sage—or if this was the Eternal Spring—I'd say that's a useful thing to know," declared the duchess sourly.

Clouds of smoke wafted upward, drifting over the narrow platform at the top of the tower. They could see swaths of the ground between the plumes, but most of their view below revealed only a smoky nightmare—and the promise of a growing inferno.

The digger scowled furiously at Bristyn, but then continued. "I'm not saying this is a great hope—but we *do* have Aura." He hefted the long, embroidered waterskin belt that he had worn since leaving Shalemont. The sack had not been tapped since he filled it from the spring on Wilderhof; now it bulged from the mass of its contents.

Rudy had listened carefully to Danri, wanting desperately to find some glimmer of hope, but now he shook his head in despair. "Are you suggesting that *you* could make us one of these cloudships, or something out of Aura, that would let us get down from here? It doesn't sound possible!"

"I know that I couldn't do it—diggers have no talent for working enchantments like that. Our skills are all focused on the ground—we like to stay in touch with dirt and bedrock."

"What do you propose, then?" pressed the Iceman.

"I'm thinkin'—maybe *you* could do it," Danri said bluntly to Rudy.

"What?" Sitting back in surprise, Rudy was ready to throw up his hands in despair. "If *that's* all you can think of, we might as well—"

"Rudy—wait! At least *listen!*" Anjell urged him. The fear in his niece's face was enough to make Rudy bite back his objections.

"What makes you think that I could do something?" he demanded instead.

Danri continued to meet the Iceman's gaze with his own blue-eyed stare. Rudy had never noticed how cold his companion's eyes could look.

"It's just that I've never heard of *any* human who could use Aura—for anything. Yet here you are—you speak our language, you see in the dark, you even sense danger down the road. Things no human should be able to do. Perhaps there's a chance you could weave something out of the Aura, make us a cloudship to float away from here."

More smoke spewed and billowed upward. The ground was fully obscured, and from the heat and vapors churning through the interior of the tower, they knew that the fire had fully penetrated the base of the structure. It was only a matter of moments before they were burned to death, suffocated, or carried to disaster by the tower's ultimate collapse.

"How—*how* does it work for these sylvan sages?"

"They spray the Aura around them," Kianna explained enthusiastically. "I've seen it *lots* of times. They do it on a pile of hot coals, so the Aura turns to steam right away. It forms a cloud, and the mage throws some kind of hook into it. Then everybody climbs on and they float away!"

Danri unslung the long waterskin and removed a long coil of his rope, which he fastened around the flexible leather sack.

"I guess we've got the supply of coals," Rudy allowed, still privately denying that this was anything other than a mad scheme to waste their remaining water of magic. Yet what use would the remaining Aura be to them, once they'd all perished in the blaze?

"I don't know how this magic works," he protested. "All I've done before is to take a drink, when I feel this certain kind of thirst. . . ."

He coughed, feeling the rasping rawness at the back of his throat, and suddenly he recognized the feeling, the craving for Aura, that had touched him only twice before.

"Let's try it," he said, beginning to wonder if, just maybe, there was a chance the plan would work. He took the proffered waterskin and gulped a short swallow, feeling the tingling sense of awareness. Slowly he stood and walked to the edge of the roof, looking into the churning smoke spewing past his face. A gust of it wafted around him and he felt the heat against his face; oddly, when he inhaled the stuff he didn't collapse into a fit of coughing. Perhaps the Aura gave his lungs protection as well as enhancing his senses.

And if that's the case, who's to say it won't make a flying ship for me? Grimly the Iceman took the rope from Danri, swinging the waterskin—still corked—through a couple of loops to get the feel of the line and its weight.

He heard Anjell coughing, and Raine too, as more smoke billowed across the roof. Noxious vapors spewed around the trapdoor they had climbed through—obviously, the fire had reached just below. The roof shuddered underfoot then, and the tower shook as an interior floor collapsed. There was no time to lose.

Turning back to the edge, Rudy pulled the cork on the waterskin and started to swing the rope through a tight, whirling circle. Cool Aura sprayed outward, mixing with the smoke, drifting downward like glittering flakes of diamond. Was it all going to waste?

Closing his eyes, Rudy prayed. He reached out to Baracan and pleaded silently for help, for power. As on every previous attempt at prayer he'd ever made, his thoughts rolled outward and vanished, without even an echo to hint that they had reached something.

The sack at the end of the rope grew lighter, almost drained of Aura. Frustration pounded in Rudy's heart—what use was Baracan to them now?

Then he saw what he should have guessed immediately—not Baracan, but *Aurianth*. "Please, O Goddess of Magic, Mistress of Faerine and Aura—*please* grant me the power to save my friends!"

For the first time in his life, Rudy spoke a prayer and knew beyond any possibility of doubt that it had been heard. He felt a great welling of relief, as if a multitude of troubles had been lifted from his shoulders. But still he didn't dare open his eyes.

"Look!" gasped Anjell, at last forcing Rudy to crack his lids.

A white cloud of vapor had coalesced before them, rising from below, from where the Aura had showered downward toward the flames. The mist seemed to hold the waterskin suspended, for the rope had become weightless in Rudy's hands. He pulled, slightly, on the line and the cloud drifted closer.

Abruptly a square of shingles exploded upward, and flames licked around their heels, greedily devouring the roof. Bristyn screamed, scrambling away from the hole. Only Raine's quick grab prevented the duchess from toppling off the edge of the roof.

"It worked!" cried Anjell, clapping her hands excitedly. "We can *ride* it!"

Before Rudy could stop her, she stepped to the edge of the roof and leaped toward the billowing mass of vapor. The Iceman's horrified cry strangled in his throat as he saw the girl plunge into space, topple forward into the cloud—and—*stop*! Kicking and crawling, Anjell climbed up the steep surface of cloud until she sat near the round top, waving excitedly to them.

"I . . . I don't believe it," Takian said, his voice numb.

"Stay here, then," Danri retorted, bounding to his feet. "*I* believe it!" With that, the digger hurled himself after Anjell, quickly coming to rest on the cloud. The force of Danri's jump carried the vaporous ship away from the tower, much as a boat would drift away from a dock under similar impetus, but Rudy still had hold of the rope. Quickly he tugged, pulling the cloud back toward them, holding it while Raine, Bristyn, and a still skeptical Takian jumped across. Kianna buzzed into the air, flying after them, while Rudy launched himself through a long dive, plunging heavily against the cloud and using his weight to force them away from the dying tower.

The tower shivered and convulsed, almost like a living thing yielding up its mortality. Stones crumbled out of the wall, and the flame-racked structure toppled like a tree, exploding into oblivion on the ground of the palace courtyard.

Freed of its tether, the cloud continued to rise, though the billowing gouts of smoke blocked any attempt to see down to the ground. The wind remained fresh, out of the north, and as the inferno blazed into ashes, the companions, on their ship of Aura, floated southward in the sky . . . toward the mountains and the Watershed, toward Taywick Pass and Faerine.

NINETEEN

Auraflight

From the serenity of the heights, one places the world
in proper perspective. Only when the entanglements
of humankind fade far below can the spirit of a lone
mortal truly soar.
—CREED OF THE CLIMBER

— 1 —

As Rudy stood at the very top of the hummock of cloud, a thought
occurred to him. He turned to Danri, who grinned like a giddy jester
beside him.

"Is there any way to steer this thing?" the Iceman asked.

"Who cares?" The digger's grin grew wider. "Actually, I don't
think so. Why? Do you think it could dump us anywhere worse than
where we were?"

"Not a chance of that, my friend. But—speaking of dumping—
how do you suppose we get down from here?"

Kianna fluttered up to their summit and sat down on the cottony
pillow of the cloud. Though still frail and wan, the fairy had stretched
her wings a bit and flown. Rudy still hadn't heard her sing, however.

"I think it just comes down, slowly, after it gets small enough,"
the twissel speculated. "It takes time, though—I know the sylves can

sail all the way from Spendorial to the Eternal Spring, if the wind is right."

"Spendorial?" Rudy had never heard of the place.

"It's their capital—some say the greatest city in the Enchanted Realms, though for my money I'll take Shalemont," Danri replied. "But if the lass is right, that's a flight that would run nearly the full length of Faerine. If we can make *half* that distance, we'll float all the way to the mountains at the edge of the Watershed.

"Of course," the digger continued, "I've heard that sometimes the sylves carry water barrels on these Auraclouds. Then they can drop the water over the side if they need to go higher, or sprinkle it over a portion of the cloud—which dissolves it—if they want to descend. Can't do much about that now, though."

"Then we might float right up against some mountain height?" Rudy guessed.

"If we're lucky. We should be pretty close to Faerine by then, but I doubt we'll have the height to float all the way over the ridge."

"Unless we go through Taywick Pass," the Iceman noted.

"Aye—then there's no telling how far we'll go."

For the time being, Rudy was less concerned with their destination than with the fact that they were all alive, unhurt—and uncaptured. A sense of vibrant energy filled the Iceman, though he still couldn't bring himself to believe that this cloud was *his* creation. Surely it was some aspect of the Aura spilling into the fire; would it not have gathered into such a billowy mass if Takian, or Danri, or Anjell had spilled the stuff of magic?

Deep within his soul, he knew that it wouldn't—though the knowledge gave him no particular sense of power or accomplishment. Instead, when he allowed himself to think about it, the feeling it aroused was one of acute vulnerability and hopeless inadequacy. Shaking the thought aside, he started down from the cloud's peak, determined to have a look at their exotic craft.

The Auracloud was a puffy, oval blob, about the size of the barge they had sneaked aboard enroute to Landrun. The center billowed upward through a series of steep, rounded ridges, like the levels of a normal cumulus cloud—except that this cloud provided secure support underfoot. Numerous ripples and hollows in the surface made comfortable places for the companions to sit or lie down—though for now everyone sought a vantage that allowed a view over the world sweeping past below.

As he stepped down, toward the "bow," Rudy felt the surface gently yielding to his weight—sort of like the mud in a soft marsh. Yet the cloud returned to its previous shape as soon as his weight was removed. He joined Bristyn, Raine, and Anjell near one edge of the flying ship, and his niece turned to him with a squeal of delight. He was relieved to see that the maidservant kept a secure grip on the back of Anjell's tunic.

"This is *fantastic*! You can see all the way to the mountains from here! And I don't think those people down there even know we're up here. Uncle Rudy—you're the greatest!"

He smiled wanly, his sense of inadequacy stronger than ever as he sat beside them and looked below.

"The army of Galtigor is on the march," the duchess observed, pointing. Rudy saw a wide track running southward from Landrun, through the forests of Galtigor. The first few miles of that route were black with marching columns of troops—even from this height he could see columns of horsemen, large supply wagons, and long, straggling formations of recruits.

"Going the same way we are," he observed.

"But they're not nearly so fast," Bristyn noted. She looked at the Iceman with an unusually serious expression. "I don't know how you did this—but we all owe you our lives," she said, and then added: "Again."

He shook his head awkwardly. "I don't know what I did—if I did anything. We were very, very lucky."

Raine smiled softly, and in that smile he sensed a depth of understanding that he himself had not begun to grasp. He felt tremendously grateful for her empathy, and had, as well, a strong urge to take her in his arms, seeking shelter in the warmth of her embrace. What would the duchess say if he did? With a sigh, he slumped onto a billowy seat, lacking the courage to find out.

Takian and Danri came down to join them, while Kianna buzzed around, seeking a look at the underside of their floating skyship.

"I wonder how long we'll stay up in the air?" This was a problem that had begun to worry Rudy. After all, they had no provisions—even their Aura was gone, now—and no way to keep warm and dry. "What if we get mixed up with a real storm—could the cloud be blown apart?"

Danri shrugged, with surprising good cheer. When Rudy scowled, the digger laughed out loud. "Look, my friend. We've not only made a dandy escape, but I'm pretty sure we left the impression on the ground that all of us were killed. Regardless of where and when we come down, as long as we're alive, we've gained a number of significant advantages! And if we don't make it down alive, well, we still get a fantastic ride before the end. All told, I think it's a sight better than standing around on the roof of that tower, waiting for it to fall."

"It did fall," Takian reminded them. "Looks like it started some fires in the palace, too. Garamis caused himself a lot of trouble for no return." The prince spoke wistfully, as if his brother's problems caused him distress.

"Well, he deserves whatever he gets!" Anjell declared forcefully. "And he still owes Uncle Rudy a whole bunch of money!"

Rudy sighed again, but found a grim confession somehow working its way out of his mouth. "You know, I started out for Galtigor fully intent on killing Prince Garamis—the only way I thought I could make up for the deaths of my brothers. I know he deserves that fate, but I haven't even thought about it for days. It seems pretty clear that our journey has grown far beyond my feud over the climb—we have to stop him from destroying all Faerine!"

"What are we going to do, now—I mean, all of us?" asked Bristyn. "I think circumstances have rendered *all* of our original tasks meaningless."

"We have to warn the Faerines—about *that*," Danri said, pointing downward to the army stretched along the roadway. "I'm not sure it'll do any good—there's a garrison of only a few hundred warriors at the pass. I know they won't be able to stand against this horde for long— but maybe I can give them the time to try."

"It's the Ice of Three Waters that will let Garamis find his way through the magical barriers, isn't it?" Anjell declared. "At least, that's what I heard. So why don't we take it away from him?"

Danri chuckled wryly, but both Takian and Rudy sat a little straighter. The two men locked eyes, as the notion settled more firmly.

"I think that's what we have to *try* and do," Rudy agreed. "Perhaps we should use both tactics. If you can warn the garrison, and we can somehow get hold of—or destroy—the Ice, we might be able to stop the army before it makes it into the lowlands of Faerine."

"*Can* the Ice be destroyed?" Takian asked. "I've seen that block—it doesn't melt."

"It might be possible to destroy it—with Aura," Danri speculated. "It's made up of all three types of waters, but Aura has the most power of them all. Of course, there's a good chance that—if it's soaked in Aura—it will explode with a lot of force."

After the proof that currently bore them, Rudy was not about to doubt any of the powers of Aura. He tried to envision The Block, as Takian had described it, and wondered if it might indeed be possible to reach that sacred talisman—and snatch it away from Garamis' army.

"Why does Garamis want to invade Faerine?" Anjell asked Takian.

The prince sighed and closed his eyes, in obvious emotional pain. "I don't know. Garamis has always enjoyed war—I mean, *really* enjoyed it, in a way that most other men find frightening. Still, he's never suffered a lack of enemies in Dalethica."

"He's a bad man," Kianna said with a shiver. "He-he *frightened* me!" Seeing the haunted look in the twissel's eyes, Anjell took her hand and patted it comfortingly.

Takian turned to the Duchess of Shalloth. "Garamis has always been opposed to the notion of peace with your people—his private legion, the Black Mantle, has borne most of the fighting in that war for the last decade."

"Indeed—their talents for battle and for butchery are well known to my people," Bristyn replied bitterly. "But why was he allowed to do this, without the consent of the king—or you?"

"King Larriac never saw Garamis' bad side. My brother was always destined to be king, and when my father was alive he felt that a ruler of Galtigor should not be held down by external constraints."

"But the Faerines?" Rudy pressed. "They're no threat to Galtigor, to *any* part of Dalethica! The only true enemy they have . . ."

"Is the Sleepstealer," Danri finished. "I suggested before—and I'm more convinced of it now than ever—that the Lord of Duloth-Trol is behind this. He's been known to reach mortals before, both in Dalethica and Faerine. I tell you, Garamis has been made a servant of the Dark. That's the only explanation!"

Takian shook his head stubbornly. "I can't make myself believe that."

"Whether you believe it or not—it *is* the only thing that makes sense. Have you looked at his sword, for example? That's not a normal weapon," Rudy added, gesturing to the armies below. "But this campaign only makes sense against a broader background, as a diversion for some scheme of the Sleepstealer's own making."

"You said the Watershed has been breached," Bristyn put in. "Can it be that Duloth-Trol is preparing for another war against the rest of the world? That hasn't occurred for a thousand years, but when it did—"

"Mankind was nearly destroyed," Rudy interjected grimly. "And yes, I think it not only *can* be—I think we're witnessing the beginning of such a war, right below us."

For a time none of them spoke. No one could think of an argument to dispute the bleak conclusion, though they all hoped that they were wrong. And indeed, as the fresh wind carried them, and the sun soared through the blue heavens overhead, it seemed impossible that the specter of all-out war could lurk anywhere within the bounds of the Watershed.

Yet later, when the sun set and the stars glittered in the remote fastness overhead, Rudy knew that they had guessed at the truth.

— 2 —

Like water surging toward a gap in a long dam, a great mass of air sought to flow southward, seeking release through the high barrier of the Watershed. Currents of wind gathered speed, channeled around obstacles of rising ground. At last, the gusts found their opening and here they howled and raged just like that stream plunging through the dam, rushing headlong to the breach known as Taywick Pass.

And as a stream carries a bobbing cork or buoyant log in its steady flow, so did the current of air carry the Auracloud of the Iceman. Between the White Range and the Mistcoast Mountains, both high barriers of the Watershed, Taywick Pass chopped downward in a deep notch.

For two days, blessed by exceptionally clear weather, the companions watched the ridge of mountains grow in depth and detail. What began as a distant and featureless horizon slowly resolved itself into rising ground, and then to a myriad of sharp mountain peaks, interconnected by sheer ridges and lofty plateaus.

The mountains here were not as tall as those of Halverica, but they were forbidding in their own right. Fringes of forest extended only to the lower slopes, and in many shady valleys gray-white glaciers lurked, awaiting the press of a century's snows to send them back to the lower valleys they had carved at the dawn of the Watershed. Most of the higher peaks were linked by sweeping ridges, with the summits of both ridge and mountain flanked by cliffs of gray, black, or red.

Despite a lack of provisions, the companions rode in surprising comfort. Since the cloud moved with the air, there was little wind to chill them, and when Anjell discovered that they could easily burrow small niches into the cloud they were able to remain snug even through the cool nights. Hunger and thirst were vague abstractions, in Rudy's mind—and so it seemed with his companions, as well. The blossomy mattress of vapor seemed to sustain them at least minimally.

Or perhaps it was simply that the sensations of the lofty ride were intoxicating, invigorating enough to overcome the body's natural needs, carrying life to some higher plane. For many hours Rudy considered whether this might not in fact be the case.

As the mountainous pillars flanking Taywick Pass drew near, however, his mind returned to more pragmatic concerns. Their cloud had shrunk to some extent at this point, but it still had plenty of buoyancy—more than enough to carry them through the pass and well into Faerine. But the garrison they needed to warn was stationed just past the summit of the gap, according to Danri. How terribly ironic, Rudy thought, if they were carried over and far beyond the place where their presence was most needed. Yet they could think of no way to exert any control over the cloud.

It was late afternoon as they drifted above the foothills, generally following the course of a meandering valley—though the Auracloud still floated higher than any of the summits around them. The full grandeur of the range rose to the near south, allowing them to look up at the snowswept heights along the Watershed.

"Look—there's the pass. That spire's called the Tor of Taywick, and it marks the place well," Danri said, pointing at a deep notch in the ridge of the horizon.

Rudy saw the tor immediately, though it was still twenty or thirty miles away. It was a tall column of stone, jutting upward from the ground in the saddle. Steep-sided and slender, the tor looked unclimbable; it was also too narrow to block the route through the pass to either side of its stony base.

Steadily they approached Taywick Pass, but in the cooling air, clouds of water began to form around them; for the first time since floating away from Landrun they found themselves surrounded by misty fog. Rudy climbed to the very peak of their cloudship, but even from there he could soon see nothing but churning gray in all directions.

A misty precipitation surrounded them, more like tiny droplets dancing in the air than actual drops of falling water. Rudy wondered if they were witnessing the birth of rain, such as occurred every day in Dalethica. If so, it seemed that Faerine was not the only place of magic in the world.

As they sailed farther, the air current became more tempestuous, causing the Auracloud to pitch and heave. Rudy felt dizzy, though he couldn't tell if the cloud spun through circles, or if it was the lack of any visual surroundings that made him queasy. Once a jagged piece of rock appeared, like some dagger thrust upward from a cloud of smoke. They careened past the obstacle, giving the Iceman his first startling impression of how fast they blew through the skies.

Lightning flashed and thunder roared all around them. More mountains rose and vanished, while their progress became capricious as a whirlwind's. A high cliff face materialized to their left; they drifted beside it for a time before slowing noticeably and whirling into a bay between two barely visible summits. Rudy sensed that they had blown adrift of the pass, and were now trapped in some lofty vale.

"We're sinking!" cried Anjell, drawing her uncle's attention below. Shocked, Rudy saw right *through* their Auracloud, watching the steeply sloping face of a glacier rapidly draw near. The surface looked like wet snow, pitted and ridged in vertical furrows, drawing closer with shocking speed.

Then his feet touched down and, instinctively, he kicked the toe of his boots into the surface. Danri, Anjell, and Raine did the same, while Kianna hovered above the snow and Takian slid downward for a few feet before he clawed himself to a halt with his hands.

The duchess, however, did not react as quickly. She came to rest on the sloping surface of the ice-gray glacier, and immediately turned on her heel to seek her companions. Her feet slipped free and she tumbled onto her back, careening down the mountainside, carving a trough through the wet snow and desperately scrabbling for purchase with her hands.

Quickly Rudy pointed his toes downslope, beginning a controlled slide in Bristyn's wake. Pulling his ice axe from his belt, he jammed the spike of the shaft into the glacier, using it to control his rapid glissade. Leaning to the side, he steered straight down the slope, picking up speed until the wind stung tears from his eyes.

A pair of deep crevasses cut across the glacier, yawning hungrily in the path of the tumbling duchess. Rudy crouched, the soles of his boots speeding over the rough crust of the snow. Bristyn tumbled like a rag doll as the yawning lip of the first crevasse expanded—but now Rudy's speed allowed him to close the distance.

Just as the duchess reached the edge of the crevasse the Iceman threw himself forward, stretching desperately to grasp her wrist as he drove the spade of his ice axe into the snow.

The blade bit deep as the woman tumbled into the crevasse. Sprawled on the snow at the lip of the snowy chasm, Rudy strained to hold on to his axe and Bristyn's hand. He felt as though he would be torn in two, until in a few moments Danri and Raine joined him. Together they pulled the woman to safety, carrying her sideways along the slope until they were past the edge of the crevasse and momentarily out of danger.

Bristyn Duftrall collapsed in tears, and at first Rudy thought she had been injured. Yet her voice was furious, not pained. "I can't do *anything*!" she cried, turning to the Iceman. "You saved me—*again*! It's always me causing trouble! Why can't I be of some *use*?"

"You saved Takian," Anjell said bluntly. "And you kept me warm when we were hiding from Lord Ugly."

"You're one of us," Rudy added gently. "Nothing more needs to be said—except, we should get down from here."

"But—"

"They're right." Takian reached for Bristyn's hand. "And I, for one, am *very* glad that you're with us."

Sniffling, the duchess allowed the prince to help her to her feet while the others looked around. They were in a high, barren vale. No trees marked the slopes, and an ice-covered lake filled most of the valley floor.

Together the companions made their laborious way around the shore of the ice-choked lake. Beyond, the land sloped steeply away, flanking a narrow, snow-filled channel; under the snow splashed a swollen stream, clearly audible.

"Keep clear of the stream," Rudy warned. "If you fall through, your body might be carried for miles before you come out from under the snow, a few dozen years from now."

Takian shuddered, veering away from the stream to match Rudy's course, which passed from one patch of rocks to another, as much as possible.

"Any idea where we are?" the Iceman asked, as Danri clumped past him for a look down the sloping valley floor.

The digger shrugged. "Somewhere in Faerine, I'd wager—because I think our speed was enough to carry us through the pass. Still, there's a chance we're in some high valley on the Dalethica side. Best thing we can do is follow this water down and see where we come out."

"Agreed," Rudy said. "At least we seem to be getting below the snow line." He indicated the steplike descent of the ground, which was relatively dry as it dropped away from them. "And there doesn't seem to be a lot of loose debris," he added, stepping down another two-foot drop to a lower shelf of rock.

"I'll say—it's too bad these steps are so high," Takian noted. "Otherwise it'd be like a regular stairway."

"They *are* very regular, aren't they," Rudy replied. He almost bumped into Danri, who had stopped to examine the mountainside behind and above them—the steplike shelves of rock they had just descended. The digger grimaced.

"It's no accident," he said ominously. "These steps were *carved* here, on purpose. . . . "

"But why so huge?" wondered Takian.

Rudy wasn't listening. Instead, he stared down the stairway at a manlike figure who stood before them, blocking their path. Three companions backed him up, the whole party advancing menacingly up the steps.

A wide black beard tangled across the fellow's great barrel-chest. He was dressed in a simple leather tunic and sandals—surprisingly light protection at this snowy altitude. In his right hand he bore a sword of battered bronze, in his left a shield of stout, metal-strapped wood.

But all of that seemed immaterial as he came closer, rising toward them with surprising speed. And then Rudy realized that his first suspicion had been correct: though manlike, with features similar to that of a bearded human, this was no man. Watching the way he easily negotiated the big steps, the Iceman realized that fellow before them was at least ten or eleven feet tall.

"Now I'm sure this is Faerine," Danri whispered hoarsely. "Unfortunately, it's the part where the gigants live!"

— 3 —

For days he raced along, sniffing the ground, the air, the trees—sniffing everywhere. Just when it seemed he should give up, that the man was gone for good, there came this faint scent, carried a very long way, that encouraged the snow lion to keep going.

But it was taking so *long* to find him. Some days he ate the rabbit or pheasant or turkey that carelessly wandered into his path. Other days he ate nothing at all. He could have stopped to hunt, of course—but that would have meant delaying his search. He knew what was important, so some days—*many* days—he went hungry.

There was a frightening interval when he couldn't smell the man at all, but at the same time, he knew he was out there. Then the smell returned, backed by other familiar odors, and he knew: the man was in the south, up in the mountains.

Mountains! The big ears pricked up; the huge paws padded eagerly along. Back to the mountains!

Then he ran, most all the days and even the nights. He was lucky—a deer came by, and with a quick pounce he had his first good meal in a long time. He needed rest then—but he couldn't close his eyes.

Instead he lumbered back to the trail, his belly dragging him down. It hurt so much that finally the big animal slumped to the ground; very gradually, he gave way to sleep.

He woke up slowly—too slowly. He didn't hear the men until it was too late, until the ropes snaked out to grab his head and his big paws. The ropes pulled tight, stretching him in all directions; he couldn't move.

He was caught.

— 4 —

Light from a flaring bonfire reflected off the high walls of the rock-bound amphitheatre, shining along sheer stone faces that stretched two or three hundred feet overhead. Even though it had been fully dark when they had been brought here, Rudy sensed that the true tops of the smooth rock walls soared far beyond their sight, well above the reach of light even from the massive blaze.

Perhaps he got this feeling from the echoes of the great stone drums, or from some lingering sensitivity left by his ingestion of Aura. Or perhaps it was just that everything else about the gigants had so far proven to be insanely, incomprehensibly *huge*.

Beginning with the creatures themselves. When the four gigants had first approached, Danri made a valiant stand on the great stairway, encouraging his companions to try and get away. Quickly—and with uncanny accuracy—one of the gigants had pitched a rock, striking the digger in the face and demonstrating to the others the folly of flight. They had been gathered roughly into a line, while one of the hulking brutes slapped Danri back to consciousness and shoved him into file with the other captives.

The first gigant to face them, who was called Hoagaran by his cohorts, was the leader of this small patrol. After warning them not to stray from the trail—at the risk of their lives—this growling fellow had led them along a twisting, narrow path. With two gigants leading the way, and another two bringing up the rear, the companions had no chance to seek escape. Rudy held Anjell's hand, and the gigants had moved them along in sullen silence.

For several miles the huge creatures had prodded their reluctant captives up winding mountain trails, past sweeping vistas and deep canyons. It had been full nightfall by the time they approached the vast hall; now they stood with a sense of dire portent, wondering what their captors intended.

Hoagaran bade the prisoners wait while he approached the fire, marching with regal dignity toward a trio of gigants who occupied huge stone thrones on a level platform below the fire. Around these gathered many of the hulking humanoids—close to a hundred, by Rudy's quick estimate. The creatures glowered and muttered, bristling with hostility.

"You bring me the digger spy and his cohorts?" demanded the gigant in the center seat.

"Yes, my chieftain. He claims that he is no spy, but how else do we explain his presence in the High Armory?"

Beside Rudy, Danri fumed silently. The digger had obviously learned his lesson, however, since his earlier protestations to Hoagaran had resulted in a painful cuff on the side of his head—adding to the damage caused by the rock that had struck him there earlier. Now

Danri's eye was nearly swollen shut, and a trickle of dried blood trailed from the corner of his mouth into the thicket of his beard.

The Iceman stepped to Danri's side and touched a hand to the digger's shoulder. Never had he seen his companion so furious, though the stocky miner continued his valiant effort to ignore the taunts of their captors.

"Do you know where this place is?" Rudy whispered. "Or how far it is to Taywick Pass?"

"The gigants have a few of these halls, always in the high mountains," the digger muttered in reply. "But I've never been to one— and I don't know how far from the pass we are right now."

"Maybe we can make them see the danger of Garamis' invasion," the Iceman said hopefully. "Even if they won't join us, perhaps they'll be willing to let us go—"

Danri snorted in disbelief. "Fat chance of that. Once they've got us here, I don't think they'll want to let us leave—after all, we've seen their sanctum."

"You are Danri, digger of Shalemont?" The booming voice pulled their attention back to the fire. The gigant on the center throne had risen, and now he stalked toward them, each footstep thudding against the ground like a felled tree.

"That's me," the digger replied. "I wish I could say it was a pleasure."

"Silence your insolent tongue!" declared one of the guards, stepping forward with upraised fist. Rudy leapt between the digger and the gigant, glaring upward at the hulking figure—who seemed somewhat taken aback by the Iceman's courage. Nevertheless, the gigant chieftain continued to speak to Danri. "Many of my kinsmen have gone to Shalemont to seek you—for many years they have failed. They claimed you ran away because you were afraid."

Danri snorted in amusement. "Nope. I've just been busy, that's all."

"The only thing worse than a digger is a digger with human friends," declared the chieftain, stomping to within a few feet of the companions.

Rudy spun back and stared at this huge creature, who was nearly twice as tall as he. Furthermore, this gigant stood nearly a head taller than most of his fellows, and the Iceman noticed that he was also more ornately dressed. A whole bearskin was draped over his massive shoulders, with the clawed forepaws dangling over his chest. Other skins, from deer and sheep as far as Rudy could tell, girded the gigant's loins. His feet were clad in sandals of heavy leather, but unlike those of his companions, his were strapped with gold wire.

"I am Gulatch, chieftain of the White Mountain gigants. This is my domain you spy upon—and it is I who will deal your punishment. Is there anything you wish to say before you begin your journey to Aurianth?"

"Why would I spy on a gigant?" demanded the digger, finding his voice with no difficulty. "Do you think I'm trying to learn how to be stupid?"

Again the guard raised a fist, but Rudy spoke before Danri was subjected to another blow.

"We're *not* spies!" he insisted. "We rode an Auracloud through Taywick Pass, and it dropped us in that valley—in the place you called the High Armory! We're not enemies—we came to warn you of danger!"

Chuckles of amusement, rumbling like a distant rockslide, rose from the gathered throng of gigants. Gulatch, however, scowled suspiciously. "How is it you speak the tongue of Faerine? This is *more* proof that you spy upon us!"

"You've just proved you're as big a fool as you look!" spat Danri. This time Rudy couldn't prevent the blow that sent the digger tumbling across the rocky ground. "And a coward to boot!" cried the unrepentant digger, spitting out a broken tooth and wiping the fresh blood from his lips. "Do you always let your lackeys do your fighting for you?"

"I let no one do my fighting for me," replied Gulatch. "My companions, however, are concerned that their chieftain is addressed with the respect appropriate to his rank."

"*I* respect you. Can I talk?" Anjell's tiny voice carried easily

through the vast amphitheatre. The girl stepped away from the quivering Kianna, whom she had been comforting. The gigant chief looked
at her in astonishment.

"Even a *child* speaks our tongue?" he wondered aloud in amazement.

"Rudy and Danri and Kianna taught me—they know an awful
lot. But they're *not* spies," Anjell declared.

"What purpose brings you to our domain?" The gigant squatted
on his massive thighs, bringing his eyes down closer to Anjell's level.

"We came to stop the war," she replied bluntly. "And we will,
too—that is, if you'll let us."

"What war? The diggers are an annoyance, but certainly no cause
for warfare. The business of Faerine is for Faerines—think you we
need humans to interfere in our affairs?"

"It's *because* of the humans!" Anjell asserted.

Rudy wanted to support his niece, but he bit back his own com-
ments; after all, the gigant seemed to be giving the girl more serious
attention than he had bestowed upon either Danri or the Iceman.

"The Prince of Galtigor—the *bad* one," Anjell amended, with an
apologetic look at Takian, "is coming to Taywick Pass with an army.
He's going to make war against Faerine—and we're trying to stop it!"

Gulatch frowned, his bushy eyebrows lowering like heavy storm
clouds. "Is this true?" he demanded, confronting Rudy and the digger
again.

"Exactly true," Rudy replied quickly, before Danri could spit out
something insulting. Somehow the infuriated digger held his tongue,
allowing the Iceman to continue. "He's coming with many thousands
of men—he'll be at the foot of the pass by tomorrow at the latest! We
were trying to land there ahead of him, to warn the garrison."

"The garrison will know," the gigant chieftain declared. "But why
does this concern you? If this prince of Galtigor is your enemy, know
that the Wards of the Watershed will guard the pass against any human
intrusion. He and his army may enter the gap, but then they will
wander around, lost—for weeks, perhaps, or longer. When at last they
march out again, they'll find themselves back in Dalethica. The pass
is inviolate to non-Faerines."

"What about non-Faerines who bear the Ice of Three Waters?" demanded Rudy. "Garamis is convinced that this treasure will grant him the power to see through the deceptions. And we know that he has had the help of a Lord Minion of the Sleepstealer!"

Gasps exploded from the gathered gigants, though the outbursts were quickly stifled. Gulatch himself bolted upward and planted his hands on his hips as Rudy spoke; still, he seemed to consider carefully what he had been told.

"You speak of things that are impossible," he said finally. "I do not know the purpose of your treachery, but it shall not be allowed to progress." He clapped his hands, and a dozen strapping gigants marched out of the assembled crowd.

"Take the prisoners to the Well of Despair," Gulatch ordered. "We will keep them there—long enough to determine what their part in the invasion is supposed to be. Only after we have learned all we can shall we proceed with the executions."

Rudy couldn't believe what he was hearing. "Don't be a fool!" he shouted, stepping aggressively toward the chieftain. Gulatch regarded him with a look akin to amusement. "If Garamis *does* get through the pass, it will be too late—for the garrison, for you, for all Faerine! Why won't you believe us?"

"Perhaps we will—but this is not something we can decide without careful consideration. That will require many days."

"We don't *have* days, many or few! Garamis might attack at any time!"

"If you are telling the truth. But there are many reasons you could be lying, and these are what we shall debate." Gulatch scowled, as if afraid he'd spoken too gently. Apparently he decided that he had.

"Then, after our debate," he growled, "you shall be put to death."

TWENTY

To the Tor of Taywick

The Watershed stands upon a foundation of rock.
Patterns of wind and rain insure that the barriers
between the realms remain intact. And as a final
measure, if physical separation fails, there are always
the Guardians. . . .
—CODEX OF THE GUARDIANS

— 1 —

The heavy wagons were mired in a steeply climbing section of the roadway. Two days earlier the army had left the East Highway, following a rutted road that gradually faded to a track. Now, as it approached the last heights before Taywick Pass, the route all but vanished. Despite the lashes and profanity of the drivers, ranks of stolid oxen stood, belly-deep in mud, refusing to continue the exhausting ascent. Behind the baggage train straggling companies of the great army began to jam together, many of the men taking the opportunity to slip into the woods for an unauthorized rest.

Garamis forced Cyric through the crowd of troops until he reached the muddy swatch of road and the string of mired wagons. The prince made his decision quickly.

"Push them off the road. Cut the oxen from their traces, and load as much cargo onto their backs as possible. We'll do without the rest."

"Aye, Your Highness," declared the grizzled freightmaster. They could abandon the smithy and some of their food; Garamis would not allow the entire army to lose a day's march just to salvage a few comforts. Besides, the field smithy was a luxury—every man had a weapon, and the horses were all shod. As to the food, they could always eat the oxen if hunting proved impractical. Once they reached Faerine, of course, they would be able to live off the plundered goods of the magic folk.

"Stand to—beside the road! Ready to march as soon as the Ice of Three Waters comes by!" commanded the prince. A dozen captains and sergeants took up the cry, cajoling their weary troops back into file along the shoulder of the road.

But Garamis didn't wait to see the results. Turning Cyric back along the track, he galloped past the assembling troops until he reached the chariot bearing the precious block of ice, as well as Wilfriz and the grinning, elated Boric. A dozen of the palace warhounds bayed and howled around the chariot, adding their own frantic element to the confusion.

"Bring that along, here," the prince commanded. "I've ordered the road cleared, and I want the chariot to the fore by the time we reach the pass."

"Aye, lord." Wilfriz held the reins, and the burly captain didn't spare the lathered chargers as his whip cracked. Bouncing over deep ruts, the chariot rolled after Garamis at a fast clip; Boric clung to the rail and bared his teeth, grinning into the wind. Soon they reached the foot of the slope and churned upward through mud gouged by the freight wagons.

The laboring horses snorted and strained, sinking past their fetlocks as the big hooves sought purchase. By brute force the steeds dragged the two-wheeled cart onto the upper stretch of dry road. Galtigor's men raised their voices in cheers as their prince galloped by, and like a single creature the army's snakelike body slithered into the road and started after.

Garamis rode past a long file of scruffy Bordermen—archers who lived along Galtigor's frontier with Falteran. The foresters raised their weapons in salute, but watched him with wary eyes. The bowmen had always been loyal to the Crown, but perhaps they were less than enthused with their current commander. Troubled by the reaction, the prince made up his mind not to use the Bordermen in any key role. No matter—as always before, he intended to employ his trusted Black Mantles for the most crucial parts of the fight.

Beyond the bowmen he came to the first companies of his personal legion, and cheers erupted as Cyric carried the prince along the line of black and red. Long pikes bristled above several huge formations— their tight blocks would provide the anvil against which any opposing attack would be smashed. Beyond the pikemen rode the light horsemen. Gleaming in their black leather tunics trimmed in crimson, these riders bore swords and shortbows and rode small, nimble horses. Now the men held their blades overhead, a line of steel glittering in the sun as their prince rode past.

More companies cheered as Garamis and the chariot thundered along. Here, slowing Cyric to an easy trot, the monarch joined his black-clad lancers. Steel breastplates and helmets reflecting like mirrors of ink, the lancers carried heavy shields, massive swords, and lances. Their mounts were huge—the Lancers of the Black Mantle had first pick of the kingdom's war horses; their charge had never failed to break an opponent's line. In this they were aided by the effect they had on the enemy's morale, for the lancers were known to be merciless on the field, and unspeakably cruel to their captives. In the past, when the Carillonn foot soldiers had seen them coming, all but the most stalwart of companies broke and ran from the field.

Now, however, the armored horsemen milled about in confusion, detachments galloping in several directions as they searched for a route. One unit of veterans attempted to lead its horses up a sheer bluff of rock, instead of across the grassy slope that stretched out before them, just a few feet away. Another unit rode straight into a soggy marsh, where the mounts sank to their bellies and the riders were forced to dismount and flounder toward dry land.

These battle-scarred warriors had all served Garamis for a decade or more, and he knew them to be steady, reliable troops. Instantly the prince guessed the nature of their current difficulties: the Ice of Three Waters had been too far away when the advance riders reached the borders of the Taywick Illusions. Now the cheering took on a deep, resonant sound, and the recently bewildered lancers urged their horses forward in the wake of the chariot. The detachment at the cliff suddenly realized what they were trying to do, and sheepishly turned back to the rest of their regiment; the same for the muddy explorers who emerged from the swamp.

"There's the trail!" cried a captain, as the chariot rolled on.

"Follow me!" Garamis shouted, waving his fist. "Behold—the illusions of Taywick dissolve before the Ice!"

Above and beyond the lancers Garamis saw the great tor that rose in the center of Taywick Pass, jutting above the smooth, rolling terrain. There was no sign of a road, but the ground was open, perfect for the deployment of his army.

The route beckoned, wide and smooth and undefended. To the men around the Ice, including Garamis, all the illusions ceased to exist and they saw the pass as it was. The prince climbed a low rise, drawing a deep breath of satisfaction as he looked at the prospective battlefield.

The ground immediately before him led straight through the pass. The right side was screened by a grove of pine or cedar; to the far left spread a low, marshy area. In between these obstacles, however, a smooth green field extended all the way to the great tor.

Beyond that smooth-sided pillar curled a stream, and Garamis could see a stone bridge to the left—the last obstacle before the open pastures of Faerine. His army could pass to the right of the pillar also; in the end, the great column of rock wouldn't stop the advance any more than an upright stick could stop a flood.

— 2 —

Rudy looked fearfully at the approaching gigants. Anjell's clever argument had bought them time, perhaps—time in a place called the Well of Despair—but she had not persuaded the hulking creatures to release them. The most galling thing of all was their powerlessness, since they had no way of fighting the stubborn, massive beings.

Abruptly the stone drums, which had pounded a steady cadence since the prisoners had first entered the hall, ceased. Gulatch spun with surprising speed to face the great, round instruments. Rudy, too, gaped in astonishment as the two gigant drummers tumbled aside, knocked down by a bizarre creature who marched forward, boldly invading the Hall of Gigants.

The Iceman saw Gulatch make some kind of protective gesture across his face—as if attempting to ward off a supernatural threat. Groans of fear rose from the ranks of assembled gigants. Rudy leaned to the side, trying to get a look at the intruder. He saw more of the strange figures behind, descending with apparent ease down the steep cliff wall that formed the border of the amphitheatre. Yet there were no more than a dozen of the creatures altogether—why did a hundred gigants cower in obvious fear?

The intruder's two legs and arms, the torso and craggy face, all bore a superficial resemblance to those parts of a human or gigant. Yet this *thing*—Rudy wasn't absolutely sure it was a living creature— seemed to be made out of stone. The face was the gray bedrock of a high glacial valley, the arms and hands the rust-red of an iron-rich crest. Knotty cracks marked the knuckles and elbows; these creased and flexed easily as the strange being advanced.

"What *is* that?" Anjell asked, completely unafraid.

"Even the gigants show fear," Rudy added, with an abrupt twinge of recognition. He remembered the slate-skinned figures he'd seen on the Glimmercrown, unsuccessfuly seeking to halt Garamis' climb.

"It's a Guardian—a *High* Guardian," Danri said. "I've never seen one before, but every digger knows what they look like."

"What does it want?" the Iceman wondered aloud. He felt strangely delighted, almost exhilarated by the Guardian's arrival—yet he had no idea why it was here. Unlike the gigants, it caused him absolutely no fear. Instead, his relief grew into a kind of giddy joy.

You must let the human go.

Rudy heard the command—or did he *feel* it in some deeper portion of his brain? No words were spoken, and the message was directed from the Guardian to Gulatch, not to the Iceman. Yet the meaning was clear and specific—the human that the Guardian referred to was none other than Rudgar Appenfell.

"Why—why do you come here?" the gigant chieftain asked plaintively, his voice like a distant horn muffled by fog. "We do not threaten the Watershed—leave us alone!"

But you do *threaten the divides of the world. This human has a destiny, and you would hold him from it.*

"This human?" Gulatch turned to study Rudy, his massive face crinkled with skepticism. "Who is he that he should have such a destiny."

He is the Man of Three Waters.

Rudy heard the name and felt a jolt. Up to that point he had been intrigued and optimistic about the strangers' arrival, wondering if they were potential rescuers. Yet with this statement the Guardians forced him into their own plans, and he was not sure he could accept that burden. He felt a hand on his arm and looked down to see Raine's taut, wondering face. She too was awe-struck, yet the knowledge that she would help him suddenly made the Iceman strong.

"Is this true?" Gulatch confronted Rudy.

"I—yes, it is."

Again the gigant chieftain turned back to the High Guardian. "Is it also true that an army of humans marches toward the pass; and that they have the means to penetrate Faerine?"

I do not know the truth or falseness of this. It is true that the Watershed is threatened; that a part of the threat will be found at Taywick Pass; and that this human is destined to stand in the path of that threat. There he will live or die.

"Then you will take him with you." Gulatch turned to the gigants who were gathered around the prisoners. "Take the others to the well, but the tall human will remain so that he can depart with the Guardians."

"No!" Rudy declared. "We will *all* go with the Guardians—I am not leaving without my companions."

"That is impossible!" boomed the gigant. "Take them away!"

The Iceman acted impulsively as the gigant warriors stepped closer. Knowing he risked everything on a desperate gamble, Rudy hurled himself at Gulatch, driving his head into the creature's gut—and staggering backward, as solidly as if he had smashed into a tree trunk.

"Insolent human!" cried the chieftain, raising a clublike fist. Rudy reeled from the force of the collision, barely sensing the threatening hand—and the imminent blow that could kill him. He hoped, desperately, that his guess about the Guardians was correct.

The stonelike figure reached forward with surprising speed, grasping the gigant's arm and twisting the hulking creature to the ground. Gulatch landed with a resonant *boom*, and enough force to drive the air from his lungs. Gasping helplessly, the massive chieftain struggled to inhale.

You must not harm this human. The Guardian's message held a hint of iron, and a stony undertone of rebuke—apparently it was not used to repeating itself.

"But he attacked me—" Drawing ragged breaths, the gigant chieftain sputtered indignantly.

"Because you threaten my friends!" Rudy brandished an aggressive fist before the gigant's nose, which he could reach only because Gulatch was still sitting on the ground. "And I'll come after you again, unless you release them—I told you, we're all going!"

Come—time is short, urged the Guardian.

"Come on—we're getting out of here," Rudy said, gesturing to his companions. Hastening, Bristyn and Kianna came forward, while Raine took Anjell's hand and led the girl, who stared wonderingly around. Danri and Takian flanked the Iceman as he brought up the rear.

A hundred gigants glowered and muttered when the Guardian turned and led the way from the amphitheatre, but as the Iceman's companions departed, none of the hulking creatures moved forward to stop them.

— 3 —

Captain Matheral guided his trotting charger with his knees, allowing his eyes to play across the panorama of heights leading to Taywick Pass. Nine knights of Carillonn rode behind him—though the once disciplined formation had grown ragged during the long ride and now extended for some distance along the woodland trail. It had been three days since any of them had seen a road, five nights since they'd slept with a roof over their heads—and that had been the roof of a forester's woodshed.

And in the time since Bristyn Duftrall's disappearance, the knight's searching had led him only to one, mysterious clue. Again he looked at the great snow lion, as the creature padded along before the war horse, accepting the tether of rope around its neck. Still glittering in that mass of fur was the silver and diamond necklace that had first caught Math's eye—the necklace that belonged to the Duchess of Shalloth.

It had been the gleam of those precious stones that first suggested to Matheral that they capture the magnificent animal, which had been sleeping off a meal in the deep forest when the knights first encountered it. They had thrown looped ropes from six directions, and fortunately four of the loops caught. Once tethered, the creature had proven surprsingly docile—even going so far as to tug on the line, pulling the knights to the south.

Not having any other clue to follow, Matheral gave the cat its head, always keeping the rope around the maned neck. Every day the creature had loped with increasing urgency, as they left the lowland forests behind and started to work their way through the foothills.

Now, as the knights and their big chargers cantered after the lion, moving up the lower slopes of the White Range, Matheral wondered again how the snow lion had come to wear the necklace. He remained mystified, but had to stick to his earlier conclusion: the animal was somehow linked to the duchess in the past. In any event, it was the only straw he could grasp in the hope of finding the lady Bristyn alive.

As the knights approached a rounded ridge line, Matheral's natural caution caused him to rein back and approach the crest at a slow walk. The woods thinned out near this narrow height, which rose toward Taywick Pass at an oblique angle. As he reached the summit, the knight stopped in surprise, and then pulled back behind the concealment of the crest.

"The army of Galtigor's down there!" he whispered to the nearby riders. "Marching on Faerine, by all appearances!"

Shaking their heads in disbelief, several of Math's men accompanied him to the summit, where they crawled forward and looked into the valley below.

The tangle of Garamis' army crept up a wide trail, churning the track into sticky mud. Matheral saw the big freight wagons, toppled off to the side, and as his eyes followed the steady, determined march of the foot columns, the knight felt a sense of grim, utter foreboding. The sight of that force was unspeakably sinister and menacing.

Wondering what to do next, he was distracted until he saw a flash of movement out of the corner of his eye. The big snow lion had been sitting alertly, sniffing the air as it had sniffed every step of the way since it had been captured. Now the animal's ears pricked up and it bounced up off its hindquarters, quivering.

Math tugged on the long leash, reminding the excited animal that it was restrained. The snow lion looked at the knight, expression pleading, almost persuasive. Then the creature sniffed at the rope. In one fluid motion it extended a forepaw, flicking a razor-sharp claw through the tether. Matheral gaped in astonishment at the loose line held firmly in his hand.

In another instant he looked up, just in time to see the snow lion's tail disappearing over the next ridge.

— 4 —

"Good thing you got me out of there before I lost my temper," Danri remarked, limping behind Rudy on the trail. "No telling how many gigants I woulda been forced to rough up—the big oafs were starting to get on my nerves."

"*Starting?*" the Iceman asked, with a shallow laugh; he shivered with the memory of how close they had come to disaster.

Though the gigant hall was no more than a couple of miles behind them, Rudy felt quite safe under the protective escort of the High Guardians. The companions had trekked through mountainous terrain, under a night sky that glittered with stars—the clouds had drifted away sometime during their brief captivity. Now, in the daylight, they saw nothing but sheer peaks and desolate gorges to all sides. Icy winds moaned down the slopes, chilling to the bone, and still there was no sign of the high tor that marked the pass.

Following a series of perilous trails, the rock-skinned beings led the companions over a lofty ridge and along the crest of a sheer cliff. Finally they descended into a high valley. Judging by the closeness of the surrounding heights, however, Rudy knew that they had not yet reached Taywick Pass.

Bristyn, her face pale, stumbled along weakly as she leaned on Takian's arm. Anjell stepped gingerly, wincing at the pain in her feet— though she bravely made no complaint. Instead, she held the fairy's hand and whispered comfortingly to Kianna, who kept her eyes downcast. Every once in a while the twissel's body was racked by shivering. And Danri still looked horrible, his faced puffed and distorted by bruises. All of them were battered and sore, with no shelter in sight, lost in the high mountains of Faerine!

An idea presented itself to Rudy suddenly, and he cursed himself for failing to think of it sooner. "Is there a spring of Aura near here?" he asked, addressing the back of the impassive stone being before him.

The High Guardian did not reply, but veered slightly in his descent of the ridge. Cutting across a slope of loosely piled boulders, he stopped beside a tiny pool of clear water nestled in the base of an overhanging cliff.

Here is Aura.

"We'll rest here for a moment, long enough to drink and restore some of our strength," explained the Iceman, again drawing no response from the stone-faced Guardian. Instead, the creature turned to his fellows, nodded once, and started to walk away, back toward the high ridge they had just descended.

"Wait!" called Rudy. "Aren't you going to stay with us—to lead us?"

How can I be your leader? The Guardian seemed genuinely puzzled.

"Where is Taywick Pass? How do we get there?"

Follow the drainage from this valley. It will carry you into the main saddle of the pass.

The communication entered Rudy's mind together with a maplike image of their route, which he saw would spill them into the pass from the western heights. Distance was hard to judge accurately, but he thought that they might be able to reach Taywick by midday. While Anjell and Raine filled a waterskin with Aura and offered it to the other companions, the Iceman argued with their stubborn rescuers.

"You—you Guardians should come with us," Rudy said.

I do not understand.

"Your purpose is to defend the Watershed. Nowhere does it face as much danger as in the center of Taywick Pass. The strength of you and your comrades would be invaluable in holding the line!"

We Guardians are neutral; we cannot join a battle in the favor of one realm over the others. It takes a power beyond that which is mortal to draw us into the struggle—and you lack this power.

"What do you mean? *What* power?" pressed the Iceman.

Great power—might exceeding that of any man, minion, or Faerine. The Guardian's emotionless reply didn't really answer Rudy's question.

"You must reconsider—at least come and witness the threat!" Rudy urged, but he found himself speaking to the Guardian's back. The stony creature made no more reply as it led its companions toward the heights.

"My feet feel *lots* better," Anjell said, dancing a step to demonstrate.

"It—it's amazing," Bristyn Duftrall allowed, standing straighter. When Rudy looked at her, he could almost see the fatigue, the pain, sloughing off her body. Danri, still bloody, opened his swollen eye and grinned; at the same time the bruises on his face faded.

Rudy looked at the pool and for a moment he powerfully envied Faerine, where illness and hurt could be swept away with a tiny drink—and pools of healing water existed seemingly on every mountainside. Roughly he forced the feeling aside; all his life he'd known that Faerine and Dalethica should not mingle, that the Watershed existed to prevent just the type of confusion that now afflicted his emotions.

"I'm betting that Garamis will attack today—tomorrow at the latest." Rudy looked up at the sun. "If we set a good pace, we'll be in Taywick Pass in the next few hours. Can everybody do it?"

Nods and a few words of assent were his reply. Takian stepped to Bristyn's side, offering her the support of his hand, and Danri all but stomped his feet in his eagerness to be on the way.

"Shouldn't we fill up our waterskins while we're here?" Anjell asked. "Who knows when we'll find another pool as nice as this one?"

"The lass is right," Danri agreed. "Aura is part of all the rivers and lakes of Faerine, but pure springs—like this—are pretty rare. If we come to a stream, it'll be about a hundred parts water to one of Aura." The digger unslung his waterbelt and immersed it in the cool liquid, while Anjell did the same with Rudy's waterskin.

Then they started down the long, rocky mountainside. The slope soon curved into a narrow vale, and the rough ground became smoother. At first there were no trees, and the clumps of brush clung to the ground in small, straggly bunches. For the most part the surface of moss, lichen, and weathered rocks made for easy walking. Beside them splashed a shallow stream, leading the way to the lower elevations.

As the companions descended the valley floor they reached a stretch of tangled ground, large boulders scattered about like the lower teeth of some monstrous creature. Scrambling through these, they moved slowly and carefully to avoid the chance of a sprained ankle or broken leg. Then the ground leveled off across a wide plateau, still above the tree line, and here the sunlight reflected off strands of glimmering water standing in a wide marsh. Rudy led the group along the sloping ground, skirting the vale without wasting time in the mud. At the far end of the marsh the waterway dropped through a series of steplike falls, spilling in a curve to the left. Shortly the companions came around the bend in the valley and found the full sweep of Taywick Pass before and below them.

Terrain of gently rolling ground, covered with green, extended across a mile-wide gap before a rising slope betokened the far side of the pass. The pillar of the tor rose like a watchtower in the middle of the gap, which was perhaps five miles long. Several small ponds and one rapid stream marked the ground throughout the pass, mingled amid a few small groves of scraggly trees, but with the exception of the narrow stream and the tor, it was a place easily negotiated by an army.

At least, so it appeared to Rudy.

"How can they call this a pass?" Anjell demanded crossly. "There's a big gorge right across the middle of it! And what about those cliffs? How's anybody supposed to climb them?" She pointed, indicating a wide swath of smooth, green meadow.

"The enchantment of Taywick," Rudy murmured. "What do you see?" he asked Takian and Bristyn.

They described similar obstacles, and Raine, too, pointed to numerous pitfalls and cul-de-sacs that she saw. The prince added that the pass appeared to stretch to the far horizon. "It looks like you could wander around in there for *weeks*, and never find your way out again," he declared. Suddenly the nobleman frowned. "Why do you ask—what do *you* see?"

Rudy, with Danri and Kianna chiming agreement, described the pastoral setting, with its wide, open pathways and dry, smooth ground. All the while the Iceman's mind struggled in adjusting to another piece of information about himself. The illusionary protections of Taywick Pass masked the eyes of all the humans who looked at it—but he, the Man of Three Waters, was unaffected! Again he felt that strange queasiness, as he found himself swept along in a direction he did not seek, nor fully comprehend.

"I see my brother has driven his army hard," Takian observed, pointing toward the north. They saw the blocks of marching men, mingling chaotically with prancing horses. The tiny form of a black chariot rolled forward in the midst of the formation.

"How do they know where to march?" Bristyn demanded. "It looks like they're wandering around in a maze."

"The Ice is doing its work," Rudy said. "They're moving right along the main approach route; there, he's halting his first regiment."

"Probably letting the rest of the army join up," Takian said. "From the length of the column, I'd guess that will take him at least the rest of the morning. But he'll be ready to attack before the day is out."

The Iceman continued to watch. Two trios of horsemen broke away from the black chariot, riding ahead. After a minute, however, the riders slowed to a walk, and the horses began to wander around aimlessly.

"It looks like Garamis tried to send outriders to check out those clumps of trees, but now they're wandering around in a field of daisies—they're lost, I think," Rudy speculated. "Apparently the illusion is dispelled only for those within a certain distance of the Ice. It looks like they started to wander when they got about five hundred paces away from the chariot."

This fact, Rudy thought, might give them some cause for hope. After all, the gap was more than twice that distance in width, so Garamis would not be able to block the pass and protect his entire army against the illusion. Then a sickening realization wiped away his optimism—Garamis didn't need to *block* the pass. He had only to mass his men into one unstoppable phalanx and march right through.

"The Taywick Garrison?" Rudy asked, suddenly sensing the urgency of the situation. "How will we find them?"

"You already have. Please don't make the mistake of taking any hostile action."

Kianna screamed and covered her eyes as the silken voice, smooth and polite and steel-firm, emerged from a small clump of boulders nearby. Rudy would have thought the rocks couldn't hide a good-sized rabbit, but now several tall warriors rose to their feet and stepped forward. Each bore a long bow, with a steel-tipped arrow pointed at the companions. Their garments were loose, whipped by the wind around slender limbs; their faces were long and lean, with huge dark eyes and pointed slender ears.

Rudy didn't have to look twice to recognize that these were sylves.

— 5 —

"I am Quenidon Daringer, warcaptain of the Taywick Garrison," the sylve announced haughtily. "You will explain your presence on my flank."

It had taken an hour for their captors to march the companions down the slope and into this shaded bower, on the Faerine side of Taywick Pass. The warriors had kept their sylvan arrows unwaveringly pointed at the prisoners, but had resisted any attempts at conversation. Apparently, Rudy realized, they were waiting to let their commander do all the talking; now that they had reached the headquarters, Daringer wasted no time.

The sylve's gleaming golden breastplate reflected the morning sun into Rudy's face, but the Iceman stared in wonder at the colorful plumes trailing from the warrior's golden helmet. The sylve's hair, of a yellow so bright that it challenged the color of his gilded armor, lay in long curls over his shoulders. Eyes of indigo flashed from a sharp, angular face—a face that was frowning with suspicion and concern.

Danri stood beside the Iceman, under a canopy of leafy branches where the ground had been cleared of rocks and underbrush. It was like a large room formed within a framework of trees, and now it served as the Taywick Garrison's command post. Besides the two companions and the warcaptain, several other sylvan warriors—including the scout who had apprehended them—stood behind their leader, listening attentively.

"You must know, already, of the army approaching from Dalethica," Rudy declared, with as much dignity as he could muster. The tongue of Faerine seemed to flow like music from his lips, and he used every nuance of tone and syntax to convince the sylve of his seriousness.

The warcaptain didn't deign to respond beyond a slight narrowing of his eyes that might have been affirmation.

"The captain of this army bears the Ice of Three Waters. The power of this artifact serves to negate the illusionary protections of Taywick Pass. Know that, in the vicinity of the Ice, the humans see the lay of the land as it truly is."

Several of the sylvan lieutenants, standing behind their captain, stiffened in alarm, or exchanged worried looks at Rudy's words. Daringer, however, merely scowled a little more seriously.

"I would be skeptical," he allowed, "were it not for the fact that you travel with two Faerines—and that this army of Galtigor has already demonstrated astonishing persistence as it penetrates the approaches to the pass. No other human explorers have made it so far."

"My companions are most disoriented," Rudy acknowledged, with a look at Anjell, Raine, and the other humans. They sat on a log outside the command post, still looking back at the route they had followed since meeting the sylvan scouts. Though it had been a gentle descent of a smooth, open slope, his human companions had been convinced that they were walking over cliffs, wading swamps, and negotiating other challenging obstacles. Only by holding tightly onto Rudy, Danri, or Kianna had the other humans been able to move. Anjell, in fact, had gone so far as to close her eyes and follow her uncle's lead; she had found the going much easier than had the adult humans, who persisted in looking around.

Now, as if sensing the development of a plan, Raine and Takian came into the command center. Another figure clumped into the room, and Danri's eyes widened in astonishment. "Blaze Smelter!" he cried, stepping forward to thump his old friend on the shoulder. "So you're still holding the duty from Shalemont!"

"Aye—my five years are almost up, but quite an ending it's lookin' to be," grunted the other digger, who was slightly taller than Danri, but lacked the latter's strapping shoulders and heavily muscled arms.

"Well, you've got my hammer to back you up," promised Danri. "And my friends here have some information—it's important."

"You can vouch for these strangers?" Quenidon Daringer inquired of Blaze.

"Danri's a trusted friend. He's been gone from Shalemont a long time, taken by the Madness. There were some who feared he'd never be coming home."

Another warrior came in, and Rudy knew this must be a sartor. The creature walked upon two goatlike legs with sharp, split hooves. Its torso and face were manlike, save for the sharp, curved horns jutting from the forehead, and the leathery roughness of the skin. This sartor wore a wide metal belt around his midsection, a shortsword resting in a scabbard at his waist.

"This is Poat Glenhollow," Blaze noted, while the sartor nodded with restrained dignity at the companions.

Blaze and Poat took their places beside Daringer. "I'm glad to see all of you," the sylvan commander admitted. "But if it's true that this army will march right through the illusions, then I don't know how much use any of us can be. For centuries that magical screen has been our primary means of defense, standing proof against explorers, miners, bandits, and any others who have tried to reach Faerine through Taywick Pass.

"Yet I have seen the force that now approaches. Know that we can meet it here only with a company of diggers, another of sartors, and a regiment of sylves. I have less than five hundred warriors to stand against at least ten times that number."

More like thirty times that number, Rudy thought grimly. He said nothing, knowing that such extremes became almost meaningless.

"Yet if we shall have to stand and fight, even if we perish in the attempt, that is what I and my warriors do willingly. The humans will know that they have been in a battle."

"Perhaps there's another way that the outcome can be influenced," Rudy suggested hesitantly. "If a lone saboteur could infiltrate the enemy army, reaching the Ice of Three Waters and either seizing or destroying it, the Galtigors would be thrown into immediate disarray."

"True," mused Daringer, intrigued. "But surely this block will be well-guarded. Perhaps held in the midst of the army?"

"Yes—the prince will keep it as far back as he dares, I'm sure, to prevent it falling into your hands during the battle. But if I can sneak around, come at it from *behind*—"

"You are offering to perform this mission?" interrupted the sylve, his eyebrows rising in a tiny gesture of surprise.

"It *has* to be me," the Iceman declared. "I'm human, and yet I can move around the pass without becoming lost in the illusions."

"On some more tranquil occasion, I mean to ask how you do that," the warcaptain said dryly.

"It's a bold plan," Takian said. "But you're not going alone—*I'm* coming along."

"One person would have the best chance of getting through—"

"That's rockwash, and you know it," Danri interjected, speaking to Rudy. "Two—or three, or even four—of you might have a better chance. At least there'll be someone there to watch your back."

"He's right," Raine added. "The three of us can pass for warriors of Galtigor until we're close. Then Takian and I can keep watch while you try to take the Ice."

Rudy's throat tightened with gratitude, his heart swelling with confidence. With companions like these, he could almost believe that the task might be accomplished.

"It's the best chance we have," Blaze Smelter declared, after Danri had translated the humans' conversation. "In the meantime, we'll meet the army in the center of the pass—and hope we can hold 'em long enough for you to reach that chariot."

"If I can, I'll try to get rid of the driver and ride it away from the army," Rudy said. "Maybe try and reach the Faerine lines, so we can destroy it."

"Destroying it will be difficult and dangerous," Quenidon cautioned. "If the Ice comes into contact with Aura, the result could be a violent explosion—many could die."

Rudy's heart sank—yet at the same time he vowed, grimly, to take this ultimate measure if it was the only way he could succeed.

"That stream flowing through the pass—is that Aura, or water?" Raine asked.

"Almost pure water," the sylvan leader replied.

"If you can get the Ice to the stream, perhaps we can throw it in the water, let the flow carry it away from the battle. The water is several feet deep—the Ice should float."

"That sounds like the best chance—but first we've got to get to it." Rudy stepped to the side, looking past the leafy canopy to the sky overhead. "It's after noon. I would expect Garamis to begin his advance within an hour or two—let's be ready for him."

"You risk much in our cause," Quenidon Daringer observed. "I am grateful, even as I wonder why you do so. Yet I also see that some of you are unarmed; will you accept a token of our appreciation that may be of use in the battle?"

While the companions nodded silently, Quenidon whispered

something to an aide, who quickly left the bower. In moments he re-turned, bearing three thin-bladed swords of brilliant, silvery metal.

"Digger steel," Quenidon remarked, with a nod at Danri and Blaze. "Few humans have held blades such as these. We have extra weapons with our garrison—please do us the honor of accepting these."

"Thank you," Rudy said, amazed at the feather-light feel of the weapon in his hand. Swiftly he and Raine slid the blades through their belts; Takian's sword dropped readily into his scabbard.

"Form the battle line!" commanded Quenidon Daringer, turning with stately grace and gesturing to his lieutenants. He turned back to the Iceman. "I thank you for your efforts on our behalf. Now it would seem that you had best prepare to leave."

TWENTY-ONE

War on the Watershed

Through the ages of history come times when
diplomacy fails to soothe the savage nature of
humanity. Then it remains for good men to take up
the sword, sacrificing blood and treasure so that evil
shall not prevail.
—SCROLL OF BARACAN

— 1 —

Captain Matheral of Carillonn had faced many devious foes in his life. Outnumbered three to one, he had bested a company of the Redsteel Guards in the marshes of the River Ariak; he had led thundering charges into the teeth of fiery Corsari bombards; and he had pledged the Warrior's Creed, a measure of valor and the indoctrinating oath for any man who would stand among the One Hundred Knights of Carillonn.

Yet never had he faced a foe so vexing, so impossibly omnipresent, as the very ground in Taywick Pass. They were hopelessly, utterly trapped by the terrain—and Math didn't even know how it had happened! Before him a rocky knoll, draped with ice-encrusted cliff, stretched across the path. To the right he was confronted with a precipitous drop to a field of splintered boulders; the ground on the left descended through a series of fetid marshes, broken by smooth patches of scum-coated pond.

Most terrifying of all, the trail *behind* the knights—the place where not ten minutes ago he had been walking—was now a broad lake, waters of such intense blue as could only signify great depth. He had led his company to an island in the lake, cut off in all directions from any traversable path.

The knights were all dismounted, clutching the bridles of their placid chargers. The horses seemed singularly undisturbed, though Matheral knew that the men around him had reached the edge of panic.

"Which way out of here?" demanded Kenton, a normally imperturbable veteran.

"By Baracan—this is sorcery!" claimed another knight, palming his heart while he looked nervously over his shoulder.

"Look out!" cried Kenton, his voice cracking in fright. The knight pointed upward, toward the overhanging shelves of the rocky knoll. Shudders rippled along the sharp, splintered cliffs.

Great boulders cracked and broke free, the sound reaching the knights after a second's delay. The stones crashed onto lower ledges, quickly gathering mass and momentum.

"Run!" shouted a frantic rider, abandoning his horse and sprinting toward the scum-coated mire. Other men, hesitantly, stumbled after.

"Hold!" Matheral's order snapped through the growing fear, bringing his men back to their training and their pride. "This *is* sorcery—the magic of Taywick Pass. But it's sorcery that seeks to deceive, not to kill!"

As he spoke, Math stood staunchly in the path of the rockslide. All his instincts compelled him to flee, but his will proved stronger. Stones clattered to the ground on all sides, but none harmed him. In moments the last of the falling rocks had tumbled past, and when he looked upward, the captain of knights was astounded to see that the rocky knoll had almost completely disappeared. In its place, a sloping glacier of gray-blue snow climbed into a steep mountain valley.

Slowly the men shuffled back, awed by his courage—and shamed by their own cowardice. Matheral walked among them, clapping a shoulder here or tousling a young warrior's head there. Each knight found his horse, taking the bridle in one hand and keeping the other free to draw a weapon.

"We can do nothing if we stay here—we've got to move. If we have to, we'll let the horses choose where to go. Form ranks of two men, and follow me!"

His face locked into a grimace of determination, Math walked in the lead. Trying to ignore the rippling terrain under his feet, he set out in the direction of the deep-watered lake.

— 2 —

Rudy, Raine, and Takian slipped around the edge of Taywick Pass, scuttling to and from the cover of brush and rockpiles, seeking an approach into the army of Galtigor's flank. Already the companies of that force had expanded across a broad front; drummers rattled out a beat that signaled imminent advance.

At least Anjell and Kianna were safe for the present, the Iceman reflected tensely—though the fairy's terror at the approaching battle was terrible to see. Together with the duchess, they had been escorted to a sheltered vale at the far end of the pass—only if the Galtigors broke completely through the Faerines would the three be threatened. Danri had joined the company of diggers, vowing to do everything within his power to see that such a breakthrough never occurred.

As the trio advanced, the Iceman held the hands of his companions, encouraging them to close their eyes as they crossed a gently sloping, grassy hillside. Anjell had shown them that so long as a person didn't look at the ground, he remained unaffected by the illusions.

Undulations in the terrain masked them from Garamis's troops, though the Iceman frequently checked their enemy's location. Thus far the companies remained clustered around the chariot at the entrance to the pass.

A flash of movement along the crest of the hill caught Rudy's eye—he wondered with a start if some of the Black Mantles had gotten behind them. There it was again: a tawny shape gliding over the crest, racing toward them over the brushy ground.

The Iceman gasped, audibly enough for Raine and Takian to open their eyes. Rudy couldn't believe his senses—surely the sorcery of Taywick was causing a cruel delusion in his mind!

"Kalland!" Raine called, beginning to dispel his doubts. The big snow lion barreled into him, knocking the Iceman to the ground and squatting possessively on his chest. Rudy squirmed free to the accompaniment of deep, rumbling yowls of pleasure. Raine threw her arms around the animal's broad neck, and Kalland took time to nuzzle the woman.

"You're the most amazing animal," Rudy declared, shaking his head in wonder. "I left you for dead—and here you are! But what is it?"

Kalland had pounced away, and now looked back at the trio in obvious agitation. With another bound, the animal tried to lead them back up the sloping ridge.

"Follow him!" urged Raine, though Rudy had already started after the big cat. Takian and Raine trotted along.

"As long as we stay in Kalland's footsteps, the ground's pretty smooth," Raine discovered as they jogged steadily upward. In a few moments they crested the rise and stopped in astonishment. A hundred yards away a party of dismounted horsemen advanced--the leader of which spotted them immediately.

"Matheral!" Raine shouted. "It's the duchess's guards!"

Quickly, with the snow lion leading the way, the companions reached the knights. "My dear," cried Matheral, embracing Raine. "I had thought you were lost forever! But tell me—the duchess? Is she—?"

"She is well—and will stay that way if this battle can be won," Raine reassured him. She introduced Rudy as he and Takian joined them.

"And the prince," Matheral noted. "Last I saw, you had taken an arrow in the back—it seemed a fatal shot."

"As it would have been, if not for the duchess and her friends. I made a full recovery—and now I seek vengeance. It grieves me to know my own brother was behind that murderous attempt, which makes it all the more important that he be stopped."

"But Kalland and you?" Raine asked the knight in wonder. "How did—"

"I saw the necklace around his neck, thought I recognized her ladyship's jewels. We roped him, and he led us south for days. Apparently he was trying to reach Taywick all along." Matheral shook his head, then scratched his fingers through the lion's mane. "Kalland you're called? It's a good name for a hero."

"Now that you're here, can you help us?" Rudy asked bluntly.

"Aye. Tell me what you need."

Quickly Raine explained their plan to the knight. "The army is a mile or two away, over these low ridges. As soon as we get some uniforms, we'll try to make our way to the chariot and its Ice."

"How are you going to find your way over there?" Matheral questioned. "It takes an hour to walk a hundred steps—and you've got to go a mile or more."

"I can find the way," Rudy said. "I don't have time to explain how."

"What can we do to help?" Matheral asked bluntly.

"You can support the Faerines," Rudy suggested. "They're terribly outnumbered." Briefly he described the thin battle line.

"Okay—but I'd also like to keep an eye on you. I could charge when a diversion is needed, if only I could find my way through this accursed nightmare-land!"

"Kalland can lead you!" Rudy said. "He wasn't affected by the illusions. Just stay in his footsteps and you'll do okay. Don't try to charge, though, unless you can first get in range of the Ice of Three Waters."

Still skeptical, the knight agreed. "I've crossed swords with these black-cloaked butchers before—and I'll not hesitate to do it again, no matter the odds!"

"Nothing will matter unless we can reach that chariot," Rudy said grimly. "But you could observe our advance from this hill. If it looks like we're getting into trouble, we could use that diversion—maybe you could feint a charge against the right wing of the army?"

"*Feint* a charge?" Matheral was insulted. "Why, the ten of us will ride all the way to Duloth-Trol if need be!"

"Excellent!" Takian declared. Horns blared from the far side of the low hillock, and they heard swords beating against shields in the rhythmic crescendo preceding the attack.

"Not much time left, now," Rudy declared. "Let's get going!"

"Wait!" Math said suddenly. He reached into his belt pouch and pulled out a small, tightly rolled sheet of parchment which he extended toward Raine. "This is from Paderon Zyloth. His last words were to me, asking that you receive it."

Too stunned to speak, Raine reached out a trembling hand and took the scroll. Quickly she tucked it into her own pouch.

"We'll wait if you want to look at it," Rudy said quietly.

The woman shook her head, hair swirling from the sharpness of the gesture. Her face was ashen, and the Iceman placed a hand gently on her arm, wanting desperately to embrace her, to shelter her from the imminent violence. Yet he sensed that it wasn't the thought of battle that caused her disquiet.

"Like you said—let's go," Raine declared, blinking quickly. Her voice was strong, and the color had returned to her face.

Kalland loped after Rudy as they started back over the slope. "Sorry, big fellow," the Iceman said, touched by the animal's devotion—but knowing that Kalland's presence would give the lie to their disguises. "Can you wait here with the captain for a little longer?"

The big cat stayed, sitting on the ground and staring after him. Before Rudy disappeared over the hill, he looked back to see Kalland's ears cocked, his nostrils sampling the air, as if to make sure that the man had really been there.

Coming off the crest, the Iceman and his companions saw the full sweep of Garamis' army. They dashed to a concealing thicket, where they paused to study their objective.

Watching the army form ranks and line up for the impending attack, Rudy saw proof that this was an experienced force—an army that had fought, and won, many battles. From the precise array of unit flags, carried by standard bearers at the front of each formation, to the gleaming display of armor worn by the tightly packed lancers, or the precise ranks of archers that marched forward on either flank, ready to shower the enemy with arrows, these were men who would fight hard and well.

At the fore of the human army came many rows of men wearing the Black Mantles of Garamis' personal guard. Rudy noticed that the prince held his light and heavy horsemen back from the first wave, however, obviously intending to throw them into the fight when the Faerine line was critically weakened or broken.

"Those archers far to the right are the Bordermen—good, loyal warriors," Takian said sadly. "Those knights around the chariot—with the red plumes on their helmets—are the Redsteel Guards. My brother's favorite bully-boys."

"Look," Rudy pointed, relieved as the plumed riders galloped away from the command post. "He's sending the guards to back up the Bordermen."

"Good news, I guess. Now, how do we mix in with Garamis' troops?" Takian wondered, crouched on the ground beside Rudy and Raine.

"How about taking the colors off some stragglers as disguises?" suggested the Iceman. They had all seen, in the wake of the army, numerous small pockets of men wandering aimlessly, lost in the illusionary maze and too far from the charm-breaking spell of the Ice.

"Here's four of them now," Raine said, pointing to a small knot of spearmen who brandished their weapons at a lilac bush as if they expected the plant to lunge savagely after them.

The trio walked slowly around the rise of ground, concealed from the view of most of the army. They approached the four men casually, watching as one spearman spotted them and raised his hand to point— high in the air over their heads.

"Hey!" the warrior of Galtigor shouted upward, when the companions were about twenty feet away. "How did you get up there? Can you see the rest of the army from there?"

"Yes!" Rudy shouted back. "Look behind you—you'll see the way up."

In unison the men turned, and the Iceman led his companions in a sudden rush. He bashed one on the back of the head with his sword, knocking the man out, while Raine dragged another to the ground and immobilized him with a sharp kick. Takian, meanwhile, dropped the last two with rapid strikes of his sword.

"Grab their tunics!" Takian urged, as hoofbeats thundered nearby.

Rudy stripped the Black Mantle tunics off three of the fallen Galtigors—choosing garments that had not been stained with blood. He threw one of these over his own clothing, and passed the others to Takian and Raine. Several horsemen galloped past, a hundred paces away, but they paid no attention to the three comrades.

Drawing a deep breath, Rudy looked toward the heart of his enemy's army. Companies advanced throughout the range of his vision, while pennants fluttered above the field. In the center of this mass came the tall chariot, twin horses pulling it forward at a slow walk.

"That's where we need to be," the Iceman declared. Raine and Takian nodded silently. "So let's get going," he urged, wondering if he was taking himself and two loyal companions to their deaths.

— 3 —

The charge of the light infantry swept forward like an ocean wave, rushing toward a frail levee of Faerine defenders. Garamis, seated on Cyric beside the great chariot, had commanded the trumpeters to sound the attack. Now he watched the advance from a low elevation near the middle of the pass. Boric, standing beside Wilfriz in the chariot, clapped and cheered.

A thin line of sylvan archers dared to occupy the field, standing now amid a riot of flowers. The slim warriors held their weapons raised, strings taut with arrows drawn fully back. Yet they didn't shoot as the swarm of infantrymen picked up their pace to a steady trot. War cries erupted from thousands of throats, while swords and shields danced over the infantry's heads, sparkling like diamonds in the bright sunshine.

Abruptly slender arrows flew, arcing high over the battle and then soaring downward, quickly vanishing into the midst of the thronging attackers. The battle cries deepened, flavored now with screams of pain and fear. A hundred arrows had been fired; as the attacking wave moved on, nearly a hundred men lay dead or dying on the crushed grass in the formation's wake.

Another volley of arrows, and a third, slashed through the sky as the sylves fired with deadly efficiency. More men screamed and died, but the press of the attack was too great. Unstoppable, a primal force as inexorable as an incoming tide, the light infantry started to sprint, sensing the overwhelming impact of the imminent clash.

A fourth volley slashed through the ranks, and suddenly the Faerine archers vanished. There was nothing magical about their disappearance. Instead, they turned and melted away, loping gracefully into the cover of a copse of densely needled evergreens. Howling in frustration, the throng of infantrymen rushed in pursuit.

"Send the light horse to swing around behind that grove," Garamis instructed. Nearby couriers stood ready beside fleet horses, while signalers held an assortment of flags beside tall staffs. "And I want my archers—the Bordermen—to screen the right flank of the trees. Cut them down if they come out of that way."

"Let's go, Garam! I want to charge!" Boric hopped restlessly into the chariot, beside the impassive Wilfriz and the Ice of Three Waters.

"Later!" snapped the elder prince. "*I* will give that order—and not until the time is right!"

"Can we tell the archers to shoot?"

Garamis ignored his brother's pout. Horns blared and additional pennants snapped in the breeze, commanding the advance of the cavalry and initiating the steady march of three long ranks of bowmen.

The sylves vanished into the trees, leaving no sign of an enemy. The prince swept his eyes from one end of the battlefield to the other, from the clump of trees on the right to the broad field in the center, and the trickling stream and marshy shoreline to the left.

"I want the pikes to advance down the middle," he ordered his assembled lieutenants. "Bring the lancers up—I want them ready to attack at a moment's notice. Place half the light swordsmen along the creek—just to guard against a trick. Then order a general advance of the militia."

He knew that the bristling array of pikes would drive any oppo-

nent from that open field—and even if the enemy came at them with
cavalry or heavily armored infantry, the hedgehog of steel would shatter
the enemy attack into fragments. By experimenting, the men had discovered that the Ice of Three Waters neutralized the illusions for all
the men within about five hundred paces of the chariot. Given this
broad range, the prince felt certain that he would be able to keep most
of the army together.

Advancing with the chariot, Garamis planned to keep the bulk of
his army under the protection offered by the Ice of Three Waters. In
a few minutes the woods to the right would be surrounded, the line to
the left well-screened. The Tor of Taywick stood beyond. That spire
would divide the attack into two sections, but both would remain
within the Ice's range.

Now the rest of his force took up the advance with a throaty cheer.
The battle was all but won.

— 4 —

"You came out in Dalethica—that's bad enough! But you mean to tell
me you've been traveling with *humans?*" sputtered Blaze Smelter, outrage and disbelief mingling in his voice with equal force.

"Maybe we should talk about it later," Danri declared curtly,
gesturing to the field just beyond the small woods where they now
stood. The dull roar of battle had grown to a crushing din, and as he
peered out between the trees it seemed that all he could see was an
onrushing horde of Galtigor swordsmen—close behind the lanky sylvan
archers who had just slipped through the digger position.

"I just don't believe it!" Blaze snorted, shaking his head for emphasis.

The sylvan archers fell back from the diggers, vanishing silently
into the heart of the grove, and at last Blaze hefted his weapon—a
heavy pickaxe—and turned toward the field. "Still, if you'd told me
you married a gigant I don't think I could be any more surprised!"

Danri wasn't listening. Tension drew him tight as a sylvan bowstring, his heart pounding with the knowledge that his first real battle was bare seconds away.

"For the mines and Aurianth!" cried Blaze Smelter, his words ringing like a trumpet call from the little grove. Two hundred diggers ducked beneath the low branches and rushed the field, full into the faces of the charging swordsmen. Danri hefted his hammer, pick side forward, and added his cry to the din raised by his fellows.

A leering, gap-toothed swordsman slashed wildly at Danri's head—a blow the digger easily ducked, bringing his hammer sharply upward. The steel pick plunged through flesh and bone and the man collapsed, uttering a scream that slowly faded to a tortured groan.

But even before the fellow died, Danri dropped two more of the enemy, as all along the line the men took the measure of the diggers, and found it fierce. The momentum of the charging Galtigors forced the Faerines back to the very fringe of the trees, but here the diggers set their feet. Hammers, axes, hatchets, picks, and poles all flashed and whirled, bruising flesh and crushing bone.

After a few moments the warriors of Garamis stumbled backward, screened by a barrier of their comrades' bodies. A half dozen diggers lay motionless, while a few others staggered or kneeled from grievous wounds, but most of the company stood unharmed and grimly furious. Danri felt his muscles tensing, rage pounding in his forehead, coloring his vision with a hazy filter of red.

"Hit 'em again!" Blaze Smelter knew this feeling, and knew how to use it. The diggers—their own throaty cries rumbling over the shaken swordsmen—sprang over the rampart of corpses, weapons bashing, and rushed against the men of Galtigor.

One man tried pathetically to defend himself from Danri, parrying a casual feint. The digger crushed the man's leg with a sharp blow, silencing his cries with an even harder bash to the head. Another Galtigor stumbled backward until Danri knocked the fellow's sword from his hand with a hard swing. The warrior turned and scrambled away, plunging through the quavering mob of his comrades.

All along the line the diggers smashed the lightly armored enemy back. Dozens of men died—even to fall down was to perish under the remorseless advance of the raging Faerines—and the survivors fled desperately from the stocky attackers. Some men dropped their weapons, others knocked their comrades aside in their panic to escape, but all of them streamed away from the stand of trees and the diggers who dashed outward from the grove.

Fury clouding his mind, Danri sprinted across the field, hammer waving, unheard curses spitting from his mouth. Only dimly did he hear Blaze Smelter's next command:

"Stop! Back to the woods! Quickly!"

Yet the order penetrated the chaos of his mind, as it did for most of the diggers in the victory-flushed company. Danri skidded to a halt and joined his fellows in trotting back toward the woods. Only a dozen of the Faerines continued the pursuit, the flight of a thousand Galtigors seeming almost comic in the face of these few.

The shower of arrows swept over them just before the bulk of digger warriors reached the shelter of the trees. Ranks of human bowmen stood revealed on the digger flank, given their chance to shoot by the retreat of the swordsmen. Danri saw dozens of his countrymen fall, pierced by the steel-tipped missiles, before he tucked himself and rolled onto the ground. More arrows struck nearby as he sprang to his feet and tumbled behind the bole of a large pine.

He looked into the field, toward the backs of the fleeing swordsmen. The valiant diggers who had continued the pursuit, he saw, were now all dead, their bodies lying like pincushions among the daisies of the field.

Blaze limped over to Danri, blood spilling from a gash along the digger warchief's leg. Still, Blaze's bearded face twisted into a crooked smile as he clasped his old friend on the shoulder.

"Guess we gave 'em something to think about that time, didn't we?"

"Aye-uh," Danri replied, but he gestured grimly into the broad fields of the pass. There Garamis' heavy infantry advanced, and the porcupine formation of the pikemen marched steadily past the grove. "It looks like there's a few more that didn't learn their lesson."

Blaze scowled. For just a moment his eyes swept across the slain diggers in the field; then he looked toward the blocks of men advancing steadily on Faerine. He slung his pick over his shoulder and looked at Danri with a shrug.

"Guess we've got a little more work to do, don't we?" he said.

Danri nodded, and the company of weary diggers turned toward the next threat.

— 5 —

Bitter disgust and vile frustration vied within Nicodareus as he thrashed around the bleak stone hallways of Agath-Trol. An overlay of supreme hatred fueled his rage, and drove him to pound his fists against the walls. When a trembling brutox tried to slip past him, the Lord Minion disemboweled the unfortunate beast with one explosive swat.

For seemingly the hundredth time, he sent his Sight to Taywick Pass, to try and see how the battle developed. As on each previous occasion, the presence of Aura in that enchanted height blocked all but the most vague impressions. About all the Lord Minion knew was that fighting raged there.

And in the midst of it stood an insolent Iceman—one who had been audacious enough to elude Nicodareus. Only recently had the Eye of Dassadec relocated the man, who now stood squarely in the path of Galtigor's army! But now, the Power of Three had been expended. There was no way for the Lord Minion to strike at this niggling foe, for without that triple blessing of Dassadec, even a Lord Minion could not travel far beyond the boundaries of Darkblood—the borders of Duloth-Trol.

Or was there, just possibly, a way?

For a long time the idea had flickered in the back of the Lord Minion's mind, but he had not dared even to consider it, much less broach it to his master. It was a power of the Sleepstealer's that had not been employed for some thirteen centuries. Indeed, Nicodareus remembered that previous occasion, and Dassadec's vow that he would never use it again.

The thing Nicodareus had in mind was a draining task even for Dassadec. At its bare minimum it required the expenditure of a full thousand minion lives. Yet it could move a Lord Minion in an eyeblink to any part of the world, and sustain him there for a short time before bringing him home with equal speed.

Finally his hatred became too great, his rage too consuming, for Nicodareus to wait any longer—he was desperate to go to the human, to kill him!

And so it was that he sought the Sleepstealer in the great throne room of Agath-Trol. Already present by the Lord Minion's order was a full legion of Dark warriors—kroaks, brutox, stalkers, and terrions. They numbered a thousand, and they were an honored legion, sworn to the Eye of Dassadec for life . . . or death.

In their presence, Nicodareus prostrated himself on the floor. His prayer was raised to the black heights, shrill with the intensity of his desperation.

"O Omnipotent One," he groveled. "I beg of you—will you grant your unworthy servant the power of Darkflight?"

TWENTY-TWO
Battle of Two Waters

The Watershed stands upon a perilous triad, for the
three realms are not equally powerful, nor equally
aggressive. Conflict between Dalethica and Faerine is
most dangerous to this equilibrium, for the weakness of both proves to the inestimable advantage of
Duloth-Trol.
—CODEX OF THE GUARDIANS

— 1 —

Rudy felt acutely self-conscious as he walked, with Raine and Takian
at his side, through the milling formations of Garamis' army. Raine
had her already short brown hair tucked under a small metal cap; even
so, her femininty seemed very obvious to the Iceman. He could only
hope that the Galtigor warriors were too preoccupied to give her a
careful look.

The area seethed with activity. A troop of lightly armored swordsmen marched past, followed by shambling columns of spearmen and
archers. Even Rudy's untrained eye could see that these troops did not
have the steady ranks and tight formations of the lead companies.

"Militia units," Takian muttered discreetly.

The Iceman nodded, suspecting that these were men and youths
who had rallied to Garamis' call to arms shortly before the campaign.
Naturally they lacked the training in tactics and drill that enabled the

warriors of the Black Mantles and the Bordermen to fight and march in such tight order.

Now sergeants cursed, resorting to whips and kicks in order to keep these men moving forward. Rudy fell in behind one of these slogging companies, thankful that the tunics of the Black Mantles secmed sufficient to persuade the bullying sergeants to leave him and his comrades alone.

The militia column veered to the right. Straight ahead, on a low hillside, Rudy saw the great chariot. Beside it reared the prancing black charger he'd first seen in Neshara. His heart pounded as he recognized Garamis, mounted astride the warhorse, Cyric.

The three companions fell out of line, striking toward a command tent that had been erected some distance behind the chariot. Takian suggested that as long as they kept moving and looked like they had somewhere to go, they were unlikely to be questioned.

When they reached the tent, Takian veered sharply toward the hill, with Rudy and Raine staying right in step. The hilltop rose before them, no more than a hundred paces away.

The chariot driver was a burly, capable-looking warrior. Beside him stood another, shorter fellow. Abruptly Takian stiffened. "Boric!" he whispered, dismayed.

Rudy recognized the name of Takian's younger brother. "Your disguise is good," he told the prince. "He won't recognize you."

Unconvinced, the grim nobleman nevertheless nodded and continued upward.

No less than a dozen signalmen stood in an arc around Garamis, and while each currently held a flagstaff or standard, they also wore swords—and would no doubt hasten to use them if their leader or the precious Ice was threatened. Several other men—trumpeters and lightly armored couriers—also stood close at hand. At least the Redsteel Guards remained occupied farther ahead on the battlefield.

Step by step the trio climbed the gently sloping ground, approaching the chariot from behind. Several horsemen galloped past, seeking the prince's decision on some aspect of the battle. Garamis pointed, and the armored riders thundered away, rejoining a group of lancers who stood in neat ranks, well behind the front lines.

Looking past the command post, Rudy suppressed a gasp as a line of stocky figures—diggers, obviously—rushed from the grove of woods, wading into the flank of the massed group of pikemen. At the same time, sylvan arrows sparkled in the sun, arcing from the woods to fall among the warriors carrying the long, tightly ordered spears.

Pikes wavered and fell as the arrows found their targets, and the diggers plunged through the gap in the block formed by the deadly missile fire. In an instant the formation of pikes had dissolved into chaos, the warriors with their long-shafted weapons helpless to combat the deadly foes who suddenly began to chop and bash within their ranks.

Another force rose from the marshy reeds beyond the woods, silvery steel gleaming as warriors rushed toward the advancing columns of men on the army's right flank. The sartors had joined the fight! Rudy saw their charge break the front of the Galtigor formation, sending several ranks of Black Mantles streaming toward the rear.

Garamis spat a curse, quickly looking across the field and then barking a command. Behind the prince, several trumpets blared, while one of the signalmen dipped his standard and then swirled the pennant through a circle. The company of militia advanced—and despite the best efforts of its sergeants, it looked like an amorphous blob spreading across the ground. At the same time, the rank of Bordermen who had flanked the grove of trees advanced, showering the woods with arrows.

Screened only by the distraction of the developing battle, the three companions marched resolutely closer. They drew within fifty paces of the chariot, continued until only thirty paces remained. Rudy noticed a pack of hounds lolling on the ground beneath the chariot's wheels, drooling and panting.

One of the signalmen turned to look at the three as they drew near the command post. The Iceman tried to keep his face impassive, turning toward the chariot and starting his measured advance, acutely aware of his companions stalking at his sides. Both occupants of the two-wheeled cart had their backs to the companions. If the trio could overwhelm them and seize the reins, perhaps they could ride from the battlefield!

"The chariot," whispered Takian. "We'll rush it together—I'll take the driver and you try to get the reins. Then we'll ride like mad to get out of here."

"Ride like mad sounds right," the Iceman murmured in agreement. "The whole thing sounds mad—but I think it's the best we're likely to do."

The companions reached the rank of signalmen without Garamis or the driver of the chariot noticing them. The curious flag-bearer, however, held up a hand, eyebrows rising questioningly. The man squinted, staring at Takian suspiciously.

"Go!" cried the young prince, suddenly drawing his sword. Rudy sprinted forward, leaping for the back of the chariot.

The flagman shouted an alarm, jabbing the tip of the staff between Takian's legs. The prince tumbled and sprawled to the ground as Raine raced past.

Hearing the commotion, Garamis turned, his face going slack with shock as he saw Rudy leaping into the back of the chariot.

"You!" cried the prince, his face flushing as he drew his black-bladed sword. The driver of the chariot, who was even taller than the lanky Iceman, spun to face Rudy.

Boric, the other occupant of the chariot, watched with round-eyed amazement. "Who are you?" he inquired.

The Iceman stabbed at the driver with his sword, but the fellow hacked with a great axe, knocking the blade to the floor of the chariot with stinging force. Raine lunged past Rudy, her own digger-steel blade driving for the man's throat, but he swiped at it with a big paw and flipped her over the edge of the chariot. She lay on the ground beneath the swords of several warriors; beside the other wheel Takian grunted and parried against the press of a half-dozen men.

Rudy found his ice axe in his hand. The burly driver smiled, his grin a leer of frightening cruelty, but before the Iceman could swing his axe, someone plucked it out of his hand from behind.

He whirled in shock, staring upward into the fiercely triumphant face of Garamis. The prince, still mounted on the snorting Cyric, had snatched away Rudy's weapon.

"Well, my young Iceman—I was told that you lived, but until

now I was skeptical. It's kind of tragic, don't you think, that you've come such a long way just to give me the chance to kill you again."

— 2 —

Danri lost track of Blaze Smelter in the chaos of the retreat. For every human they killed, ten or twenty more rushed forward, crazy for revenge. The digger's hammerblows had smashed dozens of Galtigor swords, but the men thus disarmed could always find additional blades near the bodies of their slain companions.

The overwhelming numbers had finally shattered the thin line of sylves, diggers, and sartors. Now Danri helped one of his goat-footed allies who had been slashed by a Black Mantle's sword. With grim haste they fled the advancing humans, making for the shallow stream that circled past the great Tor of Taywick Pass.

That bluff rose in the midst of the field, unscalable, like a boulder standing in a flowing stream. The sartors and a few diggers passed to the right of the huge column of stone; the sylves and the rest of the diggers circled to the left.

For a time the Faerines had held in the field and woods, aided by the vigorous attack of the sartors. Indeed, when the goat-horned Faerines rushed from the cover of the marsh, the surprise had been enough to momentarily stagger the human attack. It had taken the plodding advance of Garamis' heavily armored infantry to finally split that position; then a troop of fleet mounted lancers splashed through the shallow brook, threatening to circle around the entire defending force. Fortunately, enough sylvan archers had remained to shoot many riders from their saddles and send the rest racing for the shelter of the Galtigor lines. Still, the defense had been breached in several places, and in the press of advancing sword and pike there had been no restoring it.

And still more human companies trooped forward, threatening to sweep around the ends of the crumbling line, propelling what had begun as a careful withdrawal into a chaotic flight. A human lunged close and Danri turned, smashing him back with the gore-stained hammer.

"Leave me!" grunted the injured sartor, trying with numb fingers to draw his own sword.

"Forget it," the digger replied, his long arm wrapped around the wounded sartor's waist.

Finally the reedy bank of the last stream appeared before him. The steep-sided cliffs of the tor plunged into the water, blocking part of the bank, but for most of its course the creek was a shallow, easily forded barrier. Danri waded into the water—even though there was a stone bridge nearby, that span was jammed with retreating Faerines. Half-dragging his wounded ally, the digger stumbled all the way to the far bank. Only when they had crawled onto dry land again did the digger let go; both warriors collapsed, gasping, among the crowding ranks of their fellows.

"Rally up, Faerines!" The cry came from the base of the bridge, and Danri, with a pulse of relief, recognized Blaze Smelter's voice.

Across the stream a wall of steel-armed humankind screened the battlefield. Marching on foot or mounted upon slowly pacing horses, the army of Galtigor had delayed its pursuit long enough to allow the whole force to join up—no doubt, thought Danri, to keep as many men as possible within range of the Ice of Three Waters. Yet now that supernatural block must be on the move, to judge by the sweeping march that approached the shallow stream.

"Hold 'em at the river, fellows!" snorted another captain—Poat Glenhollow. The sartor gathered his troops and arranged them in a single line, where they could meet the humans if—as seemed inevitable—the enemy crossed the stream and tried to climb onto this bank.

Danri looked across the front to the bridge, which was finally clear of Faerines. Blaze and several diggers advanced to the center of the stone arch, and Danri hastened over to join him.

"Glad to see you here," said Blaze, giving his old companion a weary clap on the shoulder.

"Same for me—I thought we'd lost you back by the woods."

Blaze smiled, his fatigue turning the expression into a grimace. Most of the surviving Faerines had now crossed the stream, where they formed a determined, albeit thin, line of defense. For a brief moment Danri worried about Rudy—could he reach the Ice? If he couldn't, the rest of the battle was pretty hopeless.

The lancers of the Black Mantles, riding their monstrous horses, made the first rush for the bridge. Huge barrel-chested chargers pounded up the cobblestones, into a tight mass of diggers who met them with steel blunt and sharp. The Faerines staggered backward under the impetus of the attack, but then the stocky fighters held firm. A killing array of picks, hammers, axes, and swords flailed like a harvesting machine, breaking the charge into a frantic, thrashing melee.

Wishing he could strike the riders, Danri was forced instead to cripple the horses with his hammer, watching the unfortunate beasts collapse—and, if the digger was lucky, dropping the horseman into range of his weapon. Several riders went over the bridge, and some of these, weighted down by armor, perished in the shallow waters below.

A groan beside Danri drew his frantic attention as he saw Blaze Smelter go down, pierced by a Black Mantle's lance. Furiously Danri chopped at the rider's horse, and when the steed fell with a broken leg, the digger's hammer crushed the skull of the lancer. Shrill screams from the mounts mingled with the curses of men and diggers; these mortal sounds faded against the clashing, banging force of the collision, as both sides struggled for an advantage. Finally the surviving horsemen turned away, leaving dozens of dead on the cobblestones as they pounded off the bridge to regroup in the field.

Blood trickled from Blaze's mouth and nose as Danri carried his friend off the bridge. The brave digger opened his eyes with a look of gratitude—and regret.

"Good we could meet again, old friend . . . we gave 'em quite a brawl, didn't we," Blaze muttered through crimson lips.

"The biggest," Danri agreed, his voice choking as Blaze's eyes closed for the last time.

Wearily Danri looked across the stream, where the cavalry were milling about, preparing for another charge. To the right and left, infantry surged into the water, piketips shimmering in the spray, cries of battle roaring over the groans of the wounded and the tromp of booted feet. Arrows whistled overhead, volleys arcing toward targets in both armies—but the sylves could send only one precious missile for every twenty or so aimed at the Faerines.

Danri hefted his hammer and started back onto the bridge as the next assault started. Grimly determined to kill as many Galtigors as possible, he believed that the Taywick Garrison could hold for another five minutes . . . possibly ten.

Then the battle would be lost.

— 3 —

The tip of the black-bladed sword danced beneath Rudy's chin, barely an inch from the growing lump in his throat. Garamis' dark eyes—colder even than the nearby block of Ice—flashed hatred and cruel triumph. Two men stood at the back of the chariot, holding additional blades close to the Iceman's skin, while the hulking driver grinned at him through the tangle of his beard.

With bitter frustration Rudy saw the Ice of Three Waters, a gray-white block in an opened leather saddlebag near the center of the small compartment. His hand stretched for the waterskin of Aura at his waist, but he knew he could never remove and uncork the skin—three blades would pierce him at the first aggressive move. Yet he was almost desperate enough to risk the attempt, and the explosive result; he didn't try only because he didn't think he could succeed.

Seeing that Rudy was well guarded, Garamis turned to the Iceman's two companions, who crouched on the ground at each side of the chariot, under the guard of at least a dozen men of the Black Mantle.

Raine's helmet had been knocked off, and the prince leered from his saddle, chuckling at the woman's predicament. Then he shifted to the other infiltrator—and his jaw dropped, while his eyes sparked with an expression of horrified fascination.

"No! By the Nameless One—it can't be you! Takian!" he gasped. "You're dead now! I *saw* you die!"

The younger prince remained silent, meeting his brother's dark expression with a haughty glare, his blue eyes filled with their own measure of ice.

Boric, his eyes wide with wonder, looked at Garamis in complete

confusion. "What's going on, Garam? Tell me!" he demanded petu-
lantly.

"Boric! Look who's here!" cried the Iceman.

"Takian!" Boric's face creased into a grin of pure joy. "You're
not dead! Look, Garam—Tak's not dead! You said he was dead, but
he's not!"

"No thanks to Garamis," Rudy declared bluntly. "He's the one
who tried to kill him."

Boric gaped at the Iceman in silent shock.

"It's the truth," declared Takian, climbing to his feet under the
blades of many watchful guards. He stood with his back to the chariot's
wheel, facing his mounted brother.

"Why?" demanded Boric, shocked to the point of tears. Garamis
ignored him, instead twisting to face Rudy.

"How is it you keep returning to haunt me? And the tower—you
must have been there, with Takian! Both of you should have burned
to death—you *must* have burned!"

"A poor job you made of it, both times," Rudy spat, his mouth
so dry he could barely form the words.

"But . . . how did you come here? And *why*—to die again? You're
mad! Do you not fear this blade? One touch can kill you!"

"Then I'm already dead—remember?" the Iceman challenged.

"*I'll* kill him!" The chariot driver offered the grim pledge, hefting
the heavy, double-bladed axe. He stood beside the Ice, which was
barely a step in front of Rudy.

Desperately the Iceman touched his waterskin of Aura. Could he
open it, pour the liquid on the Ice, without being killed first? And if
he did, would a violent explosion kill all of them? Bile rose in his
throat—if there was any way to get out of here without harming Raine
and Takian, he *had* to wait!

"Stay your hand, Wilfriz—there are some riddles here that require my thought."

"Your Highness," interjected one of the signalmen hesitantly. He
gestured to the battlefield, where the companies of Galtigor had obeyed
the order for the general advance. Worried, Garamis looked at the Ice
of Three Waters, then at the field.

A commotion suddenly arose from the right rear of the army—cries of alarm and the pounding of heavy hooves. The hounds around the chariot started to bay in real excitement.

Rudy, with a flash of hope, saw Kalland bound into sight and streak over a low rise of ground. Immediately behind the snow lion came the tips of ten lances, and then the silvered armor and barded war horses of Matheral's knights thundered into view, charging toward the command post on the hilltop.

Below the low summit a broad, irregular column marched toward the battle—straight across the path of the charging knights. From the lack of order and casual tempo of the march, Rudy suspected these men had borne arms for all of a week or two. Now they made a valiant attempt to draw swords and stand in the face of the outnumbered knights, at the same time shouting an alarm that carried across the field.

Garamis twisted in his saddle, staring incredulously at the tiny rank of attacking knights. The horsemen struck the column of irregulars, ripping through the rank like a jagged sawblade. The sheer size of the horses crushed dozens of men, while the heavy lances struck down many more. In seconds, the chargers, without breaking stride, pounded free.

"Stop them!" cried Garamis, his voice shrill with disbelief.

Ignoring the command, the ill-trained troops fell all over each other in their scramble to get away from the crushing charge. Panic spread like fire across dry grass, opening a wide gap in the column, granting free passage for the charging knights.

"Trumpeter! Summon the Redsteel Guards!" Garamis cried. Flags waved, and the braying of a trumpet quickly rang across the field. At the same time, the pack of hounds took off toward the charging snow lion, baying savagely.

Wilfriz reacted next. Shouting to the horses, he dropped his axe and picked up a whip. Lashing the leather strand toward the startled steeds, he bellowed furiously.

Rudy lunged toward the driver; at the same time, Raine and Takian, acting with one mind, dove at the two warriors beside the wheels. As the horses sprang forward in their traces, each of the surprised

Galtigors went down, and Raine bounced to her feet on the back of the chariot.

"What are you doing?" Boric asked.

"Helping Takian! Stand back!" Rudy shouted, snatching up his silver-bladed sword. Still clutching the reins of the bucking horses, Wilfriz could only twist to shield himself from the Iceman's attack.

"Stop him!" Garamis exhorted his bodyguards, momentarily distracting them. Takian took advantage of the lapse—he seized the sword of one man, driving the others back with lightning slashes. Before the mounted prince could react, his brother's blade stabbed into Cyric's flank.

The black warhorse whinnied in shock and fury, rearing to lash at Takian with a steel-shod hoof. The nimble swordsman tumbled to the ground, somersaulting through the ring of guards and bouncing to his feet beside a signalman's horse. That mount bucked in surprise as the prince stabbed upward, cutting the rider down and springing into the still-warm saddle.

"Go!" Raine shouted urgently.

Rudy looked around to see her slamming two guards to the ground with lightning kicks to the face. She crouched in the rear of the chariot, holding further attackers at bay with her sword.

Wilfriz transferred the reins to one hand and snatched up his battleaxe. Desperately Rudy chopped at the wrist of the warrior's weapon hand, the keen blade slicing through the man's metal-strapped gauntlet.

Before the heavy battleaxe descended, Boric leaned forward and seized the man's wounded wrist in his own surprisingly strong hands. Wilfriz grunted in surprise, his face flushing with fury. Blood ran down his arm, but he pressed the weapon forward with crushing force.

"Don't!" Boric insisted. "He's a friend of Takian's!"

The burly axeman suddenly jerked his weapon away, breaking Boric's grip. A light of gleeful cruelty lit his eyes as Wilfriz turned the weapon toward the young prince.

Rudy thrust with all of his strength, driving the tip of his sword through the tangle of red beard and jowls, cutting into windpipe and jugular with brutal, murderous force. Wilfriz stiffened reflexively, leaning backward over the rail of the chariot. With a well-timed shove the Iceman pushed the corpse out of the way and grabbed the reins of the chariot.

"Go!" he yelled at the horses, slapping the reins across their flanks. Immediately the two chargers bolted into a gallop, carrying the bouncing chariot down the hill, toward the Faerine lines, between the wings of the advancing Black Mantles.

"Look out!" cried Raine, pointing to the rear.

Rudy twisted around to see Garamis astride his plunging charger. Cyric's black nostrils snorted furiously as the sleek warhorse lunged after them, sweeping toward the chariot's wheel, apparently unaffected by the wound from Takian's sword. The Iceman felt as though his life had slowed to a crawl; yet he could not force himself to react as that black-bladed sword swept closer.

Abruptly another horse came into view, as Takian's fresh mount shouldered Cyric momentarily aside. The chariot pulled away as the young prince's silver sword deflected his brother's cold black blade. Takian veered, and Garamis—his face twisted by consuming fury—turned from the chariot to pursue. In his hand, cold and purposeful, flashed the Sword of Darkblood.

— 4 —

The stand at the bridge and stream exceeded Danri's estimate by a few minutes, at the cost of dozens of Faerine lives. Humans forded at twenty, thirty different places, horses lunging across in shimmering curtains of water, heavy infantry men slogging through a racing current stained by silty mud—and, increasingly, blood.

The diggers held in a knot around the arched stone span. After a time the humans stopped trying to cross there, so deadly was the hammer of the grim warrior who stood at the center of the bridge.

To the right of the great tor fought the sylves. Their arrows exhausted, these graceful warriors now wielded blades of sharp, supple steel, weapons superior in every respect to their human-borne counterparts. Every respect, that is, but the crucial area of quantity—a dozen human swordsmen would inevitably overwhelm a single sylvan master. Even so, Quenidon Daringer's regiment held a long stretch of stream bank, driving back repeated enemy attempts to force a crossing.

On the left of the Faerine line the remnants of the sartors struggled to hold—but here the press of attacking numbers proved simply too great for even minimal success. The horned Faerines fought savagely, inflicting horrible wounds with their shortswords. With each human casualty the sartors brayed and crowed in beastly triumph—but even that eerie sound could not halt the onslaught of Galtigor. At seven or eight different fords men forced their way across, though they paid in blood for every precious footstep on the far shore. Finally one band of sartor defenders was completely overwhelmed, and then the humans spread out through the meadows and groves beyond the stream, cheering as they raced onto the far side of Taywick Pass.

From his vantage at the crest of the bridge, Danri looked at the sartor collapse, and knew that the rest of the Faerines would soon be surrounded. Somebody—probably him—should give the word for the diggers and sylves to retreat. But he was saved that indignity as the Faerine warriors seemed to sense approaching disaster. Holding their ranks as much as possible, the battered warriors—those who could still walk—fell back from the stream. Whether weary from combat or sensing that the battle was already won, the humans for the most part followed cautiously, content to allow the withdrawal without crossing weapons. The Bordermen, however, continued to shower the sartors with volleys of arrows.

Before he left the bridge for the last time, Danri grimly observed the gap of the pass before him. He saw the chariot rumbling forward from the command post, and his last hope was dashed—obviously the Galtigor prince took care to keep his army within the Ice of Three Waters' protective radius. Hastening from the bridge, he joined the other diggers in retreat, bitter shame burning in his heart.

Abruptly Danri's attention was jerked back to the sartor flank. The human advance there continued, like water spilling through a broken dam—but the sound of the battle had taken on a deeper timbre. What was the noise? Something familiar tugged at the digger's mind; the humans, too, sensed the change, as many running men slowed their advance to a more cautious walk. Before them stood a dense wall of pine—the beginning of the mountain forest that swept over a hundred miles of Faerine.

Drums! The heavy beat at last came clearly over the din, beautiful music to Danri's disbelieving ears. In moments a shower of rocks emerged from the woods, falling among the Black Mantles with bone-crushing force. Dozens of gigants burst into view, their throaty bellows burying even the resonant cadence of the mighty stone drums.

In the center of the charge raced Hoagaran, his dark beard flowing back on both sides of his fearsome face. Long hair streaming behind, he led the rush, galloping across the ground as fast as a long-legged horse. In seconds the hulking warriors trampled their first humans, bashing hundreds more to the ground with crushing blows of their crude, heavy blades.

The human archers turned, drawing back for a volley at the charging gigants, but the huge creatures paused long enough to launch another volley of rocks—each a boulder the size of a human skull or bigger. These missiles smashed bowmen to the ground like tenpins, continuing to bounce and roll with deadly effect. The Bordermen launched a few desultory arrows, but when the big warriors rushed forward again, they threw down their bows and fled in full rout.

"Charge—hit 'em from this side!" Danri had no trouble finding his voice, and his countrymen roared their approval. In an instant the diggers, their fatigue fallen away, rushed into the attack.

Yet even as the initial human companies faltered, more and more of Galtigor's troops advanced toward the fray. In the quick glance Danri stole, he thought the entire pass was blackened by their teeming numbers.

— 5 —

"I've never gone so *fast* before!" Boric exclaimed, clinging to the chariot's rail beside Raine as the two-wheeled cart bounced and jolted across the battlefield.

Rudy, desperately holding the reins, didn't answer. Instead he looked to the sides. Large columns of Galtigor's army blocked the route to either direction, forcing him to maintain his forward course—which was just as well, since he wasn't at all sure that he'd be able to turn the galloping horses.

A quick glance behind showed that Garamis and Takian had galloped off at an oblique angle. Matheral and his courageous knights carried their charge all the way to the prince's command post, where they clashed full into the Redsteel Guards who had dashed back at their prince's command. Kalland tore the head off a hound and disemboweled another, but the rest of the baying pack closed in on the snow lion with teeth flashing.

The Tor of Taywick rose before Rudy, blocking the path with its massive, cliff-draped face. Dividing the battle into two segments, the pillar of stone stood squarely between the twin columns of the advancing army. Hauling back on the reins, Rudy felt the chariot slow slightly. The chargers dropped back to a canter, and then a trot, and finally to a walk as they approached the jumble of boulders scattered around the base of the tor.

"We're taking the block where Garamis wants it!" Rudy moaned in frustration. "We just brought it forward in time for the rest of his advance."

"The Black Mantles block both sides of the tor," Raine observed, pointing to the twin wings of the enemy army.

"Why did Garamis try to kill Takian?" Boric asked, suddenly reminded of the conflict.

"Your brother Garamis is a bad man," Raine said gently. "He's fighting a war that's wrong, and Takian wants to stop him. Takian *knows* this war is wrong—and you do too, don't you, Boric?"

"But Garam said the Faerines—said that they killed Takian! But they didn't, did they?"

"No—Garamis wanted you, wanted everybody, to think so, but they didn't do anything wrong."

"Here come the Redsteel Guards," Rudy hissed, his voice taut. A dozen of the armored riders broke from the fight around the command post to charge in the chariot's wake. Frantically he looked around, realizing that they would have to abandon the chariot if they hoped to escape.

"We *can't* go around the tor!" the Iceman realized.

"Feel like making another climb?" There was a little of the familiar twinkle in Raine's eye as she cocked her head toward the looming massif of the tor. "The stream flows around the far side of this thing—from up above, you might be able to throw the Ice. . . . "

"Race you to the top," Rudy said, bringing the chariot to a full stop and seizing the saddlebag containing the Ice of Three Waters. He turned to Boric. "Remember, trust Takian—he knows what's right."

Boric scowled, but then his face cleared. "I believe you," he said.

"Come on!" Raine urged, leaping directly from the chariot onto a nearby boulder. Rudy followed, and they made their way upward across the talus, striking toward a narrow, curving ledge that presented a bare possibility of a route to the top.

TWENTY-THREE

Harvest of Hate

The ultimate achievement in life is to bring about the
death of one's most despised foe.
—TOME OF VILE COMPULSIONS

— 1 —

Garamis jabbed his spurs into Cyric's bleeding flanks, pushing the
powerful stallion to the limits of endurance. Fleeing just out of sword
range, Takian lay low across the withers of his stolen horse, lashing
the mount with the reins. The crown prince's mind was clouded with
fury, his emotions focused upon the ink-black Sword of Darkblood in
his hand. He knew a single, burning desire: kill Takian.

Yet despite his determination, and the speed of his horse, Garamis
feared that his brother might escape. Takian's steed was also fast, and
not as tired as Cyric. Thundering through the rear of the army, the
younger prince guided his fleet horse between the companies scattered
by the charge of the knights. Garamis' stallion, in pursuit, trampled
several of the cowardly wretches who had broken from those units;
kicking harder, the prince begged the black horse to close the gap.

Without warning, Cyric collapsed, groaning in agony, throwing
the prince heavily to the ground. Though the breath was driven from

Garamis' lungs, he clutched his sword and quickly staggered to his feet. The stallion tumbled several times before coming to a rest, dead; only then did Garamis see the depth of the sword wound Takian had thrust into the steed's flank.

Furious, nearly blinded by rage, Garamis shook his weapon after the rapidly fleeing figure of his brother. Not until the black blade flashed across his vision did he recall, with giddy exultation, that the weapon was more than a potent killing tool. For so long had he kept the power of Darkflight a secret, he had all but forgotten about it himself.

"Nicodareus!" he crowed, pointing the tip of the weapon at a patch of ground in Takian's path. Clutching the hilt with both hands, Garamis held on while a momentary whirlwind twisted around him. The cyclone faded as quickly as it had arisen, leaving him squarely before Takian's wheezing charger.

"Hah!" cried Garamis as his brother reined in, shocked speechless.

His lips set in a grim line—but without visible panic—Takian twisted the reins, urging the horse to gallop in a new direction.

"Nicodareus!" The prince repeated the magical command, once more popping into sight before the fleeing horseman—this time so close that Takian's horse reared back, nostrils flaring in panic. Quickly Garamis stepped in, chopping into the animal's foreleg with the black blade.

Shrieking in pain, the steed bucked frantically, tossing Takian before it slumped to its knees. With spasmodic kicks, the horse collapsed onto its side, twitched a few more times, and died.

"You can't flee the blade of Darkblood!" sneered Garamis, stepping across the carcass of the horse and advancing on Takian. The younger prince scrambled to his feet, his own silver weapon held defensively. The blade looked frail and wispy beside the Sword of Darkblood, as if the digger steel would shatter at the first solid blow.

Garamis attacked, wielding the black blade savagely, chopping high, slashing low, thrusting from the right and left. Parrying the moves with quick flicks of his own weapon, Takian fell back one step for each parry—yet that slender blade held firm even against the most crushing assaults. Still, the elder prince aggressively pressed his advantage, his brother all but stumbling in his haste to retreat.

"Your skills may buy you a few moments more of miserable life—but no more than that," Garamis taunted.

"How, Garamis—how could you fall low enough to serve the Nameless One! What about your realm, your own kind?"

"I serve the *victor*, brother! And so, under my rulership, does my realm! *My* realm, do you hear? You've desired it all your life, but it will never be yours! Taywick Pass, even all Faerine—these are just the beginning. It's a pity you won't be there to see the full height of my achievements!"

"I've lasted just long enough to see you defeated!" declared Takian, with what seemed to Garamis like remarkable aplomb. "Look!" The younger prince pointed over his brother's shoulder.

The black blade held steady for a moment, until Garamis stepped back and risked a look at the center of the battlefield—toward the rise where his command post stood. He saw men frantically running about, trying to mount horses, or cowering in panic at the sight of a plain, grassy slope. Instantly he knew—the Taywick Illusions had claimed them.

He felt a jolt of utter fear—in his bloodlust for Takian he had abandoned the Ice of Three Waters! Had the block been destroyed? With a curse of fury he whirled back to his brother, but at the same time he realized that he, himself, was not affected by the magic. Observing more men lose their bearings, he knew that the effects were sweeping closer.

"Can you see well enough to recognize disaster?" jeered Takian, jabbing his sword toward his brother. Garamis saw that the chariot, and the Ice, had moved far beyond the command post. Panic rose, momentarily paralyzing him, but then he remembered: his sword rendered such distances purely trivial. He would simply have to deal with the Iceman first.

"I'll be back for you," Garamis snarled at his brother, waving his blade enough to dissuade Takian from attacking. Then he pivoted on his heel, lifting the Sword of Darkblood toward the great tor, in the direction he had last seen the chariot.

"Nicodareus!" he cried, exulting in the name, the power. Swirling winds surrounded him for an eyeblink, until he materialized partway to the tor; repeating the command through two more instantaneous hops, he stood at the base of the great pillar of rock.

Nearby he saw the chariot, empty except for Boric—who looked at his brother reproachfully as Garamis strode forward. If Boric had noticed anything odd about his sibling's mode of transport, he didn't remark on it.

"Where is the Halverican? Where did he take my Ice?" demanded the crown prince.

Boric looked sullen. "You lied to me! I'm not telling!"

Rage flushed across Garamis' face, but he kept his voice level. "Don't let them fool you, Bor. They've stolen something important. Did they go that way?" He indicated the ground around the base of the tor.

"No, they didn't!" Inadvertently Boric's eyes swept upward. Garamis followed his brother's look just in time to see a pair of tiny figures disappear over the rim of a ledge near the top.

"That's all I need to know." The elder prince laughed, pointing upward.

"No! It's not fair!" wailed Boric. He leaped down from the chariot and ran away from Garamis, lumbering around the base of the tor toward the battle raging along the stream.

"Well, you wanted the war, my brother—let's hope it's all you imagined it would be!" said Garamis, still laughing. Then he leaned back, sighting along his blade toward a wide shelf partway up the tor, intending to make certain that he could see a good, secure landing place.

"Nicodareus!" he crowed.

And again the whirlwind blew.

— 2 —

The fourth ledge was about two hundred feet above the base of the tor, and here Rudy and Raine paused to catch their breath and select the route over the next stretch of cliff. A quick look below showed them that—thanks to the gigants' attack—the battle line had stabilized, but columns of Galtigor troops still streamed toward the fight.

"This chimney gives a good start," the Iceman observed, indicating a vertical crack that stretched a good seventy or eighty feet overheard.

"And it meets that shelf—looks like it might take us all the way to the top," Raine agreed. She brushed her short hair back from her forehead, and Rudy was startled by the look in her eyes—a haunted, wary expression of fear. But when she fastened her gaze to the cliff and started along the ledge toward the chimney, the tension vanished, leaving in its place an air of calm assurance.

Rudy felt no lingering apprehension, nothing like the despair that had dragged at him earlier. He had the Ice of Three Waters, a great wall of stone above him . . . and a climbing partner such as he had never known, never imagined.

He watched Raine with a sense of wonder as she started up the chimney, unerring in the placement of her boots, using her back and shoulders for counterpressure. He waited until she was some distance overhead before he started after. Normally, to minimize the risk of a double fall, one climber would finish the chimney before another started below, but today circumstances demanded haste.

The Ice of Three Waters was a cold weight against Rudy's back, chilling his skin even through the leather saddlebag and his tunic. The chimney proved a challenge, as it narrowed into a smooth stretch of stone where only the pressure of hands and feet against opposing walls prevented a fatal fall. Finally Raine reached the top of this stretch, collapsing onto a relatively wide ledge as Rudy joined her, panting with exhaustion.

Again the Iceman was struck by the hunted look in Raine's eyes, an expression that flickered as she looked at the pouch fastened to her belt. Abruptly, he understood.

"That piece of paper, from the priest—why are you frightened of it?"

"I'm *not*—" She halted, biting her lip on the lie and then meeting his eyes with a lucid stare. "Because . . . I think it brings me a prophecy."

Rudy waited, and she explained. "Twice before, when I came to love a place, a person—prophecy snatched me away, compelled me to new duties, new challenges not of my own desire."

"Paderon Zyloth gave you these prophecies—he told you what to do?"

"No—never before. It was Pheathersqyll at first. He told me I was the daughter of Three Stars Rising—and because of this there would be three prophecies that would rule my life. I loved him like a father—but I haven't seen him since the second prophecy sent me to Carillonn. 'Ever eastward, and always you shall serve,' " she said with uncharacteristic bitterness.

"You were sent to serve the duchess?"

"And Paderon Zyloth. I was a servant to the duchess, a student to the priest. Yet I would not have believed that the last prophecy could come from Paderon Zyloth—he placed no worth in auguries. 'Idle fantasies,' he called them. But something happened to him at the Wayfarer's Lodge . . . I think he was touched by Aurianth, during the dance. This message is the result."

Rudy was quiet for a moment. His breathing had almost returned to normal, but he couldn't make himself resume the climb yet. Indeed, he, too, had begun to fear that tiny piece of parchment.

"You could tear it up and throw it to the winds." He made the suggestion slowly, watching her eyes. She blinked, and in her smile there was pain.

"I'm glad you said that."

"You could come with me," Rudy continued, his heart pounding. "I don't even know where I'm going—but there are things happening to the Watershed, happening all over. I'm going to be a part of it, whatever it is. Please come with me—help me!" His voice grew low and firm. "I need you."

"I want to—I *can* help you. And, as well, there are ways in which I need *you*," she replied, squeezing his hand and shaking her head sadly. "But I can't throw my destiny away." Raine drew in a breath and looked upward. "Are you ready to climb?"

She stood and he joined her, slinging the Ice of Three Waters to his other shoulder for a while. "Look—this shelf curves upward here."

Raine led the way along a pleasantly smooth ledge, circling upward along the side of the tor. Shortly they came to a series of shelflike rocks and had little difficulty scrambling up to the top of the lofty pillar. They found themselves on a smooth circle of rock, perhaps fifty feet in diameter.

"The stream's off the other side—I'll see if I can get a decent throw of the Ice from here!" Rudy declared, starting across the rocky slab.

A sudden burst of wind howled in his ears, whining painfully and then vanishing as quickly it had arisen.

"What was—?" The Iceman's words were cut off in shock. Before him stood a man—a man who hadn't been here, hadn't been anywhere near here, a second earlier.

Vividly Rudy recognized that sneer of triumph, as once again he stumbled away from Prince Garamis of Galtigor, and his Sword of Darkblood.

— 3 —

A thousand minions groaned and wailed, but they could not ignore their master's command. In even ranks of ten they marched down the black steps, into the steaming ooze of the Tarlake—to certain death. Many of the pathetic creatures stayed afloat for a long time, floundering until the sticky fluid covered their noses and mouths. But most went down quickly, buried by the weight of their fellows who marched right behind.

These were kroaks, elite warriors trained twelve centuries before by the Eye of Dassadecc himself. Their loss grieved Nicodareus, and was a token of his sacrifice.

The Lord Minion himself stood upon a raised stone platform on a tower that leaned over the expanse of Darkblood. Power pulsed upward as the minions gave up their lives; the Lord Minion felt the swelling of might within him. In the distance, all around, Dassadec himself wailed from the strain of this rarely used rite—a ceremony of sacrifice to bestow Darkflight on a Lord Minion.

Yet Nicodareus knew that the suffering, the power, went for nothing less than victory in the first, crucial campaign.

Steadily the minions marched, ten at a time, until the last of the thousand vanished into the mire. Now the power, flashing with a purple glow that made Nicodareus shudder, swept upward, washed across him, and bestowed upon him in that instant the gift of Darkflight.

Another rank of minions started down the steps, followed by more, in an endless file. These additional sacrifices, brutox and kroaks together, came from additional regiments of the Eye's personal army. Ten would perish for each heartbeat of the Darkflight's duration; yet here, too, Nicodareus knew that the suffering would be worth the cost.

Then the power pulsed brightly, so that from the outside the fortress of Agath-Trol glimmered in a thousand places. When the light faded, the Eye of Dassadec was gone.

— 4 —

Rudy was vaguely aware of the battle raging below; he knew only that the defenders were strained to the breaking point. Not unlike himself, he reflected bitterly, as Garamis slowly flicked his sword from the Iceman to Raine.

"Perhaps I'll kill your wench first, eh? You could watch me cut her—that face is kind of plain, don't you think? I could pretty her up a bit."

Raine watched him, alert as a cat. Rudy saw her eyes burn with intense concentration—no longer was there even a trace of apprehension or despair.

The Iceman, on the other hand, felt a curious numbness. The hatred that had sustained him for weeks, that had carried him across Dalethica, was gone. In a flash he knew—it had never been hate that drove him. Rudy had tried to make it so, but Garamis had been only a tool in the great design that had brought him here, to the brink of the Watershed, the summit of Taywick Pass.

"Why did you do it, Garamis? You know your master—know what a threat he is to all humanity. Why would you become his tool? You're being used—he's treating you like his fool."

"Fool?" The prince snorted in contempt. "I'll have triumphs you can't even imagine—and you'll never live to see!"

"You haven't killed us yet—and we're not about to give up without a fight," Raine declared, stepping away from the cliff edge.

The black-bladed sword followed her every move, until Garamis whipped the weapon back to face Rudy. Laughing, the Prince of Galtigor gestured with the blade. "No—I haven't slain you yet, but you will die as soon as I desire it. One touch of this keen edge brings inevitable—and excruciating—death."

Garamis gestured to the teeming battlefield below. Though some formations of his army—those far to the rear—stumbled around in the obvious grip of the Taywick Illusions, many hundreds of fresh troops were just now reaching the bloodstained stream. The waterway spilled over rocks and gathered in deep pools, twisting and frothing through a curve that was farther away from the tor than Rudy had hoped.

The Iceman cast a desperate look at that gruesome flowage, not certain whether he could throw the Ice far enough to hit the water. If it would float, whether the current would carry it away from the battle—these were questions he would leave to the gods. In point of fact, he wasn't at all sure Garamis would give him the chance to make the toss.

Shifting the saddlebag on his shoulder, the Iceman tried to lower the bulk of the weight onto his forearm, to get it in position for throwing. His movement, unfortunately, caught the prince's eye.

"Drop that satchel—very carefully!" demanded Garamis, his voice deadly calm.

A sound like a thunderclap split the air and a streak of light flashed, crashing explosively into the ground between the two men. Smoke erupted, obscuring vision, but still Rudy saw a large shape there—and then the glow of two hellishly familiar eyes.

It was the Lord Minion of the Nameless One—the monster that had ravaged the Inn of Two Wells. Again the creature menaced him in all its horror, ten feet tall, coal-black except for the scalding furnace flaring from the eyes. The two batlike wings spread wide from the broad shoulders, and taloned hands reached forward, ready to rend and rip and kill.

"No!" cried Garamis, his view of Rudy blocked by the arrival of his master. "The Iceman is *mine!*"

"Silence—insolent wretch!" declared Nicodareus, turning to slap the prince roughly to the ground.

Rudy sprang toward the opposite cliff, grabbing the satchel with both hands and swinging the heavy block of Ice through a circle to build the momentum of his toss. Finally he launched the saddlebag into the air, where, flaps and thongs beating like wings, it tumbled through a long arc. The Iceman feared it would fall short, but it continued to soar farther away from the tor. Ultimately it splashed into the chill waters of the mountain stream, landing in the swirling eddies of a dark blue pool. Spray shimmered as the satchel disappeared; when it bobbed to the surface, a gray-white block floated, almost fully submerged, beside it.

"No!" Garamis uttered a wail of disbelief as he staggered to his feet. The Lord Minion ignored the prince, turning and taking a measured step toward Rudgar Appenfell.

Behind Nicodareus, Raine pounced like a cat, flying at the Prince of Galtigor. Her first kick caught him in the wrist, knocking the sword from his hand and sending him staggering toward the edge of the cliff. With a strangled gasp Garamis turned, raising his hands to shield his face as the woman flew at him again.

This time the lightning foot caught him in the groin; Raine's third kick drove the air from his lungs with a plunging blow to the gut. The prince took two steps backward—and the last one took him over the edge. With a disbelieving scream, Garamis toppled away, his terrified howl lingering for a second or more until it, too, disappeared with brutal and permanent suddenness.

In the silence it seemed to Rudy as though the whole world had stopped. He couldn't see the battlefield below them, couldn't know that a hundred skirmishes had dwindled to nothing.

Nor could he see the warriors, newly arrived to the fight, climbing quickly up the cliffs of the tor.

— 5 —

Nicodareus stood, a tower of rage, all-powerful champion of evil. Humans—foolish, pathetic wretches! Why had he tried to use them in his grand plan? The Lord Minion wanted, desperately, to kill them *all*—every mortal, red-blooded one of them. He wanted to slay great numbers, by means of unspeakable cruelty and pain; he wanted to see the diggers, and the sylves, and all the Faerines, dead.

But most of all, he wanted the Iceman of Halverica.

As the fever of his rage slowly settled into cold purpose, Nicodareus saw this victim standing alone before him. The woman was somewhere near; she didn't matter for now.

Only this lone Iceman . . .

Nicodareus calmed his seething fury, anticipating the pleasure of a lingering kill. The Eye of Dassadec stepped forward slowly, wondering if the human would try to escape, perhaps to fling himself from the cliff. Yet the man stood with uncanny courage, staring at Nicodareus as if his own, puny wrath was enough to deter a Lord Minion!

Vaguely, Nicodareus was aware that each passing heartbeat sent another ten minions marching to their deaths in distant Agath-Trol; the fatal procession would continue to deplete his army until the Eye of Dassadec willed himself back to his master's fortress. Yet despite the cost, this was an attack that Nicodareus wanted very much to savor.

He took another step forward, again amazed at the human's courage—courage that only served to fuel the fires of the Lord Minion's fury. So hotly focused were his searing eyes, so intent was his concentration, that Nicodareus did not at first notice that other figures crept over the precipice. Only when one of the newcomers stepped forward to block his path, did the Eye recognize the intruders—and then it was with numb disbelief, as if he were visited by a dream.

High Guardians. The rocky-limbed protectors of the Watershed advanced, facing Nicodareus with arms crossed, faces impassive as any cliff. In Agath-Trol more minions died—ten, twenty, thirty . . . as Nicodareus took a step backward, unwilling to accept the evidence of his eyes. Mortals, of any race, he did not fear. Even an ancient drackan would perish in battle with a Lord Minion! But the Guardians . . .

The Guardians were a different matter. Nicodareus remembered his cohort, Balzaracc, torn to pieces by High Guardians fully a thousand years before. Like the Lord Minions, the Guardians were timeless, immortal—perhaps it was these same creatures who had performed that brutal killing. Now, a wall of stone, they stood between Nicodareus and his prey.

A thousand miles away, minions marched to doom, while on the Tor of Taywick their lord wrestled with shock. Forty, sixty, eighty, and more were the lives expended to continue Nicodareus' desperate attack—and yet he would not, *could* not sacrifice himself thus.

With a ragged gasp of fury, the Eye of Dassadec released the power of Darkflight, abandoned his foothold in the world of men and magic. In the blink of an eye, he traveled back to Agath-Trol, where hundreds of minions collapsed, groaning with relief.

— 6 —

For minutes after the High Guardians emerged from the rocks at the base of the tor, warriors on both sides stood staring in awe. The creatures had been fully concealed there, detached from the battle, until— what? Danri, facing a horde of Black Mantles on the bridge, gaped at the rapid ascent of the rock-skinned creatures. Even after the Guardians reached the top of the tor, blocking off observation from below, the combatants stood in restless silence.

Hearing a sharp crack, Danri looked at the stream. He saw a brown leather satchel float beneath the bridge, borne by the current; a white block of ice floated nearby. The block was the source of the sound—the digger watched it crack again, breaking into smaller and smaller pieces. He dared to hope—had Rudy succeeded? Swiftly the current carried the objects out of sight.

"Hold on—an earthquake!" cried one of the Black Mantle riders, falling to his hands and knees and all but hugging the ground. Other humans, gathered at the base of the bridge, sought firm purchase and stared around with wide eyes.

Instantly the digger understood, though he scarcely dared to believe. He led a few of his countrymen in a ragged charge, and found their human opponents too confused to offer resistance. The diggers began to herd the disoriented men together, pushing them like sheep toward the Dalethica end of the pass.

Screams of terror attracted the digger's attention as they came around the tor; he saw sartors, drenched in blood, savagely attacking the all but helpless men of Galtigor. Humans died horribly, stumbling to the ground as they tried to flee—while the sartors, in an orgy of vengeance, hacked mercilessly through the retreating troops.

Danri was appalled to see several sartors crippling humans with blows to the legs; only when the Faerines had dozens of the enemy sprawled, screaming, on the ground did they walk slowly among them, inflicting the fatal blows.

Abruptly the digger's heart almost ceased beating—he saw a diminutive, blond-haired figure walking across the field, in the path of the blood-crazed sartors.

"Anjell!" Danri cried. Sprinting as fast as his stumplike legs could carry him, the digger raced to the girl and snatched her into his strong arms.

"Oh hi, Danri!" cried Anjell delightedly. "We got lost when the illusions came back!"

"We?" For the first time the digger noticed the young man, smiling good-naturedly beside the girl.

"I found Boric out here—and it's a good thing, too! He might have gotten hurt."

"Aye-uh," Danri agreed, shuddering. He turned the girl's face away from the sartors. "What do you say we try and find your uncle?"

"Oh, yes!" Anjell cried. "D'you think he knows the battle's over?"

"You know," the digger replied, "I kind of think he does."

— 7 —

We could not intervene to strive against any force human, minion, or Faerine, the Guardian explained patiently as Rudy, Raine, and their stony rescuers reached the bottom of the tor. *The presence here of a Lord Minion violated that fundamental compact; it is against such violations that we are allowed to act.*

"So if Nicodareus hadn't come, you couldn't have either," the Iceman concluded. The High Guardian nodded. As the climbers reached level ground, Rudy wasn't surprised when his rescuers continued to walk away from the tor, without a backward glance at the two humans.

Raine took his hand, turning to look at the mountainous tower silhouetted against the sky. "Are you sure we did the right thing— leaving his sword up there?"

Rudy shrugged uneasily. "It seemed safer than carrying it. And you and I will be the only ones who know it's there."

"You're right," she agreed. "Far better for it to rust away there than ever to be used again."

They saw Danri and Quenidon Daringer some distance away, supervising the withdrawal of the disoriented humans. Raine started toward the digger, but Rudy's gentle touch on her arm brought her to a stop.

"Wait," he said quietly. "I have to know—what about the prophecy? What are you going to do?"

"I . . ." Silently she removed the scroll, unrolled it, and read the brief message there. Rudy couldn't decipher the carefully masked expression on her face, but when she handed it to him her eyes were shining.

"I can't read the Olde Script," he demurred. "What does it say."

She cleared her throat, and when she spoke, her voice was rough. "It's the third, the last part, of my prophecy. Paderon says that he *did* undergo a revelation—he was touched by the muse of Aurianth in the North Shore Wayfarer's Lodge. The prophecy came to him that night, in a dream, and he wrote it down when he awakened."

"What does it *say?*" pressed the Iceman, scarcely daring to breathe. The thought that Raine's destiny might call her somewhere else, somewhere far away, was more than he could bear.

"This is my fate." Now, though tears welled in her eyes, Rudy could tell that Raine's expression was serene.

> *"You must seek the lion man,*
> *a man of Three Waters.*
> *He—a pillar of the Watershed,*
> *and you—his foundation, his base.*
> *The storm breeds in darkness and shadow*
> *Twice the Sleepstealer came, twice failed;*
> *And third shall be last,*
> *In utter triumph or complete dissolution*
> *Together face the Sleepstealer*
> *And together bring him down—*
> *or perish in the ashes of the world."*

— 8 —

Kianna led Bristyn through the illusions while the duchess carried heavy sacks of Aura, ministering to the multitude of wounded across the bloodstained fields of Taywick Pass. They were joined by Anjell and her friend Boric, whose strong back bore the weight of many skins of the precious, healing liquid. The twissel buzzed through the air, helping the humans negotiate the illusionary terrain between the pockets of wounded. The companions tended the injured of both armies, offering healing sips of Aura wherever they found a warrior who had been wounded but who still breathed.

Many, many more were beyond the reach of their ministrations. At first the suffering appalled Anjell to the point of tears. Though her senses never grew numb, she gradually realized that the help she could offer was the only thing that might keep great numbers of injured humans and Faerines from similar suffering. This determination kept all of them going for many hours.

Boric finally collapsed, shrugging off several heavy waterskins and looking at Bristyn bleakly. "Where's Takian?" he asked. "And Garamis?"

"I don't know," the duchess said gently. "I've been looking for your brother Takian. I hope we find him soon."

"I wanted to see the war—but I never thought so many people would get *hurt*!" groaned Boric.

"Me either," Anjell said, patting the prince's shoulder. "But at least we can help, a little."

"It-it was so bad when I was a prisoner, I didn't think anything could be worse," said Kianna Kyswyllis, shaking her head sadly. The fairy held her head up, her wings fluttering bravely. "Now I know better."

Boric nodded, and once again hefted the heavy sacks of Aura while the fairy led them toward another field of scattered, bloody forms. On a rounded hilltop near the place where the battle had started, they found Captain Matheral, lying beneath his slain horse. His knights had fallen all around; together with scores of the Redsteel Guards and many savagely ripped hounds. There was no flicker of life in the captain or in any of his warriors—the men of Carillonn had given their lives·at horrific cost to the enemy.

A patch of tawny fur showed amid the blood and mud and grass. "Kalland!" cried Anjell, for a moment yielding to her despair with a torrent of tears.

She heard a familiar huff as the great, shaggy head came weakly off the ground. The pink tongue emerged, licking her face once, before the snow lion collapsed.

"Here—have a drink of this, big fellow! You're going to be all right!" she declared, frantically trickling Aura across the huge muzzle. Kalland licked away the stuff of magic and blinked, a shine of awareness slowly returning to his eyes.

Nearby, a long procession of humans marched past, led by digger guides until they were safely past the illusions of Taywick. There was little fear that any of these men would be in a hurry to repeat the attack—especially with their prince slain. Rumors about the nature of Garamis' foul servitude were already circulating through the remnants of the army, further quelling any lingering martial spirit.

Danri, Quenidon Daringer, Rudy, and Raine joined the healers as they finally drained the last of the Aura from their once-bulging sacks.

"So many lives lost," the sylvan captain declared sadly. "But we must be grateful for those who can be saved," he added, acknowledging the efforts of Bristyn's group.

"Have you seen Takian?" the duchess asked anxiously, looking past the four warriors.

"Here, my lady—finding my way through these accursed illusions, and begging apologies for my bedraggled appearance," cried the valiant prince, climbing toward them from the other side of the low rise. "Of course, I look no different than you're used to—but now I can *try* to look like a prince again!" He limped, and his tunic and leggings were torn, but his face was creased by a smile.

"*You're* bedraggled!" declared Bristyn. "Why, it's myself that—"

"Your Grace," Takian said, reaching Bristyn and taking her hands in his own. His voice was dead serious. "Never has your beauty shone with such radiance as it does for me now, as it has for these men I've watched you save."

Sobbing, she collapsed against his chest, and the prince held her through the course of her tears. "It-it's over, now, isn't it? War?" she asked.

"*Our* war is over—in Taywick Pass, and along the border of Galtigor and Carrillon. That is, if you think we can bury the threat of strife between our peoples." Takian said, gently lifting the duchess's bloodstained chin.

She looked at the devastation around them and nodded. "I fear that we are not finished with war—but let it not be fought between your people and mine."

"There will be peace between us. And please know this, my beautiful duchess: I will not force a marriage between us—that should never have been the price of peace. But pray, my lady, allow me to still count myself among your suitors."

Bristyn looked at the prince with affection, and perhaps more, shining from her eyes. "Counting you, there is but one," she said quietly.

"Hmph," Danri muttered, embarrassed. "There's peace, and there's peace! I think the fighting's over 'tween Faerine and Dalethica, too. We were lucky that the gigants decided to throw in with us for this battle—I think the future might call for a *lot* of cooperation among us Faerines."

"There remains a breach in the Watershed, in Halverica," Rudy reminded them. He didn't want to discuss the darker aspect of Raine's prophecy, which seemed to confirm that the Sleepstealer's plans were barely beginning. "I'll return there to make sure it doesn't become a new route for minions to enter Dalethica."

"I have a slightly different idea," Bristyn Duftrall said, speaking to Danri and Daringer as well as the Iceman. "You should come to High Carillonn, all of you. The monarchs of many realms will be gathered for Summer Court; they *must* hear the tale of the dangers facing the Watershed. Won't you come, make the case for alliance and cooperation?"

"But the breach . . . it's Halverica!" Rudy objected. "And I have to take Anjell home, finally!"

"I'll send a company of good, trustworthy men to keep an eye on that tunnel," Takian pledged. "They can keep the breach bottled up until a Council of Kings is called; then all the realms will decide what to do."

The prince's eyes met Rudy's in frank understanding. "And there is the matter of the Palefee owed your family. My men will carry full payment—though I know it can't atone for the hurts done by my brother, may it lessen a small bit of the suffering."

Rudy nodded his thanks, his thoughts suddenly bleak. How many more people would lose brothers before this struggle was done?

"I, too, will send knights," Bristyn promised. "The breach is a threat to all Dalethica. Raine, when we return to Carillonn you'll have to see immediately to the announcement—"

"Your Grace." Raine's voice was strong; she looked taller than she had before. "I will not be returning with you—that is, not as your maid. I am a servant no longer."

For a moment Bristyn stiffened, frowning slightly; but in the next instant she nodded her head. "Very well." She smiled at the Iceman, and for the first time in their aquaintance, Rudy saw Raine blush.

"I'm a little homesick for the rainbow bridges," Danri groused. "But I guess I could spend a little more time in Dalethica—if you think it would do some good?"

"And I, as well," Quenidon Daringer agreed stiffly. "A warrior's place is with his troops, for the most part. However, I can see that an informal embassy to your people might yield significant benefits."

"Do we *have* to go right back home?" Anjell asked. "I always wanted to see Faerine—and we're so close!"

"Oh, yes!" Kianna chimed in. "You could come and visit me— we'd see the Eternal Spring. And I'm sure we could stop at Shalemont. And—"

"Wait!" Rudy laughed. "I, too, will see Faerine someday, Anjell. But I'm afraid your mother is going to be displeased enough as it is, when I *do* bring you home! I don't dare let you go off for sightseeing!"

But his eyes looked toward the hazy land stretching beyond the gap of this narrow pass, and he believed.

"Someday—perhaps soon—we'll be back."

It is from Aurianth that love, like music and beauty
and kindness, flows into the world.
—TALLY OF LIVES

From that moment on Taywick Pass when my destiny was made clear, I left the childhood uncertainty, the feeling I was but a cork in a current, behind. I vowed that for the rest of my life my choices would be my own. And those choices began with the Iceman, Rudgar Appenfell.

In so many ways our travails were just beginning. The might of evil massed against our world, and we had no doubt, Rudy and I, that we would be swept into the storm. Back then, of course, we had barely a glimmering of the utter violence of the imminent onslaught—and perhaps, for the sake of a short period of happiness, that was just as well.

During our darker moments, of course, we saw an image of complete horror, of obstacles too great for any mortal to overcome. Yet because we would face them together, we knew that those challenges were nothing more than the proper destiny of our lives.

And the beginnings of our love.

From: *Recollections*, by Lady Raine of the Three Waters